Dear Reader,

Private Eyes began for me with several intriguing themes:
the circumstances that might cause the disappearance
of a woman so afraid of life that she hasn't left her
house for two decades; the destructive power of
secrets; the ability of fear to paralyze generations of a
family. And more than any other Delaware novel,
this book invites you into the process of psychotherapy,
protraying how the unique bond develops between
therapist and patient.

I've been privileged to enjoy two fascinating professions—
clinical psychology and writing. What drew me to both
is a deep, and hopefully compassionate, curiosity about
people—what motivates us and, especially, how we
react to stress. I've chosen the crime novel to explore
how murder and its consequences shed some light on
human behavior. At the same time I've found great
satisfaction in entertaining other people with what I've
learned about the mysteries of the heart and the mind.

Hope you enjoy.

Sincerely,

Jonathan Kellerman

More praise for Jonathan Kellerman and *Private Eyes*

"Riveting . . . Everything works in Jonathan Kellerman's *Private Eyes* . . . As in all the Delaware novels, the best asset of *Private Eyes* is Delaware himself."
—*New York Newsday*

"Once you start this story, you won't be able to put the book down until the final page. . . . This is a tough, fast-paced, intelligent thriller with good characters and snappy dialogue."
—*The Globe and Mail* (Toronto)

"[Kellerman] has shaped the psychological mystery novel into an art form."
—*Los Angeles Times Book Review*

"Kellerman's pacing remains impeccable and . . . Delaware is as fresh and engaging as ever."
—*People*

"A swift and compelling read."
—*New York Daily News*

Please turn the page for more reviews. . . .

JONATHAN KELLERMAN

PRIVATE EYES

BALLANTINE BOOKS • NEW YORK

A Ballantine Book
Published by The Random House Publishing Group

Copyright © 1992 by Jonathan Kellerman
Excerpt from *A Cold Heart* copyright © 2003 by Jonathan Kellerman

Published in the United States by Ballantine Books, an imprint of The Random House Publishing Group, a division of Random House, Inc., New York, and simultaneously in Canada by Random House of Canada Limited, Toronto.

BALLANTINE and colophon are registered trademarks of Random House, Inc.

This edition published by arrangement with Bantam Books, a division of Random House, Inc.

www.ballantinebooks.com

ISBN 0-345-46070-7

Manufactured in the United States of America

First Ballantine Books Edition: April 2003

OPM   9

To my children,
who put everything in perspective

Special thanks to Beverly Lewis,
whose sharp eye and soft voice
make a big difference.

To Gerald Petievich, for an
insider's view—of lots of things.

And to Terri Turner,
California Parole Department,
for her efficiency and good cheer.

For all of us our own particular
creature lurks in ambush.
—HUGH WALPOLE

———————————

1

A therapist's work is never over.

Which isn't to say that patients don't get better.

But the bond forged during locked-door three-quarter hours—the relationship that develops when private eyes peek into private lives—can achieve a certain immortality.

Some patients do leave and never return. Some never leave. A good many occupy an ambiguous space in the middle—throwing out occasional tendrils of reattachment during periods of pride or sorrow.

Predicting who'll fall into which group is an iffy business, no more rational than Vegas or the stock market. After a few years in practice I stopped trying.

So I really wasn't surprised when I came home after a July night-run and learned that Melissa Dickinson had left a message with my service.

First time I'd heard from her in . . . what? It had to be nearly a decade since she'd stopped coming to the office I once maintained in a cold-blooded high-rise on the east end of Beverly Hills.

One of my long-termers.

That alone would have made her stand out in my memory, but there had been so much more. . . .

Child psychology's an ideal job for those who like to feel heroic. Children tend to get better relatively quickly and to need less treatment than adults. Even at the height of my practice it was rare to schedule a patient for more than one session a week. But I started Melissa at three. Because of the extent of her problems. Her unique situation. After eight months we tapered to twice; at year's anniversary, were down to one.

Finally, a month shy of two years, termination.

She left therapy a changed little girl; I allowed myself a bit of self-congratulation but knew better than to wallow in it. Because the family structure that had nurtured her problems had never been altered. Its surface hadn't even been scratched.

Despite that, there'd been no reason to keep her in treatment against her will.

I'm nine years old, Dr. Delaware. I'm ready to handle things on my own.

I sent her out into the world, expecting to hear from her soon. Didn't for several weeks, phoned her and was informed, in polite but firm nine-year-old tones, that she was just fine, thank you, would call *me* if she needed me.

Now she had.

A long time to be on hold.

Ten years would make her nineteen. Empty the memory banks and be prepared for a stranger.

I glanced at the phone number she'd left with the service. An 818 area code. San Labrador exchange.

I went into the library, dug into my CLOSED files for a while, and finally found her chart.

Same prefix as her original home number, but the last four digits were different.

Change of number or had she left home? If she had, she hadn't gone very far.

I checked the date of her last session. *Nine* years ago. A birth date in June. She'd turned eighteen a month ago.

I wondered what had changed about her. What was the same.

Wondered why I hadn't heard from her sooner.

2

The phone was picked up after two rings.

"Hello?" Voice of a stranger, young, female.

"Melissa?"

"Yes?"

"This is Dr. Alex Delaware."

"Oh. Hi! I didn't . . . Thanks so much for calling back, Dr. Delaware. I wasn't expecting to hear from you until tomorrow. I didn't even know if you'd call back."

"Why's that?"

"Your listing in the phone boo— Excuse me. Hold on for one second, please."

Hand over the phone. Muffled conversation.

A moment later she came back on. "There's no office address for you in the phone book. No address at all. Just your name, no degree—I wasn't even sure it was the same A. Delaware. So I didn't know if you were still in practice. The answering service said you were but that you worked mostly with lawyers and judges."

"That's basically true—"

"Oh. Then I guess—"

"But I'm always available to former patients. And I'm glad you called. How are things, Melissa?"

"Things are good," she said quickly. Clipped laugh. "Having said that, the logical question is why am I calling you after all these years, right? And the answer is that it's not about me, Dr. Delaware. It's Mother."

"I see."

"Not that anything terrible's— Oh, darn, hold on." Hand over the phone again. More background conversation. "I'm really sorry, Dr. Delaware, this just isn't a good time to talk. Do you think I could come and . . . see you?"

"Sure. What's a good time for you?"

"The sooner the better. I'm pretty free—school's out. I graduated."

"Congratulations."

"Thanks. It feels good to be out."

"Bet it does." I checked my book. "How about tomorrow at noon?"

"Noon would be great. I really appreciate this, Dr. Delaware."

I gave her directions to my house. She thanked me and hung up before I could complete my goodbye.

Having learned much less than I usually do during a preappointment call.

A bright young woman. Articulate, tense. Holding back something?

Remembering the child she'd been, I found none of that surprising.

It's Mother.

That opened up a realm of possibilities.

The most likely: She'd finally come to grips with her mother's pathology—what it meant to *her.* Needed to put her feelings in focus, maybe get a referral for her mother.

So tomorrow's visit would probably be a one-shot deal. And that would be it. For another nine years.

I closed the chart, comfortable with my powers of prediction.

I might as well have been playing the slots in Vegas. Or buying penny stocks on Wall Street.

I spent the next couple of hours on my latest project: a monograph for one of the psych journals on my experiences with a school full of children victimized by a sniper the previous autumn. The writing was more of an ordeal than I'd expected; the trick was to make the experience come alive within the confines of a scientific approach.

I stared down at draft number four—fifty-two pages of defiantly awkward prose—certain I'd never be able to inject any humanity into the morass of jargon, scholarly references, and footnotes I had no clear memory of creating.

At eleven-thirty I put my pen down and sat back, still unable to find the magic voice. My eyes fell on Melissa's chart. I opened it and began reading.

October 18, 1978.

The fall of '78. I remembered it as a hot and nasty one. With its filthy streets and septic air, Hollywood hadn't worn its autumns well for a long time. I'd just given Grand Rounds at Western Pediatric Hospital and was itching to get back to the west side of town and the half a dozen appointments that made up the rest of my day.

I'd thought the lecture had gone well. *Behavioral Approaches to Fear and Anxiety in Children.* Facts and figures, transparencies and slides—in those days I'd thought all that quite impressive. An auditorium full of pediatricians, most of them private practitioners. An inquisitive, practical-minded bunch, hungry for what worked, with little patience for academic nit-picking.

I fielded questions for a quarter of an hour and was on my way out of the lecture hall when a young woman stopped me. I recognized her as one of the frequent questioners, thought I'd seen her somewhere else as well.

"Dr. Delaware? Eileen Wagner."

She had a pleasant full face under cropped chestnut hair. Good features, bottom-heavy figure, a slight squint. Her white blouse was mannish and buttoned to the neck; her skirt, knee-length tweed over sensible shoes. She carried a black Gladstone bag that looked brand-new. I remembered where I'd seen her before: last year's House Staff Roster. Third-year resident. M.D. from one of the Ivy League schools.

I said, "Dr. Wagner."

We shook hands. Hers was soft and stubby, bare of jewelry.

She said, "You gave a lecture on fears to the Four West staff last year, when I was PL-three. I thought it was quite good."

"Thank you."

"I enjoyed today, too. And I've got a referral for you, if you're interested."

"Sure."

She shifted the Gladstone bag to another hand. "I'm in practice now, out in Pasadena, have privileges at Cathcart Memorial. But the kid I have in mind isn't one of my regular patients, just a phone-in through Cathcart's help line. They didn't know how to handle it and sent it over to me because I'm listed as having an interest in behavioral pediatrics. When I heard what the problem was, I remembered last year's talk and thought it would be right up your alley. Then, when I read the Grand Rounds schedule, I thought: perfect."

"I'd be glad to help, but my office is on the other side of town."

"No matter. They'll come to you—they have the means. I know because I went out a few days ago to see her—it's a little girl we're talking about. Seven years old. Actually I came here this morning *because* of her. Hoping to learn something that could help *me* help her. But after listening to you it's clear her problems go beyond office management. She needs someone who specializes."

"Anxiety problems?"

Emphatic nod. "She's just *racked* with fears. Multiple phobias as well as a high level of general anxiety. I'm talking really pervasive."

"When you say you went out there, do you mean a house call?"

She smiled. "Didn't think anyone did them anymore? At Yale Public Health they taught us to call them 'home visits.' No, actually I don't make a habit of it—wanted them to come into the office to see me, but that's part of the problem. They don't travel. Or rather, the mother doesn't. She's an agoraphobic, hasn't left her house for years."

"How many years?"

"She didn't get any more specific than 'years'—and I could see even that much was hard for her, so I didn't push. She really wasn't prepared for being questioned at all. So I kept it brief, focused on the kid."

"Makes sense," I said. "What did she tell you about the kid?"

"Just that Melissa—that's her name—was afraid of everything. The dark. Loud noises and bright lights. Being alone. New situations. And she often seems tense and jumpy. Some of it's got to be constitutional—genetics—or maybe she's just imitating the mother. But I'm sure some of it's the way she lives—it's a very strange situation. Big house—huge. One of those incredible mansions on the north side of Cathcart Boulevard out in San Labrador. *Classic* San Labrador—acres of land, huge rooms, dutiful servants, everything very hush-hush. And the mother stays up in her room like some Victorian lady afflicted with the vapors."

She stopped, touched her mouth with a fingertip. "A Victorian princess, actually. She's really beautiful. Despite the fact that one side of her face is all scarred and there appears to be some mild facial hemiplegia—subtle sagging, mostly when she talks. If she weren't so beautiful—so *symmetrical*—you might never notice. No keloiding, though. Just a mesh of fine scars. I'd be willing to bet she had top-level plastic surgery years ago for something really major. Most likely a burn or some kind of deep flesh wound. Maybe that's the root of *her* problem—I don't know."

"What's the little girl like?"

"I didn't see much of her, just caught a glimpse when I walked in the front door. Small and skinny and cute, very well dressed—your basic little rich girl. When I tried to talk to her she scampered away. I suspect she actually hid somewhere in her mother's room—it's a bunch of rooms, actually, more like a suite. While the mother and I were talking I kept hearing little rustles in the background and each time I stopped to listen, they'd stop. The mother never remarked on it, so I didn't say anything. Figured I was lucky enough just getting up there to see her."

I said, "Sounds like something out of a Gothic novel."

"Yes. That's exactly what it was. Gothic. Sort of spooky. Not that the *mother* was spooky—she was charming, actually. Sweet. In a vulnerable way."

"Your basic Victorian princess," I said. "She doesn't leave the house at all?"

"That's what she said. What she confessed—she's pretty ashamed. Not that shame's convinced her to try to leave the house. When I suggested she see if she could make it to my office, she started to get really tense. Her hands actually started shaking. So I backed off. But she did agree to have Melissa be seen by a psychologist."

"Strange."

"Strange is your business, isn't it?"

I smiled.

She said, "Have I piqued your interest?"

"Do you think the mother really wants help?"

"For the girl? She says she does. But more important, the kid's motivated. She's the one who called the help line."

"Seven years old and she called herself?"

"The volunteer on the line couldn't believe it either. The line's not intended for kids. Once in a while they get a teenager they refer to Adolescent Medicine. But Melissa must have seen one of their public service commercials on TV, copied down the number, and dialed it. And she was up late to do it—the call came in just after ten P.M."

She lifted the Gladstone bag chest-high, popped it open, and pulled out a cassette.

"I know it sounds bizarre, but I've got the proof right here. They tape everything that comes over the line. I had them make me a copy."

I said, "She must be pretty precocious."

"Must be. I wish I'd had a chance to actually spend some time with her—what a neat kid, to take the initiative." She paused. "What a hurt she must be going through. Anyway, after I listened to the tape I phoned the number she gave the volunteer and reached the mother. She had no idea Melissa had called. When I told her, she broke down and started to cry. But when I asked her to come in for a consultation, she said she was ill and couldn't. I thought it was something physically debilitating, so I offered to go out there. Hence, my Gothic home visit."

She held the tape out to me. "If you'd like, you can have a listen. It's really something. I told the mother I'd be talking to a psychologist, took the liberty of giving her your name. But don't feel any pressure."

I took the cassette. "Thanks for thinking of me, but I honestly don't know if I can make home visits to San Labrador."

"She can come to the other side of town—Melissa can. A servant will bring her."

I shook my head. "In a case like this, the mother should be actively involved."

She frowned. "I know. It's not optimal. But do you have techniques that can help the girl at all without maternal involvement? Just lower her anxiety level a bit? Anything you did might reduce her risk of turning out totally screwed up. It would be a real good deed."

"Maybe," I said. "If the mother doesn't sabotage therapy."

"I don't think she will. She's antsy, but seemed to really love the kid. The guilt helps us there—think how inadequate she must feel, the kid calling in like that. She knows this isn't the right way to raise a child but can't break out of her own pathology. It's got to feel horrible for her. The way I see it, this is the right time to harness the guilt. If the kid gets better, maybe Mom'll see the light, get some help for herself."

"Is there a father in the picture?"

"No, she's a widow. It happened when Melissa was a baby. Heart attack. I got the impression he was a much older man."

"Sounds like you learned a lot from a brief visit."

Her cheeks colored, "One tries. Listen, I don't expect you to disrupt your life and drive out there on a regular basis. But getting a referral closer to home wouldn't make any difference. Mom never leaves to go *anywhere*. For her, half a mile might as well be Mars. And if they do try therapy and it doesn't work, they may never try it again. So I want somebody competent. After listening to you I'm convinced you're right for the case. I'd greatly appreciate it if you could accept less than optimal. I'll make it up to you with some solid referrals in the future. Okay?"

"Okay."

"I know I sound overinvolved and maybe I am—but the whole idea of a seven-year-old calling in like that . . . And that house." She raised her eyebrows. "Besides, I figure it won't be long before my practice really gets crazy and I don't have the time to give anyone this kind of individual attention. So I might as well enjoy it while I can, right?"

Another reach into the Gladstone. "Anyway, here's the relevant data." She handed me a piece of note paper topped with the logo of a pharmaceutical company. On it she'd printed:

Pt: Melissa Dickinson, DOB 6/21/71.
Mom: Gina Dickinson.

And a phone number.

I took it and put it in my pocket.

"Thanks," she said. "At least payment won't be a hassle. They're not exactly Medi-Cal."

I said, "Are you the physician of record, or do they have someone they've been seeing?"

"According to the mother, there's a family doctor in Sierra Madre that Melissa's seen occasionally in the past—immunizations, school physicals, nothing ongoing. Physically, she's a very healthy girl. But he's not really in the picture—hasn't been for years. She didn't want him contacted."

"Why's that?"

"The whole therapy thing. The stigma. To be perfectly frank, I had to do a sell-job. This is San Labrador we're talking about; they're still fighting the twentieth century. But she will cooperate—I got a commitment out of her. As to whether or not I'll end up being their regular doc, I don't know. Either way, if you want to send me a report, I'd sure be interested in finding out how she does."

"Sure," I said. "You just mentioned school physicals. Despite the fears, does she attend classes regularly?"

"She did until recently. Servants drove her and picked her up; parent-teacher conferences were conducted over the phone. Maybe in that neck of the woods it's not that strange, but it can't have been great for the kid, the mother never showing up for anything. Despite that, Melissa's a terrific student—straight A's. The mother made a point of showing me the report cards."

I said, "What do you mean by 'until recently'?"

"Lately she's been starting to exhibit some definite symptoms of school phobia: vague physical complaints, crying in the morning, claiming she's too scared to go to school. The mother's been letting her stay home. To me that's a big fat danger sign."

"Sure is," I said. "Especially with her role model."

"Yup. The old biopsychosocial chain. Take enough histories and all you see is chains."

"Chain mail," I said. "Tough armor."

She nodded. "But maybe we can break one this time, huh? Wouldn't that be uplifting?"

I saw patients all afternoon, finished a stack of charts. As I cleared my desk I listened to the tape.

FEMALE ADULT VOICE: Cathcart help line.

CHILD'S VOICE (*Barely audible*): Hello.

ADULT VOICE: Help line. How may I help you?

Silence

CHILD'S VOICE: Is this (*Breathy, inaudible*) . . . hospital?

AV: This is the Cathcart Hospital help line. What can I do for you?

CV: I need help. I'm . . .

AV: Yes?

Silence

AV: Hello? Are you there?

CV: I . . . I'm scared.

AV: Scared of what, dear?

CV: Everything.

Silence

AV: Is there something—or someone—right there with you, scaring you?

CV: . . . No.

AV: No one at all?

CV: No.

AV: Are you in some kind of danger, dear?

Silence

AV: Honey?

CV: No.

AV: No danger at all?

CV: No.

AV: Could you tell me your name, honey?

CV: Melissa.

AV: Melissa what?

CV: Melissa Anne Dickinson. (*Starts to spell it out*)

AV: (*Breaks in*) How old are you, Melissa?

CV: Seven.

AV: Are you calling from your house, Melissa?

CV: Yes.

AV: Do you know your address, Melissa? (*Tears*)

AV: It's all right, Melissa. Is something—someone or something—bothering you? Right now?

CV: No. I'm just scared . . . always.

AV: You're always scared?

CV: Yes.

AV: But there's nothing there bothering you or scaring you right *now*? Nothing in your house?

CV: Yes.

AV: There is something?

CV: No. Nothing right here. I . . . (*Tears*)

AV: What is it, honey?

Silence

AV: Does someone at your house bother you other times?

CV: (*Whispering*) No.

AV: Does your mommy know you're calling, Melissa?

CV: No. (*Tears*)

AV: Would she be mad if she knew you were calling?

CV: No. She's . . .

AV: Yes, Melissa?

CV: . . . nice.

AV: Your mommy's nice?

CV: Yes.

AV: So you're not scared of your mommy?

CV: No.

AV: What about your daddy?

CV: I don't have a daddy.

Silence

AV: Are you scared of anyone else?

CV: No.

AV: Do you know what you are scared of?

Silence

AV: Melissa?

cv: Darkness . . . burglars . . . things.

av: Darkness and burglars. And things. Can you tell me what kinds of things, honey?

cv: Uh, things . . . all kinds of things! (*Tears*)

av: Okay, honey, just hold on. We'll get you some help. Just don't hang up, okay?

Sniffles

av: Okay, Melissa? Still there?

cv: Yes.

av: Good girl. Now, Melissa, do you know your address— the street where you live?

cv: (*Very rapidly*) Ten Sussex Knoll.

av: Could you please repeat that, Melissa?

cv: Ten. Sussex. Knoll. San Labrador. Cal. Ifornia. Nine-one-one-oh-eight.

av: Very good. So you live in San Labrador. That's really close to us—to the hospital.

Silence

av: Melissa?

cv: Is there a doctor who can help me? Without shots?

av: Of course there is, Melissa, and I'm going to get you that doctor.

cv: (*Inaudible*)

av: What's that, Melissa?

cv: Thank you.

A burst of static, then dead air. I turned off the recorder and phoned the number Eileen Wagner had written down. A reedy male voice answered: "Dickinson residence."

"Mrs. Dickinson, please. This is Dr. Delaware, regarding Melissa."

Throat clear. "Mrs. Dickinson's not available, Doctor. However, she said to tell you that Melissa can be at your office any weekday between three and four-thirty."

"Do you know when she'll be available to talk?"

"No, I'm afraid I don't, Dr. Delaware. But I'll apprise her of your call. Is that time period suitable for you?"

I checked my appointment book. "How about Wednesday? Four o'clock."

"Very good, Doctor." He recited my address and said, "Is that correct?"

"Yes. But I would like to talk with Mrs. Dickinson before the appointment."

"I'll inform her of that, Doctor."

"Who'll be bringing Melissa?"

"I will, sir."

"And you are . . . ?"

"Dutchy. Jacob Dutchy."

"And your relationship to—"

"I'm in Mrs. Dickinson's employ, sir. Now, in the matter of your fee, is there a preferred mode of payment?"

"A check would be fine, Mr. Dutchy."

"And the fee itself?"

I quoted him my hourly rate.

"Very good, Doctor. Goodbye, Doctor."

The next morning, a legal-size manila envelope arrived at the office by messenger. Inside was a smaller, rose-colored envelope; within that, a sheet of rose-colored stationery folded over a check.

The check was for $3,000 and was annotated *Medical treatment for Melissa*. At my '78 rate, over forty sessions' worth. The money had been drawn on a savings account at First Fiduciary Trust Bank in San Labrador. Printed in the upper left corner of the check was:

R.P. DICKINSON, TRUSTEE
DICKINSON FAMILY TRUST UDT 5-11-71
10 SUSSEX KNOLL
SAN LABRADOR, CALIFORNIA 91108

The stationery was heavy stock, folded in half, with a Crane watermark. I opened it.

At the top, in embossed black script:

Regina Paddock Dickinson

Below that, in a fine, graceful hand:

> *Dear Doctor Delaware,*
> *Thank you for seeing Melissa.*
> *I'll be in touch.*
> *Faithfully yours,*
> *Gina Dickinson*

Scented paper. A mixture of old roses and alpine air. But it didn't sweeten the message:

Don't call us, plebe. We'll call you. Here's a juicy check to suppress any protests.

I dialed the Dickinson residence. This time a woman answered. Middle-aged, Gallic accent, voice pitched lower than Dutchy's.

Different pipes, same song: *Madame* wasn't available. No, she had no idea when Madame *would* be available.

I left my name, hung up, looked at the check. All those digits. Treatment hadn't even begun and I'd lost control. It wasn't the way to do business, wasn't in the best interests of the patient. But I'd committed myself to Eileen Wagner.

The tape had committed me.

. . . a doctor who can help me. Without shots.

I thought about it for a long time, finally decided I'd stick it out long enough to do an intake at least. See if I could get a rapport with the little girl, get some sort of progress going—enough to impress the Victorian princess.

Dr. Savior.

Then, I'd start making demands.

During my lunch hour I cashed the check.

3

Dutchy was fiftyish, mid-size and plump, with slicked-down too-black hair parted on the right, apple cheeks, and razor-slash lips. He had on a well-cut but old-fashioned double-breasted blue serge suit, starched white shirt, linen pocket square, Windsor-knotted navy tie, and mirror-bright black bluchers with extra heel. When I came out of the inner office he and the girl were standing in the middle of the waiting room, she looking down at the carpet, he examining the artwork. The look on his face said my prints weren't passing muster. When he turned to face me, his expression didn't change.

All the warmth of a Montana hailstorm, but the girl clutched his hand as if he were Santa Claus.

She was small for her age but had a mature, well-formed face—one of those children endowed early with the countenance they'll grow old with. An oval face, just this side of pretty, beneath bangs the color of walnut shells. The rest of her hair was long, almost to her waist, and topped with a pink flowered band. She had big round gray-green eyes with blond lashes, an upturned nose lightly freckled, and a pointy pixie chin under a narrow, timid mouth. Her clothes were too formal for school: puffed-sleeve dress of pink dotted swiss sashed with white satin tied in a bow at the back, pink lace-topped socks, and white patent-leather buckle shoes. I thought of Carroll's Alice encountering the Queen of Hearts.

The two of them stood there, immobile. A cello and a piccolo, cast in odd duet.

I introduced myself, bending and smiling at the girl. She stared back. To my surprise, no terror.

No response at all, other than flat appraisal. Considering what had brought her to the office, I was doing great, so far.

Her right hand was swallowed by Dutchy's meaty left one. Rather than have her relinquish it, I smiled again and held out my hand to Dutchy. He seemed surprised by the gesture and took it with reluctance, then let go at the same time he released the girl's fingers.

"I'll be off now," he announced to both of us. "Forty-five minutes—correct, Doctor?"

"Correct."

He took a step toward the door.

I was looking at the girl, bracing myself for resistance. But she just stood there, staring down at the carpet, hands pressed to her sides.

Dutchy took another step and stopped. Chewing his cheek, he turned back and patted the girl's head. She gave him what appeared to be a reassuring smile.

" 'Bye, Jacob," she said. High, breathy voice. Same as on the tape.

The rose tint spread from Dutchy's cheeks to the rest of his face. He chewed his cheek some more, lowered his arm stiffly, and mumbled something. One last glare at me and he was gone.

After the door closed I said, "Looks like Jacob's a good friend."

She said, "He's my mother's retainer."

"But he takes care of you, too."

"He takes care of everything."

"Everything?"

"Our house." She tapped her foot impatiently. "I don't

have a father, and my mother doesn't leave the house, so Jacob does lots of things for us."

"What kinds of things?"

"*House* things—telling Madeleine and Sabino and Carmela and all the service people and the delivery people what to do. Sometimes he makes food—snacks and finger food. If he's not too busy. Madeleine cooks the big hot meals. And he drives all the cars. Sabino only drives the truck."

"All the cars," I said. "Do you have a lot?"

She nodded. "A lot. My father liked cars and bought them before he died. Mother keeps them in the big garage even though she doesn't drive them, so Jacob has to start them and drive them so they don't get sticky inside the engine. There's also a company that comes to wash them every week. Jacob watches them to make sure they do a good job."

"Sounds like Jacob keeps busy."

"He does. How many cars do you have?"

"Just one."

"What kind?"

"It's a Dodge Dart."

"Dodge Dart," she said, pursing her lips and thinking. "We don't have one of those."

"It's not very fancy. Kind of beat-up, actually."

"We have one like that. A Cadillac Knockabout."

"Cadillac Knockabout," I said. "Don't think I've ever heard of that model."

"It's the one we took today. To here. A 1962 Cadillac Fleetwood Knockabout. It's black and old. Jacob says it's a workhorse."

"Do you like cars, Melissa?"

Shrug. "Not really."

"What about toys? Do you have any favorites?"

Shrug. "Not really."

"I've got toys in my office. How about we go check them out?"

She shrugged a third time but allowed me to usher her into the consult room. Once she was inside, her eyes took flight, darting and alighting upon desk, bookshelves, toy chest, back to the desk. Never settling. She knitted her hands, pulled them apart, and began a curious rolling, kneading motion, turning one set of tiny fingers over the other.

I walked over to the toy cabinet, opened it, and pointed. "I've got lots of stuff in here. Box games and dolls and clay and Play-Doh. Paper and pencils, too. And crayons, if you like to draw in color."

"Why should I do that?" she said.

"Do what, Melissa?"

"Play or draw? Mother said we were going to talk."

"Your mother was right. We are going to talk," I said. "But sometimes kids who come here like to play or draw before they start talking. While they get used to this place."

The hands kneaded faster. She looked down.

"Also," I said, "playing and talking can help kids express how they feel—help get their feelings out."

"I can get my feelings out," she said, "by talking."

"Great," I said. "Let's talk."

She took a place on the leather sofa and I sat opposite her in my chair. She looked around some more, then placed her hands in her lap and stared straight at me.

I said, "Okay. Why don't we start by talking about who I am and why you're here. I'm a psychologist. Do you know what that means?"

She kneaded her fingers and kicked the couch with her heel. "I have a problem and you're the kind of doctor who helps children who have problems and you don't give any shots."

"Very good. Did Jacob tell you all that?"

She shook her head. "My mother. Dr. Wagner told her about you—she's my mother's friend."

I remembered what Eileen Wagner had said about a brief chat, about a little girl wandering and hiding in a big, spooky house, and wondered what friendship meant to this child. "But Dr. Wagner met your mother because of you, didn't she, Melissa? Because of your call to the help line."

Her body tightened and the little hands kneaded faster. I noticed that her finger pads were pink, slightly chafed.

"Yeah, but she likes my mother."

Her eyes left mine and stared at the carpet.

"Well," I said, backtracking, "Dr. Wagner *was* right. About the shots. I *never* give shots. Don't even *know* how to give shots."

Unimpressed, she looked at her shoes. Sticking her legs straight out, she began bobbling her feet.

"Still," I said, "even going to a doctor who doesn't give shots can be scary. It's a new situation. You don't know what's going to happen."

Her head shot up, the green eyes defiant. "I'm not scared of *you*."

"Good." I smiled. "And I'm not scared of you either."

She gave me a look that was part bafflement, mostly scorn. So much for the old Delaware wit.

"Not only don't I give shots," I said, "but I don't do anything *to* the children who come here. I work *with* them. As a team. They tell me about themselves and when I know enough about them, I show them how not to be scared. Because being scared is something we learn. So we can *un*learn it."

Spark of interest in the eyes. Her legs relaxed. But more kneading, faster.

She said, "How many other kids come here?"

"Lots."

"How many?"

"Between four and eight a day."

"What are their names?"

"I can't tell you that, Melissa."

"Why not?"

"It's a secret—just like I couldn't tell anyone that you came here today unless you gave me permission."

"Why?"

"Because kids who come here talk about things that are private. They want privacy—do you know what that means?"

"Privacy," she said, "is going to the bathroom like a young lady, all by yourself, with the door closed."

"Exactly. When kids talk about themselves, they sometimes tell me things they've never told anyone. Part of my job is knowing how to keep a secret. So everything that goes on in this room is a secret. Even the names of the people who come here are secret. That's why there's that second door." I pointed. "It goes out to the hall. So people can leave the office without going into the waiting room and seeing other people. Would you like to see?"

"No, thank you." More tension.

I said, "Is something bothering you right now, Melissa?"

"No."

"Would you like to talk about what scares you?"

Silence.

"Melissa?"

"Everything."

"Everything scares you?"

Look of shame.

"How about we start with one thing."

"Burglars and intruders." Reciting, without hesitation.

I said, "Did someone tell you the kinds of questions I'd be asking you today?"

Silence.

"Was it Jacob?"

Nod.

"And your mother?"

"No. Just Jacob."

"Did Jacob also tell you how to answer my questions?"

More hesitation.

I said, "If he did, that's okay. He's trying to help. I just want to make sure you tell me how *you* feel. You're the star of this show, Melissa."

She said, "He told me to sit up straight, speak clearly, and tell the truth."

"The truth about what scared you?"

"Uh-huh. And then maybe you could help me."

Accent on the *maybe*. I could almost hear Dutchy's voice.

I said, "That's fine. Jacob's obviously a very smart person and he takes good care of you. But when you come here, you're the boss. You can talk about anything you want."

"I *want* to talk about burglars and intruders."

"Okay. Then that's what we'll do."

I waited. She said nothing.

I said, "What do these burglars and intruders look like?"

"They're not real burglars," she said, scornful again. "They're in my imagination. Pretend."

"What do they look like in your imagination?"

More silence. She closed her eyes. The hands kneaded furiously, her body took on a faint rocking motion, and her face screwed up. She appeared to be on the brink of tears.

I leaned in closer and said, "Melissa, we don't have to talk about this right now."

"Big," she said, eyes still closed. But dry. I realized that the facial tightness wasn't a presage to tears, just intense concentration. Her eyes moved frantically beneath their lids.

Chasing images.

She said, "He's big . . . with this big hat . . ."

Sudden stillness beneath the eyelids.

Her hands untangled, floated upward, and made wide circles. ". . . and a long coat and . . ."

"And what?"

The hands stopped circling but remained in the air. Her mouth was slightly parted but no sound came out. A slack look came onto her face. Dreamy.

Hypnotic.

Spontaneous hypnotic induction?

Not uncommon in children her age: young kids readily cross the boundary between reality and fantasy; the bright ones are often the best hypnotic subjects. Combine that with the solitary existence Eileen Wagner had described and I could see her visiting the cinema in her head on a regular basis.

Sometimes, though, the feature was a horror flick. . . .

The hands dropped back into her lap, found one another, and began rolling and kneading. The trancelike expression lingered. She remained silent.

I said, "The burglar wears a big hat and a long coat." Unconsciously, I'd lowered my voice and slowed it. Taking her cue. The dance of therapy.

More tension. No reply.

"Anything else?" I said gently.

She was silent.

I played a hunch. An educated guess born of so many other forty-five-minute hours. "He's got something else besides a hat and a coat, doesn't he, Melissa? Something in his hand?"

"Bag." Barely audible.

I said, "Yes. The burglar carries a bag. For what?"

No reply.

"To put stuff in?"

Her eyes snapped open and her hands clamped down on her knees. She began rocking again, harder and faster, head held stiff, as if her neck were jointless.

I leaned over and touched her shoulder. Bird bones beneath cotton.

"Do you want to talk about what goes into the bag, Melissa?"

She closed her eyes and kept rocking. Trembled and hugged herself. A tear rolled down her cheek.

I patted her again, got a tissue, and wiped her eyes, half expecting her to pull away. But she allowed me to dab the tears.

Dramatic first session, movie-of-the-week perfect. But too much, too fast; it could jeopardize the therapy. I dabbed some more, searching for some way to slow it down.

She killed that notion with a single word:

"Kids."

"The burglar puts kids in the sack?"

"Uh-huh."

"So the burglar is really a kidnapper."

She opened her eyes, stood up, faced me, and held up her hands as if praying. "He's a murderer!" she cried, emphasizing each word with a shake. "A Mikoksi with acid!"

"A Mikoksi?"

"A Mikoksi with *acidthatmeanspoison*! *Burning* poison! Mikoksi threw it on her and he's going to come back and burn her again, and me, too!"

"Who did he throw poison on, Melissa?"

"*Mother!* And now he's going to come back!"

"Where is this Mikoksi now?"

"In jail, but he's going to get out and hurt us again!"

"Why would he do that?"

"Because he doesn't like us. He liked Mother but then he stopped liking her and he threw poison acid on her and tried to kill her but it only burned her on the face and she was still beautiful and could get married and have me!"

She began pacing the office, holding her temples, stooped and muttering like a little old woman.

"When did all this happen, Melissa?"

"Before I was born." Rocking, face to the wall.

"Did Jacob tell you about it?"

Nod.

"Did your mother talk to you about it, too?"

Hesitation. Shake of head. "She doesn't like to."

"Why's that?"

"It makes her sad. She used to be happy and beautiful. People took pictures of her. Then Mikoksi burned her face and she had to have operations."

"Does Mikoksi have another name? A first name?"

She turned and faced me, truly puzzled. "I don't know."

"But you know he's in jail."

"Yes, but he's getting out and it's no fair and no justice!"

"Is he getting out of jail soon?"

More confusion.

"Did Jacob tell you he was getting out soon?"

"No."

"But he did talk to you about justice."

"Yes!"

"What does justice mean to you?"

"Being fair!"

She gave me a challenging look and put her hands on the flat place where one day her hips would be. Tension rumpled the sliver of brow beneath her bangs. Her mouth curled and she wagged a finger. "It was no fair and stupid! They should have a fair justice! They should have killed *him* with the acid!"

"You're very angry at Mikoksi."

Another incredulous look at the idiot in the chair.

I said, "That's good. Getting really angry at him. When you're angry at him, you're not so scared of him."

Both hands had fisted. She opened them, dropped them, sighed, and looked at the floor. More kneading.

I went over to her and kneeled so that we'd be at eye level if she chose to raise her eyes. "You're a very smart girl, Melissa, and you've helped me a lot by being brave and talking about scary things. I know how much you want not to be afraid anymore. I've helped lots of other kids and I'll be able to help you."

Silence.

"If you want to talk some more about Mikoksi or burglars or anything else, that's okay. But if you don't, that's okay, too. We've got some more time together before Jacob comes back. How we spend it is up to you."

No movement or sound; the second hand on the banjo clock across the room completed half a circuit. Finally she lifted her head. Looked everywhere but at me, then homed in suddenly, squinting, as if trying to put me in focus.

"I'll draw," she said. "But only with pencils. Not crayons, they're too messy."

•   •   •

She worked the pencil slowly, a tongue tip extending from one corner of her mouth. Her artistic ability was above average, but all the finished product told me was that she'd had enough for one day: happy-face girl next to happy-face cat in front of red house and a fat-trunked tree full of apples. All of it under a huge golden sun with prehensile rays.

When she was through she pushed it across the desk and said, "You keep it."

"Thank you. It's terrific."

"When am I coming back?"

"How about in two days? Friday."

"Why not tomorrow?"

"Sometimes it's good for kids to take some time to think about what happened before they come in."

"I think fast," she said. "And there's other stuff I didn't say yet."

"You really want to come in tomorrow?"

"I want to get better."

"All right then, I can see you tomorrow at five. If Jacob can bring you."

"He will," she said. "He wants me to get better, too."

I saw her out through the separate exit and spotted Dutchy walking down the hall, a paper bag in one hand. When he saw us he frowned and looked at his watch.

Melissa said, "We're coming back to him at five tomorrow, Jacob."

Dutchy raised his eyebrows and said, "I believe I'm right on time, Doctor."

"You are," I said. "I was just showing Melissa the separate exit."

"So other kids won't see me or know who I am," she said. "It's privacy."

"I see," said Dutchy, looking up and down the hall. "I brought you something, young lady. To tide you over until dinner." The top half of the bag was accordion-folded neatly.

He opened it with his fingertips and drew out an oatmeal cookie.

Melissa squealed, took it from him, and prepared to bite into it.

Dutchy cleared his throat.

Melissa held the cookie mid-air. "Thank you, Jacob."

"You're quite welcome, young lady."

She turned to me. "Would you like some, Dr. Delaware?"

"No, thank you, Melissa." Sounding to myself like a charm school candidate.

She licked her lips and went to work on the cookie.

I said, "I'd like to talk to you for a moment, Mr. Dutchy."

He glanced at his watch again. "The freeway . . . the longer we wait . . ."

I said, "Some things came up during the session. Important things."

He said, "Really, it's quite—"

I forced a patient grin and said, "If I'm to do my job, I'm going to need help, Mr. Dutchy."

From the look on his face, I might have passed wind at an embassy dinner. He cleared his throat again and said, "One moment, Melissa," and walked several feet down the corridor. Melissa, her mouth full of cookie, followed him with her eyes.

I smiled at her, said, "We'll just be one second, hon," and joined him.

He looked up and down the hall and folded his arms across his chest. "What is it, Doctor?"

From a foot away, he was shaven clean as palmar flesh, smelling of bay rum and fresh laundry.

I said, "She talked about what happened to her mother. Some person named Mikoksi."

He flinched. "Really, sir, it's not my place."

"This is important, Mr. Dutchy. It's obviously relevant to her fears."

"It's best that her mother—"

"True. The problem is I've left several messages with her

mother that haven't been returned. Normally, I wouldn't even see a child without direct parental participation. But Melissa obviously needs help. Lots of help. I can provide that help but I need information."

He chewed his cheek so long and hard I was afraid he'd gnaw through it. Down the hall, Melissa was munching and staring at us.

He said, "Whatever happened was before the child's time."

"Chronologically, maybe. But not psychologically."

He stared at me for a long moment. A hint of moisture appeared in the corner of his right eye, no bigger than the diamond on a budget engagement ring. He blinked and made it disappear. "Really, this is quite awkward. I'm an employee. . . ."

I said, "All right. I don't want to put you in a difficult position. But please deliver the message that someone needs to talk to me as soon as possible."

Melissa scuffed her feet. The cookie was gone. Dutchy gave her a grave but oddly tender look.

I said, "I do want to see her tomorrow at five."

He nodded, took a step closer, so that we were almost touching, and whispered in my ear: "She pronounces it Mikoksi but the damned villain's name was McCloskey. *Joel* McCloskey."

Lowering his head and pushing it forward, like a turtle peeking out of its shell. Waiting for a reaction.

Expecting me to know something . . .

I said, "Doesn't ring any bells."

The head drew back. "Were you living in Los Angeles ten years ago, Doctor?"

I nodded.

"It was in the papers."

"I was in school. Concentrating on my textbooks."

"March of 1969," he said. "March third." A pained look crossed his face. "This is— That's all I can say right now, Doctor. Perhaps some other time."

"All right," I said. "See you tomorrow."

"Five it is." He let out his breath and drew himself up. Tugging at his lapels, he cleared his throat. "Getting back to the present, I trust everything proceeded as planned today."

"Everything went fine."

Melissa was coming our way. The white satin sash had come loose and hung from a single loop, scraping the floor. Dutchy rushed over and tied it, brushed crumbs from her dress, braced her shoulders, and told her to stand up straight, young lady, a curved spine simply wouldn't do.

She smiled up at him.

They held hands as they left the building.

I saw another patient a few minutes later, managed to put the cello and the piccolo out of my mind for three quarters of an hour. Leaving the office at seven, I took a five-minute drive to the Beverly Hills Library. The reading room was crowded with retirees checking out the final stock quotations and teenagers doing their homework or faking it. By seven-fifteen I was sitting at a microfilm viewer with a March '69 spool of the *Times*. March 4 rolled into view. What I was looking for was on the upper left quadrant.

ACTRESS THE VICTIM OF ACID ATTACK

(HOLLYWOOD) A quiet hillside neighborhood above Hollywood Boulevard was the scene of a grisly early-morning assault upon a former fashion model currently under contract to Apex Motion Picture Studios, that left neighbors of the victim horror-struck and wondering why.

Regina Marie Paddock, 23, 2103 Beachwood Drive, Apartment 2, was awakened at home by her doorbell at 4:30 A.M., by a man claiming to be a Western Union messenger.

When she opened the door, the man brandished a bottle and flung its contents in her face. She collapsed screaming and the assailant, described as a male Negro, five eleven to six two, 190–200 pounds, escaped on foot.

The victim was taken to Hollywood Presbyterian Hospital where she was treated for third-degree facial burns. A hospital spokesman described her condition as "serious, but stable. She's in no mortal danger but is in considerable pain, having sustained extensive tissue damage to the left side of her face. Miraculously, her eyes were unaffected."

An Apex spokesman expressed the studio's "shock and deep regret over the vicious, unprovoked attack on the talented Gina Prince [Miss Paddock's stage name]. We will do everything within our power to work with the authorities in swiftly apprehending the perpetrator of this heinous crime."

The victim was born in 1946 in Denver, Colorado, moved to Los Angeles at the age of 19, was hired as a photographic and fashion model by the prestigious Flax Agency, and quickly advanced to feature spreads in *Glamour* and *Vogue*. After leaving Flax she switched to the now defunct Belle Vue Agency, eventually left modeling, signed with the William Morris Agency and received an acting contract at Apex.

Although she has not yet been cast in a film, the studio spokesman said she had been under consideration for "several important roles. She's a very talented and beautiful young lady. We'll do everything to see that her career remains untainted by this tragic occurrence."

Police are actively searching for the assailant and request that any information be directed to Detectives Savage or Flores at the LAPD's Hollywood Division.

At the center of the article was a head shot that could have been reduced from a *Vogue* cover: oval face on a long stalk of neck, framed by straight, pale hair worn long and layered in a complex style, sophisticated for the time. Arched eyebrows, high cheekbones, huge, pale eyes, pouty mouth. The shadowy perfection of a study by Avedon or someone almost as good.

I thought of what acid could do to perfection, backed away from that, and tried to look at the photo as if it were just a photo.

The features, taken singly, were almost identical to Melissa's, but the gestalt added up to a good deal more than just this side of pretty. I wondered whether puberty would bring Melissa to her mother's level of beauty.

I turned the knob on the viewer. A brief summary of Gina Paddock's medical status appeared in the next day's paper. Condition downgraded to stable. No leads. Another message of sympathy from the studio, augmented by a $5,000 reward for information leading to capture. But no more pledges of an untainted career.

I kept dialing. Two weeks later:

SUSPECT IN ACID ATTACK NABBED
Apprehended After Police
Receive Anonymous Tip

(LOS ANGELES) Police announced the arrest of a suspect in the March 3 early-morning acid attack that left actress Gina Prince (Regina Marie Paddock) permanently disfigured.

The arrest, in South Los Angeles, of Melvin Louis Findlay, 28, was announced at an 11:00 P.M. press conference at Parker Center by Hollywood Division Squad Commander Bryce Donnemeister, who described Findlay as a known felon and recent parolee from the Men's Colony at Chino, where he served eighteen months of a three-year sentence for extortion. Findlay's other arrests and convictions include aggravated assault, robbery, and vehicular grand theft.

"Physical evidence in our possession leads us to believe we have a strong case against this individual," said Donnemeister. He refused to elaborate on whether the victim had identified Findlay and offered no details on the arrest other than to say that an anonymous phone tip had led the police to Findlay and that "subsequent investigation confirmed that the information provided to us was valid."

Miss Prince continues to convalesce at Hollywood Presbyterian Hospital, where her condition is described as good. Plastic surgeons have been called in to consult on the reconstruction of her face.

Three days after that:

FORMER EMPLOYER ARRESTED IN ACID ASSAULT ON ACTRESS

(LAS VEGAS) The former employer and onetime companion of acid attack victim Gina Prince (Regina Marie Paddock) was arrested last night by Las Vegas police as a prime suspect in the March 3 assault that left the former fashion model and actress with extensive facial disfiguration.

Joel Henry McCloskey, 34, was arrested in his room at the Flamingo Hotel, where he had registered under a false name, and was placed in the custody of the Las Vegas Police Department in compliance with a warrant issued by the Criminal Division of the Los Angeles Superior Court.

LAPD Hollywood Division Commander Bryce Donnemeister said that information provided by another suspect in the case, Melvin Findlay, 28, arrested March 18, had incriminated McCloskey.

"It appears at this time that Findlay was hired help and McCloskey did the alleged hiring."

Donnemeister added that Findlay had worked for McCloskey in 1967 in a "janitorial capacity" but declined further comment pending a full investigation.

McCloskey, a native of New Jersey and a former nightclub singer, came to Los Angeles in 1962 with aspirations of being an actor. When those failed, he opened the Belle Vue Modeling Agency. After luring Miss Prince away from the larger, more established Flax Agency, he tried to serve as her film agent, according to Hollywood sources.

McCloskey and Miss Prince are reported to have developed a personal relationship that ended when Miss Prince left Belle Vue and, in an attempt to trade fashion modeling for screen stardom, signed with the William Morris Agency. Shortly after, Belle Vue's fortunes plummeted, and McCloskey declared bankruptcy on February 9 of this year.

When asked whether revenge figured as a motive in the attack, Police Commander Donnemeister said, "We're reserving comment until the suspect has been fully and properly questioned."

Miss Prince continues to recuperate at Hollywood Presbyterian Hospital, where plans are being made for her to undergo extensive reconstructive surgery.

There was a photo with this one, too: a small, dark, slender man being led away by two detectives who dwarfed him. He had on a sport coat, slacks, and an open-neck white shirt. His head was lowered and his longish hair hung down over the top half of his face. What was visible of the bottom half was angular, grim, James Deanish, and in need of a shave.

It took a while to locate the conclusion of the case.

McCloskey's extradition and arraignment, Melvin Findlay's agreement to plead guilty and testify against McCloskey in return for a simple assault conviction, McCloskey's indictment for attempted murder, conspiracy to commit murder and mayhem. Arraignment proceedings, then a three-month lag until the trial.

The judicial process was swift. The prosecutor distributed selections from Gina Prince's modeling portfolio to the jurors, followed by close-ups of her ravaged face taken in the emergency room. A brief appearance by the victim, bandaged and sobbing. Testimony by medical experts to the effect that her face would be scarred permanently.

Melvin Findlay testified that McCloskey had hired him to "trash the [obscenity] girl's face, make sure she was no [obscenity] good for nobody, and if she died, he wouldn't have no [obscenity] problem with that, too."

The prosecution produced a taped confession that the defense tried unsuccessfully to challenge. The tape was played in open court: McCloskey tearfully admitting to hiring Findlay to maim Gina Prince but refusing to explain why.

The defense didn't dispute the facts but attempted an insanity defense, which was hampered by McCloskey's refusal to talk to the hired-gun psychiatrists. The prosecution's psychiatric pistol testified to observing McCloskey in the county jail and finding him "uncooperative and depressed, but lucid and free of serious mental disease." It took two hours for the jury to bring in guilty verdicts on all charges.

At the sentencing hearing, the judge called McCloskey "an abject monster, one of the most despicable defendants it has been my displeasure to encounter in my twenty years on the bench," and handed down a combination of sentences that added up to twenty-three years in San Quentin. Everyone seemed satisfied. Even McCloskey, who fired his lawyers and refused to appeal.

After the trial, the press tried to interview the jurors. They chose to have their foreman speak for them and he was concise:

> "Only a semblance of justice could be accomplished," said Jacob P. Dutchy, 46, an executive aide at Dickinson Industries, Pasadena. "This young lady's life will never be the same. But we did what we could to ensure that McCloskey pays the harshest penalty possible under the law."

A Mikoksi with acid.

Twenty-three years in San Q.

Time off for good behavior could cut it in half. A belated appeal might shave off more. Meaning McCloskey's release could be imminent—if it hadn't already taken place.

No doubt Dutchy would know the precise release date—he'd be the type to follow that kind of thing closely. I wondered how he and the child's mother had explained it all to Melissa.

Dutchy. Interesting fellow. Throwback to another age.

From juror to retainer. I was curious about the evolution but had little hope of satisfying my curiosity. The way things were going, I'd be lucky to get an accurate history on my patient.

I thought of Dutchy's secretiveness and devotion. Gina Dickinson had the ability to inspire strong loyalties. Was it the helplessness, the same princess-in-distress frailty that had brought Eileen Wagner out on a house call?

What did growing up with a mother like that do to a child?

Men with sacks . . .

Same dream I'd heard from so many other children, almost an archetype. Children I'd cured.

But I sensed this child would be different. No easy heroism here.

I had a deli dinner at Nate 'n Al, on Beverly Drive:

corned beef on rye accompanied by the tape-loop blather of Hollywood types shmoozing about pending deals, drove home, and phoned a San Labrador exchange that had stuck in my head.

This time an answering machine with Jacob Dutchy's voice informed me no one was available and invited me, halfheartedly, to leave a message.

I repeated my urgent desire to speak with the lady of the house at 10 Sussex Knoll.

4

No callback that evening, nor the following day, and as 5:00 P.M. approached I resigned myself to pumping Dutchy for information again—awkward position be damned.

But he didn't show up. Instead, Melissa was accompanied by a Mexican man in his sixties—broad and low-slung, hard and muscular despite his age, with a thin gray mustache, beak nose, and hands as rough and brown as cedar bark. He wore khaki work clothes and rubber-soled shoes and held a sweat-stained beige canvas hat in front of his groin.

"This is Sabino," said Melissa. "He takes care of our plants."

I said hello and introduced myself. The gardener smiled uncomfortably and muttered, "Hernandez, Sabino."

"Today we took the truck," said Melissa, "and looked down on everyone."

I said, "Where's Jacob?"

She shrugged. "Doing stuff."

At the mention of Dutchy's name, Hernandez stood up straighter.

I thanked him and told him Melissa would be free in forty-five minutes. Then I noticed he wasn't wearing a watch.

"Take a seat, if you'd like," I said, "or you can leave and come back at five forty-five."

"Okeh." He remained standing.

I pointed to a chair.

He said, "Ohh," and sat down, still holding his hat.

I took Melissa into the consult room.

Healer's challenge: Put aside my annoyance at the way the adults were fancy-dancing around me and concentrate on the child.

Plenty to concentrate on, today.

She began talking the moment she sat down, looking away from me and reciting her terrors nonstop, in a singsong oral-report voice that told me she'd studied hard for therapy. Closing her eyes as she went on, and climbing in power and pitch until she was nearly shouting, then stopping and shivering with dread, as if she'd suddenly visualized something overwhelming.

But before I could say anything, she was off again. Fluctuating between blurt and whisper, like a radio with a broken volume control.

"Monsters . . . big bad things."

"What kinds of big bad things, Melissa?"

"I don't know . . . just bad."

She went silent again, bit down on her lower lip, began rocking.

I put my hand on her shoulder.

She opened her eyes and said, "I know they're imaginary but they still scare me."

"Imaginary things can be very scary."

Saying it in a soothing voice, but she'd reeled me into her world and I was flashing mental pictures of my own: gibbering hordes of fanged and hooded shadow-things that lurked in the nightgloom. Trapdoors unlatched by the death of light. Trees turned to witches; shrubs to hunched, slimy corruptions; the moon, a looming, voracious fire.

The power of empathy. And more. Memories of other

nights, so long ago; a boy in a bed, listening to the winds whip across the Missouri flatlands . . . I broke away from that and focused on what she was saying:

". . . that's why I hate to sleep. Going to sleep brings the dreams."

"What kinds of dreams?"

She shivered again and shook her head. "I make myself stay awake but then I can't stop it anymore and I sleep and the dreams come."

I took her fingers in mine and stilled them with touch and therapeutic murmurings.

She turned silent.

I said, "Do you have bad dreams every night?"

"Yes. And more. Mother said one time there were seven."

"Seven bad dreams in one night?"

"Yes."

"Do you remember them?"

She liberated her hand, closed her eyes, and retreated to a detached tone. A seven-year-old clinician, presenting at Case Conference. The case of a certain nameless little girl who woke up cold and sweating from her sleeping place at the foot of her mother's bed. *Lurching* awake, heart pounding, clawing the sheets to keep from falling endlessly, uncontrollably, into a huge black maw. Clawing but losing her grip and feeling everything float away like a kite with a broken string. Crying out in the darkness and rolling—hurtling—toward her mother's warm body, a love-seeking missile. Mother's arm reaching out unconsciously and drawing her near.

Lying there, frozen, staring up at the ceiling, trying to convince herself it was just a ceiling, that the things crawling up there weren't—*couldn't* be—real. Inhaling Mother's perfume, listening to Mother's light snores. Making sure Mother was deep asleep before reaching out and touching satin and lace, a stretch of soft arm-flesh. Then up to the face. The good side . . . somehow she always ended up next to the good side.

Freezing again, as she said *good side* for the second time.

Her eyes opened. She threw a panicky glance at the separate exit.

A convict weighing the risks of jailbreak.

Too much, too soon.

Leaning in close, I told her she'd done well; we could spend the rest of the session drawing again, or playing a game.

She said, "I'm scared of my room."

"Why's that?"

"It's big."

"Too big for you?"

A guilty look crossed her face. Guilty confusion.

I asked her to tell me more about her room. She painted more pictures.

Tall ceiling with pictures of ladies in fancy dresses on it. Pink carpets, pink-and-gray lamb and pussycat wallpaper that Mother had picked especially for her when she was a baby in a crib. Toys. Music boxes and miniature dishes and glass figurines, three separate dollhouses, a zoo of stuffed animals. A canopy bed from somewhere else far away, she forgot where, with pillows and a fluffy comforter filled with goose feathers. Lace-trimmed windows that were round on top and went almost up to the ceiling. Windows with bits of colored glass in them that made colored pictures on your skin. A seat in front of one of the windows that had a view of the grass and the flowers Sabino tended all day; she wanted to call down and say hello to him but was afraid to get too close to the window.

"Sounds like a huge room," I said.

"Not just one room, a bunch. There's a sleeping room and a bathroom and a dressing room with mirrors and lights all around them, next to my closet. And a playroom—that's where most of the toys are, but the stuffed animals are in the sleeping room. Jacob calls the sleeping room the nursery, which means a baby room."

Frown.

"Does Jacob treat you like a baby?"

"No! I haven't used a crib since I was three!"

"Do you like having such a big room?"

"No! I hate it! I never go inside it."

The guilty look returned.

Two minutes until the session was over. She hadn't budged from her chair since she'd sat down.

I said, "You're doing a great job, Melissa. I've really learned a lot. But how about we stop for now?"

She said, "I don't like to be alone. Ever."

"No one likes to be alone for a long time. Even grownups get afraid of that."

"I don't like it *ever*. I waited until my *birthday*—till I was *seven*—to go to the bathroom by myself. With the door closed and privacy."

Sitting back, daring me to disapprove.

I said, "Who went with you till you were seven?"

"Jacob and Mother and Madeleine and Carmela kept me company till I was four. Then Jacob said I was a young lady now, only ladies should be with me, so he stopped going. Then, when I was seven I decided to go there alone. It made me cry and hurt my stomach and once I threw up, but I *did* it. With the door closed a little, then all the way—but I still don't *lock* it. No way."

Another dare.

I said, "You did great."

Frown. "Sometimes it still makes me nervous. I'd still like to have someone there—not looking, just there, keeping me company. But I don't ask them."

"Good for you," I said. "You fought your fear and beat it."

"Yes," she said. Astonished. Translating ordeal into victory for what appeared to be the first time.

"Did your mother and Jacob tell you you did a good job?"

"Uh-huh." Dismissive wave. "They always say nice things."

"Well, you did do a good job. You won a tough fight. That means you can win other fights—beat up other fears.

One by one. We can work together and pick the fears you want to fight, then plan how we'll do it, step by step. Slowly. So it's never scary for you. If you'd like, we can start the next time you're here—on Monday."

I got up.

She stayed in her chair. "I want to talk some more."

"I'd like to, too, Melissa, but our time is up."

"Just a *little*." Hint of whine.

"We really have to end now. I'll see you on Monday, which is only . . ."

I touched her shoulder. She shrugged me off and her eyes got wet.

I said, "I'm sorry, Melissa. I wish there—"

She shot out of the chair and shook a finger at me. "If your job is to *help* me, why can't you help me *now*?" Stamping her foot.

"Because our sessions together have to end at a certain time."

"*Why?*"

"I think you know."

" 'Cause you have to see other kids?"

"Yes."

"What're their names?"

"I can't talk about that, Melissa. Remember?"

"How come *they're* more important than *me*?"

"They're not, Melissa. You're very important to me."

"Then why are you kicking me *out*?"

Before I could answer, she burst into tears and headed for the door to the waiting room. I followed her, wondering for the thousandth time about the sanctity of the three-quarter hour, the idolatry of the clock. But knowing, also, the importance of limits. For any child, but especially this one, who seemed to have so few. Who'd been sentenced to live out her formative years in the terrible, unbounded splendor of a fairy-tale world.

Nothing scarier than fairy tales . . .

When I got to the waiting room she was tugging at

Hernandez's hand, crying and insisting, "Come *on,* Sabino!" He stood, looking frightened and puzzled. When he saw me, puzzlement changed to suspicion.

I said, "She's a little upset. Please have her mother call me as soon as possible."

Blank look.

"*Su madre,*" I said. "*El teléfono.* I'll see her Monday at five. *Lunes. Cinco.*"

"Okeh." He glared and squeezed his hat.

Melissa stamped her foot twice and said, "No way! I'm *never* coming back here! *Never!*"

Yanking at the rough brown hand. Hernandez stood and continued to study me. His eyes were watery and dark and had hardened, as if he were considering retribution.

I thought of all the protective layers surrounding this child, how ineffectual all of it was.

I said, "Goodbye, Melissa. See you Monday."

"No way!" She ran out.

Hernandez put on his hat and went after her.

I checked with my service at day's end. No messages from San Labrador.

I wondered how Hernandez had communicated what he'd seen. Prepared myself for a cancellation of the Monday appointment. But no message to that effect came that evening or the next day. Maybe they wouldn't offer that courtesy to a plebe.

I phoned the Dickinson household and got Dutchy on the third ring.

"Hello, Doctor." That same formality, but no irritation.

"I'm calling to confirm Melissa's appointment on Monday."

"Monday," he said. "Yes, I have that. Five o'clock, correct?"

"That's it."

"Is there anything available earlier, by chance? The traffic from our side of—"

"That's all I've got, Mr. Dutchy."

"Five it is, then. Thank you for calling, Doctor, and good eve—"

"One second," I said. "There's something you need to know. Melissa got upset today, left the office in tears."

"Oh? She seemed in fine spirits when she got home."

"Did she say anything to you about not wanting to come on Monday?"

"No. What was the trouble, Doctor?"

"Nothing serious. She wanted to stay past the appointed time, and when I told her she couldn't, she burst into tears."

"I see."

"She's used to having her way, isn't she, Mr. Dutchy?"

Silence.

I said, "I'm mentioning it because that may be part of the problem—lack of limits. For a child it can be like drifting in the ocean without an anchor. Some changes in basic discipline may be in order."

"Doctor, I'm not in any position to—"

"Of course, I forgot. Why don't you put Mrs. Dickinson on the phone right now and I'll discuss it with her."

"I'm afraid Mrs. Dickinson is indisposed."

"I can wait. Or call back, if you can let me know when she will be disposed."

Sigh. "Doctor, please. I'm not able to move mountains."

"I wasn't aware I was asking you to."

Silence. Throat clear.

I said, "Are you able to deliver a message?"

"Certainly."

"Tell Mrs. Dickinson this is an untenable situation. That although I have compassion for her situation, she's going to have to stop avoiding me if she wants me to treat Melissa."

"Dr. Delaware, please—this is quite— You really mustn't give up on the child. She's so . . . such a good, smart little girl. It would be a terrible waste if . . ."

"If what?"

"*Please*, Doctor."

"I'm trying to be patient, Mr. Dutchy, but I'm really having trouble understanding what the big deal is. I'm not asking Mrs. Dickinson to leave her house—all I want to do is *talk*. I understand her situation—I did my research. March 3, '69. Does she have a phobia of the telephone, too?"

Pause. "It's doctors. She had so many surgeries—so much pain. They kept taking her apart like a jigsaw puzzle and putting her back together again. I'm not denigrating the medical profession. Her surgeon was a magician. He nearly restored her. Externally. But inside . . . She just needs time, Dr. Delaware. Give *me* time. I'll get her to see how vital it is she contact you. But please be patient, sir."

My turn to sigh.

He said, "She's not without insight into her . . . into the situation. But after what the woman's been through—"

"She's afraid of doctors," I said. "Yet she met with Dr. Wagner."

"Yes," he said. "That was . . . a surprise. She doesn't cope well with surprises."

"Are you saying she had some sort of adverse reaction just to meeting with Dr. Wagner?"

"Let's just say it was difficult for her."

"But she did it, Mr. Dutchy. And survived. That could be therapeutic in and of itself."

"Doctor—"

"Is it because I'm a man? Would it be easier for her to deal with a female therapist?"

"No!" he said. "Absolutely not! It's not that at all."

"Just doctors," I said. "Of any gender."

"That's correct." Pause. "Please, Dr. Delaware"—his voice had softened—"please be patient."

"All right. But in the meantime someone's going to have to give me facts. Details. Melissa's developmental history. The family structure."

"You deem that absolutely necessary?"

"Yes. And it needs to be soon."

"All right," he said. *"I'll* fill you in. Within the limitations of my situation."

"What does that mean?" I said.

"Nothing—nothing at all. I'll give you a comprehensive history."

"Tomorrow at noon," I said. "We'll have lunch."

"I don't generally have lunch, Doctor."

"Then you can watch me eat, Mr. Dutchy. You'll be doing most of the talking anyway."

I picked a place midway between the west side and his part of town, one I thought sufficiently conservative for his sensibilities: the Pacific Dining Car on Sixth near Witmer, just a few blocks west of downtown. Dim rooms, polished mahogany paneling, red leather, linen napkins. Lots of financial types and corporate attorneys and political backstagers eating prime beef and talking zoning variances, sports scores, supply and demand.

He'd arrived early and was waiting for me in a back booth, dressed in the same blue suit or its twin. As I approached he half-rose and gave a courtly bow.

I sat down, called for the waiter, and ordered Chivas straight up. Dutchy asked for tea. We waited for the drinks without talking. Despite his frosty demeanor he looked out of his element and slightly pitiable—a nineteenth-century man transported to a distant, vulgar future he couldn't hope to comprehend.

Caught in an awkward position.

My ire had faded since yesterday and I'd pledged to avoid confrontation. So I started by telling him how much I appreciated his taking the time to see me. He said nothing and looked thoroughly uncomfortable. Small talk was clearly out of the question. I wondered if anyone had ever called him by his first name.

The waiter brought the drinks. Dutchy regarded his tea with the inherently disapproving scrutiny of an English peer, finally raised his cup to his lips, sipped, and put it down quickly.

"Not hot enough?" I said.

"No, it's fine, sir."

"How long have you worked for the Dickinson family?"

"Twenty years."

"Long before the trial, then."

He nodded and raised his cup again but didn't put it to his lips. "Being assigned to the jury was a stroke of fate—not one that I welcomed, at first. I wanted to apply for exemption, but Mr. Dickinson preferred I serve. Said it was my civic duty. He was a civic-minded man." His lip trembled.

"When did he die?"

"Seven and a half years ago."

Surprised, I said, "Before Melissa was born?"

"Mrs. Dickinson was expecting Melissa when it—" He looked up, startled, and swung his head to the right. The waiter was approaching from that direction, bearing the blackboard. Imperious and well-spoken and black as coal; Dutchy's African cousin.

I chose the T-bone steak, bloody rare. Dutchy asked if the shrimp was fresh that day and when informed that it *certainly* was, ordered shrimp salad.

When the waiter left I said, "How old was Mr. Dickinson when he died?"

"Sixty-two."

"How did he die?"

"On the tennis court."

The lip trembled some more but the rest of his face remained impassive. He fumbled with his teacup and tightened his mouth.

"Did your serving on the jury have anything to do with getting them together, Mr. Dutchy?"

Nod. "That's what I meant by a stroke of fate. Mr. Dickinson came with me to court. Sat in during the trial and was . . . entranced by her. He'd followed the case in the papers before I was impaneled. Had commented several times—over his morning paper—on the profoundness of the tragedy."

"Had he known Mrs. Dickinson before the attack?"

"No, not in the least. His concern, in the beginning, was . . . thematic. And he was a kind man."

I said, "I'm not sure I understand what you mean by thematic."

"Grief for beauty lost," he said, like a teacher announcing an essay theme. "Mr. Dickinson was a great aesthete. A conservationist and a preservationist. He'd spent much of his life dedicated to beautifying his world, and was terribly hurt by the degradation of beauty. However, he never allowed his concern to cross ethical bounds. When I was selected for the jury he said he'd be accompanying me to court but that both of us needed to be quite scrupulous about not discussing the case. He was also an honest man, Dr. Delaware. Diogenes would have rejoiced."

"An aesthete," I said. "What kind of business was he in?"

He looked down his nose at me. "I'm referring to Mr. *Arthur* Dickinson, sir."

Once more, no bells. This guy had a way of making me feel like a D student. Rather than come across a complete philistine, I said, "Of course. The philanthropist."

He continued to stare at me.

I said, "So how did the two of them finally meet?"

"The trial intensified Mr. Dickinson's concern—hearing her testimony, seeing her face bandaged. He visited her in the hospital. As chance had it, he'd been a benefactor of the very surgical wing in which she'd been placed. He conferred with the doctors and made sure she was receiving the very best care. Brought in the top man in the plastics field—Professor Albano Montecino from Brazil, a true genius. The man had done pioneering work in facial construction. Mr. Dickinson arranged for him to obtain medical privileges and exclusive use of an operating room."

Sweat had glossed Dutchy's brow. He pulled out a handkerchief and patted.

"Such pain," he said, facing me squarely. *"Seventeen* separate surgeries, Doctor. Someone with your background can appreciate what that means. Seventeen *invasions*—each one excruciating. Months of recuperation, long stretches of immobility. You can understand why she's taken to solitude."

I nodded and said, "Were the operations successful?"

"Professor Montecino was pleased, pronounced her one of his grand triumphs."

"Does she agree with him?"

Disapproving look. "I'm not privy to her opinions, Doctor."

"Over how long a period was she operated on?"

"Five years."

I did some mental calculations. "So she was pregnant during part of it."

"Yes, well . . . the pregnancy interrupted the surgical process—tissue changes brought about by hormones, physical risks. Professor Montecino said she'd have to wait and be monitored closely. He even suggested . . . termination. But she refused."

"Was the pregnancy planned?"

Dutchy blinked hard and drew back his head—the turtle once more—as if unable to believe what he'd heard. "Good Lord, sir, I don't pry into the *motivations* of my employers."

I said, "Excuse me if I wander into uncharted territory from time to time, Mr. Dutchy. I'm just trying to get as full a background as possible. For Melissa's sake."

He harrumphed. "Shall we talk about Melissa, then?"

"All right. She's told me quite a bit about her fears. Why don't you give me your impressions."

"My impressions?"

"Your observations."

"My observations are that she's a terribly frightened little girl. Everything frightens her."

"Such as?"

He thought for a moment. "Loud noises, for one. They can literally make her jump. Even those that aren't very loud—at times it seems to be the suddenness of it that sets her off. A tree rustling or footsteps—or even music—has the ability to put her in a crying fit. The doorbell. It seems to occur when she's been in a period of unusual calm."

"Sitting by herself, daydreaming?"

"Yes. She daydreams a lot. Talks to herself." Closing his mouth, wanting a comment from me.

I said, "What about bright lights? Have they ever scared her?"

"Yes," he said, surprised. "Yes, they have. I can recall a specific incident, several months ago. One of the maids purchased a camera with a flashbulb and was traipsing around the house trying it out." Another disapproving look. "She surprised Melissa as the child ate breakfast and snapped a picture. The sound and sight of the bulb going off distressed Melissa greatly."

"Distressed her in what way?"

"Tears, screaming, breakfast rejected. She even started hyperventilating. I had her breathe into a paper bag until her respiration returned to normal."

"Shift in arousal," I said, more to myself than to him.

"Pardon me, Doctor?"

"Sudden changes in arousal—in her psychophysiologic level of consciousness—seem to bother her."

"Yes, I suppose they do. What can be done about that?"

I held out my hand in a restraining gesture. "She told me she has bad dreams every night."

"That's true," he said. "Often more than once a night."

"Describe what she does while she's having them."

"I can't say, Doctor. When they occur she's with her moth—"

I frowned.

He caught himself. "However, I do recall observing a few

incidents. She cries a lot. Cries and screams. Thrashes around and fights comfort, refusing to go back to sleep."

"Thrashes around," I said. "Does she ever talk about what she saw in the dream?"

"At times."

"But not always?"

"No."

"When she does, are there any consistent themes?"

"Monsters, ghosts, that kind of thing. I don't really pay much mind. My efforts are concentrated on getting her settled."

"One thing you *can* do in the future," I said, "*is* pay close mind. Keep a written record of what she says during these incidents and bring it in to me." I realized I sounded imperious. Wanting to make *him* the D student. Power struggle with a butler?

But he was comfortable with the subservient role, said "Very well, sir," and raised his teacup to his lips.

I said, "Does she seem completely awake after having a nightmare?"

"No, she doesn't," he said. "Not always. Sometimes she sits up with a horrid, frozen look on her little face, screaming inconsolably and waving her hands. We— I try to wake her but it's impossible. She's even gotten out of her bed and walked around, still screaming, impossible to wake. We just wait until it subsides, then return her to bed."

"To her own bed?"

"No. Her mother's."

"She never sleeps in her own bed?"

Shake of the head. "No, she sleeps with her mother."

"Okay," I said. "Let's get back to those times when she can't be awakened. Does she scream about anything in particular?"

"No, there are no words. Just a terrible . . . howling." Wince. "It's really quite disturbing."

"You're describing something called night terrors," I

said. "They're not nightmares, which take place—as do all dreams—during light sleep. Night terrors occur when the sleeper arouses too quickly from deep sleep. Rudely awakened, so to speak. It's a disorder of arousal, related to sleepwalking and bed-wetting. Does she wet the bed?"

"Occasionally."

"How often?"

"Four or five times a week. Sometimes less, sometimes more."

"Have you done anything about it?"

Shake of the head.

"Does it bother her that she wets the bed?"

"On the contrary," he said. "She seems rather casual about it."

"So you have talked to her about it."

"Only to tell her—once or twice—that young ladies need to be careful about their personal hygiene. She ignored me and I didn't pursue it."

"How does her mother feel? How does her mother *react* to the wetting?"

"She has the sheets changed."

"It's her bed being wet. That doesn't bother her?"

"Apparently not. Doctor, what do these attacks—these terrors—mean? Medically speaking?"

"There's probably a genetic component involved," I said. "Night terrors run in families. So do bed-wetting and sleepwalking. All of it probably has something to do with brain chemistry."

He looked worried.

I said, "But they aren't dangerous, just disruptive. And they usually go away by themselves, without treatment, by adolescence."

"Ah," he said. "So time is on our side."

"Yes, it is. But that doesn't mean we should ignore them. They can be treated. And they're also a warning sign— there's more than just pure biology involved. Stress often increases the number of attacks and prolongs them. She's telling us she's troubled, Mr. Dutchy. Telling us with her other symptoms, as well."

"Yes, of course."

The waiter arrived with the food. We ate in silence, and though Dutchy had said he didn't take lunch, he consumed his shrimp with genteel fervor.

When we finished I ordered a double espresso and he had his teapot refilled.

After finishing my coffee, I said, "Getting back to the genetic issue, are there any other children—from a previous marriage?"

"No. Though there was a previous marriage. For Mr. Dickinson. But no children."

"What happened to the first Mrs. Dickinson?"

He looked annoyed. "She died of leukemia—a fine young woman. The marriage had only lasted two years. It was very difficult for Mr. Dickinson. That's when he plunged himself more deeply into his art collection."

"What did he collect?"

"Paintings, drawings and etchings, antiquities, tapestries. He had an exceptional eye for composition and color, sought out damaged masterpieces and had them restored. Some he restored himself—he'd learned the craft as a student. That was his true passion—restoration."

I thought of him restoring his second wife. As if he'd read my mind, Dutchy gave me a sharp look.

"What else," I said, "besides loud noises and bright lights, is Melissa afraid of?"

"The darkness. Being alone. And at times, nothing at all."

"What do you mean?"

"She'll throw a fit with no provocation."

"What does 'a fit' look like?"

"Very similar to what I've already described. Crying, rapid breathing, running around screaming. Sometimes she'll simply lie on the floor and kick her feet. Or clutch the nearest adult and hold on like a . . . a *limpet*."

"Do these fits generally occur after she's been refused something?"

"Not typically—there is that, of course. She doesn't take kindly to being restricted. What child does?"

"So she has tantrums, but these fits go beyond that."

"I'm referring to genuine *fear*, Doctor. Panic. It seems to come out of nowhere."

"Does she ever say what's scaring her?"

"Monsters. 'Bad things.' Sometimes she claims to hear noises. Or see and hear things."

"Things no one else hears or sees?"

"Yes." Tremble in his voice.

I said, "Does that bother you? More than the other symptoms?"

"One does wonder," he said softly.

"If you're worried about psychosis or some sort of thought disorder, don't. Unless there's something else going on that you haven't told me. Like self-destructive behavior, or bizarre speech."

"No, no, nothing like that," he said. "I suppose it's all part of her imagination?"

"That's exactly what it is. She's got a good one, but from what I've seen, she's very much in touch with reality. Children her age typically see and hear things that adults don't."

He looked doubtful.

I said, "It's all part of play. Play is fantasy. The theater of childhood. Kids compose dramas in their heads, talk to imaginary playmates. It's a kind of self-hypnosis that's necessary for healthy growth."

He remained noncommittal, but was listening.

I said, "Fantasy can be therapeutic, Mr. Dutchy. Can actually *reduce* fears by giving children a sense of control over their lives. But for certain children—those who are high-strung, introverted, those living in stressful environments—

that same ability to paint mental pictures can lead to anxiety. The pictures simply become too vivid. Once again, there may be a constitutional factor. You said her father was an excellent art restorer. Did he show any other sort of creativity?"

"Most definitely. He was an architect by trade and a gifted painter in his own right—when he was younger."

"Why'd he stop?"

"He convinced himself he wasn't good enough to justify devoting much time to it, destroyed all his work, never painted again, and began collecting. Traveling the world. His architecture degree was from the Sorbonne—he loved Europe. He built some lovely buildings before he invented the strut."

"The strut?"

"Yes," he said, as if explaining the ABC's. "The Dickinson strut. It's a process for strengthening steel, used extensively in construction."

"What about Mrs. Dickinson?" I said. "She was an actress. Any other creative outlets there?"

"I have no idea, Doctor."

"How long has she been agoraphobic—afraid to leave the house?"

"She leaves the house," he said.

"Oh?"

"Yes, sir. She strolls the grounds."

"Does she ever leave the grounds?"

"No."

"How large are the grounds?"

"Six and three-quarter acres. Approximately."

"Does she stroll them extensively—from corner to corner?"

Throat clear. Cheek chew. "She prefers to remain fairly close to the house. Is there anything else, Doctor?"

My initial question remained unanswered; he'd nit-picked his way out of giving a direct reply. "How long has she been that way—not leaving the grounds?"

"From the . . . beginning."

"From the time of the attack?"

"Yes, yes. It's quite logical, really, when one understands the chain of events. When Mr. Dickinson brought her home right after the wedding, she was in the midst of the surgical process. In great agony, still very frightened—traumatized by the . . . by what had been done to her. She never left her room, on Professor Montecino's orders—she was ordered to lie still for hours at a time. The new flesh had to be kept extremely supple and clean. Special air filters were brought in to remove particles that might pollute her. Nurses hovered around the clock with treatments and injections and lotions and baths that made her cry out in terrible pain. She couldn't have left even if she'd wanted to. Then, the pregnancy. She was restricted to total bed rest, bandaged and unbandaged constantly. Four months into the pregnancy, Mr. Dickinson . . . passed on, and she . . . It was a safe place for her. She couldn't leave. Surely that's obvious. So in a sense it's completely logical, isn't it? The way she is. She's gravitated to her safe place. You see that, don't you, Doctor?"

"I do. But the challenge now is to find out what's safe for Melissa."

"Yes," he said. "Of course." Avoiding my glance.

I called the waiter over and ordered another espresso. When it arrived, along with more hot water for Dutchy, he wrapped his hands around his teacup but didn't drink. As I took a sip he said, "Forgive my presumption, Doctor, but what, in your educated opinion, is the prognosis? For Melissa."

"Given family cooperation, I'd say good. She's motivated and bright and has a lot of insight for someone her age. But it's going to take time."

"Yes, of course. Doesn't anything worthwhile?"

Suddenly he pressed forward, hands flapping, fingers wiggling. An odd bit of fluster for such a staid man. I smelled bay rum and shrimp. For a moment I thought he was going to grab my fingers. But he stopped himself abruptly, as if at an electrified fence.

"Please help her, Doctor. I pledge everything in my power to aid your treatment."

His hands were still in the air. He noticed it and gave a look of chagrin. Ten fingers plummeted to the table like gunshot ducks.

"You're very devoted to this family," I said.

He winced and looked away, as if I'd exposed some secret vice.

"As long as she comes in, I'll treat her, Mr. Dutchy. What you can do to help is tell me everything I need to know."

"Yes, of course. Is there something else?"

"McCloskey. What does she know about him?"

"Nothing!"

"She mentioned his name."

"That's all he is to her—a name. Children hear things."

"Yes, they do. And she's heard plenty—she knows he attacked her mother with acid because he didn't like her. What else has she been told about him?"

"Nothing. Truly. As I said, children overhear—but he's not a topic of conversation in our household."

"Mr. Dutchy, in lieu of accurate information, children make up their own facts. It would be best for Melissa to understand what happened to her mother."

His knuckles were white around the cup. "What are you suggesting, sir?"

"That someone sit down and talk with Melissa. Explain to her why McCloskey had Mrs. Dickinson attacked."

He relaxed conspicuously. "Explain why. Yes, yes, I can see your point. There's just one problem."

"What's that?"

"Nobody *knows* why. The bastard never let on and *nobody* knows. Now if you'll excuse me, Doctor, I really must be going."

5

On Monday, Melissa was in a great mood, cooperative and polite, no more testing of limits, no remnants of the last session's power struggle. But reserved, less eager to talk. Asking if she could draw instead.

The typical new patient.

As if all that had happened till now had been some kind of probation and this was the real beginning.

She started with the same kind of benign productions she'd presented to me during our first session, then progressed quickly to deeper pigments, sunless skies, patches of gray, foreboding images.

She sketched sad-looking animals, anemic gardens, forlorn children in static poses, flitting from subject to subject. But by the second half of the session she found a theme that she stayed with: a series of houses without doors or windows. Bulky, drunkenly listing, visceroid structures fashioned of painstakingly rendered stone and set amidst groves of skeletal trees under a gloomy, crosshatched sky.

Several sheets later she added gray shapes approaching the houses. Gray that turned to black, and became human. Men-shapes wearing hats and long coats and bearing lumpy sacks.

Drawing with such fury that she ripped the paper. Starting over.

Pencils and crayons diminished to nubs, consumed like kindling. Every finished product was shredded with glee. She worked that way for three weeks straight. Leaving the office without comment, at session's end, marching like a little soldier.

By the fourth week she began to round out the last ten or fifteen minutes with silent stretches of game playing: Chutes and Ladders, Crazy Eights, Go Fish. No conversation. Competing with great determination and little apparent pleasure.

Sometimes Dutchy brought her to the office, but increasingly it was Hernandez, who still regarded me with a jaundiced eye. Then other chaperons began to appear: a series of dark, lean youths—young men who smelled of work-sweat and looked so alike that, in my mind, they became interchangeable. I learned from Melissa they were Hernandez's five sons.

Alternating with them was a big, doughy woman about Dutchy's age with tightly braided hair and cheeks like windbellows. The owner of the deep Gallic voice. Madeleine, the cook/maid. Invariably, she arrived sweating and looking fatigued.

All of them slipped away the moment Melissa stepped over the threshold, returning to pick her up precisely at session's end. Their punctuality—and avoidance of eye contact—smacked of Dutchy's tutelage. Dutchy, the few times he showed up, was the most adroit at escape, not even stepping into the waiting room. No follow-up on my request to collect data. I should have been resentful.

But as time went on, it bothered me less and less.

Because Melissa seemed to be getting better. Without him. Without any of them. Ten weeks since therapy had started and she was a different child, unburdened, conspicuously calm, no more kneading, no more pacing. Allowing herself to smile. Loosening up as she played. Laughing at my repertoire of grade-school jokes. Acting like a *kid*. And though she continued to resist talking about her fears—about anything substantive—her drawings had become less frantic, the sack-men were vanishing. Windows and doors sprouted like buds on the stone faces of houses that now stood plumb-straight.

Drawings that she preserved and presented to me with pride.

Progress? Or just a seven-year-old putting on a happy face for her therapist's sake?

Knowing what she was like outside the office would have helped my assessment. But those who could tell me shunned me as if I were a virus.

Even Eileen Wagner was out of the picture. I'd phoned her office several times and gotten her answering service, despite being careful to call during business hours. Slow practice, I supposed. She was probably moonlighting to make ends meet.

I called the Medical Staff Office at Western Pediatrics to find out if she had another job. They had nothing else listed. I phoned her office again, left messages that went unanswered.

Strange, considering the dedication she'd shown in arranging the referral, but everything related to this case smacked of strange, and I'd gotten used to it.

Remembering what Eileen had told me about Melissa's fulminating school phobia, I asked Melissa the name of her school, looked up the number, and called it. Presenting myself as her doctor and not clarifying when the clerk assumed pediatrician, I asked to speak with Melissa's teacher—a Mrs. Vera Adler, who confirmed that Melissa had missed a good deal of school early in the semester but since then her attendance had been perfect and her "social life" seemed better.

"Was she having social problems, Mrs. Adler?"

"I wouldn't say that, no. I mean, she was never a problem

of any sort, Doctor. But she wasn't the most outgoing child—kind of shy. Off in her own world. Now she mixes more. Was she ill before, Doctor?"

"Just the usual stuff," I said. "Just following up."

"Well, she's doing fine. We *were* starting to worry, she was absent so much, but she's fine now. A very nice, extremely bright little girl—she tests out on the Iowa at the ninety-ninth percentile. We're so glad she's gotten adjusted. . . ."

I thanked her and hung up, heartened. Said to hell with the grown-ups and continued to do my job.

By the fourth month of treatment, Melissa was treating the office as if it were a second home. Sauntering in smiling, making a beeline for the drawing table. She knew every cranny, could tell when a book had been moved from its usual place, was quick to put it back. Restoring. Showing an unusual eye for detail that jibed with the perceptual sensitivity Dutchy had described.

A child whose senses ran on full throttle. For her, life would never be boring. Could it ever be tranquil?

As the fifth month began she announced she was ready to talk again. Informing me that she wanted to be a team—just like I'd said at the beginning.

"Sure. What would you like to work on?"

"The dark."

I rolled up my sleeves, ready to muster every kernel of wisdom I'd gathered since grad school. First I taught her to recognize the physical warning signs of anxiety—how she *felt* when the fear came on. Then I trained her in deep relaxation that evolved into full-blown hypnosis because of her ease at drifting into imagery. She learned self-hypnosis in a single session, could sink into trance within seconds. I supplied her with finger signals she could use to communicate while under, and finally began the desensitization process.

Seating her in a chair, I told her to close her eyes and imagine herself sitting in the dark. A dark room. Watching as her body grew taut and her index finger popped up, I warded off the tension with suggestions of deep calm and well-being. When she'd relaxed once more, I had her return to the dark room. On/off, over and over again, until she could tolerate the image. After a week or so, she'd mastered the imaginary darkness and was ready to tackle the real enemy.

I drew the outer office drapes and manipulated the light-switch rheostat, getting her accustomed to gradually increasing dimness. Stretching the time that she sat in partial darkness and reacting to evidence of tension with instructions for deeper and deeper relaxation.

Eleven sessions into the treatment, I was able to pull the blackout drapes closed, plunging both of us into total darkness. Counting the seconds out loud and homing in on the sound of her breathing. Ready to move in at the merest catch or quickening, determined she'd never experience prolonged anxiety.

Rewarding each success with high praise and low art—cheap plastic toys that I bought in bulk at the five-and-dime. They thrilled her.

By the end of the month, she could sit in blackness—which sometimes made me lose my balance—for an entire session, free of tension, chatting about school.

Soon, she was as nocturnal as a bat. I suggested it might be a good time to work on her sleep. She smiled and agreed.

I was especially eager, because *this* was my bailiwick. During my internship I'd been presented with several cases of children with chronic night terrors and had been impressed with the level of disruption the episodes caused in kids and their families. But none of the psychologists or psychiatrists at the hospital knew how to treat the disorder. Officially, there *was* no treatment other than tranquilizers and sedatives whose effects were unpredictable in children.

I went to the hospital library, chased down references, found plenty of theory but nothing about treatment. Frustrated, I sat for a long time thinking and decided to try something outlandish: operant conditioning. Bald behavior therapy. Reward the children for *not* having terrors and see what happened.

Simple-minded—almost crude. Theoretically, it made no sense. As the senior staff was quick to inform me over their fuming pipes. How could unconscious behavior—arousal from profoundly deep sleep—be consciously manipulated? What could voluntary conditioning accomplish in the face of hard-wired deviance?

But research had emerged recently that suggested greater voluntary control over body function than had ever been imagined: patients learning how to raise and lower skin temperature and blood pressure, even mask severe pain. At Psychiatric Case Conference, I asked for permission to try to decondition night terrors, arguing that there was nothing to lose. A lot of head-shaking and words of discouragement, but consent was granted.

It worked. All my patients got better and stayed better. The senior staff started implementing my plan with their patients and achieved similar results. The chief psychologist told me to write it up for a scientific journal, listing him as co-author. I sent the article in, overcame skeptical reviewers with columns of numbers and statistical tests, and got published. Within a year other therapists had begun to replicate my findings. I received requests for reprints and phone calls from all over the world, was asked to give lectures.

Had been doing just that the day Eileen Wagner had approached. It was the lecture that had led me to Melissa.

And now Melissa was ready to be treated by the expert. But there was a problem: The technique—*my* technique—depended upon family cooperation. Someone needed to monitor the patient's sleep pattern precisely.

I buttonholed Dutchy on a Friday afternoon, before he had a chance to dash away. He gave a resigned look and said, "What is it, Doctor?"

I handed him a pad of graph paper and two sharpened pencils and, adopting the demeanor of a full professor, gave him his orders: Before bedtime, Melissa was to practice relaxation. He wasn't to badger or remind her; it would be her responsibility. His job was to record the occurrence and frequency of night terrors. Nights without terrors were to be rewarded the following morning with one of the trinkets she seemed to love so much. Nights following terrors were not to be commented on.

"But, Doctor," he said, "she's not having them."

"Not having what?"

"The terrors. Her sleep's been perfectly calm for weeks. The bed-wetting's also ceased."

I looked over at Melissa. She'd stepped behind him. Half a small face peeked out. Enough for me to see the smile.

Pure joy. Reveling in her secret, as if it were confection.

That made sense. The way she'd been brought up, secrets were the coin of the realm.

"The change has really been quite . . . remarkable," Dutchy was saying. "That's why I didn't feel it was necessary to—"

I said, "I'm really proud of you, Melissa."

"I'm proud of *you*, Dr. Delaware," she said, starting to giggle. "We're an excellent *team*."

She continued to get better more rapidly than science could explain. Leapfrogging over my clinical game plans.

Healing *herself*.

Magic, one of my wiser supervisors had once said. *Sometimes they'll get better and you won't know why. Before you've even started doing what you think is so goddam clever and hotshot scientific. Don't fight it. Just put it down to magic. It's as good an explanation as any.*

She made me feel magical.

We never got into the topics I'd thought essential to explore: death, injury, loneliness. *A Mikoksi with acid.*

Despite the frequency of sessions, her chart was thin—I had very little to record. I began to wonder if I was functioning as anything more than a high-priced babysitter, told myself there were worse things to be. And, faced with the onslaught of difficult cases that seemed to grow each month as my practice burgeoned, I was thankful for the chance to be passive and magical for forty-five minutes a day, three times a week.

After eight months she informed me that all her fears were gone. Risking her wrath, I suggested reducing our time together to two sessions a week. She agreed so readily that I knew she'd been thinking the same thing.

Nevertheless, I expected a few backward steps as the loss sank in and she attempted to buy herself time and attention. It never happened, and at year's end she was down to one session per week. The quality of the sessions changed, too. More casual. Lots of game-playing, no drama.

Therapy winding itself down. Triumph. I thought Eileen Wagner would like to know, made one more attempt to reach her, got a disconnected-number recording. Called the hospital and learned she'd closed her practice, resigned from the staff, left no forwarding address.

Puzzling. But she wasn't my concern. And one less report to write wasn't something I'd mourn.

For such a complicated case, it had turned out surprisingly simple.

Patient and doctor, slaying demons.

What could be purer?

The checks from Fiduciary First Trust kept coming, three figures at a shot.

The week of her ninth birthday, she arrived with a gift. I had none for her—had decided long ago never to buy patients anything. But she didn't seem to mind and glowed from the act of giving.

A gift too big for her to carry. Sabino brought it into my office.

Massive basket of crepe-paper-wrapped fruit, cheeses, wine samples, tins of caviar, smoked oysters and trout, chestnut paste, jars of preserves and compotes, from a gourmet shop in Pasadena.

Inside was a card.

TO DOCTOR DELAWARE, LOVE, MELISSA D.

On the reverse side was a drawing of a house. The best she'd ever done—carefully shaded, lots of windows and doors.

"This is beautiful, Melissa. Thank you very much."

"Welcome." Smiling, but her eyes had filled with tears.

"What's the matter, hon?"

"I want . . ."

She turned around and faced one of the bookcases, hugging herself.

"What is it, Melissa?"

"I want . . . It's time maybe . . . to . . . for no more . . ."

She trailed off into silence. Shrugged. Kneaded her hands.

"Are you saying you want to stop coming for sessions?"

Multiple rapid nods.

"There's nothing wrong with that, Melissa. You've done *great*. I'm really proud of you. So if you want to try it on your own, I understand and I think it's terrific. And you don't have to worry—I'll always be here if you need me."

She whipped around and faced me.

"I'm nine years *old*, Dr. Delaware. I think I'm ready to handle things on my own."

"I think you are, too. And don't worry about hurting my feelings."

She started to cry.

I went to her, hugged her. She put her head against my chest and sobbed.

"I know it's hard," I said. "You're worried about hurting my feelings. Probably been worried about that for a long time."

Wet nods.

"That's very kind of you, Melissa. I appreciate your caring about my feelings. But don't worry—I'm fine. Sure, I'll miss seeing you, but I'll always keep you in my mind. And just because you stop coming for regular sessions doesn't mean we can't stay in touch. Over the phone. Or by writing letters. You can even come in to see me when there's nothing bothering you. Just to say hi."

"Do other patients do that?"

"Sure."

"What're their names?"

Smiling mischievously.

We both laughed.

I said, "The thing that's most important to me, Melissa, is how well you've done. How you've taken charge over your fears. I'm really impressed."

"I really feel I can handle things," she said, drying her eyes.

"I'm sure you can."

"I can," she repeated, looking over at the big basket. "Have you ever had chestnut paste? It's kind of weird— doesn't taste like roasted chestnuts at all. . . ."

The following week, I phoned her. Dutchy answered. I asked how she was doing. He said, "Very well indeed, Doctor. Let me get her for you." I couldn't be sure, but I thought he sounded friendly.

Melissa came on the line, polite but distant. Letting me know she was okay, would call me if she needed to come in. She never did.

I called a couple of more times. She sounded distracted and eager to get off the phone.

A few weeks later I was doing my books, reached her ledger sheet, and realized I'd been paid in advance for ten sessions I hadn't conducted. I wrote out a check and mailed it to San Labrador. The next day a manila envelope arrived at the office by messenger. Inside was my check, in three neatly torn pieces, along with a sheet of scented stationery.

> *Dear Dr. Delaware,*
> *With much gratitude,*
> *Faithfully yours,*
> *Gina Dickinson*

Same fine graceful hand she'd used to promise me, two years ago, that she'd be in touch.

I wrote another check for exactly the same amount, made it out to Western Pediatrics Toy Fund, went down to the lobby, and posted it. Knowing I was doing it for myself as much as for the kids who'd get the toys, and telling myself I had no damn right to feel noble.

Then I took the elevator back up to my office and got ready for my next patient.

6

It was one in the morning when I put the file away. Reminiscing was strenuous exercise, and fatigue had enveloped me. I hobbled to bed, slept fitfully, did a good impression of waking at seven, and marched into the shower. A few minutes after I'd dressed, the bell rang. I went to the door and opened it.

Milo stood out on the terrace, hands in his pockets, wearing a yellow golf shirt with two wide horizontal green stripes, tan chinos, and high-top basketball shoes that had once been white. His black hair was longer than I'd ever seen it, the forelock completely hiding the brow, the sideburns nearly at jaw level. His pocked, lumpy face was flecked with three days' worth of patchy beard and his green eyes seemed filmed over—the normally startling hue dulled to the color of very old grass.

He said, "The good news is at least now you lock it. The bad news is you open it without checking to see who the hell's out there."

"What makes you think I didn't check?" I said, standing aside and letting him in.

"Latency of response from final footstep to latch-turn. Powers of detection." He tapped his temple and headed straight for the kitchen.

"Good morning, Detective. Leisure becomes you."

He grunted and didn't break step.

I said, "What's up?"

"What should be up?" he called back, face already in the fridge.

Another bona fide random drop-in. They were growing more frequent.

Terminal doldrums.

Halfway into his punishment—six months' suspension from the force without pay. The most the department could hand out short of canning him. The department hoping he'd learn to enjoy civilian life and never come back. The department deluding itself.

He scrounged for a while, found rye bread, lox spread, and milk, located a knife and a plate, and began preparing himself some breakfast.

"What are you staring at?" he said. "Never seen a guy cook before?"

I went to get dressed. When I came back he was standing at the counter, eating spread on toast and drinking milk out of the carton. He'd put on more weight—his belly approached sumo-status, meloning the nylon shirt.

"Got a busy day planned?" he said. "Thought we might go down to Rancho and shoot some golf balls."

"Didn't know you golfed."

"I don't. But a guy needs a hobby, right?"

"Sorry, I'm working this morning."

"Oh, yeah? Need me to leave?"

"No, not patients. I'm doing some writing."

"Ahh," he said, giving a dismissing wave. "I meant real work."

"It's real work for me."

"What, the old blockaroo?"

I nodded.

He said, "Want me to do it for you?"

"Do what?"

"Write your paper."

"Right."

"No, I'm serious. Scribbling always came easy for me. That's why I went as far as the master's—God knows it wasn't all the academic shit they shoved at me. Not much flair to my prose, but it was . . . *workmanlike, if a bit pedestrian.* In the words of my former academic adviser."

He crunched toast. Crumbs cascaded down his shirt-front. He made no effort to brush them off.

I said, "Thanks, Milo, but I'm not ready for a ghost-writer yet." I went to make coffee.

"Whatsamatter?" he said with a full mouth. "Don't trust me?"

"This is scientific writing. The Hale shooting for a psych journal."

"So?"

"So we're talking dry. Maybe a hundred pages of dry."

"Big deal," he said. "No worse than your basic homicide file." He used a crescent of rye crust to tick his fingers: "Roman Numeral One: Synopsis of Crime. Roman Numeral Two: Chronological Narrative. Roman Numeral Three: Victim Information. Roman—"

"I get the point."

He shoved the crust in his mouth. "The key to excellent report writing," he said between chews, "is to take every bit of passion out of it. Use an extra heaping portion of superfluously extraneous tautological redundancies in order to make it mind-numbingly *boring.* So that when one's superior officers read it, they zone out and start skimming and maybe don't notice the fact that one has been spinning one's wheels since the body turned up and hasn't solved a goddam thing. Now tell me, is that so different from what you're doing?"

I laughed. "Up till now I've been telling myself I was after the truth. Thanks for setting me straight."

"No problem. It's my job."

"Speaking of job, how'd it go downtown?"

He gave a very long, very dark look. "More of the same.

Desk jockeys with smiling faces. This time they brought in the department shrink."

"Thought you refused counseling."

"They got around it by calling it a stress evaluation. Terms of the penalty—read the small print."

He shook his head. "All those greasy-faced fuckers talking real softly and slowly, as if I was senile. Inquiring about my *adjustment*. My *stress* level. *Sharing* their concern. Ever notice how people who *talk* about sharing never really do? They were also careful to let me know that all my medical bills had been picked up by the department—therefore the department had received copies of all my lab tests and there was some concern over my cholesterol level, triglycerides, whatever. Was I really feeling up to returning to active duty?"

He scowled. "What a bunch of princes, huh? I smiled back and said it was funny how they never gave a shit about my stress level or triglycerides when I was out there doing the job."

"How'd they react to that bit of charm?"

"More smiles, then this *greasy* silence you could deep-fry potatoes in. Mind-tripping. No doubt the asshole shrink prepped them—no offense. But that's the military mind: Destroy the individual."

He looked at the milk carton, said, "Ah, low-fat. That's good. Here's to triglycerides."

I filled the coffee-maker carafe with water, spooned Kenyan into the hatch.

"Give the assholes one thing," he said. "They're getting more assertive. This time they came right out and talked pension. Dollars and cents. Actuarial tables, how much more it added up to when you threw in the interest I could earn if I invested wisely. How nice life could be with what I had coming after fourteen years. When I didn't slaver and snap, they dropped the carrot and picked up the stick, started hinting around about how the pension was by no means a foregone conclusion, given the circumstances. Blah blah blah. How timing was of the essence. Blah blah blah."

He started to work on another piece of bread.

I said, "Bottom line?"

"I let them blah on for a while, then got up, said I had a pressing engagement, and left."

"Well," I said, "if you ever do decide to quit, there's always the diplomatic corps."

"Hey," he said, "I've had it to here." Running a finger across his throat. "Give me the half-year boot, okay. Take my gun and shield and pay, okay. But just let me do my time in peace and quiet, and cool it with the fucking *follow-ups*. All that phony sensitivity."

He drank and ate. "Course, guess I can't expect much better, given the circumstances." He smiled.

"A-plus in reality testing, Milo."

He said, "Assaulting a superior officer." Bigger smile. "Has a nice ring to it, wouldn't you say?"

"You forgot the crucial part. On TV."

He grinned, started to drink more milk but was smiling too broadly and lowered the carton. "What the hell, this is the media age, right? The chief wears pancake when he plays meet-the-press. I gave them some soundbites they'll never forget."

"That you did. What's the situation with Frisk?"

"Word has it his cute little nose has healed quite nicely. The new teeth look almost as good as the old ones—amazing what they can do with plastic nowadays, huh? But he *is* gonna look a little different. Less Tom Selleck, more . . . Karl Malden. Which isn't bad for a superior officer, right? That shopworn look—implied wisdom and experience."

"He back on duty?"

"Nooo. Seems Kenny-poo's *stress* level is still pretty high, *he's* taking a long recuperation. But he'll be back, eventually. Kicked upstairs, where he can screw up on a higher level and do systematic damage."

"He's the assistant chief's son-in-law, Milo. You're lucky to still be on the force."

He put down the carton and glared. "Don't you think if

they could have shafted me, they would have? They're in a one-down position and they know it—that's why they're going the weasel route."

He slammed his big hand down on the counter. "Asshole used me for fucking *bait*. The lawyer Rick had me talk to told me I had grounds for a major-league civil suit, could have taken it to the papers and kept it there for months. He would have loved it—the shyster. Big contingency fee. Rick wanted me to do it, too. On principle. But I refused because that wasn't what it was about—bunch of goddam shysters quibbling about technicalities for ten years. This was one-on-one; it needed to be handled one-on-one. Going the TV route was my extra insurance—couple of million witnesses, so no one could say it didn't happen the way it did. That's why I hit him *after* he said what a great hero I was and gave me the commendation. So no one could say it was sour grapes. The department owes me, Alex. They should be *grateful* all I did was mess up his face. And if Frisk is smart, he'll be grateful, too—stay out of *my* face. Permanently. Fuck his family connections. He's lucky I didn't rip his lungs out and toss them at the cameras."

His eyes had cleared and his complexion had deepened to hot pink. With his hair over his forehead and thick lips, he resembled a disgruntled gorilla.

I applauded.

He rose a few inches, stared at me, then started laughing. "Ah, nothing like adrenaline to make the day take on a rosy glow. Sure you don't want to golf?"

"Sorry. I really have to get the paper done and there's a patient coming at noon. And, frankly, knocking balls around the green isn't my idea of recreation, Milo."

"I know, I know," he said. "No aerobic benefit. Bet *your* triglycerides are just peachy."

I shrugged. The coffee was done. I poured two cups, gave one to him.

"So," I said, "what else have you been doing to fill the time?"

He gave an expansive gesture and put on a brogue: "Oh, it's been just grand, lad. Needlepoint, papier-mâché, decoupage, crocheting. Little schooners and yachts made of ice-cream sticks and *glitter*—there's a wonderful world of *crafts* out there just waiting to be explored." He drank coffee. "It's been shit. Worse than a desk job. At first I thought I'd get into gardening—grab some sun, a little exercise. Back to the earth—to my roots, praise Hibernia."

"Planning to grow potatoes?"

He chuckled. "Planning to raise anything I could, other than hell. Only problem was, Rick brought in this landscape designer last year, redid the whole yard with all this southwestern shit—cactus, succulents, low-moisture ground cover. So we could cut our water usage, be ecologically sound. So much for Farmer Spud. So okay, scratch that, I figured I'd tinker around the house—fix everything that needed fixing. I used to be handy—when I worked construction in college I learned all the trades. And when I lived by myself I used to do all of it: plumbing, wiring, whatever. The landlord loved me. Only problem with that plan is, there's nothing to fix. I hadn't been around the house long enough to realize it, but after nagging me for a year or so, Rick finally took care of everything. Seems he found this handyman—fellow from Fiji, former patient. Cut himself with a power saw, nearly lost a couple of fingers. Rick sewed him up in the E.R., saved the fingers, and purchased eternal gratitude: The guy works for us basically for free, on call twenty-four hours a day. So unless he slips with the saw again, my expertise is not in demand. Scratch Mr. Fixit. What does that leave? Shopping? Cooking? Between the E.R. and the Free Clinic, Rick's never home to eat, so I grab whatever and stuff my face. Once in a while I go out to a civilian range in Culver City and shoot. I've been through my record collection twice and read more bad books than I ever want to think about."

"What about volunteer work?"

He clapped his hands over his ears and grimaced. When he removed them, I said, "What?"

"Heard it before. Every day, from the altruistic Dr. Silverman. The Free Clinic AIDS group, homeless kids, Skid Row Mission, whatever. *Find a cause, Milo, and stick with it.* Only problem is, I feel too goddam *mean. Coiled.* Like someone better not say the wrong thing to me or they're gonna end up sucking the sidewalk. This . . . *hot* feeling in my gut—sometimes I wake up with it; sometimes it just comes on. And don't tell me it's post-traumatic stress syndrome, 'cause giving it a name doesn't do squat. I've been there before—after the war—and I know nothing but time is gonna bleed it out of me. Meantime, I don't want to be around too many people—especially people with heavy-duty misery. I've got no sympathy to give. I'd end up telling them to shape up and get their goddam lives in order."

"Time heals," I said, "but time can be sped along."

He gave me an incredulous look. "What? *Counseling?*"

"There are worse things."

He slapped his chest with both hands. "Okay, here I am. Counsel me."

I was silent.

"Right," he said, and looked at the wall clock. "Anyway, I'm gone. Gonna hit little white balls and pretend they're something else."

He began barreling out of the kitchen. I held out an arm and he stopped.

"How about dinner," I said. "Tonight. I should be free by seven or so."

He said, "Charity meals are for soup kitchens."

"You're a charmer," I said, and lowered my arm.

"What, no date tonight?"

"No date."

"What about Linda?"

"Linda's still in Texas."

"Oh. Thought she was due back last week."

"She was. The stay's been extended. Her father."

"The heart?"

I nodded. "He's gotten worse. Bad enough to keep her there indefinitely."

"Sorry to hear it. When you talk to her, give her my best. Tell her I hope he mends." His anger had given way to sympathy. I wasn't sure that was an improvement.

"Will do," I said. "Have fun at Rancho."

He took a step, stopped. "Okay, so this hasn't been party-time for you either. Sorry."

"I'm doing fine, Milo. And the offer wasn't charity. God knows why, but I thought dinner would be nice. Two guys shooting the bull, all that buddy stuff, like in the beer commercials."

"Yeah," he said. "Dinner. Okay, I can always eat." He patted his gut. "And if you're still struggling with your term paper by tonight, bring a draft along. Uncle Milo will render sage editorial input."

"Fine," I said, "but in the meantime why don't you think about getting yourself a real hobby?"

7

After he left I sat down to write. For no apparent reason it went more smoothly than ever before, and noon arrived quickly, heralded by the second doorbell ring of the day.

This time I squinted through the peephole. What looked back at me was the face of a stranger, but not foreign: remnants of the child I'd once known merging with a photo from a twenty-year-old newspaper clipping. I realized that at the time of the attack her mother hadn't been that much older than Melissa was now.

I opened the door and said, "Hello, Melissa."

She seemed startled, then smiled. "Dr. Delaware! You haven't changed at all!"

We shook hands.

"Come on in."

She entered the house and stood with her hands folded in front of her.

The transition from girl to woman appeared nearly complete, and the evidence pointed to a graceful process. She had fashion-model cheekbones that asserted themselves through flawless lightly tanned skin. Her hair had darkened to a sun-streaked light brown and it hung, poker-straight and gleaming, to her waist. The straight-edge bangs had given way to a side part and flip. Below naturally arched brows her gray-green eyes were huge and wide-set. A young Grace Kelly.

A miniature Grace Kelly. She was barely five feet tall, with a cinch-waist and tiny bones. Big gold hoop earrings dangled from each shell-like ear. She carried a small lambskin handbag, wore a blue pinpoint button-down shirt, a denim skirt that ended an inch above her knees, and maroon penny loafers without socks. Maybe Preppy still ruled in San Labrador.

I showed her to a chair in the living room. She sat, crossed her legs at the ankles, hugged her knees, and looked around. "You have a very nice home, Dr. Delaware."

I wondered what my eighteen hundred square feet of redwood and glass really looked like to her. The castle she'd grown up in probably had rooms bigger. Thanking her, I took a seat and said, "It's good to see you, Melissa."

"Good to see you, too, Dr. Delaware. And thanks so much for doing it on short notice."

"My pleasure. Any trouble finding the address?"

"No. I used my Thomas Guide—I just learned about Thomas Guides. They're terrific."

"Yes, they are."

"Amazing how so much information can go in one book, isn't it?"

"Sure is."

"I've never really been up to these canyons. It's quite pretty."

Smile. Shy, but poised. *Proper.* A proper young *lady.* Was it for my benefit? Did she metamorphose into something giggly and ill-mannered when she and her friends hit the mall?

Did she go to the mall?

Did she have friends?

The ignorance born of nine years struck home.

Starting from scratch.

I smiled back and, trying not to be obviously analytic, studied her.

Posture straight, maybe a little stiff. Understandable, considering the circumstances. But no obvious signs of anxiety. Her hands remained motionless around her knees. No kneading, no evidence of chafing.

I said, "Well. It's been a long time."

"Nine years," she said. "Pretty unbelievable, huh?"

"Sure is. I don't expect you to sum up all nine of them. But I am kind of curious about what you've been up to."

"Just the usual," she said, shrugging. "School, mostly."

She bent forward, straightened her arms, and hugged her knees tighter. A sheet of hair fell across one eye. She brushed it aside and checked out the room again.

I said, "Congratulations on graduating."

"Thanks. I got accepted to Harvard."

"Fantastic. Double congratulations."

"I was surprised they took me."

"I'll bet there was never any doubt in their minds."

"That's nice of you to say, Dr. Delaware, but I think I was pretty lucky."

I said, "Straight A's or close to it?"

Return of the shy smile. Her hands remained clamped on her knees. "Not in gym."

"Well, shame on *you*, young lady."

The smile widened, but maintaining it seemed to take effort. She kept looking around the room, as if searching for something.

I said, "So when do you leave for Boston?"

"I don't know. . . . They want me to notify them within two weeks if I'm coming. So I guess I'd better decide."

"That mean you're thinking of not going?"

She licked her lips and nodded and brought her gaze to rest, meeting mine. "That's what—that's the problem I wanted to talk to you about."

"Whether or not to go to Harvard?"

"What going to Harvard *means*. In terms of Mother." She licked her lips again, coughed, and began rocking, very gently. Then she freed her hands, picked up a cut-crystal paperweight from the coffee table, and peered through it, squinting. Studying the refraction of the gold-dusted southern light streaming in through the dining room windows.

I said, "Is your mother opposed to your going away?"

"No, she's— She says she wants me to. She hasn't objected at all—as a matter of fact, she's been very encouraging. Says she *really* wants me to go."

"But you're worried about her anyway."

She put down the paperweight, moved to the edge of her chair, and held out her hands, palms up. "I'm not sure she can *handle* it, Dr. Delaware."

"Being away from you?"

"Yes. She's . . . It's . . ." Shrug. She began wringing her hands. That saddened me more than it should have.

I said, "Is she still— Is her situation the same? In terms of her fears?"

"No. I mean, she still has it. The agoraphobia. But she's better. Because of her treatment. I finally convinced her to get treatment and it's helped."

"Good."

"Yes. It is good."

"But you're not sure treatment's helped her enough to cope with being separated from you."

"I don't know. I mean, how can I be sure . . . ?" She shook her head with a weariness that made her seem very old. Lowered her head and opened her bag. After fumbling for a few moments she drew out a newspaper article and handed it to me.

February of last year. A "Lifestyles" piece entitled "New Hope for Victims of Fears: Husband and Wife Team Fight Debilitating Phobias."

She lifted the paperweight and began toying with it again. I read on.

The article was a profile of Leo Gabney, a Pasadena-based clinical psychologist, formerly of Harvard University, and his psychiatrist wife, Ursula Cunningham-Gabney, alumna and former staff member of that august institution. An accompanying photograph showed the two therapists sitting side by side at a table, facing a female patient. Only the back of the patient's head was visible. Gabney's mouth was open, in speech. His wife seemed to be looking at him out of the corner of her eye. Both doctors wore expressions of extreme earnestness. The caption read: DRS. LEO AND URSULA GABNEY COMBINE THEIR SKILLS TO WORK INTENSIVELY WITH "MARY," A SEVERE AGORAPHOBIC. The last word had been circled in red.

I studied the picture. I knew Leo Gabney by reputation, had read everything he'd written, but had never met the man. The camera revealed him to be sixty or close to it, with bushy white hair, narrow shoulders, dark, drooping eyes behind heavy black-framed glasses, and a round, smallish face. He wore a white shirt and dark tie, had rolled his sleeves up to the elbow. His forearms were thin and bony—almost womanish. My mental image had been something more Herculean.

His wife was brunette and good-looking in a severe way; Hollywood would have cast her as the repressed spinster, ripe for awakening. She was dressed in a cowl-neck knit top with a paisley kerchief draped over one shoulder. A short perm fit nicely around her face. Glasses hung from a chain around her neck. She was young enough to be Leo Gabney's daughter.

I looked up. Melissa was still turning the crystal. Pretending to be enthralled with the facets.

The knickknack defense.

I'd totally forgotten this particular knickknack. Antique French. A real find, rescued from the back shelves of a tiny curio shop in Leucadia. Robin and me . . . the amnesia defense.

I resumed reading. The article had the self-consciously laudatory tone of a p.r. release striving to sound like journalism. It recounted Leo Gabney's pioneering work in the research and treatment of anxiety disorders. Cited his "landmark success treating Korean War G.I.'s for combat trauma when clinical psychology was still an infant science, pioneering research in frustration and human learning," and tracing his career through three decades of animal and human studies at Harvard. Thirty years of prolific scientific writing.

No blockaroo for him.

Ursula Cunningham-Gabney was described as a former student of her husband's and possessor of both a Ph.D. in psychology and an M.D.

"We joke," said her husband, "that she's a paradox."

Both Gabneys had been tenured members of the staff of Harvard Medical School before relocating to southern California two years previously and establishing the Gabney Clinic. Leo Gabney explained the relocation as "a quest for a more relaxed life-style, as well as the chance to bring to the private sector our combined body of research and clinical skills."

He went on to describe the collaborative nature of the Gabney approach:

> "My wife's medical training is especially useful in terms of detecting physical disorders, such as hyperthyroidism, that present symptoms similar to those of anxiety disorders. She's also in a unique position to evaluate and prescribe some of the more recent—and superior—anti-anxiety drugs that have come along."
>
> "Several of the new medications look promising," Ursula Cunningham-Gabney elaborated, "but none is sufficient in and of itself. Many physicians tend to view medication as a magic bullet and prescribe without carefully weighing cost-effectiveness. Our research has shown that the treatment of choice in debilitating anxiety disorders is clearly a combination of behavior and carefully monitored medication."
>
> "Unfortunately," her husband added, "the typical psychologist is ignorant about drugs and, even if knowledgeable, unable to prescribe them. And the

typical psychiatrist has little or no training in behavior therapy."

Leo Gabney claims this has led to bickering
between the professions and inadequate treatment
for many patients with incapacitating conditions
such as agoraphobia—a morbid fear of open spaces.

"Agoraphobics need treatment that is multimodal as well as creative. We don't limit ourselves
to the office. Go into the home, the workplace,
wherever reality beckons."

More red circles, around *agoraphobia* and *the home*.

The rest consisted of pseudonymous case histories, which
I skimmed.

"Finished."

Melissa put down the paperweight. "Have you heard of
them?"

"I've heard of Leo Gabney. He's very well known—has
done a lot of very important research."

I held out the clipping. She took it and put it back in
her bag.

"When I saw this," she said, "it just sounded right for
Mother. I'd been looking for something—we'd started talking, Mother and I. About how she should do something
about . . . her problem. Actually, we talked for years. I
started bringing it up when I was fifteen—old enough to
realize how much it was affecting her. I mean, I always knew
she was . . . different. But when you grow up with someone,
and the way they are is the only way you know, you get used
to them."

"True," I said.

"But as I got older, started to read more psychology and
understand more about people, I began to realize how hard it
must be for her—that she was really *suffering*. And if I loved
her, my obligation was to help her. So I started talking to her
about it. At first she wouldn't talk back, tried to change the
subject. Then she insisted she was okay—I should just take

care of myself. But I just kept at it, in small doses. Like after I'd done something good—gotten a really good grade or brought home an academic award—I'd bring it up. Letting her know I deserved to be taken seriously. Finally, she started to *really* talk. About how hard it was for her, how bad she felt not being a normal mother—how she'd always wanted to be like all the other mothers but that every time she tried to leave, the anxiety just got to her. More than just psychologically. Physical *attacks*. Not being able to breathe. Feeling as if she were going to die. How it trapped her, made her feel helpless and useless and guilty for not taking care of me."

She gripped her knees again, rocked, stared at the paperweight, then back at me. "I told her that was ridiculous. She'd been a terrific mother. She cried and said she knew she hadn't but that I'd turned out wonderful anyway. Despite her, not because of her. It hurt me to hear that and I started to cry, too. We held each other. She kept telling me over and over how sorry she was, and how glad she was that I was so much better than she was. That I would have a good life, get out and see things she'd never seen, do things she'd never done."

She stopped, sucked in breath.

I said, "It must have been so hard for you. Hearing that. Seeing her pain."

"Yes," she said, letting loose a rush of tears.

I reached over, pulled a tissue out of the box. Handed it to her and waited until she composed herself.

"I told her," she said, sniffling, "that I wasn't better than she was, in any way whatsoever. That I was out in the world because I'd gotten *help*. From you. Because *she'd* cared enough about me to *get* me help."

I thought of a child's voice on a crisis line tape. Scented brush-off letters, calls unanswered.

". . . that I cared about her and wanted *her* to get help. She said she knew she needed it but that she was beyond treatment, doubted anyone could help her. Then she started crying harder and said doctors scared her—she knew that was stupid and babyish, but her fear was overpowering. That she never even talked to you on the phone. That I really had gotten better despite her. Because I was strong and she was weak. I told her strength isn't something you just have. It's something you learn. That she was strong, too, in her own way. Living through everything she'd been through and still ending up a beautiful, kind person—because she is, Dr. Delaware! Even though she never got out and did the things other mothers did, I never cared. Because she was *better* than the other mothers. Nicer, kinder."

I nodded and waited.

She said, "She feels so guilty, but really she was wonderful. Patient. Never grumpy. She never raised her voice. When I was little and couldn't sleep—before you cured me—she'd hold me and kiss me and tell me over and over that I was wonderful and beautiful, the best little girl in the world, and that the future was my golden apple. Even if I kept her up all night. Even if I wet the bed and soaked her sheets, she'd just hold me. In the wet sheets. And tell me she loved me, that everything would be okay. That's the kind of person she is and I wanted to help her—to give some of that kindness back."

She buried her face in the tissue. It turned into a sodden lump and I gave her another.

After a while she dried her eyes and looked up. "Finally, after months of talking, after we'd both cried ourselves dry, I got her to agree that if I found the right doctor, she'd try. A doctor who would come to the house. But I didn't do anything for a while because I had no idea where to find a doctor like that. I made a few calls, but the ones who phoned me back said they didn't do house calls. I got the feeling they weren't taking me seriously, because of my age. I even thought of calling you."

"Why didn't you?"

"I don't know. I guess I was embarrassed. Pretty foolish, huh?"

"Not at all."

"Anyway, then I read the article. It sounded perfect. I called their clinic and spoke to her—the wife. She said yes, they could help, but that *I* couldn't arrange treatment for someone else. The patients themselves had to call to set it up. That they insisted upon that, only accepted patients who were *motivated*. She made it sound like applying to college— as if they got tons of applications but only took a few. So I talked to Mother, told her I'd found someone, gave her the number and told her to call. She got really scared—started to have one of her attacks."

"What's that like?"

"She turns pale and grabs her chest and begins breathing really hard and fast. Gasping, as if she can't get any breath in. Sometimes she faints."

"Pretty scary."

"I guess," she said. "For someone seeing it for the first time. But like I said, I'd grown up with it, so I knew she wasn't in any danger. That probably sounds cruel but that's the way it is."

I said, "No, it doesn't. You understood what was happening. Could put it in context."

"Yes. Exactly. So I just waited until the attack was over—they usually don't last more than a few minutes and then she gets really tired and goes to sleep for a couple of hours. But I wouldn't let her sleep this time. I held her and kissed her and started talking to her, very quietly and calmly. About how the attacks were terrible, how I knew she felt terrible, but didn't she want to try to get rid of them? Not to *feel* like that anymore? She started crying. And saying yes, she did want that. Yes, she would try, she promised, but not right now, she was too weak. So I let her off the hook, and nothing happened for weeks. Finally, my patience ran out. I went up to her room, dialed the number in front of her, asked for Dr. Ursula, and handed her the phone. And stood over her. Like this."

Rising, she folded both arms over her chest and put on a stern look.

"I guess I caught her off guard, because she took the phone, began talking to Dr. Ursula. Doing a lot of listening and nodding, mostly, but at the end of it she'd made an appointment."

She let her arms drop and sat back down.

"Anyway, that's how it happened, and it seems to be helping her."

"How long's she been in treatment?"

"About a year—it'll be a year this month."

"Does she see both Gabneys?"

"At first they both came to the house. With a black bag and all sorts of equipment—I guess they were giving her a physical. Then only Dr. Ursula came, and all she brought was a notebook and a pen. She and Mother spent hours together up in Mother's room—every day, even weekends. For weeks. Then finally they came downstairs, walked around the house. Talking. Like friends."

Punctuating *friends* with just a hint of frown.

"*What* they talked about I couldn't tell you, because she—Dr. Ursula—was always careful to keep Mother away from everyone—the staff, me. Not by actually coming out and saying it—she just has a way of looking at you that lets you know you're not supposed to be there."

Another frown.

"Finally, after about a month, they went outside. To the grounds. Strolling. Did that for a long time—months—with no progress that I could see. Mother had always been able to do that by herself. Without treatment. That phase seemed to be going on forever and no one was telling me anything about what was going on. I began to wonder if they—if *she* knew what she was doing. If I'd done the right thing by bringing her into our home. The one time I tried to ask about it was pretty unpleasant."

She stopped, wrung her hands.

I said, "What happened?"

"I caught up with Dr. Ursula at the end of a session, just as she was getting into her car, and asked her how Mother was doing. She just smiled and told me everything was going well. Clearly letting me know it was none of my business. Then she asked me if anything was troubling me—but not as if she cared. Not the way *you'd* say it. I felt she was putting me down—analyzing me. It was creepy. I couldn't wait to get away from her!"

She'd raised her voice, was nearly shouting. Realized it and blushed and covered her mouth.

I gave a reassuring smile.

"But then afterward," she said, "I could understand it. I guess. The need for confidentiality. I started to think back and remembered how it had been with my therapy. I was always asking you all those questions—about other kids—just to see if you'd break the secret. *Testing* you. And then I felt very good, very comforted, when you didn't give in." She smiled. "That was terrible, wasn't it? Testing you like that."

"A hundred percent normal," I said.

She laughed. "Well, you passed the test, Dr. Delaware." The blush deepened. She turned away. "You helped me a lot."

"I'm glad, Melissa. Thanks for saying so."

"Must be a pleasant job," she said, "being a therapist. Getting to tell people they're okay all the time. Not having to cause pain, like other doctors."

"Sometimes it does get painful, but overall you're right. It is a great job."

"Then how come you don't do it anymo— I'm sorry. That's none of my business."

"That's okay," I said. "No topic's off limits here, as long as you can tolerate not always getting an answer."

She laughed. "There you go, doing it again. Telling me I'm okay."

"You are okay."

She touched a finger to the paperweight, then retracted it. "Thank you. For everything you did for me. Not only did you get rid of my fears, you also showed me people can change—they can *win*. It's hard to see that sometimes, when you're stuck in the middle of something. I've thought of studying psychology myself. Maybe becoming a therapist."

"You'd make a good one."

"Do you really think so?" she said, facing me and brightening.

"Yes, I do. You're smart. You care about people. And you're patient—from what you've told me about getting your mother help, you have tremendous patience."

"Well," she said, "I love her. I don't know if I'd be patient with someone else."

"It would probably be easier, Melissa."

"Yes, I guess that's true. 'Cause to tell the truth, I didn't *feel* patient while it was happening—all her resistance and stalling. There were times I even wanted to scream at her, tell her to just get up and *change*. But I couldn't. She's my mother. She's always been wonderful to me."

I said, "But now, after going to all the trouble of getting her into treatment, you have to watch her and Dr. Ursula stroll the grounds for months. With nothing happening. That really tries your patience."

"It did! I was really starting to get skeptical. Then all of a sudden, things started to happen. Dr. Ursula got her outside the front gate. Just a few steps, down to the curb, and she had an attack when she got there. But it was the first time she'd been outside the walls since . . . the first time I'd ever seen her do it. And Dr. Ursula didn't pull her back in because of the attack. She gave her some kind of medicine—in an inhaler, like they use for asthma—and made her stay out there until she'd calmed down. Then they did it again the next day, and again, and she kept having attacks—it was really hard to watch. But finally Mother was able to stand at the curb and be okay. After that, they started walking around the block. Arm in arm. Finally, a couple of months ago, Dr. Ursula got her to drive. In her favorite car—it's this little Rolls-Royce Silver Dawn, a '54, but in perfect condition. Coachbuilt—custom-made. My father had it built to his specifications when he was in England. One of the first to have power steering. And tinted windows. Then he gave it to her. She's always loved it. Sometimes she sat in it after it had been washed, with the engine off. But she never drove it. She must have said something to Dr. Ursula about its being her favorite, because the next thing I knew, the two of them were tooling around in it. Down the drive and right out the gates. She's at the point where she can drive with someone else in the car. She drives to the clinic with Dr. Ursula or someone else with her—it's not far, over in Pasadena. Maybe that wouldn't sound too impressive. But when you think of where she was a year ago, it's pretty fantastic, don't you think?"

"I do. How often does she go to the clinic?"

"Twice a week. Monday and Thursday, for group therapy. With other women who have the same problem."

She sat back, dry-eyed, smiling. "I'm so proud of her, Dr. Delaware. I don't want to mess it up."

"By going to Harvard?"

"By doing *anything* that would mess it up. I mean, I think of Mother as being on a scale—one of those balance scales. Fear on one side, happiness on the other. Right now it's tipping toward happiness, but I can't help thinking that any little thing could knock it the other way."

"You see your mom as pretty fragile."

"She *is* fragile! Everything she's been through has made her fragile."

"Have you talked to Dr. Ursula about the impact of your going away?"

"No," she said, suddenly grim. "No, I haven't."

"I get the feeling," I said, "that even though Dr. Ursula has helped your mother a lot, she's still not your favorite person."

"That's true. She's a very—she's cold."

"Is there anything else about her that bothers you?"

"Just what I said. About her analyzing me . . . I don't think she likes me."

"Why's that?"

She shook her head. One of her earrings caught the light and flashed. "It's just the . . . vibrations she gives off. I know that sounds . . . imprecise—but she just makes me feel uncomfortable. The way she was able to tell me to butt out without having to say it. So how can I approach her about something personal? All she'd do is put me down—I feel she wants to shut me out."

"Have you tried to talk to your mother about this?"

"I talked to her about therapy a couple of times. She said Dr. Ursula was taking her through steps and she was climbing them slowly. That she was grateful to me for getting her into treatment but that now she had to be a big girl and do things for herself. I didn't argue, didn't want to do anything that would . . . ruin it."

Wringing. Flipping her hair.

I said, "Melissa, are you feeling a little left out? By the treatment?"

"No, it's not that at all. Sure, I'd like to know more—especially because of my interest in psychology. But that's not what's important to me. If that's what it takes to work—all that secrecy—then I'm happy. Even if this is as far as it goes, it's still major progress."

"Do you have doubts it will go further?"

"I don't know," she said. "On a day-to-day basis it seems to go so slowly." She smiled. "You see, Dr. Delaware, I'm not patient at all."

"So even though your mother's come a long way, you're not convinced she's gone far enough for you to be able to leave her."

"Exactly."

"And you feel frustrated not knowing more about her prognosis because of the way Dr. Ursula treats you."

"Very frustrated."

"What about Dr. Leo Gabney? Would you be more comfortable talking to him?"

"No," she said. "I don't know him at all. Like I said, he

only showed up at the beginning, a real scientist type—walking very fast, writing things down, ordering his wife around. He's the boss in that relationship."

Following that insight with a smile.

I said, "Even though your mother says she wants you to go to Harvard, you're not sure she can handle it. And you feel you can't talk to anyone to find out if she can."

She shook her head and gave a weak smile. "A quandary, I guess. Pretty dumb, huh?"

"Not at all."

"There you go again," she said. "Telling me I'm okay."

Both of us smiled.

I said, "Who else is around to take care of your mother?"

"There's the staff. And Don, I guess—that's her husband."

Dropping that nugget into the bucket, then draping it with a look of innocence.

But I couldn't keep the surprise out of my voice. "When did she get married?"

"Just a few months ago."

The hands began kneading.

"A few months," I repeated.

She squirmed and said, "Six."

Silence.

I said, "Want to tell me about it?"

She looked as if she didn't. But she said, "His name is Don Ramp. He used to be an actor—never a big one, just a bit player. Cowboys and soldiers, that kind of thing. He owns a restaurant now. In Pasadena, not San Lab, because in San Lab you're not allowed to sell liquor and he serves all kinds of beers and ales. That's his specialty. Imported beers. And meat. Prime rib. Tankard and Blade, it's called. Armor and swords all over the place. Like in old England. Kind of silly, actually, but for San Labrador it's exotic."

"How'd he and your mother meet?"

"You mean because she never leaves the house?"

"Yes."

The hands kneaded faster. "That was my— I introduced them. I was at the Tankard with some friends, a school thing for some seniors. Don was there, greeting people, and when he found out who I was, he sat down and told me he'd known Mother. Years ago. Back in her days at the studio. The two of them had been on contract at the same time. He started asking these questions—about how she was doing. Talking on and on about what a wonderful person she'd been, so beautiful and talented. Telling me I was beautiful, too." She snorted.

"You don't think you're beautiful?"

"Let's be real, Dr. Delaware! Anyway, he seemed so nice and he was the first person I'd met who'd actually known Mother before, back in her Hollywood days. I mean, people in San Labrador don't usually come from an entertainment background. At least they don't admit it. One time another actor—a real star, Brett Raymond—wanted to move in, buy an old house and tear it down to build a new one, and there was all this talk about his money being dirty money because the movies were a Jewish business and Jewish money was dirty money, and Brett Raymond himself was really Jewish and tried to hide it—which I don't even know if it's true or not. Anyway, they—the zoning board—made his life so miserable with hearings and restrictions and whatever that he changed his mind and moved to Beverly Hills. And people said good, that's where he belonged. So you can see how I wouldn't meet too many movie people, and when Don started talking about the old days, I thought it was great. It was like finding a link to the past."

I said, "It's a bit of a leap from that to marriage."

She gave a sour smile. "I invited him over—as a surprise for Mother. This was before she was getting treatment. I was looking for anything to get her going. Get her to socialize. And when he arrived he had three dozen red roses and a big bottle of Taittinger's. I should have known then he had . . . plans. I mean, roses and *champagne*. One thing led to another. He started coming over more often. In the afternoon, before the Tankard opened. Bringing her steaks and more flowers and whatever. It became a regular thing—I just kind of got used to it. Then six months ago, just around the time she started to be able to leave the grounds, they announced they were getting married. Just like that. Brought in a judge and did it, at the house."

"So he was seeing her when you were trying to persuade her to get treatment."

"Yes."

"How'd he relate to that? And to treatment?"

"I don't know," she said. "I never asked him."

"But he didn't fight it."

"No. Don's not a fighter."

"What is he?"

"A charmer. Everyone likes him," she said, with distaste.

"How do you feel about him?"

She gave me an irritated look, brushed her hair from her forehead. "How do I feel? He doesn't get in my way."

"Do you think he's insincere?"

"I think he's . . . shallow. Pure Hollywood."

Echoing the prejudices she'd just decried. She realized it and said, "I know that sounds very San Labrador, but you'd have to meet him to understand. He's tan in the winter, lives for tennis and skiing, always smiling even when there's nothing to smile about. Father was a man of depth. Mother deserves more. If I'd known it would get this far, I'd never have started it."

"Does he have any children of his own?"

"No. He was never married. Not until *now*."

The way she emphasized "now" made me ask, "Are you concerned that he married your mother for her money?"

"The thought has occurred to me—Don's not exactly poor, but he's not in Mother's league."

She gave a wave of her hand, so choppy and awkward that it made me take note.

I said, "Is part of your conflict about Harvard a worry that she needs protection from him?"

"No, but I can't see him being able to take care of her. Why she married him I still can't figure out."

"What about the staff—in terms of taking care of her?"

"They're nice," she said, "but she needs more."

"What about Jacob Dutchy?"

"Jacob," she said, with a tremor in her voice. "Jacob . . . died."

"I'm sorry."

"Just last year," she said. "He developed some kind of cancer and it took him quickly. He left the house right after the diagnosis and went to a place—some sort of rest home. But he wouldn't tell us where. Didn't want anyone to see him sick. After he . . . Afterwards, the home called Mother and told her he was . . . There wasn't even any funeral, just cremation. It really hurt me—not being able to help him. But Mother said we'd helped by letting him do it his way."

More tears. More tissues.

I said, "I remember him as being a strong-willed gentleman."

She bowed her head. "At least it was quick."

I waited for her to say more. When she didn't, I said, "So much has been happening to you. It's got to feel overwhelming. I can see why it's hard for you to know what to do."

"Oh, Dr. Delaware!" she said, getting up and coming forward and throwing her arms around my neck. She'd put on perfume for the appointment. Something heavy and floral and much too old for her. Something a maiden aunt might wear. I thought of her making her own way through life. The trials and errors.

It made me ache for her. I could feel her hands grip my back. Her tears moistened my jacket.

I uttered words of comfort that seemed as substantial as the gilded light. When she'd stopped crying for a full minute, I pulled away gently.

She moved away quickly, sat back down, looking shamefaced. Wringing her hands.

I said, "It's all right, Melissa. You don't always have to be strong."

Shrink's reflex. Another yea-say.

The right thing to say. But in this case, was it the truth?

She began pacing the room. "I can't believe I'm falling apart like this. It's so . . . I planned for this to be so . . . businesslike. A consultation, not . . ."

"Not therapy?"

"Yes. This was for *her*. I really thought I was okay, didn't need therapy. I wanted to *show* you I was okay."

"You really are okay, Melissa. This is an incredibly stressful time for you. All the changes in your mother's life. Losing Jacob."

"Yes," she said absently. "He was a dear."

I waited several moments before continuing. "And now the Harvard thing. That's a major decision. It would be foolish *not* to take it seriously."

She sighed.

I said, "Let me ask you this: If everything else was calm, would you want to go?"

"Well . . . I know it's a great opportunity—my golden apple. But I have to— I *need* to feel right about it."

"What could help you feel right about it?"

She shook her head and threw up her hands. "I don't know. I wish I did."

She looked at me. I smiled and pointed at the couch. She returned to her seat.

I said, "What could really convince you your mother will be okay?"

"Her *being* okay! Normal! Like anyone else. That sounds terrible—as if I'm ashamed of her. I'm not. I'm just worried."

"You want to be sure she can take care of herself."

"That's the thing, she can. Up in her room. It's her domain. It's just the outside world. . . . Now that she's going out—trying to change—it's scary."

"Of course it is."

Silence.

I said, "I suppose I'd be wasting my breath to remind you that you can't go on taking responsibility for your mother forever. Being a parent to your parent. That it will get in the way of your own life and do *her* no good."

"Yes, I know. That's what N— Of course that's true."

"Has someone else been telling you the same thing?"

She bit her lip. "Just Noel. Noel Drucker. He's a friend—not a boyfriend, just a boy who's a friend. I mean, he likes *me* as more than a friend, but I'm not sure how I feel about him. But I do respect him. He's an exceptionally good person."

"How old is Noel?"

"A year older than me. He got accepted to Harvard last year, took time off to work and save up money. His family doesn't have any money —it's just him and his mother. He's been working his whole life and is very mature for his age. But when he talks about Mother, I just want to tell him to . . . stop."

"Ever let him know how you feel?"

"No. He's very sensitive. I don't want to hurt him. And I know he means well—he's thinking of me."

"Boy," I said, blowing out breath. "You're taking care of lots of people."

"Guess so." Smile.

"Who's taking care of Melissa?"

"I can take care of myself." Stating it with a defiance that pulled me back nine years.

"I know you can, Melissa. But even caretakers need to be cared for, once in a while."

"Noel tries to take care of me. But I won't let him. That's terrible, isn't it? Frustrating him like that. But I've got to do things my way. And he just doesn't understand the way it is with Mother. No one does."

"Do Noel and your mother get along?"

"The little they have to do with each other, they do. She thinks he's a nice boy. Which he is. Everyone thinks that—if you knew him you'd understand why. And he likes her well enough. But he says I'm doing her more harm than good by protecting her. That she'll get better when she really has to—as if it's her choice."

Melissa got up and walked around the room again. Letting her hands settle on things, touching, examining. Feigning sudden fascination with the pictures on the walls.

I said, "How can I best help you, Melissa?"

She pivoted on one foot and faced me. "I thought maybe if you could talk to Mother. Tell me what you think."

"You want me to evaluate her? Give you a professional opinion as to whether she really can cope with your going to Harvard?"

She bit her lip a couple of times, touched one of her earrings, flipped her hair. "I trust your *judgment*, Dr. Delaware. What you did for me, how you helped me change—it was like . . . magic. If you tell me it's okay to leave her, then I will. I'll just do it."

Years ago I'd seen *her* as the magician. But letting her know that, now, would be terrifying.

I said, "We were a good team, Melissa. You showed strength and courage back then, just like you're showing now."

"Thank you. So would you . . . ?"

"I'd be happy to talk with your mother. If she consents. And if it's okay with the Gabneys."

She frowned. "Why them?"

"I need to make sure I don't disrupt their treatment plan."

"Okay," she said. "I just hope she doesn't give you problems."

"Dr. Ursula?"

"Uh-huh."

"Any reason you think she might?"

"No. She's just . . . She likes to be in charge of everything. I can't help thinking she *wants* Mother to keep secrets. That have nothing to do with therapy."

"What kind of secrets?"

"I don't *know*," she said. "That's the thing: I've got nothing to back me up—just a feeling. I know it sounds weird. Noel says I'm being paranoid."

"It's not paranoia," I said. "You care deeply about your mother. You've been taking care of her for years. It wouldn't be natural for you to just—"

Her tension dissipated. She smiled.

I said, "There I go again, huh?"

She started to giggle, stopped, embarrassed.

I said, "I'll call Dr. Ursula today, and we'll take it from there. Okay?"

"Okay." She took a couple of steps closer, wrote down the number at the clinic for me.

I said, "Hang in there, Melissa. We'll get through this."

"I sure hope so. You can call me on my private line—that's the number you reached me at yesterday."

She walked back to the coffee table, hastily picked up her purse, and held it in front of her, waist-high.

The accessory defense.

I said, "Is there anything else?"

"No," she said, glancing at the door. "Guess we've covered plenty, haven't we?"

"We had plenty to catch up on."

We walked to the door.

She turned the knob and said, "Well, thanks again, Dr. Delaware."

Tight voice. Tight shoulders. More tense than when she'd come in.

I said, "Are you sure there's nothing else you want to talk about, Melissa? There's no rush. I've got plenty of time."

She stared at me. Then her eyes slammed shut like security shutters and her shoulders dropped.

"It's *him*," she said, in a very small voice. "McCloskey. He's back—in L.A. Totally free and I don't know what he'll do!"

8

I brought her back inside and sat her down.

She said, "I was going to mention it at the start but . . ."

"It gives a whole different dimension to your fear of leaving."

"Yes, but to be honest, I'd be worried even without him. He just adds to it."

"When did you find out he was back?"

"Last month. There was this show on TV, some documentary about the Victim's Bill of Rights—how in some states the family can write away to the prison and they'll tell you when the criminal is coming up for a parole hearing. So you can protest. I knew *he'd* gotten out—years ago—and had moved away. But I wrote anyway, trying to see if there was anything more I could learn—I guess it was part of the same thing. Trying to help her. The prison took a long time to write back, then told me to get in touch with the Parole Department. That was a real hassle—talking to the wrong people, being put on hold. In the end I had to submit a written request for information. Finally I got through and found out the name of his last parole officer. Here in L.A.! Only he wasn't seeing him anymore—McCloskey had just gone off parole."

"How long's he been out of prison?"

"Six years. *That* I found out from Jacob. I'd been bugging him for a while, wanting to know—wanting to understand. He kept putting me off, but I wouldn't give up. Finally, when I was fifteen he admitted he'd been keeping an eye on McCloskey the whole time, had found out he'd been released a couple of years before and had left the state."

She made tiny white fists and shook them. "The creep served thirteen years out of a twenty-three-year sentence— time off for good behavior. That really stinks, doesn't it? No one cares about the victim. He should have been sent to the gas chamber!"

"Did Jacob know where he'd gone?"

"New Mexico. Then Arizona and, I think, Texas— working with the Indians on the reservation or something. Jacob said he was trying to fool the Parole Department into thinking he was a decent human being and that they'd probably *be* fooled. And he was right, because they did set him free and now he can do anything he wants. The parole officer was a nice guy, just about ready to retire. His name was Bayliss and he really seemed to care. But he said he was sorry, there was nothing he could do."

"Does he think McCloskey's a threat to your mother—or anyone else?"

"He said he had no evidence of that but that he didn't know. That no one could be sure with someone like him."

"Has McCloskey tried to contact your mother?"

"No, but what's to say he won't? He's crazy—that kind of craziness doesn't change overnight, does it?"

"Not usually."

"So he's a clear and present danger, isn't he?"

I had no easy answer for that. Said, "I can see why you're concerned," and didn't like the sound of it.

She said, "Dr. Delaware, how can I leave her? Maybe it's a sign—his coming back. That I *shouldn't* leave. I mean, I can get a good education here. UCLA and USC both accepted me. In the long run, what difference is it going to make?"

Different tune from the one she'd sung just a few moments ago.

"Melissa, a person with your brains can get a good education anywhere. Is there a reason, besides education, that you considered Harvard?"

"I don't know . . . maybe it was just ego. Yes, that's probably what it was—out to show myself I could do it."

"Any other reason?"

"Well . . . there's Noel. He really wants me to go there and I thought it would be— I mean, it *is* the best college in the country, isn't it? I figured, why not apply? It was actually kind of a lark. I really didn't think I was going to get in." She shook her head. "Sometimes I think it would have been easier being a C student. Fewer choices."

"Melissa, anyone in your position—the situation with your mother—would be in conflict. And now McCloskey. But the harsh truth is that even if he does pose a danger, you're not in any position to defend your mother against him."

"So what are you saying?" she said angrily. "That I should just give up?"

"I'm saying McCloskey should definitely be looked into. By a professional. To find out why he came back, what he's up to. If he's judged to be dangerous, there are things that can be done."

"Like what?"

"Restraining orders. Security precautions. Is your home well guarded?"

"I guess. There's an alarm system and gates. And the police patrol regularly—there's so little crime in San Labrador the police are basically just like rent-a-cops. Should we be doing more?"

"Have you told your mother about McCloskey?"

"No, of course not! I didn't want to freak her out—not with how well she's been doing."

"What about your— Mr. Ramp?"

"No. No one knows. No one asks me my opinion about anything anyway, and I don't volunteer."

"Have you told Noel?"

She gave an uncomfortable look. "Yes. He knows."

"What does he say?"

"To just forget about it. But that's easy for him—it's not his mother. You didn't answer my question, Dr. Delaware— is there something else we should be doing?"

"I'm not the one to say. There are professionals who specialize in that kind of thing."

"Where do I find them?"

"Let me check," I said. "I might be able to help you with that."

"Your court connections?"

"Something like that. In the meantime, why don't we proceed as planned. I'll contact the Gabneys and see if it's okay for me to meet with your mother. If it is, I'll let you know and you can set up an appointment for me to come by. If it isn't, we'll take another look at our options. In either event, you and I should be talking some more. Want to make another appointment?"

"How about tomorrow?" she said. "Same time. If you've *got* the time."

"I do."

"Thank you—and sorry if I got too hot under the collar just now."

"You're fine," I said, and walked her to the door for the second time.

"Thanks, Dr. Delaware."

"Take care of yourself, Melissa."

"I will," she said. But she looked like a kid overloaded with homework.

After she was gone, I thought about the way she'd dropped a crumb-trail of crucial facts: her mother's remarriage, the young man in her life, Dutchy's death, McCloskey's return.

All of it delivered parenthetically. With an offhandedness that screamed self-defense.

But given everything she had to deal with—loss, ambivalence, crucial decisions, the erosion of personal control—self-defense was damn reasonable.

The control issue had to be especially hard for her. An inflated sense of personal power was the logical legacy of all those years of raising her parent. She'd used it to guide her mother to the brink of change.

Playing matchmaker. Referral service.

Only to be defeated by her own success: forced to stand back and surrender authority to a therapist. To share affection with a stepfather.

Add to that the normal strains and doubts of young-adulthood and it had to be crushing.

Who, indeed, was taking care of Melissa?

Jacob Dutchy had once filled that role.

Though I'd barely known the man, thinking of him gone saddened me. The faithful retainer, ever protective. He'd had a certain . . . *presence.*

For Melissa, that amounted to paternal loss number two.

What did that bode in terms of her relationships with men? The development of trust?

If her comments about Don Ramp—and Noel Drucker—were any example, that road hadn't been smooth, so far.

Now the folks from Cambridge, Mass., were demanding a decision, raising the specter of further surrender.

Who was really afraid of separation?

Not that her fears were totally without foundation.

A Mikoksi with acid.

Why *had* McCloskey come back to L.A., nearly two decades after his conviction? Thirteen years of imprisonment plus six on parole made him fifty-three years old. I'd seen what prison years could do. Wondered if he was nothing more than a pallid, weary old con, seeking out the comfort of like-minded losers and dead-end haunts.

Or perhaps he'd used the time at San Quentin to let his rage fester. Nursing acid-and-blood fantasies, filling his bottle . . .

A discomfiting sense of self-doubt began nagging at me, the same feeling of missing the mark that I'd experienced nine years ago—bending all my rules to treat a terrified child.

A feeling of not really having a grip on the core of the problem.

Nine years ago, she'd gotten better despite that.

Magic.

How many rabbits were left in the hat?

A machine answered at the Gabney Clinic, listing numbers and emergency beeper codes for both doctors. No other staff members were named. I left a message for Ursula Cunningham-Gabney, identifying myself as Melissa Dickinson's therapist and requesting a call-back as soon as possible. During the next few hours several calls came in, but none from Pasadena.

At ten after seven Milo arrived, wearing the same clothes he'd had on that morning, but with grass stains on the pants and sweat stains under the armpits. He smelled of turf and looked tired.

I said, "Any holes in one?"

He shook his head, found a Grolsch in the fridge, popped it, and said, "Not my sport, sport. Chasing a little white blur around the crab grass drives me crazy."

"*Putts* you crazy. We're talking short-distance, guy."

He smiled. "The only *putz* is *me,* for thinking I could go suburban." Tilting his head back, he guzzled beer. When the bottle was empty he said, "Where to, dinner-wise?"

"Wherever you want."

"Well," he said, "you know me, always pining for the *haut monde.* See, I even dressed for success."

We ended up at a taco stand on Pico near Twentieth, in the bad part of Santa Monica, inhaling traffic fumes and sitting at a knife-scarred picnic table, eating soft steamed tortillas filled with coarse-ground pork and marinated vegetables, and drinking Coca-Cola Classic over crushed ice out of waxed-paper cups.

The stand stood on a corner patch of devastated asphalt, between a liquor store and a check-cashing outlet. Homeless people, and a few people who wouldn't live in homes if they had them, loitered and scrounged nearby. A couple of them watched us collect our food at the counter and find our seats. Panhandling fantasies or worse brightened their clouded eyes. Milo kept them at bay with policeman's looks.

We ate looking over our shoulders. He said, "Basic enough for you?" Before I could answer, he was up and heading toward the order counter, one hand in his pocket. A filthy, emaciated, mat-bearded man around my age seized the moment and approached me, grinning and flapping toothless gums incoherently as he waved randomly with a short-circuited arm. The other limb was drawn up to his shoulder, frozen stiff and bent like a chicken wing.

I held out a dollar bill. The mobile arm snapped it up with crustacean precision. He was off before Milo returned with a cardboard carton full of yellow-papered parcels.

But Milo'd seen it, and scowled as he sat down. "What'd you do that for?"

"The guy was brain-damaged," I said.

"Or faking it."

"Either way, he'd have to be pretty desperate, wouldn't you say?"

He shook his head, unwrapped a taco, and bit into it. When the food had traversed his gullet he said, "Everyone's desperate, Alex. Keep doing that and they'll be all over us like fungus."

It didn't sound like something he would have said three months ago.

I looked around, saw the way the rest of the street people were regarding him, and said, "I wouldn't worry about that."

He pointed at the food parcels. "Go ahead, this is for you, too."

I said, "Maybe in a little while," and drank Coke that had turned insipid.

A moment later I said, "If you wanted information about an ex-con, how would you go about it?"

"What kind of information?" he said, forming the words around a mouthful of pork.

"How the guy behaved in prison, what he's up to now."

"This con on parole?"

"Post-parole. Free and clear."

"A paragon of rehabilitation, huh?"

"That's the question mark."

"How long's Mr. Paragon been free and clear?"

" 'Bout a year or so."

"What was he in for?"

"Assault, attempted murder, conspiracy to commit murder—he paid someone to damage someone else."

"Paid for it, huh?" He wiped his lips.

"Paid with the intent of doing serious damage or worse."

"Then just assume he'll continue to be scum."

"What if I wanted something more specific?"

"To what end?"

"It's related to a patient."

"Meaning hush-hush confidential?"

"At this point."

"Well," he said, "it's really no big deal. You—meaning a cop, 'cause a civilian's gonna have a hell of a time doing any of this—you follow the chain. The past is the best predictor of the future, right? So first link is the guy's sheet. NCIC and local. You talk to any cops who knew him back in the bad old days. Preferably the ones who busted him. Next you eyeball the D.A.'s packet—there'll be sentencing recommendations in there, shrink stuff, whatever. Step three is talk to the prison staff—find out what kind of time he served. Though the ones who'll really know him best are the assholes who served it with him. If you've got a hook into any of them, you tug. Then check out his parole officer—problem there is caseload and turnover. Lot of what they do is rubber-stamping; the chance of getting anything meaningful is slim. Final step is locating some of his current K.A.'s— known associates—the scum he's been socializing with since he's been out. Finis. Nothing profound, just legwork. And in the end it won't tell you much. So if you've got a patient who's worried, I'd tell him or her to be careful. Buy a big gun and learn how to use it. Maybe a pit bull."

"The trace you just described—could a private attorney do it?"

He eyed me over a taco. "Your average attorney? No. Not in any reasonable length of time. One with access to a good private eye could pull it off, but it would still take a private guy longer unless he's got great police connections."

"Like an ex-cop?"

He nodded. "Some of the private guys are vets. All of them bill by the hour and this kind of thing is going to build lots of hours. So having a rich client would help."

"Sound like the kind of thing you'd be interested in?"

He put his taco down.

"*What?*"

"A little private consultation, Milo. A *real* hobby. Are you allowed to work while on suspension?"

"I'm Joe Citizen, can do whatever I want. But why the hell would I want?"

"Better than chasing blurs on crab grass."

He grunted. Picked up his taco, finished it, and began unwrapping another.

"Hell," he said, "I wouldn't even know what to charge."

"That mean you're considering it?"

"Mulling. This patient of yours—is he or she the victim?"

"Victim's daughter," I said. "Eighteen years old. I treated her years ago, when she was a kid. She's been accepted at a college out of town and isn't sure about going, even though it's probably the best thing for her."

"Because of the scumbag being back?"

"There are other reasons for her to have doubts. But the scumbag's presence makes it impossible to deal with any of those. I can't encourage her to go away with this guy lurking in the background, Milo."

He nodded and ate.

"The family's got money," I said. "That's why I asked about attorneys—if they don't already have a *battalion* on retainer, they could hire one. But with you doing it I'd have confidence it was being done properly."

"Aw, shucks," he said, and took a few more bites of taco. He pulled up his shirt collar and gave a furtive look. "Milo Marlowe, Milo Spade . . . which do you think is catchier?"

"What about Sherlock Sturgis?"

"What's that make you? The New Age Watson? Sure, go ahead, tell the family if they want to go that route I'll check him out."

"Thanks."

"*No problema.*" He picked his teeth and looked down at his sweat-stained clothes. "Wrong climate for a trench coat—any such thing as a trench *shirt?*"

"Go all the way," I said. "L.A. Vice. Armani."

We drained our drinks and polished off more food. On our way to the car, another of the panhandlers approached us—a heavy man of indeterminate race and creed, wearing a shit-eating grin while doing a palsied boogaloo. Milo glared at him, then reached into his pocket and came up with a handful of pocket change. Thrusting the money at the vagrant, he wiped his hands on his pants, turned his back on the man's gibbered benedictions, and cursed as he reached for the door handle. But the epithets lacked conviction—I'd heard much better out of him.

Dr. Ursula Cunningham-Gabney had called back while I was gone, leaving a number where she could be reached for the rest of the evening. I dialed it, got a throaty, well-modulated female voice.

"Dr. Cunningham-Gabney?"

"Speaking."

"This is Dr. Delaware. Thanks for returning my call, Dr. Gabney."

"Is this by any chance Dr. *Alexander* Delaware?"

"Yes, it is."

"Ah," she said. "I'm familiar with your research—*pavor nocturnus* in children. My husband and I included it in a bibliography on anxiety-mediated disorders we compiled last year for *The American Journal of Psychiatry*. Very thought-provoking."

"Thanks. I'm familiar with your work, too."

"Where do you practice, Dr. Delaware? Children are outside of our bailiwick, so we do have occasion to make frequent referrals."

"I'm on the west side, but I don't do therapy. Just forensic work. Short-term consultations."

"I see. The message I got said you were someone's therapist."

"Melissa Dickinson. I was her therapist years ago. I remain available for my old patients. She came in to see me recently."

"Melissa," she said. "Such a *serious* young woman."

"She has a lot to be serious about."

"Yes. Of course she does. The family pathology is deep-rooted. I'm glad she's finally reached out for help."

"Her main concern seems to be her mother," I said. "Separation. How her mother will deal with her going away to Harvard."

"Her mother is very proud of her. And eager for her to go to Boston."

"Yes, Melissa's told me that. But she's still worried."

"No doubt she is," she said. "But those worries are Melissa's alone."

"So there's no chance of her mother's relapsing if Melissa goes away?"

"Hardly, Dr. Delaware. In fact, I'm sure Gina—Mrs.

Ramp—would appreciate her newfound freedom. Melissa's a bright girl and a devoted daughter, but she can get a bit . . . cloying."

"Is that her mother's term?"

"No, Mrs. Ramp would never say it that way. But she feels it. So I hope you'll be able to confront Melissa's ambivalence head-on and do it quickly enough for her to make the break. I understand there's a deadline involved. Harvard tends to be impatient—I know from experience. So she's going to have to commit. One would hate to see a technicality get in the way of forward movement."

Thinking of McCloskey, I said, "Does Mrs. Ramp have any other worries that might be transmitting themselves to Melissa?"

"Transmitting? As in emotional contagion? No, I'd say it's just the opposite—the risk is of Melissa's anxiety transmitting itself to her mother. Mrs. Ramp presented as one of the most severely phobic patients we've ever treated, and we've treated many. But she's made extraordinary progress and she'll continue to do so. Given the chance."

"Are you saying Melissa's a threat to her progress?"

"Melissa means well, Dr. Delaware. I can certainly understand her concern. Growing up with an ineffectual mother would give her a stake in being hypermature. At some level, that would be adaptive. But things change, and at this point in time, her hovering serves only to reduce her mother's self-confidence."

"How does she hover?"

"She tends to make herself rather conspicuous during crucial therapeutic moments."

"I'm still not sure I understand."

"Okay," she said, "I'll spell it out. As you may know, treatment for agoraphobia needs to be *in vivo*—to take place out in the real world, where the anxiety-provoking stimuli are. Her mother and I literally take steps together. Out the front gate, around the block. It's a slow but steady process, calibrated so that the patient experiences as little anxiety as possible. Melissa makes a point of being there during important moments. Watching. With her arms folded across her chest and this absolutely *skeptical* look on her face. It's almost comical, but of course it's a distraction. It's gotten so I've scheduled things around her—aiming for breakthroughs when she's at school. Now, however, she's out of school and more . . . conspicuous."

"Have you ever talked to her about this?"

"I've tried, Dr. Delaware, but Melissa shows no interest in talking to me."

"Funny," I said. "She sees it differently."

"Oh?"

"She perceives herself as trying to obtain information from you and getting rebuffed."

Silence. Then: "Yes, I'm sure she does. But that's a neurotic distortion. I'm not without compassion for her situation, Dr. Delaware. She's dealing with a lot of ambivalence—intense feelings of threat and jealousy. It can't be easy for her. But I need to focus on my patient. And Melissa could use your help—or someone else's, if you're not so inclined—in sorting things out."

I said, "She'd like me to talk to her mother. In order to clarify her mother's feelings so she *can* sort out the Harvard thing. I'm calling to find out if that's okay. I don't want to disrupt your treatment."

"That's wise of you. What, exactly, would you discuss with Mrs. Ramp?"

"Just her feelings about Melissa's leaving—which, from what you've told me, sound pretty clear. After hearing it firsthand, I'd be able to deal with Melissa's doubts."

"Using your advocate role to propel her forward?"

"Exactly."

"Well, I don't see any harm in that. As long as you keep your discussion circumscribed."

"Any particular topics you'd like me to stay away from?"

"At this point, I'd say everything other than Melissa's college career. Let's just keep things simple."

"Doesn't sound as if anything about this case has been simple."

"True," she said, with a lilt in her voice. "But that's the beauty of psychiatry, isn't it?"

I called Melissa at nine and she picked up on the first ring.

"I checked with my contact—he's a police detective on temporary leave so he has some free time. If you still want McCloskey looked into, it can be done."

"I want it," she said. "Tell him to go ahead."

"It may take a bit of time, and investigators usually bill by the hour."

"No problem. I'll take care of it."

"You're going to pay him yourself?"

"Sure."

"It could end up being substantial."

"I've got money of my own, Dr. Delaware—I've paid for things for a long time. I'm going to pay *your* bill, so why not this—"

"Melissa—"

"No problem, Dr. Delaware. Really. I'm a very good money manager. I'm over eighteen, meaning it's totally legal. If I'm going to go away and live independently, why not start right now?"

When I hesitated, she said, "It's the only way, Dr. Delaware. I don't want Mother even knowing he's back."

"What about Don Ramp?"

"I don't want him involved, either. It's not his problem."

"All right," I said. "We'll work out the details when I see you tomorrow. Speaking of which, I spoke to Dr. Ursula and she says it's fine for me to meet with your mother."

"Good. I already talked to Mother and she's willing to meet you. Tomorrow—isn't that great? So can we cancel our appointment and do that instead?"

"All right. I'll be there tomorrow at noon."

"Thanks, Dr. Delaware. I'll have lunch set out for you. What do you like to eat?"

"Lunch isn't necessary, but thanks anyway."

"You're sure?"

"I'm sure."

"Do you know how to get here?"

"I know how to get to San Labrador."

She gave me directions to her house.

I copied them and said, "Okay, Melissa, see you tomorrow."

"Dr. Delaware?"

"Yes, Melissa?"

"Mother's worried. About you. Even though I told her how nice you are. She's worried about what you'll think of her. Because of the way she treated you years ago."

"Tell her I understand, and that my horns only come out during the full moon."

No laughter.

I said, "I won't be in the least bit rough, Melissa. She'll be fine."

"I hope so."

"Melissa, part of what you're dealing with—a lot more important than money management—is breaking away. Finding your own identity and letting your mother do things for herself. I know it's hard—I think it's taken lots of guts for you to go as far as you have. Just *calling* me took guts. We're *going* to work it out."

"I hear you," she said. "It's just hard. Loving someone that much."

9

The stretch of freeway that connects L.A. to Pasadena announces itself with four tunnels whose entries are festooned with exquisite stonework. Not the kind of thing any city council is likely to approve nowadays, but this bit of progress was carved into the basin long ago, the city's first conduit to ceaseless motion masquerading as freedom.

It's a grubby and graceless asphalt belt now. Three narrow, street-level lanes, bordered by exhaust-warped maples and houses that range from Victorian Relic to Tobacco Road. Psychotically engineered ramps appear without warning. Concrete overpasses that have browned with time—L.A.'s stab at patina—throw spooky shadows across the blacktop. Every time I get on it I think of Nathanael West and James M. Cain—a Southern California history that probably never really existed but is gloomily gratifying to imagine.

I also think of Las Labradoras and how places like the upper-crusty parts of Pasadena, Sierra Madre, and San Labrador might as well be on the moon for all their cross-pollination with the urban tangle at the other end of the freeway.

Las Labradoras. The Farm Girls.

I encountered them years before I met Melissa. In

retrospect, the similarity between the experiences seemed obvious. Why hadn't I made the connection before?

They were women who called themselves girls. Two dozen sorority sisters who'd married very well and settled into estate living at a young age, gotten a couple of kids off to school, and started looking for ways to fill time. Seeking comfort in numbers, they banded together and established a volunteer society—an exclusive club, sorority days renewed. Their headquarters was a bungalow at the Cathcart Hotel—a $200-a-day nest they obtained gratis, including room service, because one of their husbands owned a chunk of that hostelry, and another, the bank that held the mortgage. After composing bylaws and electing officers, they searched for a *raison d'être*. Hospital work seemed admirable, so most of their early energies were focused upon remodeling and running the gift shop at Cathcart Memorial.

Then the son of one of their members was diagnosed with a rare and painful disease and transferred to Western Pediatric Hospital, the only place in L.A. where the ailment could be managed. The child survived but suffered chronically. His mother dropped out of the club in order to devote more time to him. Las Labradoras decided to offer their good services to Western Peds.

At the time, I was in my third year on staff, running a psychosocial rehab program for seriously ill children and their families. The chief of staff called me into his office and suggested I find a niche for "these girls," talking about budgetary problems for the softer sciences and emphasizing the need to "interface with positive forces within the community."

One Tuesday in May, I put on a three-piece suit and drove out to the Cathcart Hotel. Ate boiled-shrimp canapés and crustless sandwiches, drank weak coffee, and met the girls.

They were in their mid-thirties, uniformly bright and attractive and genuinely charming, projecting a noblesse oblige tainted by self-consciousness and self-awareness: They'd gone to college during the sixties, and though that consisted, typically, of four sheltered years at USC or Arizona State or some other place where the foment hadn't really taken hold, even protected *señoritas* had been touched by the times. They knew that they—their husbands, their children, the way they lived and would continue to live—were The Enemy. The privileged battlements all those unwashed radical types clamored to storm.

I wore a beard back then and drove a Dodge Dart that teetered on the brink of death. Despite the suit and my fresh haircut, I figured I had to look like Radical Danger to them. But they accepted me warmly, listened intensely to my after-lunch talk, never removed their eyes from my slide show—sick kids, IV poles, surgical theaters. The one we staffers, during the blackest of moments, called the Tear-jerker Matinee.

When it was over, they were all wet-eyed. More certain than ever that they wanted to help.

I decided the best way to make use of their talents would be to have them serve as guides for newly diagnosed families. Psychosocial docents whose goal was to cut through the procedural red tape that hospitals produce even faster than debt. Weekly two-hour shifts in tailored uniforms that they designed themselves, smiles and greetings and guided tours of the misery. Working within the system to blunt some of its indignities, but no swan dives into the deep waters of trauma and tragedy, and no blood and guts. The chief of staff thought it was a great idea.

So did the girls. I set up a training program. Lectures, reading lists, tours of the hospital, debriefings, discussion groups, role-playing.

They were first-rate students, took detailed notes, made intelligent comments. Half-jokingly asked if I planned on testing them.

After three weeks they graduated. The chief of staff presented them with diplomas bound in pink ribbon. A week before the docent rotation was scheduled to begin, I received a handwritten note on ice-colored stationery.

LAS LABRADORAS
BUNGALOW B, THE CATHCART
PASADENA, CALIFORNIA 91125

Dear Doctor Delaware,

*On behalf of my Sisters and myself, I wish to thank
you for the consideration you've shown us during these
past few weeks. We girls all agree that we learned a
tremendous amount and greatly profited from the experience.*

*We regret, however, that we will not be able to par-
ticipate in the "Welcome Mat" program, as it presents
some strategic problems for some of our members. We hope
this hasn't caused you any undue inconvenience and
have tendered a donation to the Western Pediatric Hospital Christmas Fund in lieu of our participation.*

*Best wishes for a wonderful year and our sincere
appreciation for the terrific work you do.*

Faithfully yours,
Nancy Brown
President, Las Labradoras

I found Ms. Brown's home number in my Rolodex, dialed it
the next day, at eight in the morning.

"Oh, hi," she said. "How are you?"

"Hanging in, Nancy. I just got your letter."

"Yes. I'm so sorry. I know how terrible this looks, but we
just can't."

"You mentioned strategic problems. Anything I can help
with?"

"No, I'm sorry, but— It's nothing related to your program, Dr. Delaware. Just your . . . setting."

"My setting?"

"The hospital's. The environment. L.A., Hollywood.
Most of us were amazed at how far down it's slid. Some of the
girls think it's just too far to travel."

"Too far or too dangerous?"

"Too far *and* too dangerous. Lots of the husbands are against us coming down there, too."

"We really haven't had any problems, Nancy. You'd be here during the daylight hours, using the VIP parking lot."

Silence.

I said, "Patients come and go every day with no problem."

"Well . . . you know how it is."

"Guess so," I said. "Okay. Be well."

"I'm sure it sounds silly to you, Dr. Delaware. And to be honest, *I* think it's an overreaction—I tried to *tell* them that. But our charter says we either participate as a group or not at all. We took a vote, Dr. Delaware, and this is the way it turned out. I do apologize if we've caused you problems. And we do hope the hospital accepts our gift in the spirit in which it was offered."

"No doubt the hospital does."

"Goodbye, Dr. Delaware. Have a nice day."

Notes on good paper, monetary buy-offs, phone brush-offs. Must be the San Labrador style.

I thought about it all the way to the end of the freeway, onto Arroyo Seco, then east on California Boulevard, past Cal Tech. A quick series of loops through quiet suburban streets, then Cathcart Boulevard appeared and I resumed the eastward trek, into the wilds of San Labrador.

The Farmer Saint.

A canonization that had eluded the Vatican.

The very origins of the place were grounded in a buy-off.

Once the private domain of H. Farmer Cathcart, heir to an East Coast railroad dynasty, San Labrador looked like old money but had been chartered as a city for only fifty years.

Cathcart came to Southern California at the turn of the century in order to scope out commercial possibilities for the family. He liked what he saw, began buying up downtown rail lines and hotels, orange groves, bean farms, and ranch land on the eastern borders of Los Angeles, assembling a four-square-mile fiefdom in the foothills of the San Gabriel Mountains. After building the requisite mansion, he surrounded it with world-class gardens and named the estate San Labrador—a bit of self-aggrandizement that made Episcopal tongues wag.

Then, midway through the Great Depression, he discovered his funds weren't infinite. Holding on to half a square mile, he subdivided the rest. Parceling the gardens out to other rich men—tycoons of grand but lesser stature who could afford to maintain two- to seven-acre properties. Attaching restrictive covenants to all deed transfers, which ensured his living out the rest of his life in sweet harmony with nature and the finest aspects of Western civilization.

The rest of his life didn't amount to much—he died in 1937 of influenza, leaving a will bequeathing his estate to the city of San Labrador, should such a city exist within two years. The tycoon tenants acted quickly, setting up a charter and pushing it through the L.A. County Board of Supervisors. Cathcart's mansion and grounds became a county-owned but privately funded museum-cum-botanical gardens that nobody visited—before the freeways.

During the postwar years the land was subdivided further: half-acre lots for the burgeoning professional class. But the covenants remained in place: no "coloreds," no Orientals, no Jews, no Mexicans. No multiple dwellings. No alcohol served in public places. No nightclubs or theaters or places of "base entertainment." Commercial establishments limited to an eight-block segment of Cathcart Boulevard, no commercial structure to exceed two stories; architectural style to be in the Spanish Revival mode, with plans approved by the city council.

State and federal law eventually nullified the racial restrictions, but there were ways to get around that, and San Labrador remained lily-white. The rest of the covenants withstood tests of time and litigation. Perhaps that was due to sound legal basis. Or maybe the fact that lots of judges and at least two district attorneys resided in San Labrador had something to do with it.

Whatever the reason, the district's immunity to change remained strong. As I cruised down Cathcart, nothing seemed different from the last time I'd been there. How long ago had that been? Three years. A Turner exhibition at the museum, a stroll through the library and grounds. With Robin . . .

Traffic was sparse but slow-moving. The boulevard was split by a wide greenbelt median. The same mix of shops ran along the south side, ensconced in jewel-box Spanish Revival buildings and dwarfed by the rust-tinged Chinese pistachios H. Farmer Cathcart had planted long ago. Doctors, dentists . . . lots of orthodontists. Clothiers for both sexes offering styles that made Brooks Brothers seem New Wave. A profusion of dry cleaners, florists, interior decorators, banks, and brokerage houses. Three stationers in two blocks—suddenly that made sense. Plenty of Esq.'s and Ltd.'s and *faux*-Victorian nomenclature on the signs. Nowhere to eat or drink or stretch. Frequent signs directing the meandering tourist to the museum.

A Hispanic man in blue city-issue coveralls pushed an industrial-strength vacuum cleaner along the sidewalk. A few white-haired figures walked around him. Otherwise the streets were bare.

The *haut monde* approach to exurbia. Picture-perfect. Except for the sky, soot-streaked and dingy, clouding the foothills. Because money and connections couldn't buck geography: Ocean winds blew the smog here and, trapped by the hills, it settled in for the long run. San Labrador air was poisonous 120 days a year.

Following Melissa's directions, I drove six blocks past the commercial area, took the first left-turn break in the median, and got onto Cotswold Drive, a pine-canopied straightaway that began snaking and climbing a half-mile in. Cool shade and post-nuclear silence followed: L.A.'s usual dearth of humanity, but here it seemed more pronounced.

Because of the cars—the lack of them. Not a single vehicle at the curb. The NO PARKING AT ANY TIME enforced with Denver boots and predatory fines. Rising above the empty streets were big tile-roofed houses behind sloping lawns. They got bigger as the grade climbed.

The road split at the top of the hill: Essex Ridge to the west, Sussex Knoll to the east. No homes visible here, just two-story walls of green—eugenia and juniper and red-berried toyon backed by forests of oak, ginkgo, and liquid-ambar.

I lowered my speed and cruised until I finally saw it. Hand-carved pine gates on thick doweled posts capped with verdigrised iron—the kind of hard, waxed pine you see on Buddhist temples and the counters of sushi bars. The posts sided by iron fencing and twelve-foot hedge. The numeral "1" on the left arm of the gate, "0" on the right. To the left of the "1," an electric eye and talk box.

I pulled up, reached out the driver's window, and punched the button on the box.

Melissa's voice came out of the speaker. "Dr. Delaware?"

"Hi, Melissa."

"One second."

A rumble and groan and the gates angled inward. I drove up a steep stone path that had been hosed down so recently the air was misty. Past regimentally planted fifty-foot incense cedars and a vacant guardhouse that could have housed a couple of middle-class families. Then another regiment of trees—a sky-blotting grove of Monterey pines that stretched for several moments before condescending to smaller cousins: gnarled, bonsailike cypress and mountain dogwood ringed with free-form clumps of purple rhododendron, white and pink camellia japonica.

A dark drive. The silence seemed heavier. I thought of Gina Dickinson making her way down here, alone. Gained a new appreciation for her affliction. And her progress.

The trees finally cleared and a stadium-sized lawn came

into view—ryegrass so healthy-looking it could have been fresh sod, edged with circular beds of begonia and star jasmine. I saw flashes of light at the far west end, among the cypress. Movement, glints of metal. Two—no, three—khaki-clad men, too distant to be clearly discernible. Hernandez's sons? I could see why he needed five.

The gardeners worked on the vegetation with hand clippers, barely breaking the silence with dull clicks. No air guns or power tools here. Another covenant? Or house rules?

The path ended in a perfectly semicircular drive backed by a pair of date palms. Between the knobby palm trunks, two flights of double-width Bouquet-Canyon stone steps flanked by wisteria-laced stone balustrades led to the house: peach-colored, three-storied, wide as a neighborhood.

What could have been simply monolithic grossness was merely monumental. And surprisingly pleasing to the eye, the visual flight piloted by fanciful turns of the architect's pencil. Subtly shifting angles and elevations, a richness of detail. High, arched, leaded windows grilled with teal-green, neo-Moorish wrought-iron work. Balconies, verandas, dripstones, running molds, and mullions carved from mocha-colored limestone. A limestone colonnade on the east end. Spanish roof-tiles honeycombed with mosaic precision. Stained-glass cinquefoil insets placed with a contempt for synchrony but an unerring eye for balance.

Still, the very size of the place—and the solitude—was oppressive and sad. Like an empty museum. Nice place to visit, but I wouldn't want to be phobic here.

I parked and got out. The gardeners' clicks were augmented by bird-squawks and breeze-rustle. I climbed the stairs, unable to imagine what it would have been like to grow up here, an only child.

The entry was big enough to accommodate a delivery truck: double doors of lacquered oak, trimmed with more verdigrised iron, each side divided into half a dozen raised panels. Carved into the panels were peasant scenes that evoked high-school Chaucer. They held my interest as I pressed the doorbell.

Two baritone chimes sounded; then the right door opened and Melissa stood there, wearing a white button-down shirt, pressed blue jeans, and white tennies: she looked tinier than ever. A doll in a dollhouse built to too large a scale.

She shrugged and said, "Some place, huh?"

"Very beautiful."

She smiled, relieved. "My father designed it. He was an architect."

The most she'd said about him in nine years. I wondered what else would emerge now that I'd made a house call.

She touched my elbow briefly, then drew it away.

"Come in," she said. "Let me show you around."

Around was a vast space crammed with treasures—an entry hall big enough for croquet, and at its rear a sinuous green marble staircase. Beyond the stairs, cavernous room after cavernous room—galleries built for display, vast and silent, indistinguishable from one another in terms of function. Cathedral and coffered ceilings, mirror-sheen paneling, tapestries, stained-glass skylights, kaleidoscopic Oriental and Aubusson rugs over floors of inlaid marble and hand-painted tile and French walnut parquet. So much sheen and opulence that my senses overloaded and I felt myself losing equilibrium.

I remembered feeling that way once before. Over twenty years ago. A college sophomore, backpacking solo across Europe on a second-class rail pass and $4 a day. Visiting the Vatican. Staring bug-eyed at gold-encrusted walls, the treasure-trove assembled in the name of God. Gradually pulling away from it and watching other tourists and Italian peasants visiting from the southern villages, gawking, too. The peasants never leaving a room before dropping coins in the alms boxes that stood near each door. . . .

Melissa was talking and pointing, a docent in her own home. We were in a book-lined, five-sided, windowless room. She indicated a spotlit painting over a mantel. "And this one's a Goya. 'The Duke of Montero on His Steed.' Father bought it in Spain when art was much more reasonable. He wasn't concerned with what was fashionable—this was considered a very minor Goya until just a few years ago; too decorative. Portraiture was déclassé. Now auction houses write us letters all the time. Father had the foresight to travel to England and brought back *cartons* of Pre-Raphaelites when everyone else thought they were just kitsch. Tiffany glass pieces, too, during the fifties, when the experts brushed those off as frivolous."

"You know your stuff," I said.

She blushed. "I was taught."

"By Jacob?"

She nodded and looked away. "Anyway, I'm sure you've seen enough for one day."

Turning heel, she began walking out of the room.

"Are you interested in art yourself?" I said.

"I don't know much about it—not the way Father or Jacob did. I do like things that are beautiful. If nobody gets hurt by it."

"What do you mean?"

She frowned. We left the book-filled room, passed by the open door of another huge space, this one ceilinged with hand-painted walnut beams and backed with tall French doors. Beyond the glass was more lawn and forest and flowers, stone pathways, statuary, an amethyst-colored swimming pool, a sunken area, vine-topped and walled with dark-green tennis tarp under chain link. From the distance came the hollow thump of a ball bouncing.

A couple of hundred feet back, to the left of the court, was a long, low peach-colored building that resembled a stable: ten or so wooden doors, some of them ajar, backing a wide cobbled courtyard filled with gleaming, long-nosed antique

automobiles. Amoeboid pools of water dotted the cob-
blestones. A figure in gray overalls bent over one of the cars,
chamois in hand, buffing the flaring ruby-colored fender of a
splendid piece of machinery. From the blower pipes, I guessed
it was a Duesenberg and asked Melissa for confirmation.

"Yes," she said, "that's what it is," and keeping her eyes
straight ahead, she led me back through the art-filled caverns, toward the front of the house.

"I don't know," she said suddenly. "It just seems that so
many things start off beautiful and turn hateful. It's as if
being beautiful can be a curse."

I said, "McCloskey?"

She put both hands in the pockets of her jeans and gave
an emphatic nod. "I've been thinking about him a lot."

"More than before?"

"A lot more. Since we talked." She stopped, turned to
me, blinked hard. "Why would he come *back*, Dr. Delaware?
What does he *want*?"

"Maybe nothing, Melissa. Maybe it means nothing. If
anyone can find out, my friend can."

"I hope so," she said. "I certainly hope so. When can he
start?"

"I'll have him call you as soon as possible. His name is
Milo Sturgis."

"Good name," she said. "Solid."

"He's a solid guy."

We resumed walking. A big, broad woman in a white
uniform was polishing a tabletop, feather duster in one hand,
rag in the other. Open tin of paste wax near her knee. She
turned her face slightly and our eyes met. Madeleine, grayer
and wrinkled but still strong-looking. A grimace of recognition tightened her face; then she showed me her back and
resumed her work.

Melissa and I stepped back into the entry hall. She
headed for the green stairway. As she touched the handrail I
said, "In terms of McCloskey, are you concerned about your
own safety?"

"Mine?" she said, pausing with one foot on the first step. "Why should I be?"

"No reason. But you were just talking about beauty as a curse. Do you feel burdened or threatened by your own looks?"

"Me?" Her laughter was too quick, too loud. "Come on, Dr. D. Let's go upstairs. I'll show you beautiful."

10

The top of the landing was a twenty-foot rosette of black marble inlaid with a blue-and-yellow sunburst pattern. French provincial furniture hugged the walls, potbellied, bowlegged, almost obscene with marquetry. Renaissance paintings of the Sentimental School—cherubs, harps, religious agony—competed with flocked-velvet paper the color of old port. Foot-wide white molding and coving defined three hallway spokes. Two more women in white vacuumed the one on the right. The other corridors were dark and empty. More like a hotel than a museum. The sad, aimless ambience of a resort during the off-season.

Melissa turned onto the middle corridor and led me past five white panel doors adorned with black and gold cloisonné knobs.

At the sixth, she stopped and knocked.

A voice from within said, "Yes?"

Melissa said, "Dr. Delaware's here," and opened the door.

I'd been ready for another megadose of grandeur but found myself in a small, simple room—a sitting area, no more than twelve feet square, painted dove-gray and lit by a single overhead milk-glass fixture.

A white door took up a quarter of the rear wall. The other walls were bare except for a single lithograph: A softly colored mother-and-child scene that had to be Cassatt. The print was centered over a rose-colored, gray-piped loveseat. A pine coffee table and two pine chairs created a conversation area. Bone-china coffee service on the table. Woman on the couch.

She stood and said, "Hello, Dr. Delaware. I'm Gina Ramp."

Soft voice.

She came forward, her walk a curious mix of grace and awkwardness. The awkwardness was all above the neck—her head was held unnaturally high and tilted to one side, as if recoiling from a blow.

"Pleased to meet you, Mrs. Ramp."

She took my hand, gave it a quick, gentle squeeze and let go.

She was tall—had at least eight inches on her daughter—and still model-slender, in a knee-length, long-sleeved dress of polished gray cotton. Front-buttoned to the neck. Patch pockets. Flat-heeled gray sandals. A plain gold wedding band on her free hand. Gold balls in her ears. No other jewelry. No perfume.

The hair was medium-blond and starting to silver. She wore it short and straight, brushed forward with feathered bangs. Boyish. Almost ascetic.

Her face was pale, oval, made for the camera. Strong, straight nose, firm chin, wide gray-blue eyes stippled with green. The pouty allure of an old studio photo replaced by something more mature. More relaxed. Slight surrender of contour, the merest sag at the seams. Smile lines, brow furrows, a suggestion of pouch at the junction of lips and cheek.

Forty-three years old, I knew from an old newspaper clipping, and she looked every day of it. Yet age had softened her beauty. Enhanced it, somehow.

She turned to her daughter and smiled. Lowered her

head, almost ritualistically, and showed me the left side of her face.

Skin stretched tight, bone-white and glassy-smooth. Too smooth—the unhealthy sheen of fever-sweat. The jawline sharper than it should have been. Subtly skeletal, as if stripped of an underlying layer of musculature and refurbished with something artificial. Her left eye drooped, very slightly but noticeably, and the skin beneath it was scored with a dense network of white filaments. Scars that seemed to be floating just beneath the surface of her skin—a suspension of threadworms swimming in flesh-colored gelatin.

The neck-flesh just below the jaw was ruled with three ruddy stripes—as if she'd been slapped hard and the finger marks had lingered. The left side of her mouth was preternaturally straight, offering harsh counterpart to the weary eye and giving her smile a lopsided cast that projected an uninvited irony.

She shifted her head again. Her skin caught the light at a different angle, and took on the marbled look of a tea-soaked egg.

Off-kilter. Beauty defiled.

She said to Melissa, "Thank you, darling," and gave a crooked smile. Part of the left side didn't smile along.

I realized that—just for the moment—I'd blocked out Melissa's presence. I turned, with a smile for her. She was staring at us, a hard, watchful look on her face. Suddenly, she turned up the corners of her mouth, forced herself to join in the smile-fest.

Her mother said, "Come here, baby," and went to her, holding out her arms. Hugging her. Using her height to advantage, cradling, stroking Melissa's long hair.

Melissa stepped back and looked at me, flushed.

Gina Ramp said, "I'll be fine, baby. Go on."

Melissa said, "Have fun," in a voice on the verge of cracking. Gave one more look back and walked out.

Leaving the door open. Gina Ramp walked over and closed it.

"Please make yourself comfortable, Doctor," she said, readjusting the tilt of her face so that only the good side was visible. She gestured toward the china service. "Coffee?"

"No, thanks." I sat in one of the chairs. She returned to the loveseat. Sat perched at the edge, back straight, legs crossed at the ankles, hands in lap—the identical posture Melissa had adopted at my house yesterday.

"So," she said, smiling again. She leaned forward to adjust one of the teacups, spent more time at it than she had to.

I said, "Good to meet you, Mrs. Ramp."

A pained look fought with the smile and won. "Finally?"

Before I could answer, she said, "I'm not a terrible person, Dr. Delaware."

"Of course you aren't," I said. Too emphatically. It made her start and take a long look at me. Something about her— about this place—was screwing up my timing. I sat back and kept my mouth shut. She recrossed her legs and shifted her head, as if in response to stage direction. Showing me only her right profile. Stiff and defensively genteel, like a First Lady on a talk show.

I said, "I'm not here to judge you. This is about Melissa's going away to college. That's all."

She tightened her lips and shook her head. "You helped her so much. Despite me."

"No," I said. "Because of you."

She closed her eyes, sucked in her breath, and clawed her knees through the gray dress. "Don't worry, Dr. Delaware. I've come a long way. I can handle harsh truths."

"The truth, Mrs. Ramp, is that Melissa turned out to be the terrific young woman she is in good part because she got a lot of love and support at home."

She opened her eyes and shook her head very slowly. "You're kind, but the truth is that even though I knew I was failing her, I couldn't pull myself out of my . . . out of it. It sounds so weak-willed, but . . ."

"I know," I said. "Anxiety can be as crippling as polio."

"Anxiety," she said. "What a mild word. It's more like

dying. Over and over. Like living on Death Row, never knowing . . ." She swiveled, revealing a crescent of damaged flesh. "I felt trapped. Helpless and inadequate. So I continued to fail her."

I said nothing.

She went on: "Do you know that in thirteen years I never attended a single parent-teacher conference? Never applauded at her school plays or chaperoned field trips or met the mothers of the few children she played with. I *wasn't* a mother, Dr. Delaware. Not in any true sense of the word. She's got to resent me for it. Maybe even hate me."

"Has she given any indication of that?"

"No, of course not. Melissa's a good girl—*too* respectful to say what's on her mind. Even though I've tried to get her to."

She leaned forward again. "Dr. Delaware, she puts on a brave front—feels she always has to be grown up, a perfect little lady. *I* did that to her—my weakness did." Touching her bad side. "I turned her into a premature adult and robbed her of her childhood. So I know it's got to be there—anger. All bottled up inside."

I said, "I'm not going to sit here and tell you you gave her the ideal upbringing. Or that your fears didn't influence hers. They did. But throughout it all—from what I saw during her therapy—she perceived you as being nurturant and loving, giving her unconditional love. She still sees you that way."

She bowed her head, held it with both hands, as if praise hurt.

I said, "When she wet your sheets you held her and didn't get angry. That means a lot more to a child than parent-teacher conferences."

She looked up and stared at me. The facial sag more evident than before. Shifting her head, she switched to a profile view. Smiling.

"I can see where you'd be good for her," she said. "You

put forth your point of view with a . . . force that's hard to debate."

"Is there a need for us to debate?"

She bit her lip. One hand flew up and touched her bad side again. "No. Of course not. It's just that I've been working on . . . honesty. Seeing myself the way I truly am. It's part of *my* therapy. But you're right, *I'm* not our concern. Melissa is. What can I do to help her?"

"I'm sure you know how ambivalent she is about going away to college, Mrs. Ramp. Right now she's framing it in terms of her concern about you. Worry that leaving you at this point in your therapy might upset the progress you've made. So it's important for her to hear from you— explicitly—that you'll be okay. That you'll continue to make progress with her gone. That you *want* her to go. If you do."

"Dr. Delaware," she said, looking at me straight on, "of course I do. And I *have* told her that. I've been telling her since I found out she'd been accepted. I'm thrilled for her— it's a wonderful opportunity. She *must* go!"

Her intensity caught me by surprise.

"What I mean," she said, "is that I see this as a crucial period for Melissa. Breaking away. Starting a new life. Not that I won't miss her—of course I will. But I've finally gotten to a point where I can think of her the way I should have been doing all along. As the child. I've made *tremendous* progress, Dr. Delaware. I'm ready to take some really giant steps. Look at life differently. But I can't get Melissa to see that. I know she mouths the words, but she hasn't changed her behavior."

"How would you like her to change?"

"She overprotects me. Continues to hover. Ursula—Dr. Cunningham-Gabney—has tried to talk to her about it, but Melissa's unresponsive. The two of them seem to have a personality conflict. When *I* try to tell her how well I'm doing, she smiles, gives me a pat, and says 'Great, Mom,' and walks away. Not that I blame her. I let her be the parent for so long. Now I'm paying for it."

She lowered her gaze again, rested her brow in one hand, and sat that way for a long time. Then:

"I haven't had an attack in over four weeks, Dr. Delaware. I'm seeing the world for the first time in a very long time, and I feel I can cope with it. It's like being born again. I don't want Melissa limiting herself because of me. What can I say to convince her?"

"Sounds like you're saying the right things. She just may not be ready to hear them."

"I don't want to come out and tell her I don't need her—I could never hurt her that way. And it wouldn't be true. I *do* need her. The way any mother needs any daughter. I want us always to be close. And I'm not giving her mixed messages, Doctor—believe me. Dr. Cunningham-Gabney and I have worked on that. Projecting clear communication. Missy just refuses to hear it."

I said, "Part of the problem is that some of her conflict has nothing to do with you or your progress. Any eighteen-year-old would be anxious about leaving home for the first time. The life Melissa's led up till now—the relationship between the two of you, the size of this place, the isolation—makes moving out scarier for her than for the average freshman. By focusing on you, she doesn't have to deal with her own fears."

"This place," she said, holding out her hands. "It's a monstrosity, isn't it? Arthur collected things, built himself a museum."

A trace of bitterness. Then quick cover:

"Not that he did it out of ego—that wasn't Arthur. He was a lover of beauty. Believed in beautifying his world. And he did have exquisite taste. I have no feel for things. I can appreciate a fine painting when it's placed in front of me, but I'd never accumulate—it's just not in my nature."

"Would you ever consider moving?"

Faint smile. "I'm considering lots of things, Dr. Delaware. Once the door opens, it's hard not to step through. But we—Dr. Cunningham-Gabney and I—are working together to keep me in check, make sure I don't get ahead of myself. I've still got a long way to go. And even if I was ready to dump everything and roam the world, I wouldn't do that to Melissa—pull everything out from under her."

She touched the china pot. Smiled and said, "Cold. Are you sure you don't want me to call down for fresh? Or something to eat—have you had lunch?"

I said, "I'm sure, but thanks anyway."

"What you said before," she said. "Avoiding her own conflicts by mothering me. If that's the case, how can I pull *that* out from under her?"

"She'll come to grips with your improvement naturally—gradually—as you continue to make progress. And to be honest, you may not be able to persuade her to go to Harvard before the application deadline's up."

She frowned.

I said, "It seems to me there's something else complicating the situation—jealousy."

"Yes, I know," she said. "Ursula's pointed out how jealous she is."

"Melissa's got lots to be jealous of, Mrs. Ramp. She's been hit with a lot of change over a short period of time, besides your progress: Jacob Dutchy's death, your remarriage." The return of a madman . . . "What makes it even rougher for her is the fact that she takes credit—or blame—for initiating a good deal of the change. For getting you into treatment, introducing you to your husband."

"I know," she said. "And it's true. She did get me into therapy. Nagged me into it, God bless her. And therapy's helped me cut a window in my cell. Sometimes I feel like such a fool for not doing it sooner, all those years . . ." She shifted position suddenly, showing me her complete face. Flaunting it.

Saying nothing about her second marriage. I didn't pursue it.

She stood suddenly, made a fist, held it in front of her, and stared at it. "I've got to *convince* her, somehow." Tension blanched the scarred side, marbling it again, bleaching the stripes on her neck. "I'm her *mother,* for God's sake!"

Silence. The distant whir of a vacuum cleaner.

I said, "You sound pretty convincing right now. Why don't you call her in and tell her that."

She thought about that. Lowered the fist but kept it clenched.

"Yes," she said. "Okay. I will. Let's do it."

She excused herself, opened the door on the rear wall, and disappeared through the doorway. I heard padded footsteps, the sound of her voice, got up and looked.

She sat on the edge of a canopied bed, in an immense off-white bedroom with a muraled ceiling. Mural of courtesans at Versailles, enjoying life before the deluge.

She sat slightly stooped, bad side unprotected, pressing the mouthpiece of a white-and-gold phone to her lips. Her feet rested on plum-colored carpeting. The bed was covered with a quilted satin spread and the phone rested on a chinoiserie nightstand. High crank windows flanked the bed on both sides—clear glass under pleated, gold-fringed valances. Gilt-framed mirrors, lots of lace and toile and happily pigmented paintings. Enough French antiques to put Marie Antoinette at ease.

She nodded, said something, and put the phone back in its cradle. I returned to my seat. She came out a moment later, saying, "She's on her way up. Do you mind being here?"

"If Melissa doesn't mind."

Smile. "She won't. She's quite fond of you. Sees you as her ally."

I said, "I am her ally."

"Of course," she said. "We all need our allies, don't we."

A few minutes later footsteps sounded from the hall. Gina got up, met Melissa at the door, took her by the hand, and drew her in. Placing both hands on Melissa's shoulders, she looked down at her solemnly, as if preparing to confer a benediction.

"I'm your mother, Melissa Anne. I've made mistakes and been weak and inadequate as a mother, but that doesn't change the fact that I'm your mother and you're my child."

Melissa looked at her quizzically, then whipped her head in my direction.

I gave what I hoped was a reassuring smile and shifted my glance to her mother. Melissa followed it.

Gina said, "I know my weakness has put a burden on you, baby. But that's all going to change. Things are going to be different."

At the word *different*, Melissa stiffened.

Gina saw it and drew her close, hugging her. Melissa didn't fight it, but neither did she yield. "I want us always to be close, baby, but I also want us to live our own lives."

"We do, Mother."

"No, we don't, sweetheart. Not really. We love each other and care about each other—you're the best daughter a mother could ever hope for. But what we have is too . . . tangled. We have to untangle it. Get the knots out."

Melissa pulled away a bit and stared up at her. "What are you saying?"

"What I'm saying, baby, is that going away back east is a golden opportunity for you. Your apple. You earned it. I'm so proud of you—your whole future is waiting and you have the brains and the talent to make the best of it. So take advantage of the opportunity—I *insist* you take advantage."

Melissa wriggled free. "You insist?"

"No, I'm not trying to . . . What I mean, baby, is that—"

"What if I don't *want* to take advantage of it?" Melissa's tone was soft but combative. A prosecutor building the foundation for an assault.

Gina said, "I just think you should go, Melissa Anne." Some of the conviction had left her voice.

Melissa smiled. "That's fine, Mother, but what about what *I* think?"

Gina drew her close once more and pressed her to her breast. Melissa's face was impassive.

Gina said, "What you think is the most important, baby, but I want to make sure you *know* what you really think—that your decision isn't clouded by your worries about me. Because I'm fine, and I'm going to continue to be fine."

Melissa looked up at her again. Her smile had widened but turned cold. Gina looked away from it while holding tight.

I said, "Melissa, your mother has given a lot of thought to this. She's certain she can handle things."

"Is she?"

"Yes, I am," said Gina. Her voice had risen half an octave. "And I expect you to respect that opinion."

"I respect *all* of your opinions, Mother. But that doesn't mean I have to live my *life* around them."

Gina's mouth opened and closed.

Melissa took hold of her mother's arms and peeled them off her. Stepping back, she looped her fingers in the belt loops of her jeans.

Gina said, "Please, baby."

"I'm not a baby, Mother." Still smiling.

"No. No, you aren't. Of course you aren't. I apologize for calling you that—old habits are hard to break. That's what this is all about—changing. I'm *working* on changing—you know how hard I've been working, Melissa. That means a different life. For all of us. I want you to go to Boston."

Melissa looked at me, defiant.

I said, "Talk to your mother, Melissa."

Melissa's attention swung back to Gina, then to me once more. Her eyes narrowed. "What's going on here?"

Gina said, "Nothing, ba— Nothing. Dr. Delaware and I have had a very good talk. He's helped me clarify things even further. I can see why you like him."

"Can you?"

Gina started to reply, stammered, and stopped.

I said, "Melissa, this family's going through major changes. It's rough for everyone. Your mother's searching for the right way to let you know she's really okay. So that you don't feel obligated to take care of her."

"Yes," said Gina. "Exactly. I really am okay, honey. Go out and live your own life. Be your own *person*."

Melissa didn't move. Her smile had vanished. She was wringing her hands. "Sounds like the *grown-ups* have decided what's best for little me."

"Oh, honey," said Gina. "That's not it at all!"

I said, "No one's decided anything. What's important is that the two of you keep talking—keep the channels of communication open."

Gina said, "We sure will. We'll get through it, won't we, honey?"

She walked toward her daughter, arms out.

Melissa backed away, into the doorway, braced herself by grasping the doorframe.

"This is great," she said. "Just great."

Her eyes blazed. She pointed a finger at me. "This isn't what I expected from you."

"Honey!" said Gina.

I got up.

Melissa shook her head and held her hands out, palms-front.

I said, "Melissa—"

"*Forget* it. Just *forget* it!"

She shuddered with anger and ran out.

I stuck my head out the door, watched her race down the corridor, legs flying, hair flapping.

I considered going after her, then thought better of it and turned back to Gina, trying to conjure up something profound.

But she was in no shape to listen.

Her face had gone ghostly and she was clutching her chest. Mouth open, gasping for breath. Body starting to shake.

The shakes got violent. I rushed to her. She stumbled back, shaking her head, holding me off, her eyes wild.

Reaching into one of the pockets of her dress, she fumbled for what seemed like a very long time, finally pulled out a small L-shaped white plastic inhaler. Inserting the short end in her mouth, she closed her eyes and tried to fasten her lips around the apparatus. But her teeth chattered against the plastic and she had trouble gripping it in her mouth. Our eyes met but hers were glazed and I knew she was somewhere else. Finally she clamped her jaws around the mouthpiece and managed to inhale. Depressed a metal button at the tip of the inhaler's long end.

A faint hiss sounded. Her cheeks remained hollow. The bad side more hollow. She clutched the inhaler with one hand, grabbed a corner of the loveseat for balance with the other. Held her breath for several seconds before removing the device and collapsing on the couch.

Her chest heaved. I stood there and watched as the rhythm slowed, then sat next to her. She was still shaking; I could feel the vibrations through the sofa cushions. She mouth-breathed, worked at slowing down her respiration. Closed her eyes, then opened them. Saw me and closed them again. Her face was filmed with sweat. I touched her hand. She gave a weak squeeze in return. Her flesh was cold and moist.

We sat together, not moving, not talking. She tried to say something, but nothing came out. She rested her head against the back of the loveseat and stared at the ceiling. Tears filled her eyes.

"That was a small one," she said in a feeble voice. "I controlled it."

"Yes, you did."

The inhaler was still in her hand. She looked at it, then dropped it back in her pocket. Bending forward, she took my hand and squeezed it again. Exhaled. Inhaled. Let out breath in a long, cool, minty stream.

We were so close I could hear her heart beating. But I was focusing on other sounds—listening for footsteps. Thinking of Melissa returning, seeing us that way.

When her hand relaxed, I let it go. It took a couple more minutes for her breathing to return to normal.

I said, "Should I call someone?"

"No, no, I'm fine." She patted her pocket.

"What's in the inhaler?"

"Muscle relaxant. Ursula and Dr. Gabney did the research on it. It's very good. For short term."

Her face was soaked with sweat, the feathery bangs plastered to her brow. The bad side looked like inflatable plastic.

She said, "Whew."

I said, "Can I get you some water?"

"No, no, I'll be fine. Really. It looks worse than it is. This was a small one—the first time in . . . four weeks . . . I . . ."

"It was a tough confrontation."

She put her hand to her mouth. "Melissa!"

Shooting up, she ran out of the room.

I went after her, following her slender form down one of the dark spokes, to a rear spiral staircase. Sticking close so as not to get lost in the huge house.

11

The stairway bottomed at a short hallway just outside a pantry as big as my living room. We walked through it and into the kitchen, a banquet-sized galley painted custard-yellow and floored with white hexagonal ceramic tiles. There were two walls of coolers and freezers, oiled butcher-block counters, and lots of copper pots hanging from cast-iron ceiling racks.

No cooking smells. A bowl of fruit sat on one of the counters. The industrial eight-burner stove was bare.

Gina Ramp led me out, past a second, smaller kitchen, a silver room, and a paneled dining hall that could accommodate a convention. Looking from side to side, calling out Melissa's name.

Getting silence in return.

We backtracked, made a couple of turns, and ended in the room with the painted ceiling beams. Two men in tennis whites came through the French doors, holding rackets and wearing towels around their necks. Both were big and well built.

The younger man was in his twenties, with thick shaggy yellow hair worn past his shoulders. A long thin face was dominated by narrow dark eyes and a cleft chin deep enough to hide a diamond. His tan had taken more than one summer to build.

The second man—in his early fifties, I guessed—was thickset but not flabby, a lifelong athlete who'd stayed in condition. Heavy-jawed and blue-eyed. Executive-cut black hair with gray temples, clipped gray mustache precisely as wide as his mouth. Seamed, ruddy complexion. Marlboro Man goes Country Club.

He cocked an eyebrow and said, "Gina? What's up?" His voice was mellow and resonant, the kind that seems friendly even if it isn't.

"Have you seen Melissa, Don?"

"Sure, just a minute ago." Directing his gaze at me. "Something the mat—?"

"Do you know where she is, Don?"

"She left with Noel—"

"With *Noel?*"

"He was doing the cars, she came running out like a bat out of Hades, said something to him, and the two of them drove off. In the Corvette. Something wrong, Geen?"

"Oh, boy." Gina sagged.

The mustachioed man put his arm around her shoulder. Cast another searching look at me. "What's going on?"

Gina forced a smile and fluffed her hair. "It's nothing, Don. Just a— This is Dr. Delaware. The psychologist I told you about. He and I were trying to talk to Melissa about college and she got upset. I'm sure it'll blow over."

He held her arm, pursed his lips in a way that made his mustache peak in the middle, and arched his eyebrows again. Strong and silent. Another one to the camera born . . .

Gina said, "Doctor, this is my husband, Donald Ramp. Don, Dr. Alex Delaware."

"Pleased to meet you." Ramp extended a big hard hand and we shook briefly. The younger man had retreated to a corner of the room.

Ramp said, "They can't have gotten too far, Geen. If you'd like, I can go after them, see if I can haul 'em back."

Gina said, "No, it's okay, Don." She touched his cheek. "The price of living with a teenager, darling. Anyway, I'm sure she'll be back fairly soon—maybe they just went to get gas."

The younger man was examining a jade bowl with a fascination too intense to be genuine. Lifting it, putting it down, lifting it again.

Gina turned to him. "How are you today, Todd?"

The bowl descended and stayed put. "Great, Mrs. Ramp. And you?"

"Muddling along, Todd. How did Don do today?"

The blond man gave her a toothpaste-ad smile and said, "He's got the moves. All he needs is to work."

Ramp groaned and stretched. "These old bones rebel against work." Turning to me: "Doctor, this is Todd Nyquist. My trainer, tennis coach, and all-around Grand Inquisitor."

Nyquist grinned and touched one finger to his temple. "Doctor."

Ramp said, "Not only do I suffer, I pay for it."

Obligatory smiles all around.

Ramp looked at his wife. "You sure there's nothing I can do, honey?"

"No, Don. We'll just wait. They're bound to be back soon. Noel's not finished yet, is he?"

Ramp looked out the doors, toward the cobbled courtyard. "Doesn't look like it. The Isotta and the Delahaye are both due for a wax and all he's been doing so far is washing."

"Okay," said Gina. "So they probably did go for gas. They'll be back, and then Dr. Delaware and I will take up where we left off. You go shower off, mister. Don't worry about a thing."

Tight voice. All of them tight. Squeezing out chitchat like meat through a grinder.

Tight silence.

I felt as if I'd wandered into the middle of a collaboration between Noel Coward and Edward Albee.

Gina said, "Drink, anyone?"

Ramp touched his midriff. "Not for me. I'm going for that shower. Good to meet you, Doctor. Thanks for everything."

I said, "No problem," not sure what he was thanking me for.

He used one end of the towel to wipe his face, winked at no one in particular, and began walking off. Then he stopped, looked over his shoulder at Nyquist. "Hang in, Todd. See you Wednesday. If you promise to spare the thumbscrews."

"You bet, Mr. R.," said Nyquist, grinning again. To Gina: "I could handle a Pepsi, Mrs. R. Or anything else you got that's cold and sweet."

Ramp continued to look at him, hesitated as if contemplating return, then walked off.

Nyquist flexed his knees, stretched his neck, ran his fingers through his mane, and checked the netting on his racket.

Gina said, "I'll get Madeleine to fix you something."

Nyquist said, "Sure bet," but his grin died.

Leaving him standing there, she escorted me to the front of the house.

We sat in overstuffed chairs in one of the caverns, surrounded by works of genius and fancy. Any space not filled with art was paneled with mirror. All that reflection turned true perspective into a carny joke. Nearly engulfed by cushions, I felt diminished. Gulliver in Brobdingnag.

She shook her head and said, "What a disaster! How could I have handled it better?"

I said, "You did fine. It's going to take time for her to readjust."

"She doesn't *have* that much time. Harvard needs to be notified."

"Like I said, Mrs. Ramp, it may not be realistic to expect her to be ready by some arbitrary deadline."

She didn't respond to that.

I said, "Suppose she spends a year here—watching you get better. Getting comfortable with the changes. She can always transfer to Harvard during her sophomore year."

"I guess," she said. "But I really want her to go—not for *me*." Touching her bad side. "For her. She needs to get away. From this place. It's so— It's a world to itself. All her needs met, everything done for her. That can be crippling."

"Sounds like you're afraid that if she doesn't leave now she never will."

She sighed.

"Despite all this," she said, taking in the room, "all the beauty, it can be malignant. A house with no doors. Believe me, I know."

That startled me. I thought I'd concealed it, but she said, "What is it?"

"The phrase you just used—a house with no doors. When I treated her, Melissa used to draw houses without doors and windows."

"Oh," she said. "Oh, my." Touching the pocket that held the inhaler.

"Did you ever use the phrase in front of her?"

"I don't think I did—that would be terrible if I did, wouldn't it? Putting that image into her head."

"Not necessarily," I said. Hear ye, hear ye, the great yea-sayer cometh. "It gave her a concrete image to deal with. When she got better she started drawing houses with doors. I doubt this place will ever be for her what it was for you."

"How can you be sure of that?"

"I can't be sure of anything," I said gently. "I just don't think we need to assume that your prison is hers."

Despite the gentleness, it wounded her. "Yes, of course you're right. She's her own person—I shouldn't see her as my clone." Pause. "So you think it'll be okay for her to live here?"

"In the interim."

"How long of an interim?"

"Long enough for her to get comfortable about leaving. From what I saw nine years ago, she's pretty good at pacing herself."

She said nothing, gazed at a ten-foot grandfather clock veneered with tortoise shell.

I said, "Maybe they decided to go for a drive."

"Noel hasn't finished his work," she said. As if that settled it.

She got up, walked around the room slowly, staring at the floor. I began taking a closer look at the paintings. Flemish and Dutch and Renaissance Italian. Works I felt I should have been able to identify. But the pigments were brighter and fresher than any I'd seen in museum Old Masters; some of them bordered on lurid. I remembered what Jacob Dutchy had said about Arthur Dickinson's passion for restoration. Realized how much of a dead man's aura remained in the house.

House as monument.

Mausoleum sweet mausoleum.

From across the room, she said, "I feel terrible. I meant to thank you. Right off, as soon as we were introduced. For all you did years ago, as well as what you're doing now. But we got into things and I forgot. Please forgive me. And accept my disgracefully belated thanks."

I said, "Accepted."

She looked at the clock again. "I do hope they get back soon."

They didn't.

A half hour passed—thirty very long minutes filled with small talk and a crash course in Flemish art delivered with robotic enthusiasm by my hostess. Throughout it all I kept hearing Dutchy's voice. Wondered what the voice of the man who'd taught *him* sounded like.

When she ran out of things to say, she stood and said, "Maybe they did go out for a drive. There's no sense in your waiting around. I'm so sorry for wasting your time."

Pushing myself up from the quicksand cushions, I followed her on a furniture-strewn obstacle course that ended at the front doors.

She opened one of them and said, "When she does come home, should I get right into it with her?"

"No, I wouldn't push it. Let her behavior be your guide. When she's ready to talk, you'll know it. If you want me to be there next time you have a discussion, and that suits Melissa, I can be. But she may be angry at me. Feel I betrayed her."

"I'm sorry," she said. "I didn't want to spoil things between you."

"That can be fixed," I said. "What's important is what goes on between *you.*"

She nodded. Patted her pocket. Came closer and touched my face, the way she'd touched her husband's. Gave me a close-up look at her scars—a white brocade—and kissed my cheek.

Back on the freeway. Back on planet Earth.

Sitting in the jam at the downtown interchange, I listened to the Gipsy Kings and tried not to think about whether I'd screwed up. Thought about it anyway and decided I'd done the best I could.

When I got home I phoned Milo. He picked up and growled, "Yeah?"

"Gee, what a friendly greeting."

"Keeps away scumbags trying to peddle bullshit and geeks taking surveys. What's up?"

"Ready to get to work on the ex-con thing?"

"Yeah. I've been thinking about it, figure fifty an hour plus expenses is reasonable. That going to sit okay with the clients?"

"I didn't have a chance to get into the financial details yet. But I wouldn't worry—there's no shortage of funds. And the client says she has full access to plenty."

"Why wouldn't she?"

"She's only eighteen and—"

"You want me to work for the kid herself, Alex? Jesus, how many cookie jars we talking about?"

"This is no ditsy teenager, Milo. She's had to grow up fast—too fast. And she has her own money, assured me payment would be no problem. I just need to make sure she realizes exactly what it entails. Thought I'd get to it today, but something else came up."

"The kid herself," he said. "Do I look like Mister Rogers or something?"

"Well," I said, "I know you like me just the way I am."

He said, "Jesus," again. Then: "Tell me more about this. Who, exactly, got damaged and what kind of damage."

I started describing the acid attack on Gina Ramp.

He said, "Whoa. Sounds like the McCloskey case."

"You *know* it?"

"I know *of* it. It was a few years before my time, but it was a teaching case at the academy. Interrogation procedures."

"Any particular reason?"

"The weirdness of it. And the guy who taught the course—Eli Savage—was one of the original interrogators."

"Weird in what way?"

"In terms of motive. Cops are like anyone else—they like to classify, reduce things to basics. Money, jealousy, revenge, passion, or some sort of sexual kink sums up ninety-nine percent of your violent-crime motives. This one just didn't fit any of those. The way I remember learning it, McCloskey and the victim had once had a thing going, but it ended friendly, half a year before he had her burned. No pining away on his part, no poison pen or love letters or anonymous phone calls or any of the harassment you typically see in an unrequited passion situation. And she wasn't going out with any other guys, so jealousy seemed out of the question. *Money* wasn't a strong bet because he had no insurance out on her, no one discovered any way he'd made a dime off the attack, and he actually paid out plenty to the yog who did the dirty work. In terms of revenge, there was some speculation that he blamed her for his business going bad—he had a modeling agency, I think."

"I'm impressed."

"Don't be. You don't forget a case like that—I remember they showed us photos of her face. Before and after and during—she had tons of surgery. It was a real mess. I kept wondering what kind of person could do that to someone else. Now, of course, I know better, but those were the days of sweet innocence. Anyway, in terms of the money motive, it turns out losing the agency had nothing to do with her either. McCloskey was on the skids due to his drinking and some very heavy doping, and he himself went out of his way to make that clear during his interrogation. Kept telling the detectives he'd fucked up his life, begged to be put out of his misery. Wanting everyone to know that his putting the contract out on her had nothing to do with business."

"What *did* it have to do with?"

"That's the big question mark. He refused to say, no matter how hard they pressed him. Turned deaf and mute any time the issue of motive came up. Leaving only the psychopath angle, but no one uncovered any history of violence—he was a punk and an asshole, liked to hang around gangsters, do the Vegas bit. But that was more of a pose—everyone who knew him said he was a weenie."

"Weenies can snap."

"Or get elected to office. So, sure, maybe he *was* faking it. Maybe he was a goddam sadist and hid it so well, no one ever figured it out. That was Savage's hunch—something psychological, maybe kinky. The case stuck in his craw. He prided himself on being a top-notch questioner. He ended the lecture with this speech about how McCloskey's motive didn't really matter; what counted was the asshole was behind bars for a long time, and *that* was our job: put 'em away, let the shrinks figure 'em out."

I said, "A long time's up."

"How long did he stay in?"

"Thirteen years on a twenty-three-year sentence—time off for good behavior. Then they gave him parole for six."

"Usually parole's limited to three—probably made some kind of a deal." He grimaced. "Par for the course. Burn someone's face, rape a baby, whatever, attend remedial reading class and don't get caught shanking anyone and you walk in half the time." He paused, said, "Thirteen, huh? That would be some time ago. And you're saying he just got back to town?"

I nodded. "He spent most of his parole in New Mexico and Arizona. Working on an Indian reservation."

"The old do-gooder scam."

"Six years is a long time to scam."

"But who knows if he behaved himself for six years— who knows how many dead Indians paid for it. Even if he did, six isn't that long if the alternative is shoveling shit in some landfill or doing more time. Did he also pull a Chuckie Colson and find Jesus?"

"I don't know."

"What else *do* you know about him?"

"Just that he's off parole, free and clear, and that his last parole officer's named Bayliss and he's ready to retire or already has."

"Sounds like your eighteen-year-old's a pretty good sleuth herself."

"She learned all of this from one of the servants—a guy named Dutchy, kind of a super-butler. He kept tabs on McCloskey from the time he was convicted. Very protective of the whole family. But he's dead now."

"Ah," he said. "Leaving the helpless rich to protect themselves. Has McCloskey tried to get in touch with the family?"

"No. As far as I know, the victim and her husband aren't even aware he's back in town. Melissa—the girl—knows and it's hanging over her head."

"For good reason," he said.

"So you do think McCloskey's dangerous."

"Who knows? On the one hand you've got the fact that he's been out of jail for six years and hasn't made any moves. On the other, you've got the fact that he left the Indians and came back here. Maybe there's a good reason that has nothing to do with nastiness. Maybe not. Bottom line is it would be a smart idea to find out. Or at least try."

"Ergo . . ."

"Yeah, ergo. Time to sharpen up the old private eye. Okay, if she wants me to, I'll do it."

"Thanks, Milo."

"Yeah, yeah. The thing is, Alex, even if he does have a solid reason for being back, I'd still be concerned."

"Why's that?"

"What I told you before—the motive thing. The fact that no one knows why the hell he did it. No one ever got a *fix* on him. Maybe thirteen years opened him up and he blabbed to a cellmate. Or talked to some jail shrink. But if he didn't, that means he's a secretive fucker. *Mucho patient*. And that pushes my buttons. Fact is, if I was less of a macho, invincible guy, that would goddam well scare me."

12

After he hung up I thought of calling San Labrador, but decided to let Melissa and Gina try to work things out.

I went down to the pond, tossed pellets to the koi, and sat facing the waterfall. The fish were more active than usual but seemed uninterested in food. They were chasing one another, in tight formations of three or four. Racing and splashing and bumping against the rock rims.

Puzzled, I bent down and got close to the water. The fish ignored me, continued circling.

Then I saw it. Males chasing females.

Spawn. Shiny clusters clinging to the irises that sprouted in the corners of the pond. Pale caviar, fragile as soap bubbles, glistening under the setting sun.

First time in all the years I'd had the pond. Maybe it meant something.

I crouched and watched for a while, wondering if the fish would eat the eggs before they hatched. If any of the young would survive.

I felt a sudden urge to rescue but knew it was out of my hands. Nowhere to put the spawn—professional breeders kept multiple ponds. Removing the eggs and putting them in buckets would kill all chances of survival.

Nothing to do but wait.

Nothing like impotence to round off a charming day.

I went back up to the house and made dinner: a grilled minute steak, salad, and a beer. Ate it in bed, listening to Perlman and Zukerman do Mozart on CD, most of me getting lost in the music, a small segment of consciousness standing guard, waiting for a call from San Labrador.

The concert ended. No call. Another disc cued itself. The miracle of technology. The CD player was state-of-the-art. A gift from a man who preferred machines to people.

Another dynamic duo took center stage: Stan Getz and Charlie Byrd.

Brazilian rhythms didn't do the trick either. The phone remained mute.

More of me slipped away from the music. I thought of Joel McCloskey, apparently remorseful but keeping his motive hidden. Thought of how he'd shattered Gina Paddock's life. Scars, visible and otherwise. The hooks that people embedded in one another while trolling for love. The agony when the barbs had to come out.

Impulsively, without thinking it through, I phoned San Antonio.

A stuffed-sinus female twang said, "Yay-lo." I heard TV noise in the background. Comedy from the sound of it: flat laughter that rose, peaked, and ebbed in an electronic tide.

The stepmother.

I said, "Hello, Mrs. Overstreet. This is Alex Delaware, calling from Los Angeles."

A moment of silence. "Uh—hi, Doc. How're yew?"

"Fine. And you?"

Sigh almost long enough for me to recite the alphabet. "Good as can be."

"How's Mr. Overstreet?"

"Well . . . we're all praying and hoping for the best, Doc. How's things in L.A.? Haven't been there in years. I bet everything's bigger and faster and noisier and whatever—that's the way life always seems to go, doesn't it? You should see Dallas and Houston, and down here, too, though not as much down here—we got a ways to go before our troubles get really big."

Word assault. Feeling as if I'd been hit hard in the end zone, I said, "Life goes on."

"If you're lucky, it does." Sigh. "But anyway, enough philosophizing—that isn't gonna help anyone or anything. I expect yew'll be wanting to talk to Linda."

"If she's available."

"That's all she is, sir. Available. Poor thang never leaves the house, though I keep telling her it's not natural for a girl her age to be just sittin' around, playing nursie, getting all gloomy with no letup. Not that I'm suggesting, mind you, that she go out and live the high life every night, what with her daddy being the way he is, no telling what could happen at any minute. So she daren't do anything she might feel regretful for later, mind you. But all this sitting can't bring good to anyone. To herself, especially. If you catch what I mean."

"Uh-huh."

"Gotta figure it this way: tapioca pudding that doesn't get eaten develops a skin and turns hard and crusty around the edges and soon it's no good for anyone. Same for a woman. That's as true as the Pledge of Allegiance, believe me."

"Uh-huh."

"Anyway . . . I'll go get her, tell her you're calling long distance."

Clunk.

Shouts over the network babble:

"*Leen*-da! Leen-da, it's for *yew*! . . . *Lin*da, the *pho-one*! It's *him*, Linda—*yew* know. C'mon, hurry, girl, it's long *distance*!"

Footsteps, then a harried voice: "Let me take this in another room."

A few moments later: "Okay—one second—I've got it. Hang up, Dolores!"

Hesitation. Click. Demise of the laugh-track.

Sigh.

"Hi, Alex."

"Hi."

"That *woman*. How long did she chew your ear off?"

"Let's see," I said. "Part of one lobe's gone."

She laughed without heart. "It's amazing I've got any of mine left. Amazing Daddy hasn't' . . . So . . . how are you?"

"Fine. How is he?"

"Up and down. One day he looks fine; the next he can't get out of bed. The surgeon says he definitely needs the operation but is too weak to go through it right now—too congestive, and they're still not sure how many arteries are involved. They're trying to stabilize him with rest and medicine, get him strong enough for more tests. I don't know . . . What can you do? That's the way things go. So . . . how are you? I already asked you that, didn't I?"

"Keeping busy."

"That's good, Alex."

"The koi spawned."

"Pardon?"

"The koi—the fish in the pond—are laying eggs. First time they've ever done it."

"How nice," she said. "So now you'll be a daddy."

"Yup."

"Ready for the responsibility?"

"I don't know," I said. "We're talking multiple births." If any.

She said, "Well, look at it this way. At least there'll be no diapers to deal with."

Both of us laughed, said "So . . ." at the same time, and laughed again. Synchrony. But stilted. Like bad summer-stock theater.

She said, "Been down to the school?"

"Last week. Everything seems to be going well."

"Real well, from what I hear. I spoke to Ben a couple of days ago. He's turned out to be a bang-up principal."

"He's a nice guy," I said. "Organized, too. You made a good recommendation."

"Yeah, he is. Very organized." She gave another heartless chuckle. "Wonder if I'll have a job when I get back."

"I'm sure you will. Made any plans, yet—in terms of getting back?"

"No," she said sharply. "How in the world can I?"

I was silent.

She said, "I didn't mean to snap, Alex. It's just been hell . . . waiting. Sometimes I think waiting's the hardest thing in the world. Even worse than . . . Anyway, no sense obsessing on it. It's all part of growing up and being a big girl and facing reality, isn't it?"

"I'd say you've had more than your share of reality lately."

"Yeah," she said. "Good for toughening up the old hide."

"I kind of like your hide the way it is."

Pause. "Alex, thanks for coming out last month. The three days you spent out here were the best days I've had."

"Want me to come out again?"

"I wish I could say yes, but I'd be no good to you."

"You don't have to be good."

"That's sweet of you to say but . . . no—it just wouldn't work out. I need to . . . be with him. Make sure he gets good care."

"I take it Dolores hasn't become much of a nurse?"

"You take it correctly. She's the original Helpless Hannah—a broken nail's a major tragedy. Till now she's been one of those lucky idiots, never had to deal with anything like this. But the sicker he gets, the more *she* falls apart. And when she falls apart, she talks. Lord, how she talks. I don't know how Daddy tolerates it. Thank God I'm here to shelter him. It's as if she's bad weather—a word-storm."

I said, "I know. I got caught in the downpour."

"Poor you."

"I'll survive."

Silence. I tried to conjure her face—blond hair against my chest. The feel of our bodies . . . The images wouldn't come.

"Anyway," she said, sounding very tired.

"Is there anything I can do for you long distance?"

"Thanks, but I can't think of anything, Alex. Just think good thoughts about me. And take care of yourself."

"You, too, Linda."

"I'll be fine."

"I know you will."

She said, "I think I hear him coughing. . . . Yeah, I sure do. Got to be going."

"Bye."

"Bye."

I changed into shorts, a T-shirt, and sneakers, and tried to run off the phone call and the twelve hours that had preceded it. Got home just as the sun was setting, showered, and put on my ratty yellow bathrobe and rubber thongs. After dark I went back down to the garden and ran a flashlight over the surface of the water. The fish were inert; even the light didn't arouse them.

Postcoital bliss? Some of the egg clusters seemed to have dissipated, but several remained, adhering to the pond walls.

After I'd been down there for a quarter of an hour, I heard the phone. News from San Labrador, finally. Hopefully, mother and daughter had started to talk.

I vaulted up the stairs to the landing and made it into the house in time to catch it on the fifth ring.

"Hello."

"Alex?" Familiar voice. Familiar, though I hadn't heard it in a long time. This time the images tumbled out like vending-machine candy.

"Hello, Robin."

"You sound out of breath. Everything okay?"

"Fine. Just made a mad dash up from the garden."

"Hope I'm not interrupting anything."

"No, no. What's up?"

"Nothing much. Just wanted to say hi."

I thought her voice lacked buoyancy, but it had been a while since I'd been an expert on anything to do with her. "Hi. How've you been doing?"

"Just great. Working on an arch-top for Joni Mitchell. She's going to use it on her next album."

"Terrific."

"Lots of hand-carving. I'm enjoying the challenge. What've you been up to?"

"Working."

"That's good, Alex."

Same thing Linda had said. Identical inflections. The Protestant ethic, or something about me?

I said, "How's Dennis?"

"Gone. Flew the coop."

"Oh."

"It's okay, Alex. It was long-brewing——no great shakes."

"Okay."

"I'm not trying to be a tough broad, Alex, say it didn't affect me at all. It did. In the beginning. Even though it was mutual, there's always that . . . empty space. But I'm over it. It wasn't like— What he and I had was— I mean, it had its merits as well as its problems. But it was different . . . from you and me."

"It would have to be."

"Yes," she said. "I don't know if there'll ever be anything like what we had. That's not a manipulation, just the way I feel."

My eyelids began to ache.

I said, "I know."

"Alex," she said in a pinched voice, "don't feel pressured to respond—in any way. God, that sounds so ridiculous. I'm so afraid of going out on a limb here . . ."

"What is it?"

"I'm feeling really lousy tonight, Alex. I could really use a friend."

I heard myself saying, "I'm your friend. What's the problem?"

So much for steely resolve.

"Alex," she said timidly. "Could it be face-to-face, not just over the phone?"

"Sure."

She said, "My place or yours?" then laughed too loudly.

I said, "I'll come to you."

I drove to Venice as if in a dream. Parked in back of the storefront on Pacific, impervious to the graffiti and the trash smells, the shadows and sounds that filled the alley.

By the time I reached the front door she had it open. Dim lights touched upon the hulls of heavy machinery. Wood-sweetness and lacquer-bite floated forth from the workshop, mixing with her perfume—one I'd never smelled before. It made me feel jealous and antsy and thrilled.

She had on a gray-and-black floor-length kimono, the bottom hems flecked with sawdust. Curves through silk. Slender wrists. Bare feet.

Her auburn curls were lustrous and loose, tumbling around her shoulders. Fresh makeup, age lines I'd never seen. The heart-shaped face I'd woken up to so many mornings. Still beautiful—as familiar as morning. But some region of it new, uncharted. Journeys she'd taken alone. It made me sad.

Her dark eyes burned with shame and longing. She forced herself to look into mine.

Her lip trembled and she shrugged.

I took her in my arms, felt her wrap around me and adhere, a second skin. Found her mouth and her heat, lifted her in my arms, and carried her up to the loft.

The first thing I felt the next morning was confusion—a desolate bafflement, throbbing like a hangover, though we hadn't drunk. The first thing I heard was a slow rhythmic rasp—a leisurely samba-beat from down below.

Empty bed beside me. Some things never change.

Sitting up, I looked over the loft rail and saw her working. Hand-sanding the rosewood back of a guitar clamped to a padded vise. Hunched at her bench, wearing denim overalls, safety goggles, and a surgical mask, her hair tied up in a curly knot, bittersweet-chocolate curls of wood collecting at her feet.

I watched her for a while, then got dressed and went downstairs. She didn't hear me, kept working, and I had to step directly in front of her to catch her attention. Even then there was a delay before our eyes met; her focus, narrowed and intense, was aimed on the richly patterned wood.

Finally she stopped, placing the file on the bench top and pulling down the mask. The goggles were filmed with pinkish dust, making her eyes look bloodshot.

"This is it—the one for Joni," she said, cranking open the vise, lifting the instrument, and rotating it to give me a frontal view. "Your basic carved belly, but instead of maple she wants rosewood for the back and sides with only a minimal arch—should be interesting to hear it."

I said, "Good morning."

"Good morning." She put the guitar back in the vise, kept her glance lowered even after the instrument was secured. Her fingers grazed the file. "Sleep well?"

"Great. How about you?"

"Great, too."

"Feel like breakfast?"

"Not really," she said. "There's plenty in the fridge—*mi fridge es su fridge*. Feel free."

I said, "I'm not hungry either."

Her fingernails drummed the file. "Sorry."

"For what?"

"Not wanting breakfast."

"Major felony," I said. "You're busted."

She smiled, looked down at the bench again, then back

at me. "You know how it is—the momentum. I woke up early—five-fifteen. Because I really *didn't* sleep well. Not because of— I was just restless, thinking about this." Caressing the guitar's convex back and tapping it. "Still trying to figure out exactly how I was going to get into the grain. This is Brazilian, quarter sawn—can you imagine how much I paid for a piece this thick? And how long I had to look to find one this wide? She wants a one-piece back, so I can't afford to mess it up. Knowing that jams me up—it's been slow going. But this morning I got into it pretty easily. So I kept going—I guess it just swept me along. What time is it?"

"Seven-ten."

"You're kidding," she said, flexing her fingers. "Can't believe I've been working for almost two hours." Flexing again.

I said, "Sore?"

"No, I feel great. Been doing these hand exercises to ward off the cramps and it's really working."

She touched the file again.

I said, "You're on a roll, kiddo. Don't stop now."

I kissed the top of her head. She took hold of my wrist with one hand, used the other to push the goggles up on her brow. Her eyes really were bloodshot. Poor goggle fit or tears?

"Alex, I—"

I placed a finger over her lips and kissed her left cheek. Remnants of the perfume, now familiar, tickled my nose. Mixed with wood dust and sweat—a cocktail that brought back too many memories.

I freed my wrist. She grabbed it, pressed it to her cheek. Our pulses merged.

"Alex," she said, looking up at me, blinking hard. "I didn't set it up to happen this way—please believe me. What I said about friendship was true."

"There's nothing to apologize for."

"Somehow I feel there is."

I said nothing.

"Alex, what's going to happen?"

"I don't know."

She lowered my hand, pulled away, and faced the work-bench.

"What about her?" she said. "The teacher."

The teacher. I'd told her Linda was a school principal. Demotion in service of the ego.

I said, "She's in Texas. Indefinitely—sick father."

"Oh. Sorry to hear that. Anything serious?"

"Heart problems. He's not doing too well."

She turned, faced me, blinked hard again. Memories of her own father's sludged arteries? Or maybe it was the dust.

"Alex," she said, "I don't want to— I know I have no *right* to ask this, but what's your . . . understanding with her?"

I moved to the foot of the bench, leaned on it with both hands, and stared up at the corrugations on the steel ceiling.

"There is no understanding," I said. "We're friends."

"Would this hurt her?"

"I don't imagine it would make her whoop for joy, but I'm not planning on submitting a written report."

The anger in my voice was strong enough to make her clutch the bench top.

I said, "Listen, I'm sorry. This is just a lot to deal with and I'm feeling . . . jammed up, myself. Not because of her—maybe that's part of it. But most of it is us. Being together, all of a sudden. The way it was last night . . . Shit, how long's it been? Two years?"

"Twenty-five months," she said. "But who's counting." She put her head on my chest, touched my ear, touched my neck.

"It could have been twenty-five hours," I said. "Or twenty-five years."

She inhaled deeply. "We *fit,*" she said. "I forgot how well."

She came to me, reached up and held my shoulders.

"Alex, what we had—it's like a tattoo. You've got to cut deeply to remove it."

"I was thinking in terms of fishhooks. Yanking them out."

She flinched and touched her arm.

I said, "Choose your analogy. Either way it's major pain."

We stared at each other, tried to temper the silence with smiles, and failed.

She said, "There could be something again, Alex—why shouldn't there be?"

Answers flooded my head, a babel of replies, contradictory jabber. Before I could pick a reason, she said, "Let's at least *think* about it. What can we lose by *thinking* about it?"

I said, "Even if I wanted to, I couldn't not think about it. You own too much of me."

Her eyes got wet. "I'll take what I can get."

I said, "Happy carving," and turned to leave.

She called out my name.

I stopped and looked back. She had her hands on her hips and her face was contorted in that little-girl scrunch that women never seem to outgrow. Prelude to tears—probably carried on the X chromosome. Before the valves opened full-force she yanked down her goggles, picked up her file, turned her back on me, and began to scrape.

I left hearing the same rasp-rasp samba that had greeted me upon waking. Felt no desire to dance.

Knowing I had to fill the day with something impersonal or go mad, I drove to the University Biomedical Library to seek out references for my monograph. I found plenty of stuff that looked promising on the computer screen, but little that turned out to be relevant. By the time noon rolled around I'd generated lots of heat, very little light, and knew it was time to buckle down and wrestle with my own data.

Instead I used a pay phone just outside the library to call in for messages. Nothing from San Labrador, six others, no emergencies. I returned all of them. Then I drove into

Westwood Village, paid too much for parking, found a coffee shop masquerading as a restaurant, and read the paper while chewing my way through a rubbery hamburger.

By the time I got home I'd managed to push the day along to 3:00 P.M. I checked the pond. A bit more spawn, but the fish still looked subdued. I wondered if they were all right—I'd read somewhere that they could damage themselves in the throes of passion.

The uniforms changed, but the game never did.

I fed them, picked dead leaves out of the garden. Three-twenty. Light housekeeping took up another half hour.

Bereft of excuses, I went into the library, pulled out my manuscript, and began working. It went well. When I finally looked up, I'd been going for almost two hours.

I thought of Robin. *You know how it is—the momentum.* The fit . . .

The impetus of loneliness, propelling us toward each other.

Fishhooks.

Back to work.

The drudgery defense.

I picked up my pen and tried. Kept at it until the words ran out and my chest got tight. It was seven by the time I got up from the desk, and when the phone rang I was grateful.

"Dr. Delaware, this is Joan at your service. I've got a call from a Melissa Dickinson. She says it's an emergency."

"Put her on, please."

Click.

"Dr. Delaware!"

"What is it, Melissa?"

"It's Mother!"

"What about her?"

"She's *gone*! Oh *God*, please *help* me. I don't *knowwhatodo*!"

"Okay, Melissa. Slow down and tell me exactly what happened."

"She's *gone*! She's gone! I can't find her *anywhere*—not on the *grounds* or in any of the *rooms. I* was *looking*—we all were *looking*—and she's not here! Please, Dr. Delaware—"

"How long's she been gone, Melissa?"

"Since two-thirty! She left for the clinic for her three o'clock group, was supposed to be back by five-thirty, and it's . . . seven-oh-four and *they* don't know where she is either. Oh, God!"

"Who's they?"

"The clinic. The Gabneys. That's where she went—she had a group meeting . . . from three to . . . five. Usually she goes with Don . . . or someone else. Once I took her, but this time . . ." Panting. Gulping for air.

I said, "If you feel you're losing your breath, find a paper bag and breathe into it slowly."

"No . . . no, I'm okay. Got to tell you . . . everything."

"I'm listening."

"Yes, yes. Where was I? Oh, God . . ."

"Usually she goes with someone but this ti—"

"She was supposed to go with him—Don—but she decided to go *herself*! In*si*sted on it! I told her— I didn't think that was— But she was *stubborn*—insisted she could handle it, but she *couldn't*! I *knew* she couldn't and I was right—she *couldn't*! But I don't want to be right, Dr. Delaware. I don't care about being right or having my way or anything! Oh, God, I just want her *back,* want her to be *okay*!"

"She didn't show up at the clinic at all?"

"No! And they didn't call till four to let us know. They should have called right away, shouldn't they?"

"How long a ride is it to the clinic?"

"Twenty minutes. At the *most*. She gave herself a half hour, which was more than enough. They should have known when she didn't— If they'd called right away, we could have looked for her right away. She's been gone for over four *hours*. Oh, God!"

"Is it possible," I said, "that she changed her mind and went somewhere else instead of the clinic?"

"*Where!* Where would she *go*!"

"I don't know, Melissa, but after talking to your mother, I can understand her wanting to . . . improvise. Break free of her routine. It's not that uncommon in patients who conquer their fears —sometimes they get a little reckless."

"No!" she said. "She wouldn't do that, not without *calling*. She knows how much it would worry me. Even Don's concerned, and *nothing* gets to him. He called the police and they went out looking for her but they haven't found her or the Dawn—"

"She was driving her Rolls-Royce?"

"Yes—"

"Then she shouldn't be too hard to spot, even in San Labrador."

"Then why hasn't anyone seen it? How could nobody have *seen* her, Dr. Delaware!"

I thought of the empty streets and had a ready answer for that.

"I'm sure someone did," I said. "Maybe she ran into mechanical problems—it's an old car. Even Rolls aren't perfect."

"No way. Noel keeps all the cars in top shape, and the Dawn was like new. And if she did run into problems, she'd *call*! She wouldn't *do* this to me. She's like an infant, Dr. Delaware—she can't survive out there, doesn't have any idea of what it's *like* out there. Oh, God, what if she had an *attack* and drove off a *cliff* or something and is lying there, helpless . . . I can't *take* this anymore. This is just *too* much, too *much*!"

Sobs poured out of the receiver, so loud I pulled my ear away involuntarily.

I heard a catch of breath. "Melissa—"

"I'm . . . freaking out . . . can't . . . breathe . . ."

"Relax," I commanded. "You *can* breathe. You can breathe just fine. *Do* it. Breathe regularly and slowly."

Strangulated gasp from the other end.

"*Breathe*, Melissa. Do it. In . . . and out. In . . . and out.

Feel your muscles loosen and expand with every breath you take. Feel yourself relax, just relax. Re*lax*."

"I . . ."

"Relax, Melissa. Don't try to talk. Just breathe and relax. Deeper and deeper—in . . . and out. In . . . and out. Your whole body's getting heavier, deeper and deeper relaxed. Think of pleasant things—your mother walking through the door. She's okay. She's going to be okay."

"But—"

"Just listen to me, Melissa. Do what I say. Freaking out can't help her. Getting upset can't help her. Worrying can't help her. You need to be at your best, so keep breathing and relaxing. Are you sitting down?"

"No, I uh—"

"Find a chair and sit down."

Rustle and bump. "Okay . . . I'm sitting."

"Good. Now find a comfortable position. Stretch your feet out and relax. Breathe slowly and deeply. Every breath you take will make you deeper and deeper relaxed."

Silence.

"Melissa?"

"Okay . . . I'm okay." Whoosh of breath.

"Good. Would you like me to come out there?"

A whispered *yes*.

"Then you'll have to hold on long enough for me to get out there. It will take at least half an hour."

"Okay."

"You're sure? I can stay on the phone until you're settled."

"No . . . Yes. I'm okay. Please come. Please."

"Hang in there," I said. "I'm out the door."

13

Empty streets made lonelier by the darkness. As I drove up Sussex Knoll, a pair of headlights appeared in my rearview mirror and remained there, constant as the moon. When I turned off at the pine gates of Number 10, a blinking red light appeared over the two white ones.

I stopped, switched off the engine, and waited. An amplified voice said, "Out of the car, sir."

I complied. A San Labrador police cruiser was nudging my rear bumper, its brights on, its engine running. I could smell the gasoline, feel the heat from its radiator. The red blinker colored my white shirt pink, erased it, colored again.

The driver's door opened and an officer got out, one hand on his hip. Big and wide. He lifted something. A flashlight beam blinded me and I raised an arm reflexively.

"Both hands up in the air where I can see them, sir."

More compliance. The light traveled up and down my body.

Squinting, I said, "I'm Dr. Alex Delaware—Melissa Dickinson's doctor. I'm expected."

The cop stepped closer, caught some of the light from the halogen fixture over the left gatepost, and turned into a young white man with a heavy, prognathous jaw, baby skin, and pug features. His hat was pulled low over his forehead. On a sitcom he'd be called Moose.

"Who's expecting you, sir?" The beam lowered, illuminating my trousers.

"The family."

"What family?"

"Dickinson—Ramp. Melissa Dickinson called me about her mother and asked me to come over. Has Mrs. Ramp shown up yet?"

"What'd you say your name was, sir?"

"Delaware. Alex Delaware." With a tilt of my head I indicated the talk box. "Why don't you call over to the house and verify that?"

He digested that as if it were profound.

I said, "Can I put my hands down?"

"Move to the rear of your car, sir. Put your hands on the trunk." Keeping his eyes on me, he advanced to the box. Push of a button and Don Ramp's voice said, "Yes?"

"This is Officer Skopek, San Labrador police, sir. I'm down by your front gate, got a gentleman here who claims to be a friend of the family."

"Who's that?"

"Mr. Delaware."

"Oh. Yes. It's okay, officer."

Another voice came out of the box, loud and dictatorial: "Anything yet, Skopek?"

"No, sir."

"Keep looking."

"Yes, sir." Skopek touched his hat and turned off his flashlight.

The pine gates began sliding inward. I opened the door of the Seville.

Skopek followed me and waited until I'd turned the ignition on. When I put the Seville in gear, he stuck his face in the driver's window and said, "Sorry for the inconvenience, sir." Not sounding sorry at all.

"Just following orders, huh?"

"Yes, sir."

Spotlights and low-voltage accent beams set among the trees created a nightscape Walt Disney would have cherished. A full-size Buick sedan was parked in front of the mansion. Rear searchlight and lots of antennas.

Ramp answered the door wearing a blue blazer, gray flannels, blue-striped button-down shirt with a perfect collar roll, and wine-colored pocket square. Despite the fashion statement, he looked drawn. And angry.

"Doctor." No handshake. He walked ahead of me, fast, leaving me to close the door.

I stepped into the entry. Another man stood in front of the green staircase, examining a cuticle. As I got closer, he looked up. Looked me over.

Early sixties, just under six feet and hefty, with a big, hard paunch, thin, gray, Brylcreemed hair, meaty features filling a broad face the color of raw sweetbreads. Steel-rimmed glasses over a fleshy nose, bladder jowls compressing a small, fussy mouth. He had on a gray suit, cream shirt, gray-and-black striped tie. Masonic stickpin. American flag lapel pin. VFW lapel pin. Beeper on his belt. Size thirteen wingtips on his feet.

He kept scrutinizing.

Ramp said, "Doctor, this is our police chief, Clifton Chickering. Chief, Dr. Delaware, Melissa's psychiatrist."

Chickering's first look told me I'd been the topic of discussion. The second one let me know what he thought of psychiatrists. I figured telling him I was a psychologist wouldn't alter that much, but I did it anyway.

He said, "Doctor." He and Ramp looked at each other. He nodded at Ramp. Ramp glared at me.

"Why the devil," he said, "didn't you tell us that bastard was back in town?"

"McCloskey?"

"Do you know of some other bastard who'd want to harm my wife?"

"Melissa told me about him in confidence. I had to respect her wishes."

"Oh, Christ!" Ramp turned his back on me and began pacing the entry hall.

Chickering said, "Any particular reason for the girl to keep it confidential?"

"Why don't you ask her?"

"I did. She says she didn't want to alarm her mother."

"Then you've got your answer."

Chickering said, "Uh-huh," and shot me the kind of look vice-principals reserve for teenage psychopaths.

"She could have told *me*," said Ramp, stopping his pacing. "If I'd known, I'd have looked out for her, for God's sake."

I said, "Is there evidence McCloskey was involved in the disappearance?"

"Christ," said Ramp. "He's here, she's gone. What more do you need?"

"He's been in town for six months."

"This is the first time she's been out on her own. He hung around and waited."

I turned to Chickering. "From what I've seen, Chief, you keep a pretty tight lid on things. What's the chance Mc-Closkey could have been hanging around the neighborhood for six months—stalking her without being noticed?"

Chickering said, "Zero." To Ramp: "Good point, Don. If he's behind it, we'll know it soon enough."

Ramp said, "Why all the confidence, Cliff? You haven't found him yet!"

Chickering frowned. "We've got his address, all the particulars. He's being staked out. When he surfaces, he'll be snapped up faster than a free turkey dinner on Skid Row."

"What makes you think he'll surface? What if he's off somewhere, with—"

"Don," said Chickering. "I understa—"

"Well, *I* don't!" said Ramp. "How the hell is staking out his address going to do a damn thing when he's probably long gone!"

Chickering said, "It's the criminal mind. They tend to return to roost."

Ramp gave a disgusted look and resumed pacing.

Chickering went a shade paler. Parboiled sweetbreads. "We're interfacing with LAPD, Pasadena, Glendale, and the Sheriffs, Don. Got everyone's computers on the job. The Rolls' plates are on all their alert lists. There's no car registered to him, but all the hot sheets are being scrutinized."

"How many cars on the hot sheets? Ten thousand?"

"Everyone's looking, Don. Taking it seriously. He can't get far."

Ramp ignored him, kept pacing.

Chickering turned to me. "This wasn't a good secret to keep, Doctor."

Ramp muttered, "That's for damn sure."

I said, "I understand how you feel, but I had no choice— Melissa's a legal adult."

Ramp said, "What you did was legal, huh? We'll see about that."

A voice from the top of the stairs said, "Just get off his case, Don!"

Melissa stood on the landing, dressed in a man's shirt and jeans, her hair tied back carelessly. The shirt made her look undernourished. She came down the curving flight fast, swinging her arms like a jogger.

Ramp said, "Melissa—"

She stood before him, chin up, hands fisted. "Just leave him *alone*, Don. He didn't *do* anything. *I* was the one who asked him to keep it secret, he *had* to listen, so just lay *off.*"

Ramp drew himself up. "We've heard all tha—"

Melissa screamed, *"Shut up dammit!* I don't want to hear this *crap* anymore!"

Ramp's turn to go pale. His hands quavered.

Chickering said, "I think you'd best calm down, young lady."

Melissa turned to him and shook her fist. "Don't you *dare* tell me what to do. You should be out doing your job—getting your stupid rent-a-cops to find my mother instead of standing around with *him*, drinking our scotch."

Chickering's face tensed with rage, then settled into a sick smile.

"Melissa!" said Ramp.

" 'Melissa'!" She mimicked his outraged tone. "I don't have time for this crap! My mother's out there and we have to find her. So let's stop looking for scapegoats and just figure out how to *find* her!"

"That's exactly what we're doing, young lady," said Chickering.

"How? With neighborhood patrols? What's the point? She's not in San Labrador anymore. If she was, she would have been spotted long ago."

A moment's pause before Chickering answered. "We're doing everything we can."

It sounded hollow. He knew it. The look on both Ramp's face and Melissa's drove it home.

He buttoned his coat. Tight across the midriff. Turned to Ramp. "I'll stay as long as you need me, but in your interests, I should be out on the streets."

"Sure," said Ramp dispiritedly.

"Chin up, Don. We'll find her, don't you worry."

Ramp shrugged and walked away, disappearing into the innards of the mansion.

Chickering said, "Good to meet you, Doctor." His index finger pointed like a revolver. To Melissa: "Young lady."

He saw himself out. When the door closed, Melissa said, "Idiot. Everyone knows he's an idiot—the kids all call him Prickering behind his back. There's basically no crime in San Labrador, so no one challenges him. It's not because of him, though—just that outsiders stick out like sore thumbs. And the police roust anyone who doesn't look rich."

Talking rapidly but fluently. Just a slight raise of pitch—
a tinge of the panic I'd heard over the phone.

I said, "Your basic small-town setup."

She said, "That's what this place is. Hicksville. Nothing
ever happens here." She lowered her head and shook it. "Only
now it has. It *is* my fault, Dr. Delaware. I should have *told* her
about him!"

"Melissa, there's no indication McCloskey has anything
to do with this. Think of what you just said about the police
rousting outsiders. The chance of anyone being able to stalk
her without being spotted is nil."

"Stalk." She shivered, let out breath. "I hope you're
right. Then where is she? What happened to her?"

I chose my words carefully. "It's possible, Melissa, that
nothing happened to her. That she did this on her own."

"You're saying she ran *away?*"

"I'm saying she may have taken a drive and decided to
prolong it."

"No way!" She shook her head vehemently. "No way!"

"Melissa, when I talked to your mother I got the sense
she was chafing at the bit—really yearning for some freedom."

She kept shaking her head. Turned her back on me and
faced the green staircase.

I said, "She talked to me about being ready to take giant
steps. Of standing before an open door and having to walk
through. She spoke of this house as stifling her. I got the
distinct impression she wanted out and was even considering
moving once you'd gone away."

"No! She didn't take anything with her—I checked her
room. All the suitcases are there. I know everything in her
closet and she didn't take any of her clothes!"

"I'm not saying she planned a trip, Melissa. I'm talking
about something spontaneous. Impulsive."

"No." Another sharp head shake. "She was careful. She
wouldn't do this to me."

"You are her main concern. But maybe she got . . .

intoxicated by her newfound freedom. She insisted on driving by herself today—wanted to feel in control. Maybe once she got out on the road, driving her favorite car, it felt so good she just kept going. That has nothing to do with her love for you. But sometimes when things start to change, they change fast."

She bit her lip, fought back tears, and said in a very small voice, "You really think she's okay?"

"I think you need to do everything possible to try to locate her. But I wouldn't assume the worst."

She took several breaths, punched her sides. Kneaded her hands. "Out on the road. And she just kept going. Wouldn't that be something." Wide-eyed. Fascinated by the possibility. Then fascination gave way to injury. "No, I just can't see it—she wouldn't do that to me."

"She loves you dearly, Melissa, but she—"

"Yes, she does," she said, crying. "Yes, she does love me. And I want her *back*!"

Footsteps sounded on the marble to our left. We turned toward it.

Ramp was standing there, blazer over one arm.

Melissa used her bare hands to dry her eyes hastily and ineffectually.

He said, "I'm sorry, Melissa. You were right—there's no sense blaming anybody. Sorry if I offended you, too, Doctor."

I said, "No offense taken."

Melissa turned away from him.

He came over and shook my hand.

Melissa was tapping her foot, finger-combing her hair.

Ramp said, "Melissa, I know how you fee— The point is, we're in this together. We've all got to hang together. To get her back."

Melissa spoke without looking at him. "What do you want from me?"

He gave a concerned look. It seemed genuine. Paternal. She ignored it. He said, "I know Chickering's a moron. I don't have any more confidence in him than you do. So let's put our heads together. See if we can come up with *something*, for God's sake."

He held out his hands. Frozen in supplication. Genuine pain on his face. Unless he was better than Olivier.

She said, "Whatever." Sounding that bored had to be a strain.

He said, "Look, there's no sense standing around out here. Let's go in, stay near the phone. Can I get you something to drink, Doctor?"

"Coffee, if you've got it."

"Sure bet."

We followed him through the house, settled in the rear room with the French doors and painted beams. The gardens and rolling lawns and tennis court were bathed in emerald light. The pool was a lozenge of peacock blue. All but one of the doors to the car stable were closed.

Ramp picked up a phone on an end table, punched two digits, and said, "Pot of coffee in the rear study, please. Three cups." Hanging up, he said, "Make yourself comfortable, Doctor."

I settled in a sun-cracked club chair the color of a well-used saddle. Melissa perched on the arm of a cane-backed chair nearby. Scratched her lip. Tugged at her ponytail.

Ramp remained standing. Every hair in place, but his face showed the strain.

A moment later Madeleine came in with the coffee and set it down without comment. Ramp thanked her, dismissed her, and poured three cups. Black for me and himself, cream and sugar for Melissa. She accepted it but didn't drink.

Ramp and I sipped.

No one spoke.

Ramp said, "Let me call Malibu again." He picked up the phone and punched in a number. Held it to his ear for several moments before putting it back in its cradle. Treating the apparatus with special care, as if it held his fate.

I said, "What's in Malibu?"

"Our . . . Gina's beach house. Broad Beach. Not that she'd go there, but it's the only thing I can think of."

Melissa said, "That's ridiculous. She hates the water."

Ramp punched buttons again, waited several moments, and hung up.

We sipped some more.

Ate more silence.

Melissa put her cup down and said, "This is stupid."

Before either Ramp or I could reply, the phone rang.

Melissa beat Ramp for it.

"Yes, but speak to *me,* first. . . . Just *do* it, dammit—I'm the one who . . . What! Oh, no! What do you—that's ridiculous. How can you be sure! That's stupid. . . . No, I'm perfectly capable of . . . No, you listen to me, you—"

She stood there, open-mouthed. Pulled the phone away from her face and stared at it.

"He hung up!"

"Who?" said Ramp.

"*Prick*ering! That ass hung *up* on me!"

"What did he have to say?"

Still gazing at the phone, she said, "McCloskey. They found him. Downtown L.A. The L.A. police questioned him and let him *go!*"

"Christ!" said Ramp. He snatched the phone out of her hand, punched buttons hurriedly. Twisting his shirt collar and grinding his teeth. "Cliff? This is Don Ramp. Melissa said you . . . I understand that, Cliff. . . . I know she is. It's a frightening thing, but that's no . . . All right. I know you are. . . . Yes, yes . . ." Frowning and shaking his head. "Just tell me what happened. . . . Uh-huh . . . Uh-huh . . . But how can you be sure, Cliff? This isn't some goddam *saint* we're talking about, Cliff. . . . Uh-huh . . . Yes . . . Yes, but . . . Still, wasn't there some way . . . Okay. But what if . . . Okay, I will. Thanks for calling, Cliff. Stay in touch."

Hanging up, he said, "He apologizes for hanging up on

you. Says he told you he was busy, trying to find your mom, and you continued to . . . lip off to him. He wants you to know he has your mother's best interests at heart."

Melissa stood there, glassy-eyed. "They had him and they let him go."

Ramp put his arm over her shoulder and she didn't resist. She looked numb. Betrayed. I'd seen more life in wax models.

"Apparently," said Ramp, "he can account for his whereabouts every minute of the day—they have no grounds to hold him. They had to release him, Meliss. Legally."

"The asses," she said in a low voice. "The goddam *asses*! What does it matter where he was all day? He doesn't do things himself—he *hires* people to do things." Raising her voice to a shout: "He hires *people*! So *what* if he wasn't there him*self*!"

Wrenching herself away from Ramp, she grabbed her face and let out a squeal of frustration. Ramp started to approach her, thought better of it, and looked at me.

I went over to her. She retreated to a corner of the room and faced the wall. Stood in the corner like a child being punished, sobbing.

Ramp gave a sad look.

Both of us knowing she could have used a father. Neither of us able to fill the bill.

Finally she stopped crying. But she stayed in the corner.

I said, "Neither of you has confidence in Chickering. Maybe a private investigator's called for."

Melissa said, "Your friend!"

Ramp looked at her with sudden curiosity.

She looked at me and said, "Tell him."

I said, "Yesterday, Melissa and I discussed investigating McCloskey. A friend of mine's an LAPD detective on leave. Very competent, lots of experience. He agreed to do it. He'd probably agree to look into your wife's disappearance as well. If she shows up soon, you might still want to consider checking out McCloskey. Of course, your attorneys may have someone else they work with—"

"No," said Melissa, "I want your friend. Period."

Ramp looked at her, then me. "I don't know who they use—the lawyers. We never had to deal with anything like this. Is this friend of yours really good?"

Melissa said, "He already *said* he was. I want him, and I'm paying."

"That won't be necessary, Melissa. I'll pay."

"No, *I* will. She's my mother and that's the way it's going to be."

Ramp sighed. "We'll talk about it later. In the meantime, Dr. Delaware, if you'd be kind enough to call your friend—"

The phone rang again. Both of them jerked their heads around.

This time Ramp got there first. "Yes? Oh, hello, Doctor. . . . No, I'm sorry. She hasn't . . . Yes, I understand. . . ."

Melissa said, *"Her.* If she'd called sooner, we could have started looking sooner."

Ramp covered his ear. "I'm sorry, Doctor, I couldn't hear . . . Oh. That's very kind of you. But no, I don't see any pressing reason for you to . . . Hold on."

Covering the mouthpiece with his other hand, he looked at me. "Dr. Cunningham-Gabney wants to know if she should come over. Any reason she should?"

"Does she have any . . . clinical information about Mrs. Ramp that would help locate her?"

"Here," he said, handing me the phone.

I took it, said, "Dr. Cunningham-Gabney, this is Alex Delaware."

"Dr. Delaware." The well-modulated voice stripped of some of its melody. "I'm very alarmed by today's events. Did Melissa and her mother have any sort of confrontation before she disappeared?"

"Why do you ask that?"

"Gina called me this morning and intimated there had been some unpleasantness—Melissa staying out all night with some boy?"

Keeping my eyes off Melissa, I said, "That's accurate, as far as it goes, Doctor, but I doubt it's a causal factor."

"Do you? Any unusual stress could cause someone like Gina Ramp to behave unpredictably."

Melissa was staring straight at me.

I said, "Why don't you and I get together? Discuss any clinically relevant factors that might shed light on what's happened."

Pause. "She's right there, isn't she? Hovering?"

"Basically."

"All right. I don't imagine my coming down there and provoking another confrontation is very wise. Would you like to come over to my office, right now?"

"Sounds good," I said, "if Melissa thinks that's okay."

"That child has too much power as is," she said sharply.

"Maybe so, but clinically I think it's advisable."

"Very well. Consult her."

I covered the receiver and said to Melissa: "What do you think of my getting together with her? At the clinic. To share facts—psychological data—in order to see if we can figure out where your mother is."

"Sounds like a good idea," said Ramp.

"Sure," Melissa said sourly. "Whatever." Waving her fingers. The same offhandedness she'd used two days ago to drop clinical bombs.

I said, "I'll stay here as long as you want me to."

"No, no. You can go right now. I'll be fine. Go talk to her."

I got back on the phone. "I'll be there within the half hour, Dr. Cunningham-Gabney."

"Ursula. Please. At times like this a hyphen's a damned nuisance. Do you know how to get here?"

"Melissa will tell me."

"I'm sure she will."

Before I left, I called Milo's home and got Rick's voice on a machine. Both Melissa and Ramp sagged when I told them he wasn't in, making me realize how much stake they were putting in his powers of detection. Wondering if I was doing him a favor by drawing him into the *haut monde*, I left a message for him to call me at the Gabney Clinic during the next couple of hours; at my home, after that.

As I got ready to leave, the doorbell chimed. Melissa jumped up and ran out of the room. Ramp followed her, walking with long, tennis-bred strides.

I brought up the rear, to the entry hall. Melissa opened the doors and let in a black-haired boy of around twenty. He took a step toward Melissa, looked as if he wanted to hug her. Saw Ramp and stopped himself.

He was on the small side—five seven, slim build, olive skin, full bowed lips, brooding brown eyes under heavy brows. His hair was black and curly, worn short on top and sides, longer in back. He had on a short red busboy's jacket, black slacks, white shirt, and black bow tie. A set of car keys jangled in one hand. He looked around nervously. "Anything?"

Melissa said, "Nothing."

He moved closer to her.

Ramp said, "Hello, Noel."

The boy looked up. "Everything's okay, Mr. Ramp. Jorge's handling the cars. There aren't that many tonight. It's kind of slow."

Melissa touched the boy's sleeve and said, "Let's get out of here."

Ramp said, "Where are you going?"

Melissa said, "Out. To look for her."

Ramp said, "Do you really think—"

"Yes, I do. C'mon, Noel." Tugging at the red fabric. The boy looked at Ramp.

Ramp turned to me. I played sphinx. Ramp said, "Okay, Noel, consider yourself off for the rest of the night. But be careful—"

Before he finished the sentence the two of them were out the door. It slammed shut and echoed.

Ramp stared at it for a few moments, then turned to me, weary. "Would you care for a drink, Doctor?"

"No, thanks. I'm expected at the Gabney Clinic."

"Yes, of course."

He walked me to the door. "Have kids of your own, Doctor?"

"No."

That seemed to disappoint him.

I said, "It can be tough."

He said, "She's really bright—sometimes I think that makes it rougher, for all of us, her included. Gina told me you treated her years ago, when she was just a little kid."

"Seven through nine."

"Seven through nine," he said. "Two years. So you've spent more time with her than I have. Probably know her a hell of a lot better than I do."

"It was a long time ago," I said. "I saw a different side of her."

He smoothed his mustache and played with his collar. "She's never accepted me—probably never will. Right?"

"Things can change," I said.

"Can they?"

He opened the door on Disney lights and cool breeze. I realized I hadn't gotten directions to the clinic from Melissa and told him so.

He said, "No problem. I know the way by heart. Gone there plenty. When Gina needed me to."

14

On the way to Pasadena I found myself peering up driveways, checking foliage, scanning the streets for a misplaced shadow, a flash of chrome. The crumpled outline of a woman down.

Irrational. Because the pros had been there already: I spotted three San Labrador police cruisers within a ten-block radius, one of which tailed me for half a block before resuming its prowl.

Irrational because the streets were naked—a stray tricycle could be spotted a block away.

A neighborhood that kept its secrets off the street.

Where had Gina Ramp taken hers?

Or had they been taken from her?

Despite my words of encouragement to Melissa, I hadn't convinced myself the whole thing was an impromptu vacation from phobia.

From what I'd seen, Gina had been vulnerable. Fragile. Just arguing with her daughter had set off an attack.

How could she possibly handle the real world—whatever that meant.

So I kept searching as I drove. Spitting in the face of reason and feeling a little better for it.

•   •   •

The Gabney Clinic occupied a generous corner lot in a good residential neighborhood that had begun yielding reluctantly to apartments and shops. The building had once been a house. A big two-storied, shingle-sided, brown craftsman-style bungalow set back behind a flat, wide lawn. Three giant pines shadowed the grass. A front porch spanned the width of the structure, darkened by massive eaves. Shake roof, lots of wood-relief, stingy windows in oversized casements. Ungainly and dimly lit—some architectural hack's sendup of Greene and Greene. No sign advertising what went on inside.

A low wall—rock chips in cement—fronted the property. A gateless gap in the center provided access to a cement walkway. On the left, a wood-plank gate had been propped open, exposing a long, narrow driveway. A white Saab Turbo 9000 was parked at the mouth of the drive, blocking further motor access. I left the Seville parked on the street—Pasadena was more tolerant than San Labrador—and made my way up the walk.

A white porcelain sign the size and shape of an hour cigar was nailed to the front door; GABNEY was painted on it in black block letters. The knocker was a snarling lion chewing on a brass ring, top-lit by a yellow bug bulb. I lifted it and let it fall. The door vibrated—C-sharp, I was pretty sure.

A second porch light went on. A moment later the door opened. Ursula Cunningham-Gabney stood in the doorway wearing a burgundy-colored scallop-necked knit dress that ended two inches above her knees and accentuated her height. Vertical ribs ran through the fabric, accentuating further. High-heeled pumps were the topper.

The perm she'd worn in the newspaper photo had been replaced by a glossy fudge-colored wedge. John Lennon eyeglasses hung from a chain around her neck, competing for chest-space with a string of pearls. The chest itself was convex and concave exactly where it should have been. Her waist was small, her legs sleek and very, very long. Her face was squarish, finely molded, much prettier than in the picture. Younger, too. She didn't appear to be much older than thirty. Smooth neck, tight jawline, big hazel eyes, clear features that didn't need camouflage. But she was wearing plenty: pale foundation, artfully applied blush, mauve eye shadow, deep-red lipstick. Aiming for severe and hitting the target.

"Dr. Delaware? Come in."

"Alex," I said. "Fair is fair."

That confused her for a moment; then she said, "Yes, of course. Alex." And smiled. And turned it off.

She motioned me into what would have seemed like a generous entry hall if I hadn't just done time at Dickinson Manor. Parquet floors, architecturally paneled oak walls stained shoe-polish brown, plain-wrap craftsman benches and coat trees, a clock that said SANTA FE below the 12 and RAILROAD above the 6. On the walls was a scattering of muddy California plein-air landscapes—the kind of stuff the galleries in Carmel had been trying to palm off as masterpieces for years.

The living room was to the left, visible through half-open sliding wooden doors. More oak walls, more landscapes—Yosemite, Death Valley, the Monterey coast. Black-upholstered straight-backed chairs arranged in a circle. Heavy drapes hid the windows. What would have been the dining room was to the right, set up as a waiting area with mismatched couches and magazine tables.

She stayed a couple of steps in front of me, heading for the rear of the first floor. Quick, deliberate steps. Tight dress. Fluid glutei. No chitchat.

She stopped, opened a door, and held it.

I stepped into what had probably been a maid's room. Small and dim and gray-walled, with a low ceiling. Furnished with simple contemporary pieces: a low-backed pine and gray-leather stenographer's chair behind a pine table-desk. Two side chairs. Three bracketed shelves full of textbooks on the wall behind the desk. Diplomas filling the wall to the left. A single window on a side wall was covered by a gray pleated shade.

A single piece of art, next to the shelves. Cassatt drypoint etching. Soft color. Mother and child.

Yesterday I'd seen another piece by the same artist. Another simple gray room.

Therapeutic rapport taken to the nth?

Chicken-egg riddles jumped into my head.

Ursula Cunningham-Gabney went behind the desk, sat, and crossed her legs. The dress rode up. She left it that way. Put on her glasses and stared at me.

She said, "No sign of her yet?"

I shook my head.

She frowned, pushed the glasses higher on her thin, straight nose. "You're younger than I expected."

"Ditto. And you squeezed in two doctorates."

"It really wasn't that remarkable," she said. "I skipped two grades in elementary school, started Tufts at fifteen, went to Harvard for grad school at nineteen. Leo Gabney was my major professor and he guided me through —helped me avoid some of the nonsense that can trip a person up. I did a double major in clinical and psychobiology—had taken all the premed courses as an undergrad. So Leo suggested I go to med school. I did my dissertation research during the first two years, combined my psych internship with my psychiatric residency, and ended up with licensure in both fields."

"Sounds pretty hectic."

"It was wonderful," she said, without a trace of smile. "Those were wonderful years."

She removed her glasses, set her hands flat on the desk.

"So," she said. "What are we to make of Mrs. Ramp's disappearance?"

"I thought *you* could clue *me* in."

"I'd like to take advantage of the fact that you saw her more recently than I did."

"I thought you saw her every day."

She shook her head. "Not for some time. We've cut our

individual sessions to two to four times a week, depending upon her needs. The last time I saw her was Tuesday—the day you called. She was doing quite well. That's why I felt it was acceptable for you to speak with her. What happened with Melissa that upset her so?"

"She was trying to let Melissa know she was fine, that it was perfectly okay for her to go away to Harvard. Melissa got angry, ran out of the room, and her mother had an anxiety attack. But she handled it—inhaled a drug she described as a muscle relaxant and worked on her breathing until she'd recovered."

She nodded. "Tranquizone. It shows great promise. My husband and I are among the first to use it clinically. The major advantage is that it's very focused—works directly on the sympathetic nervous system and doesn't appear to impact the thalamus or the limbic system. In fact, so far no one's found any CNS impact at all. Which means the addictive potential is lower—none of the problems you get with Valium or Xanax. And respiratory administration means you get improved breathing quickly, which generalizes to the entire anxiety syndrome. The only drawback is that the effects are very short-lived."

"It worked for her. She calmed down pretty quickly, felt good about handling the attack."

"That's what we work on," she said. "Self-esteem. Using the drug as a springboard for cognitive restructuring. We give them a success experience, then train them to see themselves in a power role—see the attack as a challenge, not a tragedy. To zero in on small victories and build from there."

"It was definitely a victory for her. After she calmed down, she realized the issue with Melissa was still unresolved. That upset her, but the anxiety didn't recur."

"How *did* she react to being upset?"

"She went looking for Melissa."

"Good, good," she said. "Action-orientation."

"Unfortunately, Melissa was gone—had left the house with a friend of hers. I sat with Mrs. Ramp for about half an hour, waiting for her to come back. That's the last I saw of her."

"What was Mrs. Ramp's demeanor while you waited?"

"Subdued. Worried about how she'd work things out with Melissa. But no panic—actually, she seemed quite calm."

"When did Melissa finally show up?"

I realized I didn't know and said so.

"Well," she said, "the whole thing must have affected Gina more than she let on. Even to me. She called me this morning and said there'd been a confrontation. Sounded tense but insisted she was all right. The ability to perceive herself as masterful is so essential to the treatment that I didn't argue with her. But I knew we had to talk. I offered her the choice of an individual session or discussing it in group. She said she'd try group—the next one was today—and if that didn't resolve things for her, maybe she would stay late and talk one-on-one. That's why I was especially surprised when she didn't show up—I'd expected it to be an important session for her. When the group took its midsession break at four, I called her at home, spoke to her husband, and found out she'd left for group at two-thirty. I didn't want to alarm him but I did suggest he call the police. Before the sentence was out of my mouth, I heard screaming in the background."

She paused, pressed forward so that her breasts rested atop the desk. "Apparently Melissa had come into the room—hovering—asked her stepfather what was going on, found out, and gone hysterical."

Another pause. The breasts remained there, like an offering.

I said, "You don't seem to like Melissa very much."

She lifted her shoulders, moved back against the chair. "That's hardly the issue, is it?"

"Guess not."

Tugging, now, at her hemline. Pulling harder when it didn't yield.

"All right," she said. "You're her advocate. I know child

people get into that kind of thing all the time—perhaps sometimes it's necessary. But that's totally irrelevant to the issue at hand. We've got a crisis situation here. A severely phobic woman—one of the most impaired patients I've ever treated, and I've treated lots. We've got her out on her own, dealing with stimuli she's totally unprepared for, having broken her treatment regimen—taken steps she wasn't ready for, due to pressure exerted by her relationship with an *extremely* neurotic teenage girl. And that's where *my* advocacy comes in. I have to think about *my* patient. Surely you can see that the relationship between the two of them is pathological."

Blinking hard several times. Real color deepening the rouge on her cheeks.

I said, "Maybe. But Melissa didn't invent the relationship. She was made, not born, so why blame the victim?"

"I assure you—"

"I also don't see why you feel the need to pin the disappearance on mother-daughter conflict. Gina Ramp never let Melissa get in the way of her pathology before."

She wheeled her chair back several inches, never breaking eye contact. "Now who's blaming the victim?"

"All right," I said. "This isn't productive."

"No, it isn't. Have you any other information for me?"

"I assume you're familiar with the circumstances leading up to her phobia—the acid attack?"

Barely moving her lips, she said, "You assume correctly."

"The man who did it—Joel McCloskey—is back in town."

Her mouth formed an O. No sound came out. She uncrossed her legs, pressed her knees together.

"Oh, shit," she said. "When did this happen?"

"Six months ago, but he hasn't called or harassed the family. There's no evidence he has anything to do with this. The police questioned him and he had an alibi, so they released him. And if he wanted to cause trouble, he's had plenty of time—been out of prison for six years. Never contacted her or anyone else in the family."

"Six years!"

"Six years since his release from prison. He spent most of it out of state."

"She never said a thing."

"She didn't know."

"Then how do *you* know?"

"Melissa found out recently and told me."

Her nostrils widened. "And she didn't tell her mother?"

"She didn't want to alarm her. Planned to hire a private investigator to check McCloskey out."

"Brilliant. Just brilliant." Shaking her head. "In light of what's happened, do you concur with that judgment?"

"At the time it seemed reasonable not to traumatize Mrs. Ramp. If the detective learned McCloskey was a threat, it would have been communicated."

"How did Melissa find out McCloskey was back?"

I repeated what I'd been told.

She said, "Unbelievable. Well, the child has initiative, I'll grant her that. But her meddling is—"

"It was a judgment call and it's still far from clear that it was wrong. Can you say for sure *you* would have told Mrs. Ramp?"

"It would have been nice to have had the choice."

She looked more hurt than angry.

Part of me wanted to apologize. The other wanted to lecture her about proper communication with the patient's family.

She said, "All this time I've been working on showing her the world's a safe place, and he's been out there."

I said, "Look, there really is no reason to believe anything ominous has happened. She could have had car trouble. Or just decided to stretch her wings a bit—the fact that she chose to drive over here by herself may indicate she was yearning to stretch."

"This man's being back doesn't bother you at all? The possibility that he might have been stalking her for six months?"

"You were at that house frequently. When you walked around the block with her did you ever notice him—or anyone else?"

"No, but I wouldn't have. I was focusing on her."

"Even so," I said. "San Labrador's the last place you could stalk anybody and get away with it. No people, no cars—making intruders conspicuous is exactly why they do it. And the police function as private guards. Keeping an eye out for strangers is their specialty."

"Granted," she said. "But what if he didn't sit around and make himself obvious? What if he just drove around—not every day, just once in a while? Different times of day. Hoping to grab a glimpse of her? And today he succeeded—spotted her leaving the house alone and went after her. Or maybe it wasn't him at all—he hired someone to hurt her once, could have done it again. So the fact that he has an alibi is meaningless as far as I'm concerned. What about the man who actually attacked her—the one McCloskey paid? Maybe he's back in town, too."

"Melvin Findlay," I said. "Not the man I'd choose for the job."

"What do you mean?"

"A black man driving around San Labrador without a good reason wouldn't last two minutes. And Findlay served hard time in prison for being hired help. It's hard to believe he'd be stupid enough to go after her again."

"Maybe," she said. "I hope you're right. But I've studied the criminal mind, and I long ago gave up assuming anything about human intelligence."

"Speaking of the criminal mind, did Mrs. Ramp ever say what McCloskey had against her?"

She took off her glasses, drummed her fingers, picked a piece of lint from the desk, and flicked it away. "No, she didn't. Because she didn't know. Had no *idea* why he hated her so much. There'd once been a romance, but they'd parted as friends. She was truly baffled. It made it even more difficult for her—not knowing, not understanding. I spent a long time working on that."

She drummed some more. "This is totally uncharacteristic of her. She was always a good patient, never deviated from plan. Even if it is nothing more than car trouble, I have an image of her stranded somewhere, panicking and going out of control."

"Does she carry medication with her?"

"She should—her instructions are to have her Tranquizone with her at all times."

"From what I saw, she knows how to use it."

She stared at me, gave a close-lipped smile that tightened her jawline. "You're quite the optimist, Dr. Delaware."

I smiled back. "Gets me through the night."

Her face softened. For a moment I thought she might actually show me some teeth. Then she grimaced and said, "Excuse me. I'm feeling a real lack of closure—have to deal with it."

She reached for the phone, punched 911. When the operator came on the line, she identified herself as Gina Ramp's doctor and asked to be put through to the chief of police.

As she waited I said, "His name is Chickering."

She nodded, held up an index finger, and said, "Chief Chickering? This is Dr. Ursula Cunningham-Gabney, Gina Ramp's physician. . . . No, I haven't. . . . Nothing . . . Yes, of course . . . Yes, she did. Three o'clock this afternoon . . . No, she didn't, and I haven't . . . No, there's nothing. . . . No, not in the least." Look of exasperation. "Chief Chickering, I assure you she was in *full* possession of her faculties. Absolutely . . . No, not at all . . . I don't feel that would be prudent or necessary. . . . No, I assure you, she was totally rational. . . . Yes. Yes, I understand. . . . Excuse me, sir, there is one thing I thought you might want to consider. The man who attacked her . . . No, not him. The one who actually threw the acid. Findlay. Melvin Findlay—has he been located? . . . Oh. Oh, I see. . . . Yes, of course. Thank you, Chief."

She hung up and shook her head. "Findlay's dead. Died in prison several years ago. Chickering was offended that I even asked—seems to think I'm casting aspersions on his professional abilities."

"It sounded as if he's questioning Gina's mental stability."

She gave a look of distaste. "He wanted to know if she was 'all *there*'—how's that for a choice of words?" Rolling her eyes. "I actually think he *wanted* me to tell him she was crazy. As if that would make it acceptable for her to be missing."

"Make it acceptable if he didn't find her," I said. "Who can be responsible for the actions of a crazy person?"

She blinked several more times. Gazed down at the desk top and let all the severity drop from her face. I was willing to bet her beauty had bloomed late. For a moment I saw her as a myopic little girl. Growing up smarter than her peers. Unable to relate. Sitting up in her room, reading and wondering if she'd ever fit in anywhere.

"We're responsible," she said. "We've taken on the responsibility to care for them. And here we sit, ineffectual."

Frustration on her face. My eyes drifted to the Cassatt print.

She noticed and appeared to grow even more tense. "Wonderful, isn't it?"

"Yes, it is."

"Cassatt was a genius. The expressiveness, particularly the way she brought out the essence of children."

"I've heard she didn't like children."

"Oh, really?"

"Have you had the print for a long time?"

"A while." She touched her hair. Another locked-jaw smile. "You didn't come here to discuss art. Is there anything else I can do for you?"

"Can you think of any other psychological factors that might explain Gina's disappearance?"

"Such as?"

"Dissociative episodes—amnesia, fugue. Could she have had some sort of break, be out there wandering, unaware of who she is?"

She thought for a while. "There's nothing like that in her history. Her ego was intact—remarkably so, considering everything she's been through. In fact I always thought of her as one of my most *rational* agoraphobics. In terms of the origin of her symptoms. With some of them, you never know how it starts—there's no trauma you can put your finger on. But in her case the symptoms manifested following a tremendous amount of physical and emotional stress. Multiple surgeries, prolonged stretches of time when she was ordered to remain in bed so that her face could heal—medically prescribed agoraphobia, if you will. Combine that with the fact that the assault took place when she stepped out of her home and it would be almost irrational for her *not* to behave the way she did. Maybe even in a biological sense—data are coming out showing actual structural change in the midbrain following trauma."

"Makes sense," I said. "I suppose even after she turns up, we may never know what happened."

"What do you mean?"

"The life she leads—the insularity. In her own way she's quite self-sufficient. That can lead a person to treasure secrecy. Even luxuriate in it. Back when I treated Melissa, I remember thinking that for this family, secrets were the coin of the realm. That an outsider would never really know what was going on. Gina may have stockpiled plenty of coins."

"That's the goal of therapy," she said. "To break into that stockpile. Her progress has been remarkable."

"I'm sure it has. All I'm saying is that she still may decide to hold on to a private reserve."

Her face tightened as she prepared to defend against that. But she waited until she'd calmed before speaking. "I suppose you're right. We all hold on to something, don't we? The private gardens we choose to water and feed." Turning away from me. " 'Gardens brimming with iron flowers. Iron roots and stems and petals.' A paranoid schizophrenic once told me that, and I do believe it's an apt image. Not even the deepest probing can uproot iron flowers when they don't want to be dug up, can it?"

She faced me again. Looking hurt once more.

"No, it can't," I said. "Still, if she does choose to dig them up, you'll probably be the one she hands the bouquet."

Weak smile. Teeth. White and straight and gleaming. "Are you patronizing me, Dr. Delaware?"

"No, and if it sounds that way, I'm sorry, Dr. Cunningham hyphen Gabney."

That pumped some strength into the smile.

I said, "What about the members of her group? Would they know anything useful?"

"No. She never saw any of them socially."

"How many are there?"

"Just two."

"Small group."

"It's a rare disorder. Finding motivated patients and those with the financial means to embark on the extensive treatment we offer cuts the number even further."

"How are the other two patients doing?"

"Well enough to leave home and come to group."

"Well enough to be interviewed?"

"By whom?"

"The police. The private detective—he'll be looking for her in addition to investigating McCloskey."

"Absolutely not. These are fragile individuals. They're not even aware she's missing, yet."

"They know she didn't show up today."

"No-shows aren't unusual, given the diagnosis. Most of them have missed sessions at one time or another."

"Has Mrs. Ramp missed any before today?"

"No, but that's not the point. No one's absence would be especially noteworthy."

"Will they be curious if she doesn't show up by next Monday?"

"If they are, I'll deal with it. Now if you don't mind, I'd prefer not to discuss the other patients. They haven't lost their right to confidentiality."

"Okay."

She started to cross her legs again. Thought better of it and kept her feet flat on the floor.

"Well," she said, "this hasn't been very profitable, has it?"

She stood, smoothed her dress, looked past me toward the door.

I said, "Would there be any reason for her to walk out—voluntarily?"

She snapped her head around. "What do you mean?"

"The great escape," I said. "Trading in her life-style for something new. Jumping the therapeutic gun and going for total independence."

"Total independence?" she said. "That makes no sense at all. Not a lick."

The door swung open before she was able to get me to it. A man charged in and race-walked across the entry hall. Leo Gabney. But even though I'd seen his photo just a few days ago, I had to look twice before his identity registered.

He noticed us mid-stride, stopped so suddenly I expected to see skid marks on the parquet.

It was his get-up that had thrown me off: red-and-white flannel western shirt, pipestem blue jeans, pointy-toed bullhide boots with riding heels. His belt was tooled cowhide, the buckle a big brass letter *psi*—the Greek alphabet's contribution to psychology's professional identity. A retractable key ring was attached to the belt.

Urban Cowboy, but he lacked the brawn to make it

work. Despite his age, his build was almost boyish. Five nine, 130, sunken thorax, shoulders narrower than his wife's. The bushy hair stark white over a face sun-baked the color of sour-mash whiskey. Active blue eyes. Bristly white brows. Liver-spotted cranial dome high enough to host half a dozen worry lines; prominent, high-bridged nose with pinched nostrils; less chin than he deserved. His neck was wattled. A bramble of white chest hair ended at his gullet. The entire assemblage elfin but not whimsical.

He gave his wife a peck on the cheek, gave me a laboratory look.

She said, "This is Dr. Delaware."

"Ah, Dr. Delaware. I'm Dr. Gabney."

Strong voice. Basso profundo—too deep a tone for such a narrow box. A New England accent that turned my name into *Dullaweah*.

He extended his hand. Thin and soft—he hadn't been roping steers. Even the bones felt soft, as if they'd been soaked in vinegar. The skin around them was loose and dry and cool, like that of a lizard in the shade.

"Has she shown up yet?" he said.

She said, "I'm afraid not, Leo."

He clucked his tongue. "Hellish thing. I came down just as soon as I could."

She said, "Dr. Delaware informed me that McCloskey— the man who assaulted her—is back in town."

The white eyebrows tented and the worry lines became inverted V's. "Oh?"

"The police located him but he had an alibi, so they let him go. We were discussing the fact that his previous *modus* was to hire someone—there's no reason to think he wouldn't do it again. The man he hired the first time is dead, but that doesn't rule out another scoundrel, does it?"

"No, of course not. Dreadful. Letting him go was absurd—absolutely premature. Why don't you call the police and remind them of that fact, dear?"

"I doubt they'd pay much attention. Dr. Delaware also

feels it's unlikely anyone could have watched her without being noticed by the San Labrador police."

He said, "Why's that?"

"The bare streets, the fact that the local police's area of competence is looking out for strangers."

"Competence is a relative term, Ursula. Call them. Tactfully remind them that McCloskey's behavioral style is contractor, not contractee. And that he may have contracted again. Sociopaths often repeat themselves—behaviorally rigid. Cut out by a cookie cutter, the lot of them."

"Leo, I don't—"

"Please, darling." He took both of her hands in his. Massaged her smooth flesh with his thumbs. "We're dealing with inferior minds, and Mrs. Ramp's welfare is at stake."

She opened her mouth, closed it, said, "Certainly, Leo."

"Thank you, darling. And one more thing, if you'd be so kind—pull the Saab in a bit. I'm sticking out into the street."

She turned her back on us and walked quickly to her office. Gabney watched her. Following her sway—almost lasciviously. When she closed the door, he turned to me for the first time since we'd shaken hands. "Dr. Delaware, of *pavor nocturnus* fame. Come into my office, won't you?"

I followed him to the rear of the house, into a wide, paneled room that would have been the library. Drapes of cranberry-colored velvet under gold-edged valances covered most of one wall. The rest was bookcases carved with near-rococo abandon and murky paintings of horses and dogs. The ceiling was as low as the one in his wife's study, but adorned with moldings and centered with a plaster floral medallion from which hung a brass chandelier set with electric candles.

A seven-foot carved desk sat in front of one of the bookcases. A silver and crystal pen-and-inkwell set, bone-bladed letter opener, antique fold-up blotter, and green-shaded banker's lamp shared the red leather top with an In/Out box and piles of medical and psychological journals, some still in their brown paper wrappers. The case directly behind him was filled with books with his name on the spine and letter-files tagged PEER REVIEW ARTICLES and dated from 1951 through the last year.

He settled himself in a high-backed leather desk chair and invited me to sit.

Second time, in just a few minutes, on the other side of the desk. I was starting to feel like a patient.

Using the bone-knife to slit the wrapper on a copy of *The Journal of Applied Behavioral Analysis,* he opened to the table of contents, scanned, and put the magazine down. Picking up another journal, he flipped pages, frowning.

"My wife's an amazing woman," he said, reaching for a third journal. "One of the finest minds of her generation. M.D. and Ph.D. by the age of twenty-five. You'll never find a more skillful clinician, or one more dedicated."

Wondering if he was trying to make up for the way he'd just treated her, I said, "Impressive."

"Extraordinary." He put the third journal aside. Smiled. "After that, what else could I do but marry her?"

Before I'd figured out how to react to that, he said, "We like to joke that she's a paradox." Chuckling. Stopping abruptly, he unsnapped one shirt pocket and pulled out a packet of chewing gum.

"Spearmint?" he said.

"No, thanks."

He unwrapped a stick and got to work on it, weak chin rising and falling with oil-pump regularity. "Poor Mrs. Ramp. At this stage of her treatment she's not equipped to be out there. My wife called me the moment she realized something was wrong—we keep a ranch up in Santa Ynez. Unfortunately, I had little to offer by way of wisdom—who could expect such a thing? What on earth could have happened?"

"Good question."

He shook his head. "Very distressing. I did want to be down here in case something developed. Abandoned my duties and zipped down."

His clothes looked pressed and clean. I wondered what

his duties were. Remembering his soft hands, I said, "Do you ride?"

"A bit," he said, chewing. "Though I don't have a passion for it. I'd never have bought the beasts in the first place, but they came with the property. It was the *space* I wanted. The place I settled on included twenty acres. I've been thinking about planting Chardonnay grapes." His mouth was still for a moment. I could see the gum wadded up inside one cheek, like a plug of tobacco. "Do you think a behaviorist is capable of producing a first-rate wine?"

"They say great wine is the result of intangibles."

He smiled. "No such thing," he said. "Only incomplete data."

"Maybe so. Good luck."

He sat back and rested his hands on his belly. The shirt billowed around them.

"The air," he said between chews, "is what really draws me up there. Unfortunately my wife can't enjoy it. Allergies. Horses, grasses, tree-pollens, all sorts of things that never bothered her back in Boston. So she concentrates on clinical work and leaves me free to experiment."

It wasn't the conversation I'd have imagined having with the great Leo Gabney. Back in the days when I used to imagine things like that. I wasn't sure why he'd invited me in.

Perhaps sensing that, he said, "Alex Delaware. I've followed all your work, not just the sleep studies. 'Multimodal Treatment of Self-Damaging Obsessions in Children.' 'The Psychosocial Aspects of Chronic Disease and Prolonged Hospitalization in Children.' 'Disease-Related Communication and Family Coping Style.' Et cetera. A solid output, clean writing."

"Thank you."

"You haven't published in several years."

"I'm working on something currently. For the most part I've been doing other things."

"Private practice?"

"Forensic work."

"What kind of forensic work?"

"Trauma and injury-related cases. Some child custody."

"Ugly stuff, custody," he said. "What's your opinion about joint custody?"

"It can work in some situations."

He smiled. "Nice hedge. I suppose that's adaptive when dealing with the legal system. Actually, parents should be strongly *reinforced* for *making* it work. If they fail repeatedly, the parent with the best child-rearing skills should be selected as primary custodian, regardless of gender. Don't you agree?"

"I think the best interests of the child are what counts."

"Everyone *thinks* that, Doctor. The challenge is how to operationalize good intentions. If I had my way, no decisions about custody would be made until trained observers actually lived with the family for several weeks, keeping careful records using structured, valid, and reliable behavioral scales and reporting their results to a panel of psychological specialists. What do you think of that notion?"

"Sounds good, theoretically. In practical terms—"

"No, no," he said, chewing furiously. "I speak from practical experience. My first wife set out to murder me legally—this was years ago, when the courts wouldn't even hear what a father had to say. She was a drinker and a smoker and irresponsible to the core. But to the idiot judge that heard the case, the crucial factor was that she had ovaries. He gave her everything—my house, my son, sixty percent of the paltry estate I'd accumulated as an untenured lecturer. A year later, she was smoking in bed, dead-drunk. The house burned down and I lost my son forever."

Saying it matter-of-factly, the bass voice flat as a foghorn.

Resting his elbows on the desk, he placed the fingertips of both hands together, creating a diamond-shaped space that he peered through.

I said, "I'm sorry."

"It was a terrible time for me." Chewing slowly. "For a

while it seemed as if nothing would ever have reinforcement value again. But I ended up with Ursula, so I suppose there's a silver lining."

Heat in the blue eyes. Unmistakable passion.

I thought of the way she'd obeyed him. The way he'd looked at her rear. Wondered if what turned him on was her ability to be both wife and child.

He lowered his hands. "Soon after the tragedy I married again. Before Ursula. Another error in judgment, but at least there were no children. When I met Ursula, she was an undergraduate applying for graduate school and I was a full professor at the university and the medical school as well as the first non-M.D. associate dean the medical school had ever appointed. I saw her potential, set out to help her realize it. Most satisfying accomplishment of my life. Are you married?"

"No."

"A wonderful convention if the proper confluence can be achieved. My first two were failures because I allowed myself to be swayed by *intangibles*. Ignored my training. Don't segregate your scholarship from your life, my young friend. Your knowledge of human behavior gives you great advantage over common, bumbling *homo incompetens*."

He smiled again. "Enough lecturing. What's your take on this whole thing— poor Mrs. Ramp?"

"I don't have a take, Dr. Gabney. I came here to learn."

"This McCloskey thing—very distressing to think such a man is roaming free. How did you find out?"

I told him.

"Ah, the daughter. Managing her own anxiety by attempting to control her mother's behavior. Would that she'd shared her information. What else do you know about this McCloskey?"

"Just the basic facts of the assault. No one seems to know why he did it."

"Yes," he said. "An atypically close-mouthed psychopath—usually those types love to brag about their misdeeds.

I suppose it would have been nice to know from the beginning. In terms of defining variables. But in the end, I don't feel the treatment plan suffered. The key is to cut through all the talk and get them to change their behavior. Mrs. Ramp has been doing very well. I hope it hasn't all been for naught."

I said, "Maybe her disappearance is related to her progress—enjoying her freedom and deciding to grab a bigger chunk."

"An interesting theory, but we discourage breaks in schedule."

"Patients have been known to do their own thing."

"To their detriment."

"You don't think sometimes they know what's best for them?"

"Not generally. If I did, I couldn't charge them three hundred dollars an hour in good faith, could I?"

Three hundred. At that rate—the kind of intensive treatment they did—three patients could carry the whole clinic.

I said, "Is that for both you and your wife?"

He grinned, and I knew I'd asked the right question. "Myself alone. My wife receives two hundred. Are you appalled by those figures, Dr. Delaware?"

"They're higher than what I'm used to, but it's a free country."

"That it is. I spent most of my professional life in academia and in public hospitals, ministering to the poor. Setting up treatment programs for people who never paid a penny. At this stage in my life I thought it only fair that the rich be offered the benefit of my accumulated knowledge."

Lifting the silver pen, he twirled it and put it down. "So," he said, "you feel Mrs. Ramp may have run away."

"I think it's a possibility. When I spoke to her yesterday, she hinted that she was planning to make some changes in her life."

"Really?" The blue eyes stopped moving. "What kind of changes?"

"She implied that she didn't like the house she was living in—too big, all the opulence. That she wanted something simpler."

"Something simpler," he said. "Anything else?"

"No, that's about it."

"Well, disappearing like this can hardly be thought of as a simplification."

"Do you have any clinical impressions that would explain what's happened?"

"Mrs. Ramp is a nice lady," he said. "Very sweet. Instinctively, one wants to help her. And clinically, her case is fairly simple, a textbook case of classically conditioned anxiety strengthened and maintained by operant factors: the anxiety-reducing effects of repeated avoidance and escape strengthened by the positively reinforcing qualities of reduced social responsibility and increased altruism of others."

"Conditioned dependency?"

"Exactly. In many ways she's like a child—all agoraphobics are. Dependent, ritualistic, routinized to the extent that they cling to primitive habits. As the phobia endures, it gains strength, and their behavioral repertoire drops off sharply. Eventually they become frozen by inertia—a sort of psychological cryogenics. Agoraphobics are psychological reactionaries, Dr. Delaware. They don't move unless prodded sharply. Every step is taken with great trepidation. That's why I can't see her gaily running off in search of some ill-defined Xanadu."

"Despite her progress?"

"Her progress is gratifying but she has a ways to go. My wife and I have each mapped out extensive plans."

That sounded more like competition than collaboration. I didn't comment.

Unwrapping another stick of gum, he slid it between his lips. "The treatment is well thought out—we offer full value in return for our appalling fees. In all probability, Mrs. Ramp will return to the roost and avail herself of it."

"So you're not worried about her."

He chewed hard, made squirting noises. "I'm concerned, Dr. Delaware, but worrying is counterproductive. Anxiety-*producing*. I train my phobics to stay away from it and I train myself to practice what I preach."

15

He walked me to the door, talking about science. As I made my way across the lawn I noticed the Saab had been moved forward into the driveway. Behind it was a gray Range Rover. The windshield was dusty, except for wiper arcs.

I visualized Gabney behind the wheel, forging through the mesquite, and drove away thinking what an odd couple the two of them were. At first glance she was an ice queen. Combative, accustomed to fighting for her rights—I could see why she and Melissa had raised each other's hackles. But the frost was so thin it melted on scrutiny. Underneath, vulnerability. Like Gina's. Had that formed the basis for an exceptional empathy?

Who'd introduced whom to small gray rooms and the art of Mary Cassatt?

Whatever the reason, she seemed to care. Gina's disappearance had shaken her up.

In contrast, her husband seemed intent upon distancing himself from the whole affair. Shrugging off Gina's pathology as routine, reducing pain to jargon. Yet, despite his nonchalance, he'd *zipped* down to L.A. all the way from Santa Ynez—a two-hour drive. So perhaps he *was* as worried as his wife and simply better at concealing it.

The old male-female split.

Men posture.

Women bleed.

I thought of what he'd told me about losing his son. *How* he'd told me. The ease with which he'd spun his tale suggested he'd mouthed it a thousand times before.

Working it through? Desensitization?

Or maybe he really *had* mastered the art of putting the past behind him.

Maybe one day I'd call him up and ask for lessons.

It was nine-fifty by the time I got back to Sussex Knoll. A single police cruiser was still patrolling the streets. I must have passed inspection because no one stopped me from pulling up to the gates.

Over the talk box Don Ramp's voice was dry and tired.

"No, nothing," he said. "Come on up."

The gates yawned. I sped through. More outdoor bulbs had been switched on, creating a false daylight, bright and cold.

No other cars in front of the house. The Chaucer doors were open. Ramp stood between them in his shirtsleeves.

"Not a damned thing," he said, after I'd climbed the steps. "What'd the doctors say?"

"Nothing significant." I told him about Ursula's call regarding Melvin Findlay.

His face fell.

I said, "Have you heard anything more from Chickering?"

"He called about half an hour ago. Nothing to report, she's probably fine, not to worry—it's not *his* wife out there. I asked him about contacting the FBI. He claims they won't get involved unless there's evidence of abduction, preferably something involving interstate transport of the victim."

He threw up his hands, let them fall limply. "The victim. I don't even want to think of her as that, but . . ."

He closed the doors. The entry hall was lit, but beyond it the house was in darkness.

He headed for a light switch on the other side of the entry, making scuffing sounds as he crossed the marble.

I said, "Did your wife ever say why McCloskey did it?"

He stopped, half-turned. "Why do you ask?"

"In terms of understanding her—how she dealt with the assault."

"Dealt with it in what way?"

"Victims of crime often go on fact-finding missions—wanting to know about the criminal, his motives. What turned them into victims. In order to try to make some sense out of it and protect themselves from future victimizations. Did your wife ever do that? Because no one seems to know what McCloskey's motive was."

"No, she didn't." He resumed walking. "At least not as far as I know. And she had no idea why he did it. Frankly, we don't talk much about it—I'm part of her present, not her past. But she did tell me that the bastard refused to say—the police couldn't get it out of him. He was a drinker and a drug-fiend, but that doesn't explain it, does it?"

"What kind of drugs did he use?"

He reached the switch, flicked, illuminated the huge front room in which Gina Ramp and I had waited yesterday. Yesterday seemed like ancient history. A swan-necked decanter filled with something amber and very clear sat alongside several old-fashioned glasses on a portable rosewood bar. He held out a glass to me. I shook my head. He poured a finger for himself, hesitated, doubled it, then stoppered the decanter and sipped.

"I don't know," he said. "Drugs were never my thing. This"—raising the glass—"and beer is about as daring as I get. I never knew him very well—just a bit from the studios. He was a hanger-on. Hung around Gina like a little leech. A nothing. Hollywood's full of them. No talent of his own, so he got girls to pose for pictures."

He walked farther into the room, stepped on carpeting

that dampened his footsteps and restored the house to silence.

I followed him. "Is Melissa back yet?"

He nodded. "Up in her room. She went straight up, looked pretty beat."

"Noel still with her?"

"No, Noel's back at the Tankard—my restaurant. He works for me, parking cars, busing, some waiting. Good kid, real up-from-the-bootstraps story—he's got a good future. Melissa's too much for him, but I guess he'll have to learn that for himself."

"Too much in what way?"

"Too smart, too good-looking, too feisty. He's madly in love with her and she walks all over him—not out of cruelty or snobbery. It's just her style. She just forges straight ahead, not thinking."

As if trying to compensate for the criticism, he said, "That's one thing she isn't—a snob. Despite all this." Waving his free hand around the room. "Christ, can you imagine growing up here? I grew up in Lynwood when it was still mostly white. My dad was an independent truck driver with a bad temper. Meaning there were plenty of times nobody hired him. We always had enough to eat, but that was about it. I didn't like having to scrounge, but I know now that it made me into a better person—not that Melissa's not a good person. Basically she's a real good kid. Only she's used to having her way, just plows ahead when she wants something, regardless of what anyone else wants. Gina's . . . situation made her grow up fast. Actually it's kind of amazing she developed as well as she did."

He sat down heavily on an overstuffed couch. "Guess I don't need to tell you about kids—I'm just going on because frankly I'm pretty rattled by all this. Where the hell could she be? What about this detective—you reach him yet?"

"Not yet. Let me try again."

He sprang up and brought back a cellular phone.

I dialed Milo's home, got the recorded message, then heard it break.

"Hello?"

"Rick? This is Alex. Is Milo there?"

"Hi, Alex. Sure. We just got in—saw a bad movie. Hold on."

Two seconds, then: "Yeah?"

"Ready to start early?"

"On what?"

"Private-eyeing?"

"It can't wait till morning?"

"Something's come up." I looked over at Ramp. Staring at me, haggard. Choosing my words carefully, I recounted what had happened, including McCloskey's questioning and release, and the news of Melvin Findlay's death in prison. Expecting Milo to comment on either or both. Instead, he said, "She take any clothes with her?"

"Melissa says no."

"How can Melissa be sure?"

"She says she knows the contents of her mother's closet, could tell if anything was missing."

Ramp looked at me sharply.

Milo said, "Even a skimpy little negligee?"

"I don't think it was anything like that, Milo."

"Why not?"

I shot a glance over at Ramp. Still staring, his drink untouched. "It doesn't fit."

"Ah. Hubby at close proximity?"

"Correct."

"Okay, let's switch to another lane. What have the local cops done, other than drive around?"

"That's it as far as I know. No one's too impressed with their level of competence."

"They're not known as stone geniuses out there, but what else should they be doing? Going door to door and antagonizing the trillionaires? Lady staying out late isn't Judge

Crater. It's only been a few hours. And with the kind of car she's driving, someone might actually see it. They put out bulletins—for what they're worth?"

"The police chief said they did."

"You hobnobbing with police chiefs now?"

"He was here."

"The personal touch," he said. "Ah, the rich."

"What about the FBI?"

"Nah, those guys won't touch it unless there's definite evidence of a crime, preferably one that will make the headlines. Unless your affluent friends have heavy-duty political connections."

"How heavy-duty?"

"Someone in a position to call Washington and lean on the director. Even then, she's gonna have to be missing for a couple of days for the Feds—for anyone—to take it seriously. Without some kind of evidence of a bona fide crime, what they'll do is eventually send over a couple of agents who look like actors, to take a report, march around the house in their junior G-man shades, French-kissing their walkie-talkies. What's it been, six hours?"

I looked at my watch. "Closer to seven."

"It doesn't scream major felony, Alex. What else have you got to tell me?"

"Nothing much. I just got back from talking to her therapists. They had no major insights."

"Well," he said, "you know those types. Better at asking questions than answering them."

"You have any you want to ask?"

"I could go through some motions."

Ramp was sipping and eyeing me over the rim of his glass. I said, "That might be useful."

"I guess I could make it over there in a half-hour or so, but basically it's going to be a placebo routine. Because the kind of stuff you want to do in a real missing-persons case— financial searches, credit-card checks—has to take place during working hours. Anybody think of checking hospitals?"

"I assume the police have. If you'd like to—"

"No big sweat making a few calls. In fact, I can do plenty from right here rather than spend thirty minutes getting over there."

"I think it would be a good idea to do it face-to-face."

"You do, huh?"

"Yup."

"Lots of shaky knees? Power of placebo?"

"Yup."

"Hold on." Hand over receiver. "Yeah, okay, Dr. Silverman's not happy but he's being saintly about it. Maybe I can even get him to pick out my tie."

Ramp and I waited without talking much. He, drinking and sinking progressively lower into one of the overstuffed chairs. Me, thinking about how Melissa would be affected if her mother didn't return soon.

I considered going up to her room to see how she was doing, remembered what Ramp had said about her being beat, and decided to let her rest. Depending on how things turned out, she might not be sleeping well for a while.

Half an hour passed, then another twenty minutes. When the chimes sounded I got to the door ahead of Ramp and opened it. Milo padded in, dressed as well as I'd ever seen him. Navy hopsack blazer, gray slacks, white shirt, maroon tie, brown loafers. Clean-shaven and he'd gotten a haircut—the usual lousy one, cropped too close at the back and sides, the sideburns trimmed to mid-ear. Three months off duty and he still looked like the arm of somebody's law.

I did the introductions. Watched Ramp's face change as he got a good look at Milo. Eyes narrowing, mustache twitching as if plagued by fleas.

Flinty suspicion. Marlboro Man staring down rustler

varmints. Gabney's cowboy suit would have looked better on *him*.

Milo must have seen it, too, but he didn't react.

Ramp stared a while longer, then said, "I hope you can help."

More suspicion. It had been a while since Milo's picture had been on TV but maybe Ramp had a good memory. Actors—even stupid ones—often did. Or perhaps his memory had been prompted by good old-fashioned homophobia.

I said, "Detective Sturgis is on leave from the Los Angeles Police." Pretty sure I'd mentioned that before.

Ramp stared.

Milo finally began to return the favor.

The two of them remained locked in a stare-fest. I thought of rodeo bulls in adjacent pens, snorting and pawing and butting the boards.

Milo broke first. "This is what I've been given so far." He repeated, almost word for word, what I'd told him. "Accurate?"

. "Yes," said Ramp.

Milo grunted. Pulling a note pad and pen out of a jacket pocket, he turned pages, stopped, pointed with a thick finger. "I've confirmed that the San Labrador police put out countywide bulletins on her. Which is usually a waste of time, but with this car, maybe not. They've got the car listed as a 1954 Rolls-Royce sedan, license plate AD RR SD, Vehicle Identification Number SOG Twenty-two. Correct?"

"Correct."

"Color?"

"Black over shell-gray."

"Better than a Toyota," said Milo, "in terms of conspicuousness. Before I came out I called a few of the local emergency rooms. No one fitting her description's been brought in."

"Thank God," said Ramp. Sweating.

Milo looked up at the ceiling, lowered his eyes and took

in the front rooms with one sweeping glance. "Nice house. How many rooms?"

The question caught Ramp off guard. "I'm not really sure—never counted. About thirty, thirty-five, I guess."

"How many does your wife actually use?"

"Use? Basically, she just uses her suite. It's three rooms—four including the bathroom. Sitting area, bedroom, plus a side room with bookshelves, a desk, some exercise equipment, a refrigerator."

"Sounds like a home within a home," said Milo. "Do you have one, too?"

"Just one room," said Ramp, coloring. "Right next to hers."

Milo wrote something down. "Any reason you can think of why she decided to drive to the doctor alone?"

"I don't know.—that wasn't the plan. I was supposed to go with her. We were going to leave at three. She called me at two-fifteen—I was at my restaurant—and told me not to bother coming home, she'd be driving herself. I questioned it, but she said she'd be fine. I didn't want to weaken her confidence, so I didn't press the matter."

"Thirty-five rooms," said Milo, writing again. "Besides her suite, did she frequent any of the others? Keep stuff around?"

"Not to my knowledge. Why?"

"How large is the property?"

"Just under seven acres."

"She walk around it much?"

"She's comfortable walking around it, if that's what you mean. She used to stroll quite a bit. I strolled with her, back when it was the only place she went. Lately—the last few months—she's been leaving the property, taking short walks with Dr. Cunningham-Gabney."

"Besides the front gate, is there another way to get in or out?"

"Not as far as I know."

"No rear alleys?"

"No. The property abuts another estate—Dr. and Mrs. Elridge's. There are high hedges in between. Ten feet or higher."

"How many outbuildings?"

Ramp thought. "Let's see, if you count the garages—"

"Garages? How many?"

"Ten. One long building with ten stalls, actually. It was built for her first husband's antique car collection. Some of the vehicles are priceless. The doors are kept bolted at all times. Only the Dawn's stall was left open."

Milo jotted quickly, looked up. "Go on."

Ramp looked puzzled.

Milo said, "Other buildings on the property."

"Buildings," said Ramp. "A potting shed, pool cabanas, a changing room off the tennis court. That's it, unless you count the gazebo."

"What about servants' quarters?"

"The staff lives here in the house. One of the corridors upstairs leads to their quarters."

"How many on the staff?"

"There's Madeleine, of course. Two maids and the gardener. The gardener doesn't live on the premises. He's got five sons, none of whom work for us full time but all of whom are here from time to time, helping out."

"Any of the staff actually see your wife leave?"

Ramp said, "One of the maids was polishing the entry, saw her walk out the door. I'm not sure if anyone actually saw her drive off. If you want to question them I can go get them right now."

"Where are they?"

"Up in their rooms."

"When do they go off shift?"

"At nine. They don't always retire right away. Sometimes they stay in the kitchen—talking, having coffee. I sent them up early tonight. Didn't want any hysteria."

"They pretty upset?"

Ramp nodded. "They've known her a long time, tend to be protective."

"What about other homes?"

"Only one. At the beach. Broad Beach. Malibu. She's never gone there, to my knowledge. Doesn't like the water—she doesn't even swim in the pool here. But I called over there anyway. Twice. Nothing."

"Did she say anything recently—over the past few days or even weeks—about taking off? Going away by herself?"

"Absolutely not, and I—"

"No hints dropped? Remarks that didn't seem to mean anything then but do now?"

"I said no!" Ramp's color deepened. He squinted so hard, *my* head began to ache.

Milo tapped his pen and waited.

Ramp said, "That wouldn't make sense. She wanted *more* involvement with other people, not less. That was the whole point of her treatment—getting back *into* the social whirl. And frankly, I don't see the point of this line of questioning—who the hell cares what she *talked* about? She didn't go on vacation, for Christ's sake! Something happened to her out there. Why don't you drive downtown and shake up that psychopath McCloskey! Teach the idiots who let him go something about police work!"

Breathing hard. Temple veins swollen.

Milo said, "Before I came here, I spoke to the detective at Central Division who interviewed McCloskey. Fellow named Bradley Lewis—not the best cop, but not the worst, either. McCloskey's alibi is ironclad—he was feeding the homeless at the mission where he lives. Peeling potatoes and washing dishes and ladling out soup all afternoon. Dozens of people saw him, including the priest who runs the place. He never left from noon till eight. So there's no way the police could have kept him in custody."

"What about as a material witness?"

"No crime, no witness, Mr. Ramp. As far as they're

concerned it's just a situation of some lady who stayed out late."

"But look who we're talking about—what he *did*!"

"True. But he served his time; his parole's over. Far as the law's concerned, he's Joe Citizen. The police have zero hold over him."

"Can't *you* do anything?"

"My hold's *less* than zero."

"I wasn't referring to legal niceties, Mr. Sturgis."

Milo smiled, took a deep breath. "Sorry. Donated my rubber hose to Goodwill."

"I'm serious, Mr. Sturgis."

The smile died. "So am I, Mr. Ramp. If that's the kind of help you're after, you've dialed a very wrong number."

He put his pen away.

Ramp said, "Look, I didn't mean to—"

Milo held out a hand. "I know this is hell. I know the system stinks. But rousting McCloskey right now is not in your wife's best interest. Central Division said after they let him go, they drove him home—guy doesn't have a car— and he went to bed. Let's say I go over there, wake him up. He refuses to let me in. So I force my way in, play Dirty Harry. In the movies that works great—the power of intimidation. He confesses all, and the good guys win. In the real world, he hires a lawyer. Sues my ass, and yours, and the media find out. Meanwhile your wife comes waltzing in—she had car trouble, couldn't get to a phone. A real happy ending except now she's back on page one. The main feature on *A Current Affair.* Not to mention having to watch you cough up some dough to McCloskey or play defendant for a couple of years. What's that gonna do for her psychological progress?"

Ramp said, "Christ, this is insanity," and shook his head.

"I asked Central Division to keep a watch on him. They said they'd try, but to be truthful that's not worth a lot. If she's not back by morning, I'll pay him a visit. If you can't handle waiting, I'll drive down there right now. When he doesn't let me in, I'll sit out there all night watching his door, write you a detailed surveillance report that sounds pretty impressive. I'm charging you seventy dollars an hour plus expenses. A bullshit hour gets billed the same as a productive one. But I just figured for that kind of money, you're entitled to some independent judgment on my part."

"And what is your independent judgment, Mr. Sturgis?"

"At this point, there are better ways of spending my time."

"Such as?"

"Such as making more hospital calls. Phoning all-night service stations. The auto club—if you're members."

"We are. Those sound like things I can do."

"You can. Feel free. The more people working on it, the faster we'll get it done. If you want to do it yourself, I'll write you up a list of the other things you can do and be on my way."

"What kinds of things?"

"Hooking up with the paramedics and the independent ambulance companies, keeping in touch with the traffic divisions of the various police departments in order to make sure information doesn't get lost in the shuffle—it happens a lot, believe me. If you want to go further, check out airlines, air charter services, car rental agencies. Run credit-card traces—find out what cards she carries, have the companies flag the numbers, so when they're used to make a purchase, we know where and when and get the information as soon as possible. If she's not back by morning, I'd also get to work on her bank records, see if she made any major withdrawals recently. Do you cosign on her accounts?"

"No, our finances are independent."

"No shared accounts?"

"No, Mr. Sturgis." Ramp had folded his arms across his

chest. Each word seemed to crank him tighter. "With-drawals, airlines—what are you saying? That she deliberately ran *away*?"

"I'm sure she didn't, but—"

"She *definitely* didn't."

Milo ran his hand over his face. "Mr. Ramp, let's hope she walks in any minute. If she doesn't, it's got to be approached as a missing-persons case, and missing-persons cases aren't great for the ego—the egos of those left waiting. Because to do the job properly, you've got to assume anything's possible. It's like a doctor biopsying a lump—chances are it's benign. The doctor quotes you statistics, smiles, and tells you he's almost positive it's nothing to worry about. But he cuts it open anyway and sends it to the lab."

He unbuttoned his jacket, jammed both hands in his trouser pockets, put the weight of one leg on its heel and arced it back and forth, like a runner doing an ankle stretch.

Ramp looked down at the foot, then up at Milo's green eyes.

"So," he said, "I'm going to get cut."

"It's your choice," said Milo. "The alternative is just to sit tight and wait."

"No, no—go ahead, do all those things. You can do them faster. I suppose you'll want a check before you begin."

Milo said, "I'll want one before I leave—seven hundred dollars, which is a ten-hour advance. But first round up the servants, call the gardener, and get him back here, along with any sons who were working today and might have seen her. Meantime, I'd like to check out her suite, go through her stuff."

Ramp started to question that, didn't like the answers he created for himself, and swallowed them.

Milo said, "I'll be as tidy as possible. You want to watch, that's okay."

Ramp said, "No, that's fine. Go ahead. This way." Pointing to the staircase.

The two of them began climbing, side by side, sharing the same wide marble step but keeping maximum distance.

I followed two steps behind, feeling like the guy who introduced Ali to Foreman.

When we got to the top, I heard a door open, saw a sliver of light slant across the floor of one of the corridor spokes, two doors down from Gina Ramp's room. It widened to a triangle, then was darkened by shadow as Melissa walked out into the hall, still in shirt and jeans, socks on her feet. Walking groggily, rubbing her eyes.

I called her name softly.

She started, turned. Ran toward us. "Is she—"

Ramp shook his head. "Nothing yet. This is Detective Sturgis. Dr. Delaware's . . . friend. Detective, Ms. Melissa Dickinson, Mrs. Ramp's daughter."

Milo held out a hand. She barely grazed it, withdrew, looked up at him. There were crease marks on her face—the false scars of slumber. Her lips were dry and her eyelids were swollen. "What are you going to do to find her? What can *I* do?"

"Were you here at home when your mother left?" said Milo.

"Yes."

"What kind of mood was she in?"

"Okay. Excited about going out by herself—actually, nervous, and she was covering it by trying to look excited. I was worried she'd have an attack. I tried to talk her out of it, told her I'd go with her. But she refused—she even raised her *voice* to me. She'd *never* raised her voice to me. . . ."

Biting back tears.

"I should have insisted."

Milo said, "Did she say why she wanted to go by herself?"

"No. I kept asking her that, but she refused. It wasn't like her at all—I should have known something was wrong."

"Did you actually see her drive away?"

"No. She told me not to follow her—ordered it." Biting her lip. "So I went to my room. Lay down and listened to music and fell asleep—just like I did now. I can't believe it—why am I sleeping so much?"

Ramp said, "Stress, Meliss."

She said to Milo: "What do you think happened to her?"

"That's what I'm here to find out. Your stepdad will be calling the staff together, see if anyone knows anything. In the meantime, I'll be checking out her room and making phone calls—you can help with some of those, if you want."

"Calls to where?"

"Routine stuff," said Milo. "Gas stations, the auto club. The Highway Patrol. Some of the local hospitals—just to be careful."

"Hospitals," she said, putting a hand on her chest. "Oh, God!"

"Just to be careful," Milo repeated. "The San Labrador cops have already called a few. So have I, and she hasn't been reported injured. But it pays to be careful."

She said "Hospitals" again and began crying. Milo put a hand on her shoulder.

Ramp pulled out a handkerchief, said, "Here." She glanced at it, shook her head, used her hand to wipe her eyes.

Ramp looked at the cloth, put it back in his pocket, and took a couple of steps back.

Melissa said to Milo, "Why do you want to see her room?"

"To get a feel for the type of person she was. See if anything's out of order. Maybe she left some clue. You can help me with that, too."

"Shouldn't we be *doing* something—be out there looking for her?"

Ramp said, "Waste of time."

She turned on him. "That's your opinion."

"No, it's Mr. Sturgis's opinion."

"Then let him tell me himself."

Ramp squinted, motionless except for tiny flexes along the jawline. "I'll go get the staff," he said, and walked away quickly down the left-hand corridor.

When he was out of earshot, Melissa said, "You should be keeping an eye on *him*."

Milo said, "Why's that?"

"She's got a lot more money than he does."

Milo looked at her. Ran a hand over his face. "You think he might have done something to her?"

"If he thought it might get him something, who knows? He sure likes the things money can buy—tennis, living here, the beach house. But everything belongs to Mother. I don't know why they got married—they don't sleep together or do anything together. It's like he's just visiting—some damned houseguest who refuses to leave. I don't see why she married him."

"They fight much?"

"Never," she said. "But big deal. They're not together enough to fight. What could she see in him?"

"Ever ask her?" I said.

"In a roundabout way—I didn't want to hurt her feelings. I asked her what to look for in a man. She said kindness and tolerance were the most important things."

"That describe him?" said Milo.

"I think he's just smooth. Out for luxury."

"Does he get her money if something happens to her?"

It was more than she was willing to confront. Her hand flew to her mouth. "I . . . I don't know."

"Easy enough to find out," he said. "If she doesn't show up tomorrow morning, I'll start looking into her finances. Maybe I'll find something up in her room right now."

"Okay," she said. "You don't really think something happened to her, do you?"

"No reason to. And in terms of what you mentioned before—going out there looking for her—your local cops are already patrolling extensively. I saw them on the way over and it's what they do best. There are also countywide bulletins out for her—I checked myself, didn't take that on faith. Dr. Delaware will tell you I'm the original skeptic. That doesn't mean all those police departments are gonna go out of their way to look for your mother. But a Rolls-Royce may just catch their eye. If she's not back soon, we can have the bulletins expanded, can even tell the papers she's missing— but once *those* guys sink their teeth in, they never let go, so we've gotta be careful."

"What about McCloskey!" she said. "Do you know about him?"

Milo nodded.

"Then why don't you go out there and . . . pressure him? Noel and I would have done it if we knew where he lived— maybe I'll find out and do it."

"That's not a very good idea," said Milo and repeated the speech he'd given Ramp.

"I'm sorry," she said, "but she's my mother and I've got to do what I think is right."

"How do you think your mother would like seeing you in a drawer in the morgue?"

Her mouth dropped open. She closed it. Drew herself up. Next to Milo she looked tiny, almost comically so. "You're just trying to scare me."

"You're right."

"Well, it won't work."

"Damn shame." He looked at his Timex. "Been here a quarter hour and I've done diddly. Wanna stand around talking or work?"

"Work," she said. "Of course—"

"Her room," said Milo.

"Over here. C'mon." She ran down the hall, all traces of sleepiness gone.

Milo watched her and muttered something I couldn't make out.

We followed her.

She'd reached the door, was holding it open. "Here," she said. "I'll show you where everything is."

Milo walked into the sitting room. I went in after him.

She slid past me and faced Milo, blocking the door to the bedroom. "One more thing."

"What?"

"*I'm* paying you. Not *Don*. So treat me like an adult."

16

Milo said, "If you don't like the way I'm treating you, I'm sure you'll let me know. In terms of payment, work it out with him."

He pulled out his pad again and looked around the sitting room. Went to the gray couch. Poked at the pillows, ran his hand under them. "What is this, a waiting room for visitors?"

"A sitting room," said Melissa. "She didn't have visitors. My father designed it this way because he thought it was genteel. It used to be different—very elegant, lots more furniture—but she cleaned it out and put this in. She ordered it from a catalogue. She's basically a simple person. This is really her favorite place—she spends most of her time here."

"Doing what?"

"Reading—she reads a lot. Loves to read. And she exercises—there's equipment back there." Crooking a finger in the direction of the bedroom.

Milo peered at the Cassatt.

I said, "How long's she had that print, Melissa?"

"My father gave it to her. When she was pregnant with me."

"Did he have other Cassatts?"

"Probably. He had lots of works on paper. They're stored upstairs on the third floor. To keep them out of the sunlight. That's why it's perfect for here. No windows."

"No windows," said Milo. "That doesn't bother her?"

"She's a sunny person," said Melissa. "She makes her own light."

"Uh-huh." He went back to the gray couch. Removed the cushions and put them back.

I said, "How long ago did she change the decor?"

Both of them looked at me.

"Just curious," I said. "About any changes she might have made recently."

Melissa said, "It was recent. A few months ago—three or four. The stuff that was in here was Father's taste—really ornamental. She had it put up on the third floor, in storage. Told me she felt kind of guilty because Father had spent so much time picking it out. But I told her it was okay—it was her place; she should do what she wanted."

Milo opened the door to the bedroom and stepped through.

I heard him say, "She didn't change this too much, did she?"

Melissa hurried after him. I walked in, last.

He was standing in front of the canopied bed. Melissa said, "I guess she likes it the way it is."

"Guess so," said Milo.

The room seemed even bigger from the inside. At least twenty-five feet square, with fifteen-foot ceilings embroidered with crown moldings fashioned to resemble braided cloth. A six-foot white marble mantel was topped with a gold clock and a menagerie of miniature silver birds. A gold eagle sat perched atop the clock, eyeing the smaller fowl. Groupings of Empire chairs upholstered in olive-green silk damask, a baroque threefold screen painted in *trompe l'oeil* flowers, a scattering of tiny gold-inlaid tables of doubtful function, paintings of country scenes and bosomy maidens with uncertainty in their eyes.

The braids snaked toward the center of the ceiling, terminating in a plaster knot from which a crystal and silver chandelier dangled like a giant watch fob. The bed was covered with a quilted off-white satin spread. Tapestry pillows were arranged at the head in a precise overlapping row, like fallen dominoes. A silk robe lay neatly across the foot. The bed was set on a pedestal, adding to its already considerable height. The finials of the posts nearly touched the ceiling.

Weak light shone from crystal wall sconces beside the bed, transforming the off-white color scheme to the color of English mustard, and turning the plum carpeting gray. Milo flipped a switch and flooded the room with the high-watt glare of the chandelier.

He looked under the bed, straightened, and said, "You could eat off it. When was the room made up?"

"Probably this morning. Mother usually does it herself—not the vacuuming or anything strenuous. But she likes to make her own bed. She's very neat."

I followed his glance to the chinoiserie nightstands. Ivory pseudo-antique phones on both. Bud vase with red rose centered on the one to the left. A hardcover book next to it.

All the draperies were drawn. Milo went to one of the casement windows, pulled aside the curtains, cranked, and looked out. Fresh air puffed in.

After studying the view for a while, he turned, walked to the left side of the bed, picked up the book, and opened it. Skimmed a few pages, turned it upside down, and gave it a couple of shakes. Nothing fell out. Opening the door of the stand, he bent and peered in. Empty.

I went over and looked at the book's front cover. Paul Theroux's *Patagonia Express.*

Melissa said, "It's a travel book."

Milo said nothing, kept looking around.

The wall opposite the bed was occupied by a nine-foot walnut-and-gilt armoire and a wide carved fruitwood dresser inlaid with marquetry herbs and flowers. Perfume bottles and a marble clock sat atop the dresser. Milo opened the top section of the armoire. Inside was a color TV, a Sony 19-inch that looked to be at least ten years old. Atop the television was a *TV Guide*. Milo opened it, flipped through it. The bottom of the armoire was empty.

"No VCR?" he said.

"She doesn't go in for movies much."

He moved down to the dresser, slid open drawers, ran his hands through satin and silk.

Melissa watched for several moments, then said, "What exactly are you looking for?"

"Where does she keep the rest of her clothes?"

"Over there." She pointed to carved swinging doors on the left side of the room. Indian rosewood doors inlaid with vines of copper and brass and topped with a motif that conjured up the Taj Mahal.

Milo shoved them open unceremoniously.

On the other side was a short, squat foyer with three more doors. The first opened to a green marble bathroom accented with champagne-tinted mirrors and equipped with a sunken whirlpool tub expansive enough for family bathing, gold fixtures, green marble commode and bidet. The medicine cabinet was camouflaged as just another mirrored panel. Milo pushed, looked inside. Aspirin, toothpaste, shampoo, lipstick tubes, a few jars of cosmetics. Half-empty.

"She take anything as far as you can tell?"

Melissa shook her head. "This is all she keeps. She doesn't use much makeup."

Beyond the second door was a room-sized closet outfitted with a makeup table and padded bench at the center and organized as precisely as a surgical scrub tray: champagne-colored padded hangers, all facing the same way. Two walls of cedar, two of pink damask. Double-hung hardwood dowels.

Clothes organized by type, but there wasn't much to organize. Mostly one-piece dresses in pale colors. A few gowns and furs at the back, some still bearing their sales labels. Perhaps ten pairs of shoes, three of them sneakers. A collection of sweats folded in storage compartments along the back wall. No more than a quarter of the dowel-space filled.

Milo took his time there, checking pockets, kneeling and inspecting the floor beneath the garments. Finding nothing and going into the third room.

Combination library and gym. The walls lined floor to ceiling with oak shelves, the floor high-lacquer hardwood tile. Interlocking rubber mats covered the front half. A stationary bicycle, rowing machine, and motorized treadmill sat on the rubber along with a free-standing rack of low-weight, chrome-plated dumbbells. A cheap digital watch hung from the handlebars of the bike. Two unopened bottles of Evian water stood atop a small refrigerator alongside the weight rack. Milo opened it. Empty.

He moved to the back and ran his finger along some of the bookshelves. I read titles.

More Theroux. Jan Morris. Bruce Chatwin.

Atlases. Books of landscape photography. Travelogues dating from the Victorian age to modern times. Audubon birding guides to the West. Fielding Guides to everywhere else. Seventy years of *National Geographic* in brown binders. Bound collections of *Smithsonian, Oceans, Natural History, Travel, Sport Diver, Connoisseur.*

For the first time since he'd arrived at the mansion, Milo looked troubled. But only momentarily. He scanned the rest of the bookcases, said, "Seems like we've got a theme going here."

Melissa didn't answer.

Neither did I.

No one daring to put the obvious into words.

We went back into the bedroom. Melissa seemed subdued.

Milo said, "Where does she keep her bankbooks and financial records?"

"I don't know. I'm not sure she keeps anything here."

"Why's that?"

"Her banking's handled for her—by Mr. Anger, over at First Fiduciary Trust. He's the president. His father knew mine."

"Anger," said Milo, writing it down. "Know the number offhand?"

"No. The bank's on Cathcart—just a few blocks from where you turn off to get here."

"Any idea how many accounts she keeps there?"

"Not the foggiest. I have two—my trust account and one that I use for expenses." Meaningful pause. "Father wanted it that way."

"What about your stepdad? Where does he bank?"

"I have no idea." Kneading her hands.

"Any reason to think he's in any financial trouble?"

"I wouldn't know."

"What kind of restaurant does he run?"

"Steak and beer."

"Does he seem to do pretty well?"

"Well enough. He brings in lots of imported beers. In San Labrador, that's considered exotic."

"Speaking of which," said Milo, "I could use a drink— juice or soda. With ice. Is there a refrigerator up here with something in it?"

She nodded. "There's a service kitchen at the end of the staff wing. I can get you something from there. What about you, Dr. Delaware?"

"Sure," I said.

Milo said, "Coke."

I said I'd have the same.

She said, "Two Cokes." Waited.

"What is it?" said Milo.

"Are you finished in here?"

He looked around one more time. "Sure."

We passed through the sitting room and went out into

the hall. Melissa closed the door and said, "Two Cokes. I'll be right back."

When she was gone, I said, "So what do you think?"

"What do I think? That money sure don't buy no happiness, brutha. That room"—cocking a thumb at the door—"it's like a goddam hotel suite. Like she came in on the Concorde, unpacked, went out to see the sights. How the hell could she *live* like that, not leaving a piece of herself anywhere? And what the hell did she *do* with herself all day?"

"Read and toned her muscles."

"Yeah," he said. "Travel books. It's like a bad joke. Some shlock movie director's version of irony."

I said nothing.

He said, "What? Think I've lost my sense of compassion?"

"You're talking about her in the past tense."

"Do me a favor, don't interpret. I'm not saying she's dead, just that she's gone. My gut feeling is she's been planning to fly the coop for a while, *finally* gathered enough courage and did it. Probably jamming that Rolls along Route 66 with the windows open, singing at the top of her lungs."

"I don't know," I said. "I can't see her abandoning Melissa."

He gave a small, hard laugh. "Alex, I know she's your patient and you obviously like her, but from what I've seen, the kid *grates*. You heard what she said about Mommy never raising her voice to her. That normal? Maybe Mommy finally blew her stack. See the way she treated Ramp? And suggesting to me I investigate him without any solid reason to? I couldn't put up with that shit for very long. Course, I don't have a Ph.D. in kiddy psych. But neither does Mommy."

I said, "She's a good kid, Milo. Her mother's disappeared. Time to cut her a little slack, don't you think?"

"Was she sweetness and light before Mommy split? You

yourself said she pulled a fit and ran out on Mommy yesterday."

"Okay, she can be difficult. But her mother cared about her. The two of them are close. I just don't see her running out."

"No offense," he said, "but how well do you really know the lady, Alex? You met her once. She used to be an actress. And in terms of their being close, think of it: never yelling at a kid. For eighteen years? No matter how good a kid is, they're gonna bear some yelling once in a while, right? The lady must have been sitting on a powder keg. Anger at what McCloskey did to her. At losing her husband. At being stuck up here because of her problems. That's one giant keg, right? The fight with the kid was what finally lit it—the kid mouthed off one time too many. Mom waited a long time for her to come back, and when she didn't, she said fuck it, to hell with reading about distant places, let's go see some."

I said, "Assuming you're right, do you think she'll come back?"

"Yeah, probably. She didn't take much with her. But who knows?"

"So what's next? More placebo?"

"Not *more*. The placebo hasn't started yet. When I scoped out the room it was for real. Trying to get a feel for her. As if it were a crime scene. And you know, even with all the bloody rooms I've been in, that place ranks up there on the Freaky Scale. It felt . . . empty. Bad vibes. I saw jungles in Asia that made me feel like that. Dead silent, but you knew something was going on beneath the surface."

He shook his head. "Listen to me. Vibes. I sound like some New Age asshole."

"No," I said. "I felt it, too. Yesterday, when I was here, the house reminded *me* of an empty hotel."

He rolled his eyes, flashed a Halloween mask grimace, clawed his hands, and scraped at the air.

"The *Rrrich* Motel," he said in a Lugosi accent. "They check in, but they don't check out."

I laughed. Totally tasteless. But it felt cruelly good. Like the jokes that flew around at staff meetings back in my hospital days.

He said, "I figure the best thing to do is give it a couple of days of my time. Chances are she'll be back by then. The alternative is for me to quit right now, but all that would do is spook both the kid and Ramp and send them rushing to someone else. At least with me they won't get ripped off. Might as well be *my* seventy an hour."

"Meant to ask you about that," I said. "You told me fifty."

"It *was* fifty. Then I drove up and saw the house. Now that I've seen more of the interior, I'm sorry I didn't make it ninety."

"Sliding scale?"

"Absolutely. Share the wealth. Half an hour in this place and I'm ready to vote socialist."

"Maybe Gina felt the same way," I said.

"What do you mean?"

"You saw how few clothes she had. And the sitting room. The way she redecorated. Ordering from a catalogue. Maybe she just wanted out."

"Or maybe it's just reverse snobbery, Alex. Like owning expensive art and storing it upstairs."

I was about to tell him about the Cassatt in Ursula Cunningham-Gabney's office but was interrupted by Melissa, returning with two glasses. At her heels were Madeleine and two stocky Hispanic women in their thirties who came up to the Frenchwoman's shoulder, one with long plaited hair, the other with a short shag cut. If they'd removed their white uniforms for the evening, they'd put them back on. Along with fresh makeup. They looked hyper-alert and wary, travelers passing through Customs at a hostile port.

"This is Detective Sturgis," Melissa said, handing us the Cokes. "He's here to figure out what happened to Mother.

Detective, meet Madeleine de Couer, Lupe Ortega, and Rebecca Maldonado."

Milo said, "Ladies."

Madeleine folded her arms across her bosom and nodded. The other two women stared.

Melissa said, "We're waiting for Sabino—the gardener. He lives in Pasadena. It shouldn't take long." To us: "They were waiting in their rooms. I couldn't see any reason why they shouldn't be able to come out. Or even why you shouldn't get started right now. I already asked them—"

The doorbell cut her short.

She said, "One sec," and ran down the stairs. I watched her from the top of the landing, followed her descent to the front door. Before she got there, Ramp was opening it. Sabino Hernandez walked in, trailed by his five sons. All six men had on short-sleeved sports shirts and slacks and stood at parade rest. One wore a bolo tie; a couple had on sparkling white guayaberas. They began glancing around—awestruck by circumstances or the scale of the house. I wondered how many times, after all these years, they'd actually been inside.

We assembled in the front room. Milo standing, note pad and pen out, everyone else sitting on the edges of the overstuffed chairs. Nine years had turned Hernandez into a very old man—white-haired, hunched, and loose-jawed. His hands had a permanent tremor. He looked too frail for physical labor. His sons, transformed from boys to men by the same stretch of time, surrounded him like stakeposts protecting an ailing tree.

Milo asked his questions, told them to search their memories very carefully. Got wet eyes from the women, bright stares from the men.

The only new development was an eyewitness account of Gina's departure. Two of the Hernandez sons had been working in the front of the house at the time Gina Ramp had driven out. One of them, Guillermo, had been pruning a tree near the driveway and had actually seen her drive by. Seen her clearly, because he'd been standing to the right of the right-hand drive Rolls-Royce, and the tinted window had been rolled down.

The señora hadn't been smiling or frowning—just a serious look.

Both hands on the steering wheel.

Driving very slowly.

She hadn't noticed him or said goodbye.

That was a little unusual—the señora was usually very friendly. But no, she hadn't looked frightened or upset. Not angry, either. Something else—he searched for the word in English. Conferred with his brother. Hernandez Senior looked straight ahead, seemed cut off from the proceedings.

Thinking, said Guillermo. She looked as if she'd been thinking about something.

"Any idea what?" Milo asked.

Guillermo shook his head.

Milo addressed the question to all of them.

Blank faces.

One of the Hispanic maids began crying again.

Madeleine prodded her and stared straight ahead.

Milo asked the Frenchwoman if she had something to add.

She said Madame was a wonderful person.

Non. She had no idea where Madame had gone.

Non, Madame hadn't taken anything with her other than her purse. Her Judith Leiber black calfskin purse. The only one she owned. Madame didn't like a lot of different things but what she had was excellent. Madame was . . . *très classique.*

More tears from Lupe and Rebecca.

The Hernandezes shifted in their seats.

Lost looks from all of them. Ramp stared at his knuckles. Even Melissa seemed drained of fight.

Milo probed gently, then more insistently. Doing as deft a job as I'd ever seen.

Coming up with nothing.

A tangible sense of helplessness settled over the room.

During the course of Milo's questions, no pecking order had emerged, no one stepping forth to speak for the group.

Once upon a time it had been different.

Looks like Jacob's a good friend.

He takes care of everything.

Dutchy had never been replaced.

Now this.

As if the big house were being assaulted by destiny, allowed to crumble, piece by piece.

17

Milo dismissed the staff and asked for a place to work. Ramp said, "Anywhere's okay."

Melissa said, "The downstairs study," and led us to the windowless room with the Goya painting. The desk at the center was white and French and much too small for Milo. He sat behind it, tried to get comfortable, gave up, and swung his glance from wall to book-lined wall.

"Nice view."

Melissa said, "Father used it as his study. He designed it without windows for maximum concentration."

Milo said, "Uh-huh." He opened desk drawers and closed them. Took out his note pad and placed it on the desk. "Got any phone books?"

Melissa said, "Here," and opened a cabinet beneath the shelves. Removing an armful of directories, she piled them in front of Milo, obscuring the bottom half of his face. "The black one on top's a San Labrador private directory. Even people who don't list their numbers in the regular phone book put them in here."

Milo divided the books into two short stacks. "Let's start with her credit-card numbers."

"She has all the major ones," said Ramp, "but I don't know the numbers offhand."

"Where does she keep her statements?"

"At the bank. First Fiduciary, here in San Labrador. The bills go straight there and the bank pays them."

Milo turned to Melissa. "Know any numbers?" She shook her head and gave a guilty look, like a student caught unprepared.

Milo scribbled. "What about her driver's license number?"

Silence.

"Easy enough to get from the DMV," said Milo, still writing. "Let's go for vital statistics—height, weight, birthdate, maiden name."

"Five eight and a half," said Melissa. "Around a hundred and twenty-five pounds. Her birthday's March twenty-third. Her maiden name's Paddock. Regina Marie Paddock." She spelled it.

Milo said, "Year of birth?"

"Nineteen forty-six."

"Social security number?"

"I don't know."

Ramp said, "I've never seen her card—I'm sure Glenn Anger can get you the number from her tax returns."

Milo said, "She doesn't keep any papers around the house?"

"Not as far as I know."

"The San Labrador police didn't ask you for any of those things?"

"No," said Ramp. "Maybe they figured on getting the information elsewhere—from the city rolls."

Melissa said, "Right."

Milo put down his pen. "Okay, time to get to work." He reached for the phone.

Neither Ramp nor Melissa budged.

Milo said, "Feel free to stick around for the show, but if you're drowsy, I promise this will finish you off."

Melissa frowned and left the room quickly.

Ramp said, "I'll leave you to your duties, Mr. Sturgis," and turned heel.

Milo picked up the phone.

I went looking for Melissa and found her in the kitchen, looking in one of the wall lockers. She pulled out a bottle of orange soda, twisted the cap, got a glass from an upper cabinet, and poured. Carelessly. Some of the soda spilled on the counter. She didn't attempt to clean it.

Still unaware of my presence, she raised the glass to her lips and gulped so quickly it made her cough. Sputtering, she slapped her chest. Saw me and slapped harder. When the paroxysms died, she said, "Oh, *that* was attractive." In a smaller voice: "Can't do anything right."

I came closer, ripped a piece of paper towel from a roll impaled upon a wooden holder, and mopped up the spill.

She said, "Let me do that," and took the towel. Wiped spots that were already dry.

"I know how rough this has been for you," I said. "Two days ago we were talking about Harvard."

"Harvard," she said. "Big damned deal."

"Hopefully it'll return to being a big deal soon."

"Yeah, right. As if I could ever leave now."

Wadding up the towel, she tossed it onto the counter. Lifted her head and looked straight at me, inviting debate.

I said, "In the end, you'll do what's best for you."

Her eyes flickered with uncertainty, shifted to the soda bottle.

"God, I didn't even offer you any. I'm sorry."

"It's okay. I just had that Coke."

As if she hadn't heard, she said, "Here, let me get you some." She reached up into the cupboard and retrieved another glass. As she placed it on the counter, her arm jerked and the glass skidded across the shelf. She caught it before it dropped on the floor. Dropped it and fumbled to catch it again. Staring at it, breathing hard, she said, "Damn!" and ran out of the room.

I followed her again, searched for her throughout the ground floor of the house, but couldn't find her. Went up the green stairs and headed toward her room. The door was open. I looked in, saw no one, called out her name, got no answer. Entering, I was hit by deceitful memories: crystalline recollections of a place I'd never been.

The ceiling was painted with a mural of gowned courtesans enjoying a place that could have been Versailles. Carpeting the color of raspberry sherbet covered the floor. The walls were pink-and-gray lamb-and-pussycat wallpaper broken by lace-trimmed windows. The bed was a miniature of her mother's. Shelves brimming with music boxes and miniature dishes and figurines lined the room. Three dollhouses. A zoo of stuffed animals.

The precise images she'd described nine years ago.

The place she'd never slept.

The only concession to young adulthood was a desk to the right of the bed bearing a personal computer, dot-matrix printer, and a pile of books.

I inspected the books. Two manuals on preparation for the SAT. *The College Game: Planning Your Academic Career. Fowler's Guide to American Universities.* Information brochures from half a dozen first-rate colleges. The one from Harvard, dogeared, a bookmark inserted in the Psychology section.

Manuals for the future in a room that clung to the past. As if her mind had developed while the rest had stagnated.

Had I been fooled, nine years ago, into believing she'd changed more than she had?

I left the room, considered looking for her on the second and third floors, and realized how daunting that would be.

I went downstairs and stood alone in the entry hall. Man without a function. A ten-foot marble clock, with a face almost too ornate to read, said 11:45. Gina Ramp had been gone almost nine hours.

I'd been hanging around for more than half of it.

Time to catch some sleep, leave the detecting to the pros.

I went to tell the pro I was leaving.

He was standing behind the desk, tie loosened, sleeves rolled carelessly mid-forearm, phone tucked under his chin, writing rapidly. "Uh-huh . . . Is he generally reliable? . . . He does? Didn't know you guys were doing that well. . . . That so? . . . Really . . . Maybe I should be thinking about that, yeah. . . . Anyway, what time was this? . . . Okay, yeah, I know where it is. I appreciate your talking to me at this stage of the game. . . . Yeah, yeah, officially, though I don't know that they're actively involved—San Labrador is. . . . Yeah, I know. Just for strokes, though . . . Yeah, thanks. Appreciate it. Bye."

He hung up, said, "That was the Highway Patrol. Looks like my freeway theory's getting some validation. We've got a possible sighting of the car. Three-thirty this afternoon, on the 210, heading east, out near Azusa. That's about a ten-mile drive from here, so it makes sense time-wise."

"What do you mean 'possible sighting,' and why did it take so long to find out if it was spotted that long ago?"

"The source is an off-duty motorcycle guy. He was hanging out at home, listening to his scanner, happened to hear the bulletin and called in. Seems at three-thirty he'd pulled some speeder off onto the left shoulder of the westbound 210, was in the process of writing out a ticket when he happened to notice the Rolls, or one just like it, zip by on the east-bound. It happened too fast for him to get the plates, other than to notice they were English. That answer both your questions?"

"Who was driving?"

"He didn't see that either. Not that he would've if it was her, because of the smoked windows."

"Did he notice smoked windows?"

"Nope. It was the car he was looking at. The body-style. Seems he's some sort of collector, has a Bentley from around the same period."

"Cop with a Bentley?"

"That was my reaction, too. The guy I was just talking to—sergeant at the San Gabriel chippy station—is a buddy of the first guy. The call came in to him, personally—he's also a motorhead, collects Corvettes. Lots of cops are into wheels—they work extra jobs to pay for their toys. Anyway, he informs me that some of the old Bentleys aren't that expensive. Twenty grand or so, cheaper if you buy a wreck and fix it up yourself. Rolls from the same year cost more 'cause they're rarer—only a few hundred of those Silver Dawns were made. That's why the first guy noticed it."

"Meaning it's probably hers."

"Probably. But not definitely. The guy who saw it thought it was black over gray, but he couldn't be sure—it might have been all black or dark gray over light gray. We're talking a sixty-mile-an-hour zip-by."

"How many old Rolls would there be driving around, that time, that place?"

"More than you might imagine. Apparently, a hell of a lot of them ended up in L.A. back when the dollar was worth something. And there are plenty of collectors concentrated in the Pasadena–San Labrador area. But yeah, I'd say we've got a ninety-percent-plus chance it was her."

"East on the 210," I said, picturing the wide-open highway. "Where would she be heading?"

"Anywhere, but she'd have had to make a decision fairly soon—the freeway ends around fifteen miles from there, just short of La Verne. North is Angeles Crest and I don't see her as the type to rough it. South, she could have caught any number of other freeways—the 57 going straight south. Or 10, in either direction, which would take her anywhere from the beach to Vegas. Or she could have continued on surface streets up into the foothills, checked out the sights at Rancho Cucamonga—what the hell is out there, anyway?"

"I don't know. But my guess is she'd probably stay near civilization."

He nodded. "Yeah. Her type of civilization. I'm thinking Newport Beach, Laguna, La Jolla, Pauma, Santa Fe Springs. Still doesn't narrow it much. Or maybe she turned around and headed for her own place in Malibu."

"Ramp called there twice and she didn't answer."

"What if she wasn't in the mood to pick up the phone?"

"Why would she go in one direction, then reverse herself?"

"Let's say the whole thing started out impulsively. She's just driving, for the hell of it. Gets on the freeway, gets swept along—going east by chance. Maybe it's just a matter of it being the first on-ramp she sees. When the freeway ends she decides upon a specific destination. Closest thing to home: home number two. Or let's say she was heading east intentionally. That means Route 10 and a whole bunch of other possibilities: San Berdoo, Palm Springs, Vegas. And beyond. The great beyond, Alex—she could drive all the way to Maine, if the car held up. If it didn't, with her dough she could've ditched it, gotten another one fast. All you need to chew up the open road is time and money, and neither of those is her problem."

"An agoraphobic doing the scenic route?"

"You said yourself she was in the process of getting cured. Maybe the freeway helped it along—all that blacktop, no stoplights. It can make you feel powerful. Make you wanna forget about the rules. That's why people move out here in the first place, isn't it?"

I thought about that. Thought of my first time on the open road, heading west for college at sixteen. The first time I'd driven over the Rockies, seeing the desert at night, thrilled and terrified. My first view of the dirt-brown haze looming over the L.A. basin, heavy and threatening but incapable of dimming the gilded promise of the city at twilight.

"Guess so," I said.

He came around from behind the desk.

I said, "What now?"

"Deliver the news, then get the bulletin expanded—it's better than even money she's out of the county by now."

"Or the car is."

He raised his eyebrows. "Meaning what?"

"It is possible that something happened to her, isn't it? That someone else is behind the wheel."

"Anything's possible, Alex. But if you were a bad guy, would *that* be the car you'd rip off?"

"Who was it told me long ago it's only the stupid ones you catch?"

"You wanna think foul play, fine. At this point I'd have to see something ugly to consider it anything more than an adult runaway. And not one that's likely to turn me into a hero."

"What do you mean?"

"Runaways are the hardest m.p.'s to locate under any circumstances. Rich ones are the worst of the worst. Because the rich get to make their own rules. Buying for cash, avoiding jobs, credit unions—all the stuff that leaves a paper trail. What just happened with Ramp and the kid is a perfect example. Your average husband would be a hell of a lot more in touch with his wife's credit cards and social security number. Your average couple shares. These people live separately—at least where money's concerned. The rich know the power of the buck—they rope their funds off and protect them like buried treasure."

"Separate bank accounts and separate bedrooms," I said.

"Real intimate, huh? He doesn't seem to *know* her. Wonder why she married him in the first place—the kid has a point."

"Maybe she liked his mustache."

He gave a short, sad smile and walked to the door. Looking back at the windowless room, he said, "Designed for concentration. I couldn't spend too much time here without going stir-crazy."

I thought of another windowless room, said, "Speaking of interior design, when I was over at the Gabney Clinic, I was struck by the similarity between Ursula Gabney's office decor and the way Gina furnished that sitting room upstairs. Exact same color scheme, same style of furniture. And the only art in Ursula's office was a Cassatt lithograph. Mother and child."

"So what's it mean, Doctor?"

"I don't know exactly, but if the print was a gift, it was a hell of a generous one. The last time I checked an auction catalogue, Cassatt prints in good shape were pricey."

"How pricey?"

"Twenty to sixty grand for black-and-white. A color one would go for more."

"The doctor's print is a color one, too?"

I nodded. "Very similar to Gina's."

"Sixty grand plus," he said. "What's the current wisdom on therapists accepting gifts?"

"It's not illegal but it's generally considered unethical."

"You think there's some kind of Svengali thing going on?"

"Maybe nothing that ominous," I said. "Just over-involvement—possessiveness. Ursula seems resentful of Melissa—the way one sibling might resent another. Almost as if she wants Gina all to herself. Melissa sensed it. On the other hand, maybe it's just professional pride. The treatment's been intensive. She's brought Gina a long way—changed her life."

"Changed her furniture, too."

I shrugged. "Maybe I'm overinterpreting. Or seeing it backwards. Patients influence therapists, too. It's called countertransference. Ursula could have bought her Cassatt because she saw Gina's and liked it. With the fees the clinic charges, she could sure afford it."

"Big bucks setup?"

"Megabucks. When both Gabneys work, they bill five hundred an hour per patient. Three for his time, two for hers."

"Didn't she ever hear of equal pay for equal work?"

"Her work's more than equal—my impression is she does most of the actual therapy while he sits back and plays mentor."

He clucked his tongue. "She's not doing too bad as a mentee, is she? Five hundred." He shook his head. "Sweet deal. Get a handful of rich folk in serious psychic pain and you wouldn't need much else to fuel the gravy train."

He took a step, paused. "You think this Ursula's holding back?"

"Holding back what?"

"Knowledge of the whole thing. If they were as close as you're suggesting, Gina could have let her in on her plans for the great escape. Maybe old Ursula even thought getting away would be good for her—therapeutic. Hell, maybe she even helped plan it—Gina disappeared on the way to the clinic."

"Anything's possible," I said. "But I doubt it. She seemed genuinely upset by the disappearance."

"What about the other one—the husband?"

"He mouthed the right words but didn't come across too stressed. He claims he doesn't worry. Trained himself not to."

"Doctor heal thyself, huh? Or could be he's just not as good an actor as his wife."

"The three of them in cahoots?" I said. "Thought you didn't like conspiracy theories."

"I like what fits—not that any of it does at this point. We're just head-tripping."

"There are two other women in Gina's group," I said. "If she did plan to run away, she might have mentioned it to them. When I suggested to Ursula that they be interviewed, she got really defensive: told me Gina didn't socialize with them—they couldn't be any help. If she is hiding something, that could have been stonewalling."

He gave a small smile. "Stonewalling? I thought you guys called it confidentiality?"

I felt myself go hot.

He patted my shoulder. "Now, now, what's a little reality between friends? Speaking of which, I'd better deliver the news to my clients."

We found Ramp sitting and drinking in the rear room with the painted beams. The drapes were drawn across the French doors and he was staring off into space, eyes half-closed. His face had taken on a ruddy glow and his shirt was wilting around the edges. When we came in he said, "Gentlemen?" in a hearty, greeter's voice.

Milo asked him to get Melissa and he called her room, using an intercom on the phone. When she didn't answer, he tried several other rooms without success, then looked up helplessly.

Milo said, "I'll catch her later," and told him about the car being sighted.

"The 210," said Ramp. "Where would she be going?"

"Can you think of anything?"

"Me? No, of course not. None of this makes any sense to— Why would she be driving the freeway? She just started driving, period. This is just crazy."

Milo said, "It would be a good idea to have that bulletin expanded statewide."

"Of course. Go ahead, do it."

"It's got to come from a police agency. Your local cops have probably been informed of the sighting by now, may have requested it already. If you want, I can call to confirm."

"Please," said Ramp. He got up and walked around the

room. A shirttail had come loose in front. It was monogrammed with a red DNR.

"Driving the freeway," he said. "That's nuts. They're sure
it was her?"

"No," said Milo. "The only thing they're sure of is that it
was a car just like hers."

"So it had to be her. How many damned Silver Dawns
could there be?"

He looked down, tucked in his shirt hastily.

Milo said, "The next step would be to call airline companies, then get to the bank tomorrow morning and take a
look at her financial records."

Ramp stared at him, groped like a blind man along the
edge of a nearby armchair, and lowered himself into it, still
staring. "What you said at the beginning—about this being
. . . about her running away. You think that for certain now,
don't you?"

"I don't think anything yet," Milo said with a gentleness
that surprised me and raised Ramp's head a couple of inches
higher. "I'm taking it step by step—doing the things that
need doing."

A door slammed somewhere in the house.

Ramp bounded up and left the room, returning a few
moments later trailing Melissa.

She had on a khaki safari vest over her shirt, and boots
encrusted with mud and grass.

"I had Sabino's boys check the grounds," she said. "Just
in case." A brief glance at Ramp. "What's going on?"

Milo repeated what he'd learned.

"The freeway," said Melissa. One of her hands found the
other and kneaded.

Ramp said, "It doesn't make any sense, does it?"

She ignored him, put her hands on her hips, and faced
Milo. "Okay, at least she's all right. What next?"

Milo said, "Phone work till morning. Then I head over to
the bank."

"Why wait till morning? I'll call Anger right now and tell him to get down here. It's the least he can do—all the business this family's given him."

"Okay. Tell him I'll need to go over your mother's records."

"Wait here. I'll go call him right now."

She left the room.

Milo said, "Yes, ma'am."

18

She came back with a scrap of paper and handed it to Milo. "He'll meet you there—here's the address. I had to tell him what it was about, let him know I expected him to keep it to himself. What should I do while you're gone?"

"Call airlines," said Milo. "See if anyone bought a ticket to anywhere using your mom's name. Say you're her daughter and it's an emergency. If that doesn't work, embellish it— someone's sick, you really need to know for medical reasons. Check departures from LAX, Burbank, Ontario, John Wayne, and Lindbergh. If you want to be really thorough, check under your mom's maiden name, too. I'll only come back here if something profound happens at the bank. Here's my number at home."

Scrawling on the back of the paper she'd just handed him, he tore off half and gave it to her.

"Call me if you learn *anything*," she said. "Even if it seems unimportant."

"Will do," said Milo. Turning to Ramp, he said, "Hang in there."

Ramp remained in his chair and gave a dull nod.

I said to Melissa, "Is there anything I can do for you?"

"No," she said. "No, thanks. I don't really feel like talking. I want to *do* something—no offense, okay?"

"No offense."

"I'll call you if I need you," she said.

"No problem."

"Sayonara," said Milo, heading for the door.

I said, "I'll walk out with you."

"If you insist," he said, coasting down the driveway. "But if I had a chance at some shuteye, I'd grab it."

He'd brought Rick's white Porsche 928. A portable scanner had been mounted on the dash since the last time I'd seen the car. He had the volume on low and the machine emitted a steady stream of mumbles.

"Hoo hah," I said, tapping the box.

"Christmas gift."

"From whom?"

"From me to me," he said, accelerating. The Porsche hummed in agreement. "I still think you should go to sleep. Ramp's already looking wilted and the kid's running on adrenaline. Sooner or later you're gonna be back here doing your thing."

"Not tired," I said.

"Too keyed up?"

"Uh-huh."

"It'll hit you tomorrow. Just in time for a panic call."

"No doubt."

He chuckled and gunned the engine.

The gates to the property were open. He turned left on Sussex Knoll, then left again. Giving the Porsche's wheel a rightward turn, he oversteered a bit and had to straighten before turning onto Cathcart Boulevard. The businesses along the commercial strip were all dark. The streetlights cast an opaline light that expired before it reached the grassy median.

"Yeah, there it is, all lit up," he said, pointing across the street to a floodlit one-story Greek Revival building. White limestone. Boxwood hedges, small lawn with a flagpole. FIRST FIDUCIARY TRUST BANK, FDIC in gold letters over the door.

I said, "Doesn't look big enough to store cookie-sale proceeds."

"Quality, not quantity, remember?"

He pulled up in front of the bank. To the right was a twenty-space parking lot fronted by twin iron posts and a chain that had been lowered to the ground. A black Mercedes sedan sat alone in the first spot on the left side. As we got out of the Porsche, the black car's door opened.

A man exited, closed the door, and stood there, one hand on the roof of the car.

Milo said, "I'm Sturgis."

The man came forward into the streetlight. He had on a gray gabardine sack suit, white shirt, yellow tie with blue dots. Matching handkerchief in his breast pocket, black wingtips on his feet. Quick midnight dresser.

He said, "Glenn Anger, Mr. Sturgis. I hope Mrs. Ramp's in no danger."

"That's what we're trying to find out."

"Come this way." Pointing toward the bank's front door. "The security system's been disarmed but there are still these to contend with."

Pointing to a quartet of deadbolt locks arranged in a square around the doorknob. He pulled out a ring crammed with keys, fingered one, inserted it in the upper right-hand lock, turned, and waited until a click had sounded before pulling it out. Working quickly and efficiently. I thought of a professional safecracker.

I took a good look at him. Six feet, 160, gray crewcut, long face that would probably show tan in the daylight. Nub of nose, skimpy mouth, diminutive close-set ears. As if he'd purchased his features on sale and had settled for one size too small. Thick, dark eyebrows made his pale eyes look even tinier than they were. His age was somewhere between forty-five and fifty-five. If he'd been roused from sleep, he'd made a good recovery.

Before inserting the fourth key, he stopped and looked up and down the deserted street. Then at us.

Milo's return look communicated nothing.

Anger turned the key, pushed the door open an inch. "I'm very concerned about Mrs. Ramp. Melissa made it sound quite serious."

Milo gave a noncommittal nod.

Anger said, "What exactly is it you think I can do for you?" Then he looked at me.

Milo said, "This is Alex Delaware." As if that settled it. "The first thing you can do is get me the numbers on her credit cards and her checking accounts. The second is you can educate me about her general financial situation."

"Educate you," said Anger, his hand still on the knob.

"Answer a few questions."

Anger moved his lower jaw back and forth. Curving his arm around the jamb, he reached in and turned on some lights.

Inside the bank was polished cherry wood, royal-blue carpeting, brass fixtures, and a ceiling with a relief of a bald eagle at the apex. Three teller's stations and a door marked SAFE DEPOSIT took up one side; three desk-and-chair sets filled the other. In the center of the room was a service kiosk.

The place smelled of lemon wax and ammonia and money so old it had begun to grow mold. Seeing it empty made me feel like a burglar.

Anger pointed forward and took us to a door at the rear that said W. GLENN ANGER, CHAIRMAN AND PRESIDENT over a seal that looked awfully similar to the one Ronald Reagan had just stopped using.

Two locks on this one.

Anger opened them and said, "Come on in."

His office was small and cool and smelled like a new car.

It was furnished with a squat desk—bare except for a gold
Cross pen and a black-shaded lamp—and two brown tweed
chairs with a low square table between them. Several leather-
bound books sat on the table. To the right of the desk was a
personal computer on a wheeled stand. Family photos filled
the rear wall, each featuring the same brood: blond wife
resembling Doris Day after six months of overeating, four
blond boys, two beautifully groomed golden retrievers, and a
grumpy-looking Siamese cat.

The other walls were taken up by a pair of Stanford
diplomas, a collection of Norman Rockwell plates, a framed
replica of the Declaration of Independence, and a ceiling-
high rack of athletic trophies. Golf, squash, swimming,
baseball, track. Awards dating back twenty years and in-
scribed to Warren Glenn Anger. More recent ones made out
to Warren Glenn Anger, Jr., and Eric James Anger. I wondered about the two boys who hadn't brought home any
gold-plate and tried to pick them in the photos but couldn't.
All four were smiling.

Anger took a seat behind the desk, shot his cuffs, and
looked at his watch. Dark curly hair with red tips sprouted
along the tops of his hands.

Milo and I sat in the tweed chairs. I looked down at
the table. The leather-bound books were membership
directories—rosters of three private clubs still battling the
city over admission of women and minorities.

"You're a private detective?" said Anger.

"That's right."

"What kind of education are you after?"

Milo took out his pad. "Mrs. Ramp's net worth for starts.
How her assets are divided. Any significant withdrawals
recently."

Anger's eyebrow dipped at the center. "Why exactly do
you need all this, Mr. Sturgis?"

"I've been hired to hunt for Mrs. Ramp. A good hunter
gets to know his quarry."

Anger frowned.

Milo said, "Her banking patterns might tell me something about her intentions."

"Intentions in terms of what?"

"A pattern of unusually large withdrawals might suggest she was planning to take a trip."

Anger gave several very small nods. "I see. Well, that hasn't been the case. And her net worth? What would that tell you?"

"I need to know what's at stake."

"At stake in terms of what?"

"In terms of how long she can stay out of sight—if her disappearance is voluntary."

"Are you suggesting—"

"In terms of who stands to inherit, if it isn't."

Anger's jaw moved back and forth. "That sounds ominous."

"Not really. I just need to define my parameters."

"I see. And what *do* you think's happened to her, Mr. Sturgis?"

"I don't have enough information to think anything. That's why I'm here."

Anger tilted back in his chair, rolled the bottom of his tie upward, then let it unfurl.

"I'm really concerned for her welfare, Mr. Sturgis. I'm sure you're aware of her problem—the fears. The thought of her out there by herself . . ." Anger shook his head.

"We're all concerned," said Milo. "So why don't we get to work?"

Anger swiveled his chair to one side, lowered it, and faced center again. "The problem is that a bank needs to maintain certain levels of—"

"I know what a bank needs to do, and I'm sure you do it really well. But there's a lady out there whose family wants her found a.s.a.p. So why don't we cut to the chase?"

Anger didn't move. But he looked as if he'd slammed his finger in a car door and was trying to tough it out.

"Who, exactly, is your client of record, Mr. Sturgis?"

"Both Mr. Ramp and Ms. Dickinson."

"I haven't heard from Don on this."

"He's a bit stressed right now, trying to get some rest, but feel free to call him."

"Stressed?" said Anger.

"Concerned for his wife's welfare. The longer she's gone, the greater the stress. With luck the whole thing will resolve itself, and the family will be extremely grateful to those who helped them in their time of need. People tend to remember that kind of thing."

"Yes, of course. But that's part of my dilemma. Having the matter resolve itself only to have made Mrs. Ramp's finances needlessly public without proper legal justification. Because only Mrs. Ramp has the legal justification to request release of that information."

"You've got a point," said Milo. "If you want we'll walk out of here and record the fact that you opted not to cooperate."

"No," said Anger. "That won't be necessary. Melissa *has* reached her majority—if barely. In light of the . . . situation, I suppose it's appropriate for her to make these types of family decisions in her mother's absence."

"What situation's that?"

"She's her mother's sole heir."

"Ramp gets nothing?"

"Just a small sum."

"How small?"

"Fifty thousand dollars. Let me qualify that by saying those are the facts as I know them today. The family attorneys are Wresting, Douse, and Cosner downtown. They may have drafted new papers, though I doubt it. Generally I'm kept well informed of any changes—we do the family's accounting, receive copies of all documents."

"Give me those lawyers' names again," said Milo, pen poised.

"Wresting. Douse. And Cosner. They're a fine old

firm—Jim Douse's great-uncle was J. Harmon Douse, the California Supreme Court justice."

"Who's Mrs. Ramp's personal lawyer?"

"Jim Junior—Jim Douse's son. James Madison Douse, Junior."

Milo copied it down. "Got his number handy?"

Anger recited seven numbers.

"Okay," said Milo. "The fifty thousand that goes to Ramp—that the result of a prenuptial agreement?"

Anger nodded. "The agreement states—to the best of my recollection—that Don forfeits claim to any part of Gina's estate beyond a single cash payment of fifty thousand dollars. Very simple—shortest one I've ever seen."

"Whose idea was it?"

"Arthur Dickinson's essentially—Gina's first husband."

"Voice from the grave?"

Anger shifted in his chair and gave a look of distaste. "Arthur wanted Gina well taken care of. He was acutely aware of the difference in their ages. And her fragility. He specified in his will that no subsequent husband be eligible to inherit."

"Is that legal?"

"You'd have to consult an attorney on that, Mr. Sturgis. Don certainly showed no desire to challenge it. Then, or since. I was present when the agreement was signed. Notarized it personally. Don was totally amenable. More than that—enthusiastic. Stated his willingness to forgo even the fifty thousand. It was Gina who insisted on sticking to the letter of Arthur's will."

"Why's that?"

"The man is her husband."

"Then why didn't she try to give him more?"

"I don't know, Mr. Sturgis. You'd have to ask—" Self-conscious smile. "Yes, well, I can only guess, but I suppose she was a bit embarrassed—this was a week before the wedding. Most people don't like dealing with financial matters at a time like that. Don reassured her it was irrelevant to him."

"Sounds like he didn't marry her for her money."

Anger gave a cold look. "Apparently not, Mr. Sturgis."

"Any idea why he *did* marry her?"

"I assume he *loved* her, Mr. Sturgis."

"They pretty happy together, far as you know?"

Anger sat back and folded his hands across his chest. "Investigating your own client, Mr. Sturgis?"

"Trying to fill in the picture."

"Art was never my strong suit, Mr. Sturgis."

Milo looked at the trophies and said, "Would it help if I phrased it in sports terms?"

"Not one bit, I'm afraid."

Milo smiled and scribbled. "Okay, back to basics. Melissa's the sole heir."

"That's correct."

"Who inherits the estate if Melissa dies?"

"I believe her mother does, but we're really getting out of my field of expertise."

"Okay, let's move back into it. *What's* inherited? How big of an estate are we talking about?"

Anger hesitated. A banker's prudishness. Then: "About forty million. Give or take. All of it in highly conservative investments."

"Such as?"

"State of California tax-free municipal bonds rated double-A or above, blue-chip stocks and corporate bonds, treasury bills, some holdings in the secondary and tertiary mortgage markets. Nothing speculative."

"How much yearly income does she get from all that?"

"Three and a half to five million, depending on yields."

"All interest?"

Anger nodded. Talking figures had drawn him forward and relaxed his posture. "There's nothing else coming in.

Arthur did some architecture and development early on, but most of what he accumulated was the result of royalties on the Dickinson strut—it's a process he invented, something to do with strengthening metal. He sold all rights to it just before he died, which is just as well—there've been newer techniques that have superseded it."

"Why'd he sell?"

"He'd just retired, wanted to devote all his time to Gina—to her medical problems. You're aware of her history—the attack?"

Milo nodded. "Any idea why she was attacked?"

That startled Anger. "I was at college when it happened—read about it in the papers."

"That doesn't exactly answer my question."

Anger said, "What exactly was your question?"

"The motive behind the attack."

"I have no idea."

"Any local theories you're aware of?"

"I don't engage in gossip."

"I'm sure you don't, Mr. Anger, but if you did, is there something you would have heard?"

"Mr. Sturgis," said Anger, "you need to understand that Gina's been out of circulation for a long time. She's not a topic of local gossip."

"What about at the time of the attack? Or shortly after, when she moved to San Labrador. Any gossip then?"

"From what I recall," said Anger, "the consensus was that he was out of his mind—the maniac who did it. Does a madman need a motive?"

"Guess not." Milo scanned his notes. "Those highly conservative investments you mentioned. They also Dickinson's idea?"

"Absolutely. The rules of investment are spelled out in the will. Arthur was a very cautious man—collecting art was his only extravagance. He would have bought his clothes off the rack if he could."

Milo said, "Think he was too conservative?"

"One doesn't judge," said Anger. "With what he'd put together from the strut royalties, he could have invested in real estate and parlayed it into a really sizable estate—two or three hundred million. But he insisted on security, no risks, and we did as told. *Continue* to do so."

"You've been his banker since the beginning?"

"Fiduciary has. My father founded the bank. He worked directly with Arthur."

Anger's face creased. Sharing credit with reluctance. No portraits of The Founder in here. None out in the main room of the bank, either.

None of Arthur Dickinson in the house he'd built. I wondered why.

Milo said, "You pay all her bills?"

"Everything except small cash purchases—minor household expenditures."

"How much do you pay out each month?"

"One moment," said Anger, swiveling to face the computer. He turned on the machine, waited until it had booted up and beeped a welcome, then hunted and pecked, waited, typed some more, and sat forward as the screen was filled with letters.

"Here we go—last month's bills totaled thirty-two thousand two hundred fifty-eight and thirty-nine cents. The month before that, a little over thirty—that's about typical."

Milo got up, walked behind the desk, and looked at the screen. Anger began to shield it with his hand, protecting his data like a Goody Two-Shoes kid guarding an exam. But Milo was looming over him, already copying, and the banker let his hand drop.

"As you can see," he said, "the family lives comparatively simply. Most of the budget goes to cover staff salaries, basic maintenance on the house, insurance premiums."

"No mortgages?"

"None. Arthur bought the beach house for cash and lived there while he built the main house."

"What about taxes?"

"They're paid out of a separate account. If you insist I'll call up the file, but you'll learn nothing from it."

"Humor me," said Milo.

Anger rubbed his jaw and typed a line. The computer made digestive noises. He rubbed his jaw again and I noticed that the skin along his mandible was slightly irritated. He'd shaved before coming over.

"Here," he said as the screen flashed amber. "Last year's federal and state taxes amounted to just under a million dollars."

"That leaves about two-and-a-half to four million to play with."

"Approximately."

"Where does it go?"

"We reinvest it."

"Stocks and bonds?"

Anger nodded.

"Does Mrs. Ramp take any cash out for herself?"

"Her personal allowance is ten thousand dollars per month."

"Allowance?"

"Arthur set it up that way."

"Is she allowed to take more?"

"The money's hers, Mr. Sturgis. She can take whatever she wants."

"Does she?"

"Does she what?"

"Take more than ten."

"No."

"What about Melissa's expenses?"

"Those are covered by a separate trust fund."

"So we're talking a hundred twenty thousand a year for how many years?"

"Since Arthur died."

I said, "He died just before Melissa was born. That makes it a little over eighteen years."

"Eighteen times twelve is what," said Milo. "Around two hundred months . . ."

"Two sixteen," said Anger reflexively.

"Times ten thou is over two million dollars. If Mrs. Ramp put it in another bank and earned interest, it could have doubled, right?"

"There'd be no reason for her to do that," said Anger.

"Where is it, then?"

"What makes you think it's anywhere, Mr. Sturgis? She probably spent it—on personal items."

"Two million plus worth of personal items?"

"I assure you, Mr. Sturgis, that ten thousand dollars a month for a woman of her standing is hardly worth considering."

Milo said, "Guess you're right."

Anger smiled. "It's easy to be staggered by the idea of all those zeroes. But believe me, that kind of money is inconsequential and it goes fast. I have clients who spend more on a single fur coat. Now is there anything else I can help you with, Mr. Sturgis?"

"Mr. and Mrs. Ramp share any accounts?"

"No."

"Mr. Ramp do his banking here, too?"

"Yes, but I'd prefer you talk to him directly about his finances."

"Sure," said Milo. "Now how about those credit-card numbers?"

Anger's fingers danced across the keyboard. Machineburp. Flash. "There are three cards. American Express, Visa, and MasterCard." He pointed. "These are the numbers. Below each are the credit allowances and purchase totals for the current fiscal year."

"This all of it?" said Milo, writing.

"Yes, it is, Mr. Sturgis."

Milo copied. "Between all three, she's got around a fifty-thousand monthly credit line."

"Forty-eight thousand five hundred and fifty-five."

"No purchases on the American Express—not much on any of them. Looks like she doesn't buy much."

"No need to," said Anger. "We take care of everything."

"Kind of like being a kid," said Milo.

"Beg pardon?"

"The way she lives. Like being a little kid. Getting an allowance, having all her needs taken care of, no fuss, no muss."

Anger's hand clawed above the keyboard. "I'm sure it's amusing to ridicule the rich, Mr. Sturgis, but I've noticed you're not immune to material amusements."

"That so?"

"Your Porsche. You chose it because of what it means to you."

"Oh, that," said Milo, rising. "That's borrowed. My regular transportation's much less meaningful."

"Really," said Anger.

Milo looked at me. "Tell him."

"He drives a moped," I said. "Better for stakeouts."

"Except when it rains," said Milo. "Then I take an umbrella."

Back in the Porsche, he said, "Looks like little Melissa may have been wrong about Stepdaddy's intentions."

"True love?" I said. "Yet they don't sleep together."

Shrug. "Maybe Ramp loves her for the purity of her soul."

"Or maybe he intends one day to contest the prenuptial."

"What a suspicious guy," he said. "In the meantime, there's all that allowance money to wonder about."

"Two million?" I said. "Chump change. Don't get staggered by a few zeroes, Mr. Sturgis."

"Heaven forfend."

He got back on Cathcart, drove slowly. "Thing is, he's got a point. Her kind of income, a hundred twenty a year, *could* seem like petty cash. If she *spent* it. But after being up in her room, I don't see where it went. Books and magazines and a home gym don't add up to a hundred twenty gees a year—hell, she didn't even have a VCR. There's the therapy, but that's only for the last year. Unless she's got some secret charity, eighteen years' worth of unspent allowance would have accumulated to something pretty tidy. By anyone's standards. Maybe I should have checked her mattress."

"Could be that's where the money for the Cassatt came from—both Cassatts."

"Possible," he said. "But that still leaves plenty. If she did deposit it in another bank, we'd be hard-pressed to find it any time soon."

"How could she deal with another bank without leaving the house?"

"That kind of money at stake, plenty of banks would come to her."

"Neither Ramp nor Melissa mentioned any visits from bankers."

"True," he said. "So maybe she just stashed it. For a rainy day. And maybe the rainy day came and she's got it clutched in her hot little hand right now."

I thought about that.

He said, "What?"

"Rich lady hauling megabucks in a Rolls. It spells victim."

He nodded. "In a hundred goddam languages."

We drove back to Sussex Knoll to get my car. The gates were closed but two floodlights above them had been switched on. Welcome Home lights. A stretch at optimism that seemed pitiful in the stillness of the early morning hours.

I said, "Forget the car. I'll pick it up tomorrow."

Without a word, Milo turned around and headed back toward Cathcart, putting on speed and handling the Porsche better than I'd ever seen. We sped west onto California, made the transition to Arroyo Seco in what seemed like seconds. Then the freeway, barren and dark and wind-lashed.

But Milo kept searching anyway, turning his head from side to side, checking the rearview. Waiting until we'd hit the downtown interchange before cranking the volume up on the scanner and listening to the hurts people were choosing to inflict on one another as a new day began.

19

When I got home I was still wound up. I went down to the pond and found clusters of spawn clinging bravely to some of the plants at the edge of the water. Heartened, I climbed back up to the house and wrote. Made myself drowsy in fifteen minutes and barely got my clothes off before tumbling into bed.

I awoke at six-forty A.M. Friday and called Melissa an hour later.

"Oh," she said, sounding disappointed it was me. "I already talked to Mr. Sturgis. Nothing new."

"Sorry."

"I did exactly as he said, Dr. Delaware. Called every airline at every airport—even San Francisco and San Jose, which he didn't mention. Because she could have headed north, right? Then I phoned every hotel and motel I could find in the Yellow Pages, but no one had any record of her checking in. I think he's starting to realize it might be serious."

"Why's that?"

"Because he agreed to talk to McCloskey."

"I see."

"Is he really good, Dr. Delaware? As a detective?"

"Best I know."

"I think he is, too. I actually like him better than when I first met him. But I've really got to be sure. Because no one else seems to care. The police aren't doing anything—Chickering acts as if I'm wasting his time by calling. And *Don's* gone back to work—can you believe that?"

"What are you doing?"

"Staying right here and waiting. And praying—I haven't prayed since I was a little kid. Before you helped me." Pause. "I keep going back and forth between expecting her to walk in at any moment and feeling really sick to my stomach when I realize she could be—I've got to stay here. I don't want her coming home to an empty house."

"Makes sense."

"In the meantime, I think I'm going to try some hotels up north. Maybe Nevada, too, because that really isn't very far by car, is it? Can you think of anywhere else that would be logical?"

"I guess any of the bordering states," I said.

"Good idea."

"Is there anything you need, Melissa? Anything I can do for you?"

"No," she said quickly. "No, thanks."

"I'll be coming out there today anyway. To get my car."

"Oh. Sure. Whatever."

"If you want to talk, just let me know."

"Sure."

"Take care, Melissa."

"I will, Dr. Delaware. Better keep this line open, just in case. Bye."

The phone barked: *"Sturgis."*

"Well," I said, "it's a lot better than 'Yeah?' "

"Hey, I'm a working man now. What's up?"

"I just got off the phone with Melissa. She told me the two of you conferred."

"She talked; I listened. If that's conferred, I guess we did."

"Sounds as if she's been keeping herself busy."

"She worked all night. Kid's got energy."

"Adrenaline overdrive," I said.

"Want me to tell her to cool it?"

"No, it's okay for the time being. She's dealing with her anxiety by making herself feel useful. I am concerned about what'll happen if her mother doesn't show up soon and her defenses start to crack."

"Yeah. Well, she's got you for that. Any time you want her to ease off, just let me know."

"As if she'd listen."

"True," he said.

"So," I said, "nothing new?"

"Not a damn thing. The bulletin has been expanded statewide and into Nevada and Arizona, and the credit checks are all in place. So far no big-ticket purchases have been phoned in. Small stuff is tabulated when the merchants mail in the receipts, so we'll have to wait on that. I double-checked some of the places Melissa called—mostly airlines and luxury hotels. No one fitting Mommy's description checked in during the night. I'm waiting for the passport office to open at eight, just in case she opted for long-distance travel. Told Melissa to keep working the local lines. Actually, she's a damn good assistant."

"She said you agreed to see McCloskey."

"I told her I'd do it some time today. Can't hurt—nothing else is panning out."

"What time were you planning on visiting him?"

"Fairly soon. I've got a call in to Douse—the lawyer. He's supposed to get back to me by nine. I want to verify some of the things Anger told me. If Douse is willing to answer my questions over the phone, I'll take on McCloskey soon as I'm finished. If not, it'll mean a couple of hours' delay hassling Downtown. But McCloskey doesn't live that far from the law office, so either way I should be there before noon. Whether or not I find him's another story."

"Pick me up."

"Got plenty of free time?"

"Free enough."

"Fine," he said. "You buy lunch."

He came by at nine-forty, honking the horn of his Fiat. By the time I got outside, he'd parked in the carport.

"Lunch *and* transportation," he said, pointing to the Seville I'd picked up from Melissa's house. Milo had on a gray suit, white shirt, and blue tie.

"Where to?"

"Downtown. I'll direct you."

I drove down the Glen to Sunset, got on the 405 south, then switched to the Santa Monica Freeway east. Milo pushed his seat back as far as it went.

"How'd it go with the lawyer?" I said.

"More of the same doublespeak we got at First Fidoosh— I had to engage in the requisite pissing contest before he cooperated. But once he gave in, the guy's inherent laziness took over—more than happy to talk on the phone. Probably bill the estate for every second of it. Basically he confirmed everything Anger had said: Ramp gets fifty thou; Melissa takes the rest. Mom inherits if anything happens to Melissa. If both of them go before Melissa's had kids, all of it goes to charity."

"Any specific charities?"

"Medical research. I asked him to send me copies of all the documents—he said he'd need Melissa's written permission for that. Which I don't see as any big problem. I also asked him if he had any idea how Gina spent her allowance. Like Anger, he didn't seem to think a hundred and twenty grand was anything worth messing with."

Traffic was light until a mile before the interchange, where it started to curdle.

"Get off at Ninth and take it to L.A.," said Milo.

I followed his directions north on Los Angeles Street, drove through run-down blocks filled with fashion outlets shrieking bankruptcy bargains, discount appliance stores, import-export concerns, and pay parking lots. To the west a range of mirror-glass high-rises rose like synthetic mountains built on soft soil, Federal redevelopment funds, and Pacific Rim optimism. To the east was the industrial belt that divided Downtown from Boyle Heights.

Downtown was doing its usual split-personality routine: Fast-talking, fast-walking Power Dressers, Wannabee Tycoons, and stiff-lipped secretaries sharing turf with bleary-eyed, filth-encrusted human shells transporting their life stories in purloined shopping carts and verminous bedrolls.

At Sixth Street, the shells took over, hordes of them congregating on street corners, slumping in the doorways of boarded-up businesses, sleeping in the shadows of overflowing dumpsters. I caught a red light at Fifth. The taxi in the next lane shot the light and nearly ran over a long-haired, smudge-eyed blond man dressed in a sleeveless T-shirt and torn jeans. The man began cursing at the top of his lungs and, with scabbed tattooed hands, slapped the trunk of the cab as it sped on. Two uniformed cops issuing a jaywalking citation to a young Mexican girl across the street paused to observe the tantrum, then returned to their paperwork.

Half a block later I saw two skinny black men in baseball caps and topcoats veer off the sidewalk and come face-to-face under the sagging portico of a half-demolished SRO hotel. They lowered their heads and did a palm-slapping routine so well-coordinated it could have been choreographed by Balanchine. Then one man flashed a small wad of bills and the other bent quickly and retrieved something from his sock. A quick exchange and the two of them were on their way, heading in opposite directions. The entire transaction had taken ten seconds.

Milo saw me watching. "Ah, free enterprise. There's the place—park wherever you can."

He was pointing to a wide, flat-roofed three-story building on the east side of the street. The ground floor was faced with off-white tiles that brought to mind a bus station lavatory. The upper facade was pale-aqua stucco. A single row of barred windows ran along the top of the first story, too high to be reached from the street. The rest of the structure was a blank slab. Four or five men, mostly black, all ragged, congregated drowsily near the front door, which was topped by a dead neon deco-style sign that read ETERNAL HOPE MISSION.

All the parking spots in front of the building were taken, so I drove up ten yards and nosed into a space behind a Winnebago with MOBILE MEDICAL painted on the back. A larger and more energetic group of derelicts hovered nearby—at least two dozen men and three or four women, yapping and shuffling and rubbing their arms. As I turned off the ignition I noticed it wasn't health care they were after. A loose line had formed in front of an accordion-grated storefront. Another neon sign, these tubes flashing: $$ FOR PLASMA.

Milo removed a piece of paper from his pocket, unfolded it, and placed it in the Seville's front window. A 10 by 12 card reading LAPD VEHICLE: IN SERVICE.

"Be sure to lock," he said, slamming his door.

"Next time we take yours," I said, watching a bald, eye-patched man engage in an angry conversation with a dead elm tree. "You did it!" the man kept repeating, slapping the trunk of the tree every third or fourth utterance. The palms of his hands were bloody but there was a smile on his face.

"No way—they'd eat mine," said Milo. "C'mon."

The men hanging out in front of the mission noticed us long before we got to the front door, and stepped aside. Their shadows and their stench lingered. Several of them looked hungrily at my shoes—brown loafers, purchased a month ago, that still looked new. I thought how far $120,000 would go in this neighborhood.

Inside, the building was overheated and brightly lit. The front room was large, aqua, crowded with men sitting and lying across randomly placed green plastic chairs. The floors were black-and-gray linoleum, the plaster bare except for a single wooden crucifix tacked high to the welcoming wall.

More body odor, mixed with disinfectant, the bilious reek of stale vomit, and the suety smell of something simmering in broth. A young black man in a white polo shirt and tan slacks circulated among the men, carrying a clipboard and chained pen and a handful of brochures. A name tag above the tiger embroidered on his chest said GILBERT JOHNSON, STUDENT VOLUNTEER. He made his way among the men, consulting the board from time to time. Stopping and bending to talk to someone. Handing out a leaflet. Once in a while he got a response.

None of the men moved much. No conversation that I could see. But there was still noise from afar. Metallic rattles and machine pulses and a rhythmic baritone drone that had to be prayer.

I thought of a depot filled with travelers who'd lost their way.

Milo caught the young black man's eye. The man frowned and came over.

"Can I help you?" On the clipboard was a list of names, some of them followed by check marks.

"I'm looking for Joel McCloskey."

Johnson sighed. He was in his early twenties, had broad features, Asian eyes, a cleft chin, and skin not that much darker than Glenn Anger's tan.

"Again?"

"Is he here?"

"You'll have to speak to Father Tim first. One second."

He disappeared down a hallway to the right of the crucifix and came back almost immediately with a thin white man in his early thirties wearing a black shirt, clerical collar, and white jeans over high-top black-and-white basketball shoes.

The priest had jug ears, short light-brown hair, a wispy drooping mustache, and skinny hairless arms.

"Tim Andrus," he said in a soft voice. "I thought it was all cleared up with Joel."

"Just a few more questions," said Milo.

Andrus turned to Johnson. "Why don't you get back to bed-count, Gilbert? It's going to be tight tonight—we'll need to be really accurate."

"Sure thing, Father." Johnson shot a quick look at Milo and me, then returned to the men. Several of them had turned around and were staring at us.

The priest gave them a smile that wasn't reciprocated. Turning to us, he said, "The police were here quite a while last night and I was assured everything had been taken care of."

"Like I said, Father, just a few more questions."

"This kind of thing is very disruptive. Not so much for Joel. He's patient. But the rest of the men—most of them have had experiences with the police. Lots of them are mentally disturbed. The upset in routine . . ."

"Patient," said Milo. "Good of him."

Andrus gave a short, hard laugh. His ears had turned scarlet. "I know what you're thinking, Officer. Another bleeding-heart liberal do-gooder—and maybe I am. But that doesn't mean I'm unaware of Joel's history. When he came here six months ago he was totally forthright—he hasn't forgiven *himself* for what he did all those years ago. And it was a terrible thing, so of course I had my reservations about allowing him to serve. But if I stand for anything it's the power of forgiveness. The right to *be* forgiven. So I knew I couldn't turn him away. And over the past six months he's proved me right. No one's served more selflessly. He's not the same man he was twenty years ago."

"Good for him," said Milo. "But we'd still like to talk to him."

"She still hasn't shown up? The woman he . . ."

"Burned? Not yet."

"I'm so sorry. I'm sure Joel is, too."

"Why? He express his regrets, Father?"

"He still bears the burden of what he did—never stops blaming himself. Talking to the police brought it all back. He didn't sleep at all last night—was in the chapel, on his knees. I found him and we knelt there together. But he couldn't have had anything to do with her disappearance. He's been here all week, never left the building. Working double shifts. I can attest to that."

"What kind of work does he do?"

"Anything we need. For the past week it's been kitchen and latrine duty. He requests latrine duty—would do it full time."

"He have any friends?"

Andrus hesitated before answering. "Friends he'd hire to do wrong?"

"That's not what I asked, Father, but now that you mention it, yeah."

Andrus shook his head. "Joel knew that's exactly the way the police would think. He hired someone to sin once before; therefore it was inevitable that he'd do it again."

"Best predictor of the future's the past," said Milo.

Andrus touched his clerical collar and nodded. "It's an incredibly difficult job you do, Officer. A vital job—God bless all honest policemen. But one of the side effects can be fatalism. A belief that nothing ever changes for the better."

Milo looked around at the men on the plastic chairs. The few who were still staring turned away.

"You get to see much change around here, Father?"

Andrus twisted one end of his mustache. "Enough," he said, "to maintain my faith."

"McCloskey one of those who's maintained your faith?"

The flush spread from the priest's ears to his neck. "I've been here five years, Officer. Believe me, I'm not naïve. I don't take convicted felons off the street and expect them to turn into someone like Gilbert. But Gilbert's had a good home, nurturance, education. He's starting from a different baseline. Someone like Joel has to earn my trust—earn a higher trust. It did help that he brought references."

"From where, Father?"

"Other missions."

"Here in town?"

"No. Arizona and New Mexico. He worked with the Indians, put six years of his life into helping others. Paying his legal debt and enlarging himself as a human being. Those he worked with had only good things to say about him."

Milo said nothing.

The priest smiled. "And yes, that did help him obtain parole. But he came here as a free man, Officer. In a legal sense. He works here because he chooses to, not because he has to. And in answer to your question about friends, he has none—sticks to himself, denies himself worldly pleasures. A very tough cycle of work and prayer constitutes his entire life."

"Sounds pretty darn saintly," said Milo.

Anger tightened the priest's face. He struggled to fight it and managed to put on a calm expression. But when he spoke, his voice was constricted. "He had nothing to do with that poor woman's disappearance. I really don't see why there's a need to—"

"That poor *woman* has a *name*," said Milo. "Gina Marie Ramp."

"I'm aware of tha—"

"*She's* been sticking to herself, too, Father. Cut off from worldly pleasures. But in her case, it's not out of choice. For twenty years, since the day McCloskey's hired creep destroyed her face, she's been living up in a room, too scared to go out into the world. No parole for her, Father. So I'm sure you can understand why lots of people are upset at the fact that she's disappeared. And I hope you'll find it in your heart to forgive *me* if I try to get to the bottom of it. Even if it means inconveniencing Mr. McCloskey."

Andrus bowed his head and clasped his hands in front of him. For a moment I thought he was praying. But he looked

up and his lips were still. All the color was gone from
his face.

"Forgive *me,* Officer. It's been a hard week—two men
died in their beds; two more were sent over to County
General with suspected tuberculosis." He cocked his head
toward the men in the chairs. "We've got a hundred more
heads than beds, no letup in sight, and the archdiocese wants
me to raise a larger share of my own funds." His shoulders
dropped. "One searches for small victories. I've been trying
to think of Joel as one."

"Maybe he is," said Milo. "But we'd still like to talk
to him."

The priest shrugged. "Come, I'll take you to him."

He'd never asked to see ID. Didn't even know our names.

The first door in the hall led to an enormous dining hall
where food smells finally overtook the stink of unwashed
bodies. Wooden picnic tables covered by peacock-blue oilcloth were arranged in tandem, creating five long rows. Men
sat hunched over their food, cradling their plates protec-
tively. Prison dining. Spooning and chewing nonstop with
all the joy of wind-up toys.

Along the back wall was a steam table fronted by a glass
partition and aluminum counter. Men were lined up holding
their plates out, Oliver Twist–style. Three figures dressed in
white shirts and aprons and hairnets ladled out food.

Father Andrus said, "Wait here, please," and we stood by
the door as he walked behind the steam table and said
something to the middle server. Still working, the man
nodded, handed his ladle to the priest, and stepped backward. Father Andrus began distributing food. The man in
white wiped his hands on his apron, stepped around the
table, through the line, and came toward us.

He was about five five, with a stoop that robbed him of
an inch he couldn't spare. The apron reached below his knees
and was stained with food. He shuffled, barely raising his
feet from the linoleum, and his arms remained at his sides as

if glued there. Strands of white hair straggled from under the hairnet and adhered to a pasty, moist forehead. The face below was long and sallow, thin yet flabby. An aquiline nose had conceded defeat to gravity. White eyebrows. No fat under his chin, but a flap of loose flesh shook as he came closer. His eyes were hooded, dark, deep-set, very tired.

He walked up to us, expressionless, and said, "Hello," in a flat, phlegmy voice.

"Mr. McCloskey?"

Nod. "I'm Joel." Listless. Open pores on nose and cheeks. Deep crevices flanking a down-turned, dry-lipped mouth. Eyes nearly shut under the heavy lids, yellowish scleras surrounding nearly black irises. I wondered when he'd last had a liver-function test.

"We're here to talk about Gina Ramp, Joel."

"She hasn't been found." A statement.

"No, she hasn't. Any theories you'd like to share about what might have happened to her?"

McCloskey's eyes shifted to one of the tables. Some of the men had stopped eating. Others cast covetous glances at the untouched food.

"Could we talk in my room?"

"Sure, Joel."

He shuffled out the door and turned right into the corridor. We passed dormitories crammed with folding cots, some of them occupied, and a closed door marked INFIRMARY. Moans of pain filtered through plywood and echoed along the hall. McCloskey turned toward the sound, briefly, but didn't break step. Redirecting his gaze forward, he shuffled toward a brown-painted staircase at the back of the hall. The treads were covered with hard rubber, and the banister felt greasy.

We followed his steady, slow climb up three flights. Now the disinfectant smell triumphed.

Just off the landing on floor three was another closed door taped with a piece of shirt cardboard. JOEL was written on it in black marker.

The knob had a keyhole, but he turned it and the door opened. He held it and waited for us to enter.

The room was half the size of Gina Ramp's closet—no more than eight by eight, with a cot covered by a gray wool blanket, a wooden nightstand painted white, and a narrow three-drawer, wood-grain chest. A Bible sat atop the drawer, along with a hot plate, a can opener, a cellophane-wrapped cracker-and-peanut-butter combo, a half-empty jar of pickled beets, and a tin of Vienna sausage. A calendar painting of a haloed Jesus looked down approvingly on the cot. A yellowed, fly-specked shade was half drawn on a single barred window. Beyond the bars was a wall of gray brick. Light came from a bare bulb in the center of a ceiling spotted with mildew.

Barely enough room to stand. I felt like holding on to something but didn't want to touch anything.

McCloskey said, "Sit. If you want."

Milo looked at the cot and said, "That's okay."

The three of us remained standing. Close together, but miles apart. Like subway straphangers resolute upon isolation.

Milo said, "Any theories, Joel?"

McCloskey shook his head. "I've thought about it. A lot. Since the other police were here. I hope what happened is she got well enough to go out by herself and . . ."

"And what?"

"And liked it."

"You want the best for her, do you?"

Nod.

"Now that you're a free man and the state can't tell you what to do."

A faint smile formed on McCloskey's pale lips. The corners of his mouth were crusted with something white and flaky.

"Something funny, Joel?"

"Freedom. That's long gone."

"For Gina, too."

McCloskey closed his eyes, opened them, sat heavily on the cot, removed his hairnet, and rested his brow in one hand. The crown of his head was bald, the hair around it white and gray, cut short and spiky. It might have looked fashionable on an eighteen-year-old Melrose marauder. On an old man it resembled exactly what it was: a do-it-yourself job.

Old man.

Fifty-three.

He looked seventy.

"What I want doesn't matter," he said.

"Not unless you're still after her, Joel."

The jaundiced eyes squeezed shut again. The neck-flap trembled. "I wasn't— No. I'm not."

"Not what?"

McCloskey held the hairnet with both hands, fingers poking through the mesh. Stretching it. "After her." A sub-whisper.

"Were you starting to say you never *were* after her, Joel?"

"No. I . . ." McCloskey scratched his head, then shook it. "It was a long time ago."

"Sure was," said Milo. "But history has a way of repeating itself."

"No," said McCloskey, very quietly but with force. "No, never. My life is . . ."

"What?"

"Over. Everything's out."

"What's out, Joel?"

McCloskey put one hand on his gut. "The fire. The feelings." The hand dropped. "All I do is wait."

"Wait for what, Joel?"

"Peace. Blank space." A fearful glance at Milo, then over at the picture of Jesus.

"Pretty religious guy, are you, Joel?"

"It . . . helps."

"Helps what?"

"Waiting."

Milo bent his knees, cupped his hands on them, and lowered his face until it was nearly level with McCloskey's.

"Why'd you burn her, Joel?"

McCloskey's hands began to shake. He said, "No," then crossed himself.

"Why, Joel? What'd she do to make you hate her so much?"

"No."

"C'mon, Joel. What would it hurt to tell after all these years?"

Headshakes. "I—it's not . . ."

"Not what?"

"No. I . . . sinned."

"Confess your sin, Joel."

"No . . . please." Tears. More trembling.

"Isn't confession part of salvation, Joel? *Full* confession?"

McCloskey licked his lips, put his hands together, and mumbled something.

Milo bent lower. "What's that, Joel?"

"Done my confession."

"Have you?"

Nod.

McCloskey swung his legs onto the bed and lay down on his back. Arms folded over his chest. Staring up at the ceiling, mouth agape. Beneath the apron his trousers were ancient tweed, tailored for a man thirty pounds heavier and two inches taller. The cuffs were frayed and rimmed stiff with black grime. The soles of his shoes were perforated in several places and clotted with dried food. Gray yarn peeked through some of the holes, bare flesh through others.

I said, "For you it may be all in the past. But understanding it would help her. And her daughter. After all these years the whole family's still trying to comprehend."

McCloskey stared at me. His eyes moved back and forth, as if following traffic. His lips moved soundlessly.

Deliberation. For a moment I thought he was going to open up.

Then he gave his head a violent shake, sat up, untied his apron, and slipped it over his head. His shirt bagged on him. Undoing the top three buttons, he pulled the fabric apart and exposed a hairless chest.

Hairless, but not unmarked.

Most of his skin was the color of spoiled milk. But a splotch of pink, puckered flesh, twice as wide as a hand, gnarled as briar, covered most of his left breast. The nipple was gone; in its place was a glossy, clabbered depression. Scar streaks flowed from the primary splash, like rosy paint, ending midway down his rib cage.

He stretched the shirt farther, thrust the ruined tissue forward. A heartbeat pulsed the lumpy mound. Very fast. His face was white, drawn, anointed with sweat.

"Someone do that to you at Quentin?" said Milo.

McCloskey smiled and looked back at Jesus again.

A smile of pride.

"I would take her pain away and eat it," he said. "Swallow it and let it be me. All of it. Everything."

He placed one hand on his chest, crossed the other arm over it.

"Sweet Lord," he said. "The sacrament of pain."

Then he began to mumble in something that sounded like Latin.

Milo looked down at him.

McCloskey kept praying.

"Have a nice day, Joel," said Milo. When McCloskey didn't respond, he said, "Have a nice wait."

No break in the white-haired man's benedictions.

"All this self-flagellation notwithstanding, Joel, if there's something you could be doing to help us find her, your salvation's not worth a goddam."

McCloskey looked up—just for a second—the yellow eyes filled with terror: the panic of someone who'd wagered everything on a deal gone very sour.

Then he dropped to his knees, so hard it had to hurt, and resumed his supplication.

As we drove away, Milo said, "So, what's the diagnosis?"

"Pathetic. If what we just saw was real."

"That's what I'm asking—was it?"

"I can't be sure," I said. "My instinct is to assume someone who'd hire a hit man wouldn't balk at a bit of theatrics. But something about him was believable."

"Yeah," he said. "I thought so, too. Would you call him schizophrenic?"

"I didn't see any overtly disturbed thinking, but he didn't say much, so maybe." I drove half a block. "*Pathetic* fits better than anything technical."

"What do you think drove him that far down?"

"Drugs, booze, prison, guilt. Singly or in combination. Or all of the above."

"Boy," he said, smiling, "you sound like a hard guy."

I looked out the car window at the derelicts and junkies and bag ladies. Urban zombies squandering their allotment of breath on a wet-brained haze. A very old man was sleeping on the curb, dirt-caked belly-up, snoring through rotted gums. Or maybe he wasn't old at all. "Must be the environment."

"Miss the green hills of San Labrador?"

"No," I said, realizing it as the words left my mouth. "How about something in the middle?"

"How about." He let out a tension-sloughing laugh. It wasn't enough, and he ran his hand over his face. Drummed the dashboard. Opened the window and closed it and stretched his legs without attaining comfort.

"His chest," I said. "Think it was self-inflicted?"

"Cross his heart and hope to die? That's obviously what he wanted us to think. The sacrament of pain. Shit."

Growling with contempt, but he looked ill at ease.

I made a stab at mind reading. "If he's still into pain he might still be into inflicting it on others?"

He nodded. "All the guilty talk and praying, the guy told us exactly nothing. So maybe he isn't all that fucked up, mentally. *My* instinct doesn't yell Prime Suspect, but I'd hate to be caught in an aw-shucks situation if our combined hunch quotient turns out to be low."

"So what's next?"

"First find me a phone booth. I wanna call in, see if anything's turned up on the lady. If it hasn't, let's go talk to Bayliss—the probation officer."

"He's retired."

"I know. I got his home address before I came by. Middle-class neighborhood. You should feel comfortable."

20

I found a phone booth near the Children's Museum and waited in a no-parking zone as Milo used it. He was on the line long enough for two meter maids to drive by, prepare to cite me, only to be held at bay by the LAPD cardboard. Most fun I'd had in a long time. I savored it while watching parents herd their young toward the entrance to the museum.

Milo came back jingling change and shaking his head. "Nothing."

"Who'd you speak to?"

"Highway Patrol, again. Then one of Chickering's lackeys and Melissa."

"How's she doing?" I said, pulling into traffic.

"Still hyper. Making calls. She said one of the Gabneys phoned just a while ago—the husband. Expressing concern."

"The goose with the golden egg," I said. "Planning on telling Melissa about the Cassatt?"

"Any reason to?"

I thought about that. "Not that I can see—no use getting her riled up about something else."

"I told her about McCloskey. That from what I could see we were talking brain death, but that I'd keep my eye on him. It seemed to calm her down."

"Placebo?"

"Got anything stronger?"

I picked up the Harbor Freeway at Third, switched to the 10 west, and exited at Fairfax, heading north. Milo directed me to Crescent Heights, then farther north, just past Olympic, where I turned left on Commodore Sloat, passed a block of office buildings, then entered the Carthay Circle district, a tree-shaded enclave of small, exceedingly well-kept Spanish and mock-Tudor houses.

Milo recited an address and I matched the numerals to a shake-roofed, brick and madder-stucco cottage set on a corner lot two blocks up. The garage was a miniature clone of the house behind a hedge-bordered cobbled drive. A twenty-year-old Mustang, white and shining, sat in the drive. Moisture pools beneath the chassis and a neatly coiled garden hose rested near the rear tire.

The front yard was rich green lawn worthy of Dublin, edged with beds of flowers—taller plantings of camellias, azaleas, hydrangeas, agapanthus, backing impatiens, begonia, and a white fringe of alyssum. A cobbled path ran up the middle. To the left was a weeping paper-birch triplet. A high-waisted gray-haired man in khaki shirt, blue pants, and a pith helmet inspected its branches and plucked away dead leaves. A chamois cloth hung out of one rear pocket.

We got out. Traffic from Olympic was a baritone drone. Birds sang harmony. Not a particle of trash on the streets. The man turned as we walked up the path. Sixtyish, narrow shoulders, long arms, large hands. Long, hound-dog face under the helmet. White mustache and goatee, black-framed eyeglasses. It was only when we were a few feet away that I realized he was African-featured. Skin as light as mine, dotted with freckles. Eyes golden-brown, the color of school-desk oak.

One hand remained on the tree as he watched us. He lowered it, ground a birch cone between his fingers. The particles showered to the ground.

"Gilbert Bayliss?" said Milo.

"Who's asking?"

"My name's Sturgis. I'm a detective—private—working on the disappearance of Mrs. Gina Ramp. Several years ago she was victimized by someone you used to handle at the Parole Department. Joel McCloskey."

"Good old Joel," said Bayliss, removing his hat. His hair was a thick, nappy, salt-and-pepper cap. "Private eye, huh?"

Milo nodded. "For the time being. On leave from LAPD."

"Voluntary?"

"Not exactly."

Bayliss peered at Milo. "Sturgis. I know that name—know your face, too."

Milo didn't move a muscle.

Bayliss said, "I got it. You're the one hit the other cop on TV. Something about interdepartmental intrigue—news never did make clear what it was all about. Not that I want to know. I'm out of all that."

"Congratulations," said Milo.

"Earned it. So how long they cooling you out for?"

"Six months."

"Paid or unpaid?"

"Unpaid."

Bayliss clucked his tongue. "So in the meantime you're paying bills. I wasn't allowed to do that. One thing that bothered me about the job—no room to expand opportunities. How do you like it so far?"

"It's a job."

Bayliss looked at me. "Who's this? Another LAPD bad boy?"

"Alex Delaware," I said.

"Dr. Delaware," said Milo. "He's a psychologist. Treating Mrs. Ramp's daughter."

"Melissa Dickinson," I said. "You talked to her about a month ago."

"I seem to remember something like that," said Bayliss.

"Psychologist, huh? I wanted to be one of those once. Figured what I was doing was mostly psychology, anyway—why not get paid better? Took some classes at Cal State—got enough credits for a master's but no time to write a thesis or take the exams, so that was that." He peered at me more closely. "What're you doing running around with him? Psychoanalyzing everyone?"

"We just paid a visit to McCloskey," I said. "Detective Sturgis thought it might be useful for me to observe him."

"Aha," said Bayliss. "Good old Joel. You seriously suspect he's been up to something?"

"Just checking him out," said Milo.

"Getting paid by the hour and piling up those hours—Don't get yourself worked up, soldier. I don't have to talk to you if I don't want."

"I realize that, Mr.—"

"Twenty-three years I spent following routine, taking orders from people a heck of a lot stupider than me. Working toward a twenty-five-year pension so that my wife and I could go traveling. Two years short she had the bad manners to leave me. Massive stroke. Got one kid in the army, over in Germany, married a German girl, never comes home. So the last two years I've been making my own rules. Last six months I've been getting good at it. Understand?"

Milo gave a long, slow nod.

Bayliss smiled, put his helmet back on. "Just as long as we've got a meeting of the minds on that."

"We do," said Milo. "If there's something you can tell us about McCloskey that might help us find Mrs. Ramp, I'd be much obliged."

"Good old Joel," said Bayliss. He touched his goatee, stared at Milo. "You know, there were plenty of times during those twenty-five years that I wanted to punch someone. Never did it. 'Cause of the pension. The trip the wife and I were going to take. When you punched that paper-pusher, it made me smile. I was in a low mood, thinking about things that had happened and those that hadn't. You gave me a chuckle, lasted through the evening. That's why I remember you." He smiled. "Funny thing, your walking up like this. Must be destiny. Come on in the house."

His living room was dark, neat, furnished with heavy carved pieces not quite old or good enough to be antiques. Lots of doilies and figurines and feminine touches. On the wall above the mantel were framed black-and-white photos of big bands and jazz combos, the musicians all black, and one close-up of a young, clean-shaven, pomaded Bayliss, dressed in a white dinner jacket and formal shirt and tie, and holding a slide trombone.

He said, "That was my first love. Trained classically—at Juilliard. But no one was hiring colored trombonists, so I settled for swing and bebop, did the rib circuit—traveled with Skootchie Bartholomew for five years. Ever hear of him?"

I shook my head.

He smiled. "No one did. Tell the truth, the band wasn't that good. Shooting heroin before every gig and thinking they were playing better than they actually were. I didn't want to live like that, so I quit, came out here, tooted for whoever would listen, did a few record things—you listen to 'Magic Love' by the Sheiks, some of that other doo-wop foolishness, that's me in the background. Finally got a trial run with Lionel Hampton."

He went over and touched one of the photos. "This is me, first row. That band was all power, really heavy on the brass. Playing with 'em was like trying to ride a big brass hurricane, but I did okay—Lionel kept me on. Then the big-band market dried up and Lionel took the whole outfit to Europe and Japan. I didn't see any point in that, went back to school, took the civil service. Haven't played since. My wife liked the pictures. . . . I've got to take them down, get some real art. You want some coffee?"

Both of us declined.

"Sit if you want."

We did. Bayliss settled in a soft-looking floral chair with lace antimacassars on the arms.

"Good old Joel," he said. "Wouldn't worry too much about him in terms of major felonies."

"Why's that?" said Milo.

"He's a nothing." Bayliss tapped his head. "Nothing there. When I read his file I expected some serious psychopath. Then this skinny little *nothing* walks in, all yessirs and nosirs, not an ounce of fight left in him. And I'm not talking bootlicking. Not the usual routine you get from your active psychopath—you know how they try to come across like good boys. Every joker I dealt with over twenty-five years thought he was Oscar-quality, smarter than everyone else. Just had to put on the act and no one'd see through him."

"That's the truth," said Milo. "Even though it rarely works."

"Yeah. Funny how they never stop to think about why they're spending most of their lives in six-by-six cells. But old Joel was different—this was no act. The man had everything stripped out of him. Course if you just saw him, you know that."

"How often did he come to see you?" I said.

"Just a few times—four or five. By the time he got to L.A., he really wasn't on official parole. The Department *requested* he check in until he got settled. Covering its derrière, just in case. They're really sensitive to playing it by the rules, so if something goes wrong and the victim's family gets on *Geraldo*, they can produce paperwork and show they've done the right thing. So it was really more a formality—he could have ignored it, but he didn't. Showed up once a week. We spent our ten minutes and that was it. Tell the truth, I wish I'd had more like him. Toward the end my caseload was sixty-three crooks, and some of them really did bear looking into."

Milo said, "Parole's usually three years. How come he did six?"

"Part of a deal. After he got out of Quentin, he asked to leave the state. The Department said okay if he could obtain structured placement and double his time. He found some sort of Indian reservation—out in Arizona, I think. Did three years there, then moved somewhere else, another state—I don't recall exactly—and did three there."

"Why the move?" I said.

"From what I recall," he said, "the first place was funded by a grant that got canceled, so he had to move on. The second place was Catholic—I guess he figured unless the Pope canceled, he'd be okay."

"Why the move to L.A.?"

"I asked him about that and he didn't have much of an answer—not one that made sense, anyway. Something about original sin, a lot of mumbo-jumbo about salvation. Basically what I think he was getting at was that he'd sinned here—against your missing lady—so he had to be a *good* boy *here* to even the score with the Almighty. I didn't push him on it—like I said, he wasn't even obligated to show up. It was a formality."

"Any idea what he did with his time?" said Milo.

"Far as I know he was over at that mission, full time. Cleaning toilets and washing dishes."

"Eternal Hope."

"Yeah, that's the one. Found himself another Catholic place. From what I could tell, he never left his room, never consorted with known felons or used dope. The priest confirmed it over the phone. If I'da had sixty-three like him, my job would have been a breeze."

"Did he ever talk about his crime?" I said.

"I talked to *him* about it—first time he came in. Read from his sentencing report, the judge calling him a monster and all that. I liked to do that with all of them at the outset. Establish some ground rules, let them know *I* knew who I was dealing with, eliminate a lot of nonsense. Most of them leave stir still claiming they're innocent as Baby Jesus. You try to break through that delusion, get some insight going, if there's gonna be any hope. Like doing psychoanalysis, right?"

I nodded.

"Did McCloskey develop any insight?" said Milo.

"Didn't need to. He came in *breathing* guilt, told me straight out he was worthless and didn't deserve to live. I told him that was probably true, then read the sentencing report out loud to him. He just sat there and took it—like it was some kind of medical treatment that was for his own good. About as close to a walking dead man as I'd ever seen. After a couple of times with him I found myself actually getting sorry for him—the way you feel sorry for a dog that's been hit by a car. And that's something that doesn't come easy to me. I've worked a long time fighting my sympathies."

"He ever say why he burned her?" said Milo.

"Nope," said Bayliss. "And I asked him about that, too. Because his file said he'd never owned up to any motive. But he didn't have much to say—kind of mumbled and wouldn't get into that."

A scratch of the goatee. Bayliss removed his glasses, wiped them with a handkerchief, and replaced them. "I tried to work on him a bit—think I phrased it to him in terms of his duty to her, how once he'd done a crime like that, she owned him. In a spiritual sense—I was trying to appeal to his religious side. Whenever they tried the religious stuff I turned it right back on them. But it didn't work with him— he just sat there and stared at the floor. It was all I could do to keep a conversation going for the ten minutes. And he wasn't faking it—after twenty-five years I can tell. We're talking nothing. Total zombie."

"Any idea why?" I said. "What got him to that state?"

Bayliss shrugged. "You're the psychologist."

"Okay," said Milo. "Thanks. Anything else?"

"Nothing. What's the story with the lady?"

"She left her house, drove off, and hasn't been heard from since."

"Left when?"

"Yesterday."

Bayliss frowned. "One day gone and they hire a P.I.?"

"It's not your typical situation," said Milo. "She's been housebound for a long time. Hardly left her home."

"How long's a long time?"

"Since he burned her."

"She's been severely agoraphobic since then," I said.

"Oh. That's too bad." He looked as if he meant it. "Yeah, I can see why her folks would be worried."

We walked back outside. Bayliss looked thoughtful. He accompanied us all the way to the car.

"Hope you find her soon," he said. "If there was something I could tell you about Joel that would help you, I would. But I doubt he has anything to do with it."

"Why's that?" said Milo.

"Inertia. The dead zone. He's like a snake that got stepped on one time too many and lost its poison."

I drove home on Olympic. Though his seat was pushed all the way back, Milo positioned himself with his knees drawn up. Opting for discomfort. Looking out the window.

At Roxbury, I said, "What's up?"

He kept his eyes on the landscape. "Guys like McCloskey. Who the hell knows what's real and what's not? Bayliss is so sure the asshole's run out of steam, but he admitted he barely knew him. Basically, he took McCloskey at face value because the sleaze showed up voluntarily and didn't make waves—your typical bureaucratic response. Shit flushes through the system and as long as the pipes don't back up, no one cares."

"You think McCloskey bears further watching?"

"If the lady doesn't show up real soon and no new leads develop, I'm gonna mosey on by again, try to catch him off guard. But before I do that, I'm gonna get to a phone, call in some markers, and try to find out if the scumbag's been consorting with any known felons. You got anything planned for yourself?"

"Nothing urgent."

"If you feel like it, take a run out to the beach. Check out the second house, just in case she's bunked out there and not telling anyone. It's a long drive and I don't want to kill that much time—course I don't think it'll lead anywhere."

"Sure."

"Here's the address," he said.

I took the slip of paper and continued to drive.

He looked at his watch. "Might as well leave soon. While the sun's still out. Play sleuth and work on your tan—hell, take out your boogie board and catch a wave."

"Watson goes gnarly?"

"Something like that."

21

No messages at home. I stayed long enough to give the fish a heavy feed, hoping to keep them away from the few egg clusters that remained. Then back on Sunset, heading west, by two-thirty.

Day at the beach.

I pretended it was going to be fun.

I hit Pacific Coast Highway, saw blue water and brown bodies.

Robin and I had done this drive, so many times.

Linda and I had done it once. The second time we'd been out together.

Alone was different.

I stayed away from those thoughts, paid attention to the Malibu coastline. Never the same, always inviting. Kama Sutra real estate.

Probably why people went into hock in order to get a piece of it. Living with black flies and corrosion and highway mayhem, and waxing amnesiac about the inevitable cycle of mud slides, fires, and killer storms.

Arthur Dickinson's piece was choice. Five miles up from Point Dume, past the sprawling public beach at Zuma, and a left turn onto Broad Beach Road just past the rodeo rink at Trancas Canyon.

Western Malibu, where the tacky motels and surf shops have long disappeared, ranches and tree farms fill the land-side of Pacific Coast Highway, and the dinner hour is domi-nated by sunsets of unlikely hue.

The address Milo had given me took me to the far end of the road. A half mile of white silicon heaped into sine-wave dunes. Fifty-by-a-hundred-foot mounds of dubious geology going for four million plus. At that price, architecture be-comes a competitive sport.

The Dickinson/Ramp place was a one-story saltbox with silvered wood sides and a flat brown gravel roof, behind a low chain-link fence that provided no privacy and gave the public visual access to the beach. The house was flanked on both sides by free-form, two-story ice cream scoops. One was vanilla stucco, still under construction; the other, pistachio trimmed with raspberry. Both lots were blocked by prison-bar electric gates. Green tennis-court tarp behind Vanilla. A FOR SALE sign in front of Pistachio. Alarm warnings on both.

But no security system for the saltbox. I lifted the latch and walked right in.

No landscaping, either—just a thorny mess of orange bougainvillea climbing part of the fence. Instead of a garage, a cement pad over sand, wide enough for two vehicles. A yam-colored VW van with a ski rack on its roof was parked carelessly, taking up both widths. Nowhere to conceal a Rolls-Royce.

I approached the house, absorbing the heat of the sand through the soles of my shoes. Still wearing a jacket and tie and feeling like a salesman for something. I could smell the tang of the ocean, see the high-tide spray percolate over the dunes. A V-formation of brown pelicans cut through the sky. A hundred feet beyond the breakers, someone was windsurfing.

The front door was brine-eaten pine with a knob that had greened and crusted. The windows were cloudy and moist to the touch and someone had finger-written CLEAN ME on one of the panes. Glass wind chimes dangled over the doorway, swaying and striking one another, but the roar of the ocean killed their song.

I knocked. Got no answer. Knocked again, waited, and went over to one of the streaked windows.

Single room. Unlit. Hard to make out details, but I squinted and discerned a small, open-shelved kitchen to the left, combo bedroom and living area filling the rest of the space. Futon unrolled on a dull pine floor. A few pieces of furniture—bargain rattan with Hawaiian print cushions, beanbag chair, plain-wrap coffee table. On the beach side, sliding glass doors led to a shaded patio. Through them I could see a couple of folding lounges, a rise of dune, and teal-colored water.

A man stood out on the sand, directly in front of the patio. Knees bent, back rounded, curling a barbell.

I walked around.

Todd Nyquist. The tennis instructor was braced ankle-deep in the sand, wearing skimpy black briefs, a leather power-lifter's girdle, and fingerless weight gloves, straining and grimacing as he hefted and lowered. The iron discs on the bar were the size of manhole covers. Two on each end. His eyes were clenched shut, his mouth was open, and his long yellow hair was wet and limp and drooping down his back. Sweating and grunting, he kept lifting, keeping his back immobile, putting all the strain on his arms. Curling in rhythm to the beat that blared from a boombox near his feet.

Rock 'n' roll. Thin Lizzie. "The Boys Are Back in Town."

Manic beat. It had to be torture keeping up with it. Nyquist's biceps were engorged flesh carvings.

He did six more solid reps, then a few shaky ones, until the music stopped. Letting out a hoarse cry that could have been pain or triumph, he bent his knees further and, with his eyes still closed, lowered the barbell into the sand. He exhaled noisily, began to straighten, shook his head and sprayed sweat. The beach was nearly empty. Despite the weather, only a handful of people strolled along the shoreline, mostly with dogs.

I said, "Hello, Todd." He hadn't come fully upright and the surprise nearly knocked him off his feet.

He recovered gracefully, planting his soles, then bouncing like a dancer. Opening his eyes wide, he stared, processed, and gave a wide smile of recognition.

"The doctor, right? I met you over at the big house."

"Alex Delaware." I came closer and held out my hand. My shoes filled with sand.

He looked at his gloved hands and kept them up in the air. "Wouldn't, if I were you. Pretty rank, Doc."

I lowered mine.

"Just doing my pumps," he said. "What brings you out here?"

"Looking for Mrs. Ramp."

"Here?" He seemed genuinely baffled.

"They're looking for her everywhere, Todd. Asked me to come down here and check."

"That's really weird," he said.

"What is?"

"Uh, the whole thing. Her disappearing. It really is freaky. Where could she be?"

"That's what we're trying to find out."

"Yeah. Right. Well, you won't find her here, that's for sure. She's never been here. Not once. At least not since I've been living here." He turned toward the ocean, stretched, and inhaled. "Can you imagine owning a place like this and never being here?"

"It is gorgeous," I said. "How long have you been living here?"

"Year and a half."

"You rent the place?"

He smiled wider, as if proud to possess some important secret. Removing the gloves, he fluffed his hair. More sweat droplets flew.

"It's a trade thing," he said. "Tennis and personal training for Mr. R. in return for a place to stay. But it's not really my crib. Mostly I'm other places, traveling around—last year I went on two cruises. Up to Alaska, and down to Cabo. Did an exercise class for old ladies. I also give lessons at the Brentwood Country Club, and I've got lots of friends in the city. I sleep here maybe once or twice a week."

"Sounds like a good deal."

"It is—do you know what this place would rent for? Even being dinky."

"Five thousand a month?"

"Try ten for an all-year-round, eighteen to twenty during the summer, and that's with the heat not even working. But Mr. and Mrs. R., they've been really cool about letting me stay here when I want, just as long as I make the drive over to Smogsville and give Mr. R. a good workout when he wants."

"He never comes here?"

His smile eroded. "Not really. Why should he?"

"No reason. It just seems like a good place for a workout."

We heard female conversation and turned toward it. Two string-bikinied girls, around eighteen or nineteen, were walking a sheepdog. The dog kept veering away from the water, tugging on its leash, making the girl on the other end work. She fought for a while, finally gave up and let the dog lead her diagonally across the beach. The other girl jogged along. The dog stopped straining when it reached the property line of the vanilla scoop. The three of them headed our way.

Nyquist hadn't taken his eyes off them. Both had manes of long, thick, sun-coarsened hair. One blonde, one redhead. Tall and long-legged, with perfect thighs and laughing California girl faces straight out of a soft drink commercial. The blonde's bikini was white; the redhead's, acid green. When they were a few feet away, the dog stopped and coughed and began shaking itself. The redhead bent and petted it, revealing heavy, freckled breasts.

Nyquist whispered, "Whoa." Raising his voice: "Yo! Traci! Maria!"

The girls turned.

"Hey," he said, still shouting, "how's it going, ladies?"

"Fine, Todd," said the redhead.

"Hey, Todd," said the blonde.

Nyquist stretched and grinned and rubbed a washboard abdomen. "Looking good, ladies. Whatsamatter, old Bernie still afraid of the water?"

"Yeah," said the redhead. "What a chicken." To the dog: "Aren't you, baby? Isn't Bernie just a little old wussy chicken-dog."

As if comprehending the insult, the dog turned away, kicked sand, and coughed again.

"Hey," said Nyquist, "sounds like he's got a cold."

"Naw, he's just chicken," said the redhead.

"Vitamin C'll do something for that. And B-12—crush it up and put it in his chow."

"Who's this, Todd?" said the blonde. "A new friend?"

"Friend of the landlord's."

"Oh," said the redhead, smiling. She looked at the blonde, then at me. "Gonna raise Todd's rent?"

I smiled.

Nyquist said, "One sec, Doc," and bounded over to the girls. Putting his arms around them, he drew them in, as if for a football huddle. They seemed surprised but were pliant. He muttered to them, smiling all the while. Rubbing the back of the blonde's neck. Massaging the redhead's waist. The dog nosed his ankle but he ignored it. The girls looked uncomfortable but Nyquist seemed oblivious to that, too. Finally, they drew away.

Nyquist held on to their wrists for a moment, let go, stretched his grin, patted both their rumps as they ran off. The dog followed, lumbering.

He came back. "Pardon the interlude. Got to keep the wenches in line."

Aiming for sexual bravado but coming across too strong—almost caricaturist. It reminded me of his interaction with Gina a couple of days ago. Nuances of tension that I hadn't thought much of at the time.

I could handle a Pepsi, Mrs. R. Or anything else you got that's cold and sweet.

I'll get Madeleine to fix you something.

Older woman, young stud? Tennis for hubby, other kind of lessons for the lady of the house?

Hardly original, but people so seldom were when they transgressed.

I said, "Any idea where Mrs. R. might be, Todd?"

"No," he said, scrunching his face. "It's really a mystery. I mean, where could she go, being afraid and all that?"

"She ever talk to you about her fears?"

"No, we—not at all. But hanging around someone's house you just pick stuff up." He glanced toward the house. "Wanna have a beer or something?"

"No, thanks. Got to be heading back."

"Bummer," he said, but he looked relieved. "You look in pretty good shape. What do you do in terms of workout?"

"Bit of running."

"How much?"

"Six to ten miles a week."

"Better watch it—running's ultra high-impact. Four times your weight every stride. Bad for the joints. Bad for the spine, too."

"I've got a cross-country ski machine now."

"Excellent—the ultimate aerobic. If you alternate that with some muscle-lengthening weight-training, you'll be doing yourself the ultimate favor."

"Thanks for the advice."

"No prob. If you're interested in some one-on-one training, give me a call. I don't have any cards with me but you can always get me through Mr. and Mrs.— through Mr. R." Shaking his head. "Shee, that was dumb. Sure hope they find her—she's a real nice lady."

I walked back to the Seville and took a few moments to

look at the ocean. The windsurfer was out of view but the pelicans had returned and were swooping and retrieving. Seagulls and terns followed in their wake, content with the leavings. A couple of oblong gray cigars were visible floating atop the horizon. Oil tankers making their way up the coast. I wondered what it would be like to live at sea. To be reminded, constantly, of insignificance and infinity.

Before I could take that any further I heard engine noise, then happy shouts that turned into "Hey! Mr. Landlord!"

A white VW Golf with the top down had pulled up next to me. The blonde from the beach was behind the wheel, a cigarette fuming between her fingers. The redhead sat next to her, eating from a box of Fiddle Faddle and holding an open can of Coors. Both girls had put gauzy white shirts over their bathing suits but had left them unbuttoned. Bernie the dog sat in the back seat, panting and lolling and looking motion-sick.

"Hi," said the redhead. "Neat old car. My dad had one just like it."

I smiled at the thought of the Seville as an antique. Ten years old. The day I'd bought it, these two had probably been in third grade.

"Do you, like, garage it?" said the blonde.

"Uh-huh."

"Neat."

"Thanks."

"You really with the landlord? 'Cause Traci and me are looking for a place closer to the beach. We're across PCH, now, down at Las Flores, and the beach there isn't a keeper—too wet, lots of rocks. We're willing to work—light *au pair,* babysitting, whatever, like for a trade? Todd said he'd help but we figure we can talk for ourself."

"Sorry," I said. "I do know Todd's landlord but I'm not in the real-estate business."

The blonde's face managed to turn ugly while retaining its beauty. "What a firp! Told you, Mar, it was total bullshit!"

The redhead wrinkled her nose and looked injured.

I said, "What's the matter?"

"Todd," said the redhead. "He bullshat us royal."

"How?"

"Said you were a real-estate stud and if we were nice to him, he'd talk to you about finding us a place here on Broad. We used to live here—*au pair*ing for Dave Dumas and his wife when they rented last summer, so people think we still live here and don't hassle us when we come down, but we want to be right here all the time, or at least somewhere dry."

"Dave Dumas the basketball player?"

"Yeah. Mr. Stretch." Shared giggles.

"We took care of his kids," said the blonde. "Really big kids from a *really* big guy." She laughed some more, then turned abruptly serious.

"We'd *really* like to get back here to Broad—the beach is a total keeper and the concerts at the Trancas Café are heating up. Last week Eddie Van Halen showed up to jam."

"We're willing to work," said the redhead. "Todd said he could get us a trade."

"Fag-wuss!" said the blonde. "Last time we're nice to him." She gunned the Golf's engine. The dog jerked in alarm.

I said, "What exactly did he want from you?"

"He was, like, act like we thought he was hot. Let him *touch* us in front of you." Turning to the redhead: "Told you, Mar. I was like, sure, Todd, you *might ever be*."

"Todd's not hot in real life?"

Giggles all around. The redhead picked a piece of popcorn out of the box and handed it back to the dog.

"He likes it," she said. "Bernie's got a sugar thing."

"Enjoy, Bernie," I said, walking over and petting the dog. His fur was matted and clogged with salt and dirt. As I rubbed his neck, he whined with pleasure.

"So Todd's no keeper," I said.

A wary look came into the blonde's eyes. Up close her face was hard, ready to age, already starting to leather from too much sun and risk-taking.

"You're not like a good friend of his or anything?" she said.

"Not at all," I said. "I do know the people who own the house. But I only met Todd once before."

"So you're not, like—" The blonde smiled, gave an arch look, and raised her wrist limply.

"Tra-ace! That's like *so* ru-ude!"

"So?" said the blonde. "*He's* the one who *does* it! *He* should be embarrassed!"

I said, "Todd's gay?"

"For sure," said the redhead.

"A muscle-fag," said the blonde.

"Wasted buff," said the redhead. The dog coughed. She said, "Don't stress out, Bern."

"That's why it was rank," said the blonde. "Using us to make like he's into girls—I mean, maybe he's got a buff body but his head's not buff, that's for sure."

"How do you know he's gay?" I said.

"Well," said the blonde, laughing and gunning the engine again, "it's not like we go around watching him *do* it or anything."

"He's got guys coming in and out all the time," said the redhead. "He says he's *training* them, but one time I saw him and this guy holding hands and kissing."

"Rank!" said the blonde, elbowing her friend. "You never *told* me."

"Yeah, it was a long time ago. When we were still with Big Dave."

"Big Dave," said the blonde, giggling.

"How long ago was that?" I said.

Bafflement. Both of them looked as if they were struggling with a difficult word problem.

Finally the redhead said, "A long time ago—maybe five weeks. Buffy Todd and this other guy were walking in back of the house. Right over there, I was walking Bernie." She pointed to the cement pad. "And they touched their hands. Then the other guy got in his car—white five-sixty SEC with these brushed-steel custom wheels—and Todd leaned in and gave him a little kiss."

"Rank," said the blonde.

"Kind of sweet, actually," said the redhead, looking as if she meant it. But the empathy didn't fit, and she squirmed and burst into nervous laughter.

I said, "Remember what this other guy looked like?"

She shrugged. "He was old."

"How old?"

"Older than you." Even.

"Forties?"

"Older."

"Maybe he was Todd's *dad,*" said the blonde, smirking. "You can kiss your *dad,* right, Mar?"

"Maybe," said the redhead. "Little Todd and his dad, kissing."

They looked at each other. Shook their heads, giggled some more.

"No way," said the redhead. "This was true love." She gave a reflective look. "Actually, the old guy was kind of buff. For an old guy. Kind of like Tom Selleck."

I said, "He had a mustache?"

The redhead strained. "I think so. Maybe. I just remember he reminded me of Tom Selleck. An *old* Tom Selleck. Buff tan. Big chest."

"How come," said the blonde, "so many of *them* are buff? What a *waste.*"

"It's 'cause they're rich, Trace," said the redhead. "They can afford to buy special supplements, get lipoed-out, whatever."

"Suck and tuck," said the blonde, touching her own flat midriff. "If I ever need that, put me to sleep." She stuck her hand in the box of Fiddle Faddle and groped around.

"Geez, don't *touch* everything!" said the redhead, tugging on the box.

The blonde held fast and said, "Almonds." Smile. "*Here* we go." She pulled out a nut and placed it between her teeth.

Looked at me, flicked it with her tongue, and bit down slowly.

I said, "That the last time you saw this old guy around— five weeks?"

"Yup," said the redhead, looking wistful. "It's been a long time since we hit dry sand."

"So," said the blonde, "can you do anything for us?"

"Like I said, I'm not in the real-estate business, but I do know some people—let me check around. Why don't you write down your names and numbers."

"Sure!" said the redhead, beaming. Then she grew grave. "What is it?"

"No pen."

"No prob," I said, resisting the impulse to wink. I went back to the Seville, found a ballpoint and an old mechanic's receipt in the glove compartment, and handed it to her. "Write on the back."

Using the Fiddle Faddle box as a desk, she wrote laboriously as the blonde looked on. The dog planted a wet nose on the back of my hand and wheezed in gratitude when I rubbed him again.

"Here." The redhead thrust the paper at me.

Maria and Traci. Looping script. Hearts over the I's. An address on Flores Mesa Drive. A 456 exchange.

I smiled and said, "Great, I'll do what I can. In the meantime, good luck."

"We've already got it," said the blonde.

"Got what?" said the redhead.

"Luck. We always get what we want, right, Mar?"

Giggles and a cloud of dust as the Golf shot forward.

I watched them speed to the northern end of Broad Beach Road and disappear. It took a second to register that they were around Melissa's age.

I made a three-point turn and headed back for the highway.

Older man and young stud.

Older man with a mustache and a tan.

Lots of tan, mustachioed gay men in L.A. Lots of white Mercedes.

But if Don Ramp drove a white 560 SEC with brushed-steel wheels, I was willing to go out on a limb and assume.

I joined the southbound traffic on PCH and drove home assuming even *without* proof. Casting Ramp as Nyquist's lover and recasting the tension that I'd witnessed between Nyquist and Gina.

Another macho charade on his part?

Anger on *hers*?

Did she *know*?

Did that have something to do with her hints about making a life-style change?

Separate bedrooms.

Separate bank accounts.

Separate lives.

Or had she known about Ramp when she'd married him?

Why, after living a bachelor life for so long, had *he* married *her*?

Gina's banker and lawyer seemed certain it hadn't been for money, citing the prenuptial agreement as proof.

But prenuptials—and wills—could be contested. And life-insurance policies could be taken out without bankers and lawyers being informed.

Or perhaps inheritance had nothing to do with it. Maybe Ramp simply needed a cover for the good, conservative folks of San Labrador.

Hearth and home and a child who hated his guts.

What could be more all-American?

22

I got home just after five. Milo was out. He'd recorded a new greeting on his machine. No more misanthropy. Business-like: *Please* leave your message. I asked him to *please* call when he had a chance.

I phoned San Labrador and got Madeleine.

Mademoiselle Melissa was not feeling well. She was sleeping.

Non, Monsieur was not there, either.

A catch in her voice. Click.

I paid bills, straightened the house, fed the fish some more and noticed that they looked tired—especially the females. Did thirty minutes on the ski machine and showered.

Next time I looked at my watch, it was seven-thirty.

Friday night.

Date night.

Without thinking it through, I called San Antonio. A man answered with a wary "Hello?" When I asked for Linda, he said, "Who's this?"

"A friend from Los Angeles."

"Oh. She's over at Behar—at the hospital."

"Her dad?"

"Yeah. This is Conroy, her uncle—his brother. I'm over from Houston, came down today."

"Alex Delaware, Mr. Overstreet. I'm a friend from L.A. Hope it's nothing serious."

"Yeah, well, that's what I'd like to hope, too, but I'm sorry to say that's not the case. My brother passed out this morning. They revived him but it wasn't easy—some kinda problem with circulation and the kidneys. They've got him over in intensive care. The whole family's over there. I just came back to get some things and caught your call."

"I won't keep you."

"Thank you, sir."

"Please tell Linda I called. If there's anything I can do, let me know."

"I'll be sure to do that, sir. Thank you for offering."

Click.

Wrong reason to do it, but I did it anyway.

"Hello."

"Alex! How are you?"

"Got a date tonight?"

She laughed. "A *date*? No, just sitting here by the phone."

"Care to change your luck?"

More laughter. Why did it sound so good?

"Hmm, I don't know," she said. "My mother always told me not to go out with any boy who didn't ask by Wednesday night."

"Good old Mom."

"Then again, she was full of shit about lots of other things. What time?"

"Half an hour."

She came out of the front door of her studio just as I pulled in front of the building. She was wearing a thin black silk turtleneck and tight black jeans tucked into black suede boots. Lips glossed, eyes shadowed, curls full and gleaming. I wanted her, badly. Before I could get out, she opened her own door, scooted next to me, radiating heat. One hand in my hair. Kissing me before I had a chance to catch my breath.

We necked fiercely. She bit me a couple of times, seemed almost angry. Just as I ran out of breath, she broke it off and said, "What's for dinner?"

"I was thinking Chinese." Thinking of all the times we'd eaten takeout in bed. "Of course, we could call out for it and stay here."

"Never mind that. I want a *date*."

We drove to a place in Brentwood—the standard Mandarin/Szechuan menu and paper lanterns, but always reliable—and feasted for an hour, then headed over to a comedy club in Hollywood. A lighthearted place we used to enjoy together. Neither of us had been there with anyone else.

The ambience was different now: black felt walls, murderous looking bouncers with ponytails and steroid complexions. Calcutta level density, stale smoke, and hostility. Tables crowded with heavy-eyed night-crawlers and their significant others, coming down from one trip or another, demanding an entertainment-fix or else.

The first few acts were raw meat for that crowd—mumble-mouthed novice stand-ups reciting the stuff that had always cracked up their friends but didn't make the transition to Sunset Boulevard. Sad clowns veering wildly, like drunks on ice skates—staggering between silences more painful than any I'd encountered doing therapy and stutter-bursts of manic word salad. Just before midnight, things got more polished but no more friendly: slick, trendily dressed young men and women who'd been shaped on the late night talk show lathe, spitting out the four-letter wit they couldn't get away with on TV. Rage-laced relationship humor. Ugly-spirited ethnic jokes. Screaming scatology.

Had the city gotten meaner, or had I just lost my edge?

I looked over at Robin. She shook her head. We left. This time she allowed me to open her door. Pressed herself against it the moment she was inside and stayed that way.

I began driving. Reached for her hand. She squeezed mine a couple of times and let go.

"Sleepy?" I said.

"No, not at all."

"Everything okay?"

"Uh-huh."

"So . . . Where to?"

"Do you mind just driving for a while?"

"Not at all."

I was on Fountain going west. Turning right on La Cienega, I crossed Sunset up into the Hollywood Hills, climbing slowly and steadily until I found myself on a series of narrow, hairpin residential streets named after birds.

Robin remained tight against the door, like a nervous hitchhiker. Eyes shut, not talking, her face directed away from me. She crossed her legs and placed one hand on her belly, as if it ached.

A few moments later she put her head back and straightened her legs. Despite her denial of fatigue, I wondered if she'd fallen asleep. But when I switched on the radio and found a late night jazz show, she said, "That's nice."

I kept driving, with no idea where I was going, ended up somehow on Coldwater Canyon, took it all the way to Mulholland Drive, and turned left.

A bit of forest, then clearings that revealed sheer cliff above the incandescent grid of the San Fernando Valley. Fifty square miles of lights and motion, leering through night-haze and treetops.

Bright lights, pseudo city.

Being up here felt strangely adolescent. Mulholland was the quintessential parking spot, as consecrated by Hollywood. How many make-out scenes had been filmed here? How many splatter flicks?

I lowered my speed, enjoying the view, keeping my eyes out for drag-racers and other nuisances. Robin opened her eyes. "Why don't you pull over somewhere?"

The first few turnoffs were occupied by other vehicles. I

found a eucalyptus-shaded spot several miles from the Cold-water junction, parked, and killed my lights. Not far from Beverly Glen; just a quick southward dip and we'd be home—at least *I* would.

She was still up against the door, looking out at the Valley.

"Nice," I said, setting the emergency brake and stretching.

She smiled. "The stuff of picture postcards."

"It's good being with you." I made another reach for her hand. No return squeeze this time. Her skin was warm but inert.

"So," she said, "how's your friend in Texas?"

"Her dad took a turn for the worse. He's in the hospital."

"I'm so sorry."

She cranked open her window. Stuck her head out.

"Are you okay?"

"Guess so," she said, pulling her head back in. "Why'd you call me, Alex?"

"I was lonely," I said, without thinking. Not liking the pitiful sound of it. But it seemed to cheer her. She took my hand and played with my fingers.

"I could use a friend, too," she said.

"You've got one."

"Things have been rough. I don't want to whine—I know I have a tendency to do that and I'm fighting it."

"I never thought of you as a whiner."

She smiled.

"What is it?" I said.

"Dennis. He used to complain that I whined."

"Well, fuck him, the churl."

"He didn't just leave. I kicked him out."

I said nothing.

"I got pregnant and had an abortion. It took me a week to decide that was what I was going to do. When I told him, he agreed right away. Offered to pay for it. That made me angry—that he had no conflict about it. That it was so simple for him. So I kicked him out."

Suddenly she was out of the car, walking around to the front and standing by the grille. I got out and stood next to her. The ground was thick with dead eucalyptus leaves. The air smelled like cough drops. A couple of cars drove by, then silence, then another headlight parade.

Finally, a stillness that endured.

"When I found out," she said, "I felt so strange. Disgusted at myself for being so careless. Happy that I was able to—biologically. And scared."

I remained silent, dealing with my own feelings. Anger: all the years we'd been together. The care we'd taken. Sadness . . .

"You hate me," she said.

"Of course I don't."

"I don't blame you."

"Robin, it happens."

"To other people," she said.

She stepped toward the cliff. I put both arms around her waist. Felt resistance and let go.

"The procedure itself was nothing. My OB-GYN did it, right in the office. She said we'd caught it real early—as if it were a disease. Vacuum pump and a receipt for insurance as a routine D and C. Later, I had cramps, but nothing terrible. The old Castagna pain threshold. Couple of days of Tylenol, then cold turkey."

She'd slipped into a flat voice that unnerved me.

I said, "The main thing is you're okay," and felt as if I were reading from a script. Melodrama at Make-out Mountain. Check your theater listings. . . .

"Afterward," she said, "I got paranoid. What if the pump had done damage and I could never conceive again? What if God punished me for killing what was inside me?"

She took several steps to the side. "Everyone talks about it so abstractly," she said. "The paranoia lasted for a month. I developed a rash, convinced myself I was going to get cancer. The doctor said I was fine and I believed her, was okay for a few days. Then the feelings came back. I fought them and won. Convinced myself I was going to live. Then I cried nonstop for another month. Wondering what might have been . . . Eventually, that stopped, too. But some of that sadness stuck around—in the background. It's still there. Sometimes, when I smile, I feel as if I'm really crying. It's like a hole, in here." Prodding her abdomen. "Right here."

I took hold of her shoulders and managed to turn her around. Pressed her face into my jacket.

"With *him,* dammit," she said, muffled by fabric. Then she drew away and forced herself to look at me. "He was fast-food—something to fill space. Kind of obscene that it would happen with him, huh? Like one of those horrible jokes they were telling tonight."

She was dry-eyed. My eyes began to hurt.

"Sometimes, Alex, I still lie awake at night. Wondering. It's as if I've been *sentenced* to wondering."

We stood staring at each other. Another caravan of cars zoomed by.

"Some *date,* huh?" she said. "Whine, whine, whine."

"Stop," I said. "I'm glad you told me."

"Are you?"

"Yes— I— Yes, I am."

"If you hate me, I understand."

"Why should I *hate* you?" I said, with sudden anger. "*I* had no claim on you. It had nothing to *do* with me."

"True," she said.

I let go of her shoulders. Threw up my arms and let them fall.

"I should have kept my mouth shut," she said.

"No," I said. "It's all right— No, it's not. Not right at the moment. I feel lousy. Mostly for what *you've* been through."

"Mostly?"

"Okay. For myself, too. For not being a part of your life when it happened."

She nodded mournfully, embracing that bit of gloom. "You would have wanted me to keep it, wouldn't you?"

"I don't know what I would have wanted. It's too theoretical—and there's no sense flogging yourself over it. You didn't commit any crime."

"Didn't I?"

"No," I said, taking hold of her shoulders again. "I've seen the real item. I know the difference. People being deliberately cruel—being *bestial* to one another. God knows how many times it's happening right now—down in that light show."

I pointed her toward the valley view. She allowed herself to be molded.

"The hell of it is," I said, "the ones who *should* feel guilty—the really bad ones—never do. It's the good ones who torture themselves. Don't get sucked into that. You're not doing anyone any favors by not drawing distinctions."

She looked up at me, seemed to be listening.

I said, "You made a *mistake*—and not an earthshaking one in the greater scheme of things. You'll recover. You'll go on. If you want babies, you'll have them. Meanwhile, try to enjoy life a little bit."

"Do you enjoy life, Alex?"

"I sure try. That's why I ask good-looking women out on dates."

She smiled. A tear rolled down her cheek.

I put my arms around her, from behind. Felt her belly. Toned muscle under a layer of softness. I stroked it.

She cried.

"When you called I was glad," she said, "and worried."

"About what?"

"That it would be just like a few days ago. Not that I didn't enjoy it—God, it was great. First real pleasure I'd had in so long. But afterwards, I——" She put her hand over mine and pressed. "I guess what I'm saying is I could really use a friend right now. More than a lover."

"Like I said, you've got one."

"I know," she said. "Hearing you—seeing you like this. I know I do."

She turned and we held each other.

A car sped by, trapping us momentarily in its high-beams. A teenage face appeared in the open window and shouted, "Go for it, dude!"

We looked at each other. And laughed.

She came back to the house with me and I ran her a hot bath. She soaked for half an hour, came out looking pink and drowsy. We got into bed and played gin while absently attending to a one-star western on TV. By 2:00 A.M. we'd finished a dozen games—six wins each. It seemed as good a time as any to go to sleep.

No callback from Milo on Saturday. No news from San Labrador. I phoned, got Madeleine again, and was told Melissa was still sleeping.

Robin and I spent most of the day together. Brunch and grocery-shopping at Farmer's Market, a drive out to the Self-Realization Fellowship in Pacific Palisades to look at the lake and the swans. Light dinner at a seafood place near Sunset Beach, then back to her place by seven, where I called in for messages and she played the tape on her machine.

Nothing for me, but a famous singer had called her three times an hour for the past three hours. Famous raspy baritone tight with panic.

"Emergency, Rob. Sunday concert in Long Beach. Just got back from a gig in Miami. Humidity popped Patty's bridge. Call me at the Sunset Marquis, Rob. Please, Rob, I won't go anywhere."

She turned off the machine and said, "Wonderful."

"Sounds pretty serious."

"Oh, yeah. When he calls himself, instead of getting a roadie to do it, that means nervous breakdown time."

"Who's Patty?"

"One of his guitars. Fifty-two Martin D-twenty-eight.

He's got two others, Laverne and . . . I forgot the other. They're named after the Andrews sisters—who was the other Andrews sister?"

"Maxene."

"Right. Maxene. Patty and Laverne and Maxene. All fifty-twos, sequential serial numbers. I've never heard three instruments sound so similar. But of course he *has* to play Patty tomorrow."

She shook her head and walked into the kitchenette. "Something to drink?"

"Nothing right now, thanks."

"Sure?" Looking edgy. Glancing back at the phone.

"Positive. Aren't you going to call him back?"

"You don't mind?"

I shook my head. "Actually, I'm a little tired. You're wearing an old man out."

She was about to respond when the phone rang. She answered it and said, "Yes, I just got in. . . . No, it's better if you bring it here. I can do a better job here. . . . Okay, see you soon."

She hung up, smiled, and shrugged.

She walked me to the car, we kissed lightly, avoiding conversation, and I left her to her work. Left myself to enjoy life.

But I was into a preaching mode, not a practicing one, and after driving a few blocks, I pulled into a service station and used the pay phone to try Milo again.

This time Rick answered. "He just walked in, Alex, and went right out. Said he'd be tied up for a while but that you should call him. He's got my car and the cellular phone. Here's the number."

I copied it down, thanked him, hung up, and dialed. Milo picked up after the first ring.

"Sturgis."

"It's me. What's up?"

"The car," he said. "It was found a couple of hours ago. Out near San Gabriel Canyon—Morris Dam."

"What about—"

"No trace of her. Just the car."

"Does Melissa know?"

"She's out here. I brought her myself."

"How's she doing?"

"She seems pretty shell-shocked. The paramedics looked at her, said she was okay physically, but to keep an eye on her. Any specific advice, dealing with her?"

"Just stay with her. Give me directions."

23

I shot onto the freeway at Lincoln. Traffic was gummy and hot-tempered all the way to the 134 east—weekend partyers and RV jockeys coming and going. But by Glendale it had started to thin, and by the time I reached the 210 transition, the highway was mine.

I drove faster than usual, speeding along the northern rim of Pasadena, passing the on-ramp Gina had probably taken two days ago.

Lonely road, made lonelier by the darkness, separating the city from the chalky, high desert at the base of the San Gabriel mountains. Daylight would reveal budget housing developments, industrial outcroppings, an eventual decline to gravel pits and scrubby hills. All of it hidden mercifully by a starless night. A bad night to be looking for someone.

A mile before the Highway 39 exit I slowed down to get a look at the spot where the highway patrolman had seen the Rolls-Royce. The freeway was bisected by window-high cement sound-barriers. The only thing that would have been visible—even to a car fanatic's eye—was the top of the unmistakable grille chased by a blur of lacquer.

Amazing he'd noticed anything.

But he'd been right.

I exited onto Azusa Boulevard and drove through the outskirts of a town that looked as if it had never forgotten the fifties: full-service filling stations, lodge halls, small store-fronts, all dark. Occasional streetlamps brightened some of the signs: TACK AND SADDLE, CHRISTIAN BOOKS, TAX PREPA-RATION. A present-tense intrusion appeared at the end of the third block. AM-PM mini-mart, open for business but no one was buying and the clerk looked asleep.

I crossed a railroad track and Route 39 turned into San Gabriel Canyon Road. The Seville bounced over old asphalt, speeding through a neighborhood of sad little stucco houses and trailer parks insulated from the street by cinder block walls.

No graffiti. Guess that made it the country. Cars and pickups were parked in peewee front yards. Old cars and pickups, nothing that would ever be a classic. The Rolls would have stuck out like frankness during election year.

As the road began to climb, the houses gave way to larger parcels—boarding stables and horse ranches behind stake-and-post fencing. A Park Service sign a hundred yards up was top-lit, announcing the entrance to Angeles Crest Na-tional Forest above small-print fire and camping regulations. An information booth just off the road was boarded up. The air began to smell sweet. Before me was two-lane asphalt cutting through granite bulk. The rest, darkness.

Using my brights, the speed bumps in the center of the road, and blind faith to guide me, I drove faster. A couple of miles in, I heard a deep mechanical stutter. It grew louder, deafening, seemed to be descending upon me.

Two sets of cherry-red lights appeared at the top of my windshield, then lowered and ranged directly in front of my field of vision before rising sharply and pulling ahead on a northward trajectory. Twin searchlights began scything the darkness, highlighting treetop and fissure, brushing over the mountainside, exposing momentary flashes of shimmer and luster to the east.

Water. Another peek of it around a curve.

Then a crest of concrete. Concrete piers, a sloping spill-way.

I tried to follow the copters' light-strokes, saw the dam rising a quarter mile above the water table.

Round-edged WPA architecture.

A staked placard by the road: MORRIS DAM AND RESER-VOIR. L.A. FLOOD MAINTENANCE DISTRICT.

A long time since floods had needed to be maintained in Southern California; the current drought was four years running. Still, the depth of the reservoir had to be substantial. Hundreds of millions of gallons, inky and secretive.

Milo had said to look for a utility road on the dam side. The first two I passed were blocked by padlocked metal swing gates. Five miles later, as the road looped sharply to accommodate the northern ridge of the reservoir, I saw it: sparking road flares, flashing amber emergency lights atop orange-and-white sawhorses. A convention of vehicles, some idling and huffing out white smoke.

Azusa Police black-and-whites. L.A. Sheriffs. Three Park Service Jeeps. Fire Department paramedic van.

Behind one of the Jeeps, a foreign contingent: the bowl-butt of Rick's white Porsche. And another white car: Mercedes 560 SEC. Brushed-steel wheels.

A sheriff's deputy stepped into the middle of the road and halted me. Young, female, blond ponytail. A figure that lent the beige uniform more style than it deserved.

I stuck my head out the window.

"Sorry, sir, the road's closed."

"I'm a doctor. Mrs. Ramp's daughter is my patient. I was asked to be here."

She asked me my name, requested ID to back it up. After looking at my license, she said, "One moment. Meantime, why don't you turn off your engine, sir."

Stepping to the side of the road, she talked into a hand-held radio and returned, nodding.

"Okay, sir, you can just leave your car right here with the keys in, as long as you don't mind my driving it if I have to."

"Be my guest."

"They're all down there." Pointing to an open swing-gate. "Be careful, it's steep."

The path was a vehicle-wide swath through mesquite and young conifers. Paved, but a slight softness beneath my soles said it had been recent. The blacktop provided some traction, but I still had to walk sideways to maintain balance on the fifty-degree slope.

I sidestepped my way down a quarter mile before I saw the bottom. Flat area, maybe sixty feet square, leading to a small wooden dock that bobbed on the banks of the reservoir. Hazard lanterns had been rigged on high poles, flooding the space with sallow light. People in uniforms crowded around looking at something to the left of the dock, trying to talk over the roar of the copters. From where I was standing none of the conversation was audible.

I continued to descend and saw the object of attention: A Rolls-Royce, its rear end submerged in the water, its front wheels lifted several feet off the ground. The driver's door was open. Hanging open—hinged near the center-post. The kind of doors old Lincoln Continentals used to have—suicide doors.

I peered into the crowd, saw Don Ramp in shirtsleeves next to Chief Chickering, staring at the car, one hand on his head, the other clutching his trousers, gathering a handful of worsted. As if trying, literally, to hold himself together.

No immediate sign of Milo. Finally I spotted him off to one side, out of the light. He had on a plaid shirt and jeans and his arm was around Melissa. A dark blanket covered her shoulders. Their backs were to the car. Milo's lips were moving. I couldn't tell if Melissa was listening.

I made my way down to them.

Milo noticed me coming and frowned.

Melissa looked up at me but remained under his arm. Her face was white and still, like a Kabuki mask.

I spoke her name.

She didn't respond.

I took both of her hands and gave them a squeeze.

She said, "They're still under," in a disembodied voice.

Milo said, "The divers," in the practiced tone of an interpreter.

One of the helicopters circled lower over the reservoir, using its beam to sketch spheres of light in the black water. The sketches decayed before they were complete. Someone shouted. Melissa yanked her hand free and turned toward the sound.

One of the park rangers held a flashlight near the shoreline. A wet-suited diver surfaced, pulling up his mask and shaking his head. As he stepped completely out of the water, another diver emerged. Both of them began removing their scuba tanks and weight belts.

Melissa made a groaning sound, like gears grinding, then shouted, "No!" and ran over to them. Milo and I went after her. She reached the divers and screamed, "No! You can't stop now!"

The divers backed away from her and lowered their gear to the ground. They looked at Chickering, who'd come over, accompanied by a deputy sheriff. Some of the other men were glancing our way. Ramp hung back, still fixated on the car.

"What's the situation?" Chickering asked the divers. He had on a dark suit, white shirt, and dark tie. The toes of his wingtips were coated with mud. Uniforms were assembling behind him, watchful, like a nighttime posse itching to ride.

"Black as coal," said one of the divers. He shot an uneasy glance at Melissa, turned back to the San Labrador chief. "Really dark, sir."

"Then use *light*!" said Melissa. "People night-dive all the time with lights, don't they!"

"Miss," said the diver. "We . . ." He searched for words. He was young—not much older than she. Freckled, with a downy blond mustache under a peeling nose. A thread of algae clung to his chin. His teeth began to chatter and he had to clench his jaws to make them stop.

The other diver, just as young, said, "We did use lights,

miss." He bent over and picked something off the ground. Black-cased bulb attached to a rope lanyard. He let it swing a few times and put it back down.

"*Swat Submersible,* miss. We used the yellow bulbs—they're excellent for this kind of . . . The problem here is that even during the day it's pretty murky. At night . . ." Shaking his head, he rubbed his arms, looked down at the ground.

The blond diver had seized the opportunity to move several feet away. Standing on one leg, he pulled off a flipper, switched legs, and began to tug at the other. Someone brought him a blanket identical to the one around Melissa's shoulders. The other diver looked at it longingly.

"It's a reservoir, dammit!" said Melissa. "It's *drinking* water—how can it be muddy?"

"Not muddy, miss," said the dark-haired diver. "*Murky.* Kind of opaque. It's the natural color of the water—minerals. Come here during the day and you'll see the color's this real deep green—" He stopped himself, looked to the crowd for confirmation.

The deputy stepped forward. A brass tag above one pocket said GAUTIER. Below it were rows of ribbons. He looked about fifty-five. His eyes were tired and gray.

"We're going to do everything to find your mother, Miss Dickinson," he said, showing even, tobacco-stained teeth. "The helicopters will keep going, covering a twenty-mile semicircle above the highway, which will take us well above the Crest Highway. As far as the reservoir, those boats the dam people sent out right at the beginning went over every square inch of surface. The copters are going over it again, just to make sure. But in terms of below the surface, there's really nothing we can do right now."

He spoke softly and deliberately, trying to communicate horror without being horrible. If Gina was below the surface, there was no need for urgency.

Melissa kneaded her hands, glared at him, working her mouth.

Chickering frowned and took a step closer.

Melissa shut her eyes, threw up her hands, and let out a wrenching cry. Slamming both hands over her face, she bent at the waist, as if gripped by cramps. "No, no, no!"

Milo made a move toward her but I got there first and he retreated. Taking hold of her shoulders, I drew her to me.

She fought, kept repeating the word *no*.

I held her fast, and gradually she loosened. Too loose. I put a finger under her chin and lifted her face. She was cold and plastic to the touch. It was like positioning a mannequin.

Conscious, breathing normally. But her eyes were static and unfocused and I knew if I let go, she'd sink to the ground.

The crowd of uniformed men watched. I drew her away.

She moaned and some of them flinched. One man turned his back, then others. Gradually, most of them began drifting back to the Rolls.

Chickering and Gautier lingered. Chickering stared at me, puzzled and irritated, shook his head, joined the car crowd. Gautier watched him leave with a raised eyebrow. Turning back to me, he glanced down at Melissa and gave a look of concern.

"It's okay," I said. "We're going to get out of here if that's okay with you."

Gautier nodded. Chickering was looking at the water.

Don Ramp stood alone, in muck up to his ankles. He'd somehow turned into a frail-looking, stooped man.

I tried to catch his attention, thought I had when he turned toward me.

But he was staring past me with eyes as muddy as his shoes.

The helicopters had moved on, emitting fly-on-carrion buzzes from somewhere in the north. Suddenly, my senses expanded, like the lens of a camera. I heard water lapping against the shore. Smelled the chlorophyll tang of the underbrush, the hydrocarbon stink of leaking motor fluids.

Melissa stirred, opening, too.

Like a wound. Crying softly, rhythmically. Her grief rising to a high mewl that danced above the water and the hard-data chorus of the men at the shore.

Milo frowned and shifted his weight from one foot to the other. He'd been standing behind me and I hadn't noticed.

Maybe it was that movement that snapped Ramp out of his trance. He walked toward us, took half a dozen halting steps before thinking better of it and turning around.

24

Milo and I half-walked, half-carried Melissa up to my car. He returned to the Rolls and I drove her home, prepared for therapy. She put her head back and closed her eyes, and by the time I reached the bottom of the mountain road, she was snoring lightly.

The gates to the house on Sussex Knoll were open. I carried her up to the front door and knocked. After what seemed like a long time, Madeleine answered, wearing a white cotton dressing gown buttoned to the neck. No surprise on her broad face; she had the weathered look of one used to grieving alone. I walked past her, into the huge front room, and deposited Melissa on one of the overstuffed couches.

Madeleine hurried off and came back with a blanket and a pillow. Sinking to her knees, she propped up Melissa's head, slid the pillow under it, removed Melissa's sneakers, spread the blanket over her, and tucked the corners under her feet.

Melissa turned on her side, facing the back of the sofa. There was squirrely movement under the blanket. A couple of shifts of position, then a hand peeked out, thumb extended. The hand wormed its way totally free and the thumb came to rest on Melissa's lower lip.

Still kneeling, Madeleine brushed the hair from Melissa's face. Then she stood, straightened her dress, and gave me a hard, hungry look that demanded information.

I curled a finger and she followed me across the room, out of Melissa's earshot.

When we stopped, she was standing very close to me, breathing hard, heavy bosom heaving. Her hair was braided tightly. She'd put on some kind of rosewater cologne.

"Only the car, monsieur?"

"Unfortunately." I told her about the helicopter search.

Her eyes remained dry but she brushed them hastily with her knuckles.

I said, "She may still be in the park somewhere. If she is, they'll find her."

Madeleine said nothing, pulled at a finger joint until it cracked.

Melissa made sucking sounds around her thumb.

Madeleine looked at her, then back at me. "You stay, monsieur?"

"For a while."

"I am here, monsieur."

"Good. We'll take shifts."

She didn't respond.

Not sure if there'd been a language problem, I said, "We'll take turns. Make sure she's not alone."

She didn't acknowledge that, either. Just stood there, eyes like granite.

I said, "Is there anything you want to tell me, Madeleine?"

"*Non,* monsieur."

"Then feel free to rest."

"No tired, monsieur."

We sat together on opposite sides of the couch where Melissa dozed. Madeleine got up a few times to fuss with the blanket, even though Melissa had barely moved. Neither of us talked. Every so often, Madeleine cracked a knuckle. She was working on the tenth one when the doorbell chimed. Hurrying to the entry with as much grace as her bulk would allow, she opened the door and let in Milo.

"Monsieur Sturgis." Once more eager for news.

"Hello, Madeleine." He shook his head, gave her hand a quick pat. Looking past her, he said, "How's our girl?"

"Sleeping."

He came into the room and stood over Melissa. Her thumb was still in her mouth. Some hair strands had come loose, veiling her face. He made a move, as if to brush them away, stopped himself, and whispered, "How long's she been out?"

"Since I got her in the car," I said.

"That okay?"

The two of us shifted several feet away. Madeleine moved in, close to Melissa.

"Given the circumstances," I said.

Madeleine said, "I will stay with her, Monsieur Sturgis."

"Sure," said Milo. "Dr. Delaware and I will be in the downstairs study."

She gave a small nod.

As Milo and I walked to the windowless room, I said, "You seem to have made a friend."

"Old Maddy? Not exactly a giggle a moment but she's loyal and makes a great pot of coffee. She's originally from Marseilles. I was there twenty years ago. Stopover on my way home from Saigon."

Papers covered with Milo's handwriting obscured the blotter on the small white desk. Another set of notes and a cellular phone lay atop a fruitwood writing table. The phone's antenna was extended. Milo pushed it closed.

"This was Melissa's work station," he said, pointing to the table. "We set up Info Command Central in here. She's a smart kid. Industrious. We were on the horn all day—none of it led anywhere, but she didn't let it get to her. I've seen rookie detectives who didn't handle frustration nearly as well."

"She was motivated."

"Yeah." He went behind the desk and sat down.

"How'd you find out about the car?" I said.

"We took a sandwich break at seven. She was joking about ditching Harvard and becoming a private eye—first time I'd seen her smile. I figured at the least I was keeping her mind off it. While we were eating I made a routine check with Baldwin Park CHP. Been doing it once per shift so as not to be seen as a giant pain in the ass. Didn't really expect it to lead anywhere. But the gal at the desk said, Oh yeah, that one just turned up, and told me the details. Melissa must have seen the look on my face and dropped her food. So I had to tell her. She insisted on coming with me."

"Better than waiting around."

"Guess so." He got up, walked back to the writing table, and toed a dark spot on the cream border of the Aubusson carpet. "Here's where it dropped. Her tuna and mayo, nice little grease spot."

He faced the Goya portrait and rubbed his eyes. "Before it happened, she was telling me some of the things she'd been through—how you helped her. Kid's lived a lot in eighteen years. I was too rough on her, wasn't I? Too damn judgmental."

"Occupational hazard," I said. "But you obviously did something right—she trusts you."

"I really didn't think it was going to turn out nasty." He turned and faced me. For the first time I noticed that he needed a shave and his hair looked oily. "What a fucking mess."

"Who found the car?"

"Park ranger on routine patrol. He noticed the service gate was open, went over to close it, and decided to check. The areas at the bottom are used by the dam people for taking water samples. They like to keep John Q. Public out—no peeing in the drinking water. The lock on this one was missing. But apparently that's not too weird. Sometimes the dam people forget to lock up. It's kind of a running joke between them and the rangers—he almost didn't bother to go down and check."

"No one saw the car from the dam?"

He shook his head. "It's a good couple of miles from the dam to that part of the reservoir, and the dam people generally keep their eyes glued on dials and gauges."

Milo sat back down again, looked at the papers on the desk, flipped them absently.

"What do you think happened?" I said.

"Why she drove out there in the first place and why down that road? Who knows? Chickering made a big deal about her phobia—he's convinced she got lost and started to panic and was looking for a place to get hold of herself. The others bought it. Make sense to you?"

"Maybe. If she felt a need to practice her breathing and take her medicine she would have wanted privacy. But how'd the car get into the water?"

"Looks like an accident," he said. "She parked close to the shore—the tire marks put it at eighteen inches away. The gearshift was set to neutral. For that particular model, Reverse is the parking gear, once the engine's off. She wasn't exactly an experienced driver and the prevailing wisdom was that she lost control and it rolled in. Apparently these old Rolls have servo drum brakes that take a few seconds to engage. If the hand brake's not set, they can roll a bit even after the engine's off and you really have to stomp on the main brake to stop them."

"Why didn't it roll all the way in?"

"There're these steel flanges extending several feet out from the wall of the dam. Like steps, for maintenance. The rear wheels got lodged between a couple of them. Really tight. Sheriff's investigators said it would take a winch tow."

"Was the driver's door open when the ranger found it?"

"Yes. First thing he did was take a look if anyone was trapped. But it was empty. Water was up to the seats. The doors may have flipped open accidentally—they're put on backwards, attached to the center post, so gravity would have pulled them back. Or maybe she was trying to get out."

"What's the prevailing wisdom on whether she succeeded?"

He stopped, looked at his papers again. Gathered a handful, crumpled it, and left it balled on the desk. "Most popular theory is that she either hit her head trying to get out or passed out due to anxiety and fell in. The reservoir's deep—even with the drought, over a hundred and twenty-five feet. And there are no gradations like a swimming pool—it just drops straight off. She would have sunk in seconds. Melissa says she wasn't a strong swimmer. Hadn't gone in the pool for years."

"Melissa said she didn't like water," I said. "So what was she doing out there in the first place?"

"Who the hell knows? Maybe it was all part of her do-it-yourself therapy. Confronting what scared her—that make sense to you?"

"It doesn't feel right," I said. "Do you remember your comment after the car was spotted? We were looking at the map—looking at the 210—and you thought it was unlikely she'd gone north 'cause north was Angeles Crest and you didn't see her as the type to rough it?"

"So what are you saying?"

"I don't know," I said. "But this whole tragic accident bit is based upon the assumption that she was alone. What if someone drove her there and dumped her? Weighed the body down to make sure it sank, then tried to push the car in to make it look like an accident but was prevented by the flanges?"

"Where'd this other person go?"

"Into the great beyond—the forest is huge. You once told me it's a prime dumping ground for bodies."

"Didn't know you listened so carefully."

"All the time."

He crumpled some more papers and ran his hand over his face.

"Alex, all these years on the job, you don't have to talk me into seeing the worst in people. But so far nothing screams out foul play. Give me a who and a why."

"Who do you usually suspect first when a rich woman dies?"

"The husband. But this one doesn't profit, so what's his motive?"

"Maybe he does profit. Despite what Anger and the lawyer said, prenuptials can be challenged. With an estate this size, even if he ended up with one or two percent it would be significant. And insurance policies can be taken out without lawyers and accountants—or the insured— knowing. Also, he's got another secret." I told him what I'd learned at Malibu.

He pushed the chair back to the bookshelves, stretched without appearing to achieve comfort. "Old macho Don. Living in a big old walk-in closet."

I said, "It could explain why he was so hostile when he first met you. He knew who *you* were from TV, was worried you might possibly know about him."

"Why would I?"

"Common contacts in the gay community?"

"Yeah, that's me," he said. "Mr. Activist. Direct line to the gay community."

"He'd have no way of knowing unless he himself was involved in the gay community. Given the fact that he serves food to San Labrador folk, I think that's unlikely. Or maybe it wasn't rational. Maybe it was just a gut response—your being there threatened him. Reminded him of his secret."

"Threatened," he said. "You know, it occurred to me, too—that he knew something about me. I thought he was just being a homophobe fascist, came this close to saying fuck you and walking. Then he just seemed to forget about it, so I did, too."

"Once he could see you were focusing on Gina and not him, he figured his secret was safe."

He gave a sour smile. "Didn't take long to *bust* his secret."

"Now that I think back, it was probably on his mind from the beginning. He was the first one to mention the beach house. Called over there himself. Twice. Figuring that would take care of it. He had no way of knowing I'd go out there. Even after I did, it was a fluke I found out. If Nyquist hadn't overdone it with those two girls and if I hadn't run into them later, I wouldn't have suspected a thing."

"What's this Nyquist like, besides being an overacter?"

"Blond, good-looking, pumps iron, surfs. The girls said he has guys in and out all the time. Claims to be training them."

"Golden hustler," he said. "What a cliché."

"That's exactly what I thought," I said. "Back when I suspected *Gina* of fooling around with him."

That raised his eyebrows. "When was *this*?"

"Right at the beginning, but I didn't put it into focus till yesterday. The first time I was here, Gina and I were downstairs, looking for Melissa, after their blowup. Ramp and Nyquist came in from playing tennis. Then Ramp left to shower, and Nyquist hung around for no apparent reason. Kind of casually snotty. He asked Gina for something to drink and somehow made it sound lascivious. Nothing explicit—it was the way he said it. She must have heard it, too, because she put him in his place right away. He didn't like it but he kept his mouth shut. The whole interchange took less than a minute—I forgot about it until I saw Nyquist play stud with the beach bunnies. Then the girls told me about him and Ramp and I realized it was just a front."

"Maybe it wasn't."

"What do you mean?"

"Maybe Todd's a creative fellow."

"Playing both ends?"

He smiled. "It's been known to happen."

I'd been standing since we'd entered the room. Realized it and sat down in an armchair.

"Money and jealousy and passion," I said. "A whole slew of classic motives for the price of one. Remember how Melissa said Gina told her she prized kindness and tolerance in a man? Maybe what she liked about Ramp was that he was tolerant of more than her phobia. Maybe she was referring to his acceptance of her fooling around with Nyquist and/or some other sexual explorations. But what if that tolerance wasn't mutual? Infidelity's one thing—crossing sexual preference lines is another. If Gina found out she was sharing Todd with Ramp, it could have blown her mind."

"Even if she and Nyquist *had* nothing going, learning Ramp was gay or bisexual could have blown her mind," said Milo.

"Whatever the specifics, she learned something that led her to decide she'd had enough. Time to make her escape, psychologically and physically. Take a giant step through an open door."

"Big change for Ramp if she boots him out."

I nodded. "No more mansion, no more beach house, no more tennis court—people do get accustomed to a certain standard. And if her *reason* for divorcing him ever got out, he'd lose a lot more than luxuries. He'd be finished in San Labrador."

"Outing him," he said softly.

"What?"

"Dragging him out of the closet whether he wanted it or not. It's something angry people do, and hell hath no fury."

"True," I said, "but the only thing is, I haven't picked up any exceptional hostility between Gina and Ramp. Neither has Melissa, and you can bet she'd be looking for it."

"Yeah," said Milo, "but both of them used to act, right? They'd be good at faking marital bliss. Isn't that the San Labrador way? Heavy starch on the upper lip?"

"True. So where do we go with it?"

"Go?" he said. "If you're asking, could I convince Chickering or the Sheriffs to investigate Ramp on the basis of his having a secret sex life, you know the answer to that. Should I do a little research on him and Golden Boy? What could it hurt?"

"Another day at the beach?" I said.

"Remind me to bring *my* boogie board."

"Did you get over to see McCloskey again?"

"This afternoon. He was sleeping when I got there. The priest didn't want me to bother him, but I snuck up the back way, went to his room. He didn't even look surprised to see me—resigned, the way old cons get."

"Learn anything?"

He shook his head. "Just the same old religious crap. I tried all my cop tricks. Nothing fazed him. I'm starting to think the guy's a genuine head case." He tapped his cranium. "*Nada aqui.*"

"But that doesn't preclude his hiring someone to get her."

He didn't answer, looked preoccupied.

"What is it?"

"You got me going—on Ramp. It would be nice to know how much Gina actually knew about his sexuality. Think she discussed it with those therapists?"

"Quite possibly, but I don't see them breaking confidentiality."

"Are dead people entitled to confidentiality?"

"Ethically, they are. I'm not sure about the legal end of it. If foul play was suspected they could probably be forced to open their records eventually. But without that, I don't see them being too forthcoming. Any publicity can only hurt them."

"Yeah," he said. "Patient in the lake doesn't shout Nobel Prize for medicine."

My mind drifted to black water and stayed there. A hundred plus feet of muck. "If she is at the bottom of the reservoir, what's the chance of finding the body?"

"Not terrific. Like the diver said, visibility's lousy, the area's huge—you can't drain it the way you could a lake. And a hundred and twenty-five's getting close to maximum scuba depth before you need to get into deep-sea equipment. We're talking major expense, major time commitment, with little chance of success. The Sheriff's guys weren't jumping to fill out the requisition forms."

"Sheriff's got sole jurisdiction?"

"Uh-huh. Chickering was happy to punt. The prevailing wisdom was to let nature take its course."

"Meaning?"

"Wait for her to float."

I thought of a gas-filled, suppurating lump rising to the surface of the dam. Wondered what comfort I'd be able to dredge up for Melissa if and when that happened.

Wondered what I'd tell her when she woke up . . .

"Despite the prevailing wisdom," I said, "do you think there's any chance she escaped from the car and made it back to shore?"

He gave me a puzzled look. "Abandoning your murder/mayhem scenario?"

"Exploring alternatives."

"If that's the case, why didn't she just wait by the side of the road until someone came by? It's *not* well-traveled, but eventually she would have been found."

"She might have been in shock, disoriented—maybe she even suffered a head injury, wandered off, and lost consciousness."

"No blood traces were found."

"Closed head injury. You don't need blood for a concussion."

"Wandered off somewhere," he said. "If you're searching for a happy ending, that ain't it. Not if the copters don't find her damned soon. We're talking fifty-plus hours of exposure. If I had a choice of which way to die, I'd opt for the lake."

He stood again. Paced.

"Can you handle more ugly?" he said.

I spread my arms, thrust my chest forward. "Hit me."

"There are at least two *other* scenarios we haven't considered. One: She got to shore, waited by the road, and someone did pick her up. Someone nasty."

"Psycho motorist?"

"It's an alternative, Alex. Good-looking woman in a wet dress, helpless. It would appeal to a certain . . . appetite. Lord knows we see it often enough—women stranded on the freeway, Good Samaritans turning out not to be."

I said, "That is ugly. No one deserves to suffer that much."

"Since when has deserving had anything to do with it?"

"What's Two?"

"Suicide. Gautier—the sheriff brought it up. Right after you and Melissa left, Chickering started explaining to everyone that you were her shrink, got into this little monologue about Gina's problems—bad genetics. About San Labrador having lots of eccentrics. He may guard the rich folk's palaces, but he doesn't have much affection for them. Anyway, Gautier said, given all that, why not suicide? Apparently they've had other people jump in the reservoir. Chickering loved it."

"What did Ramp have to say about that?"

"Ramp wasn't there—Chickering wouldn't have mouthed off in front of him. He didn't even realize *I* was listening."

"Where was Ramp?"

"Up on the highway. He started to look queasy—the paramedics took him to the ambulance for an EKG."

"He okay?"

"EKG-wise he is. But he looked pretty shitty. When I left he was still getting tea and sympathy."

"Acting?"

He shrugged.

"Chickering's psychological insights notwithstanding," I said, "I don't see suicide. When I talked to her there was no evidence of depression—not even a hint of it. On the contrary, she was optimistic. She had twenty years of pain and misery to contemplate doing away with herself. Why would she do it just at the point where she was looking forward to some freedom?"

"Freedom can be scary."

"Just a couple of days ago, you had her getting *high* on freedom—driving to Vegas to whoop it up."

"Things change," he said. Then: "You always have a way of complicating my life."

"What better basis for friendship?"

25

We went to check on Melissa. She was lying on her side, face to the sofa back, the blanket twisted around her in a tight cocoon.

Madeleine sat at the foot of the sofa, only a small portion of her substantial buttocks making contact with the cushion. Crocheting something pink and formless and concentrating on her hands. She glanced up as we entered.

I said, "Has she been up at all?"

"*Non,* monsieur."

Milo said, "Has Mr. Ramp come home yet?"

"*Non,* monsieur." Her fingers stilled.

I said, "Why don't we put her to bed."

"*Oui,* monsieur."

I lifted Melissa, carried her up the stairs to her room, Madeleine and Milo behind me. Madeleine turned on the light, dimmed it, and drew back the covers of the four-poster. She spent a long time tucking Melissa in, then pulled a chair to the side of the bed and sat. Reaching into a dressing-gown pocket, she drew out her crocheting and placed it in her lap. Sitting motionless, careful not to rock.

Melissa shifted position under the covers, moved again so that she was on her back. Her mouth was open and her breathing was slow and steady.

Milo watched the rise and fall of the comforter for a moment, then said, "I'm gonna get going. How about you?"

Remembering a small child's night terrors, I said, "I'll stay for a while."

Milo nodded.

"I stay also," said Madeleine. She engaged her yarn, looped it around her needle, and began dipping and tilting.

"Good," I told her. "I'll be downstairs. Call me if she wakes up."

"*Oui,* monsieur."

I sat in one of the overstuffed chairs and thought about things that kept me awake. The final time I checked my watch, it was just after 1:00 A.M. I fell asleep, still sitting, and awoke stiff and cotton-mouthed, my arms tattooed.

Dazed and confused, I jerked upright. The tattooing shifted kaleidoscopically.

Luminous blue and red and emerald and amber splotches.

Sunlight sieved through lace curtains and daubed by stained glass.

Sunday.

I felt sacrilegious. As if I'd dozed off in a church.

Seven-twenty.

Silent house.

Overnight, a stale smell had settled in. Or maybe it had been there all along.

I rubbed my eyes and tried to clear my head. Stood, with some pain, straightened my clothes, ran my hand over my stubbled face, and stretched until it was obvious that the ache wasn't ready to depart.

In a guest bathroom near the entry hall, I splashed water on my face, massaged my scalp, and headed upstairs.

Melissa was still asleep, hair spread on her pillow, too perfectly arranged to be accidental.

It reminded me of a Victorian funeral photo. Angelic children in lace-edged coffins.

I worked my way past that, smiled at Madeleine.

The pink thing was still formless but had stretched to a couple of feet. I wondered if she'd slept at all. Her feet were bare, bigger than mine. A pair of corduroy slippers was arranged neatly on the floor next to the rocker. Next to them was a telephone that she'd removed from Melissa's nightstand.

I said, *"Bonjour."*

She looked up, clear-eyed and grim, began working her needle faster.

"Monsieur." She reached down and replaced the phone.

"Did Mr. Ramp come home?"

Glance at Melissa. Shake of the head. The movement made the chair creak.

Melissa opened her eyes.

Madeleine shot me an accusing look.

I approached the bed.

Madeleine began rocking. The chair complained louder.

Melissa looked up at me.

I smiled down at her, hoping it didn't look ghoulish.

She widened her eyes. Moved her lips, seemed to be struggling.

"Hi," I said.

"I—what—" Her eyes darted, unable to settle. Panic crossed her face. She pushed her head forward, fell back. Closed her eyes and opened them again.

I sat down and took her hand. Soft and hot. Felt her forehead. Warm, but not feverish.

Madeleine rocked faster.

Melissa was squeezing my fingers. "I— Wha— Mama."

"They're still looking for her, Melissa."

"Mama." Tears. She closed her eyes.

Madeleine was there with a tissue for her and a look of reproach for me.

A moment later Melissa was sleeping again.

I waited around until her slumber deepened, got what I needed from Madeleine, and went downstairs. Lupe and

Rebecca were downstairs, vacuuming and scrubbing. When I passed, they averted their eyes.

I left the house, stepping out into sooty light that grayed the forest shielding the mansion. As I opened the door to the Seville, a white Saab Turbo came roaring up the drive. It came to a short stop, the engine quieted, and both Gabneys got out, Ursula from the driver's side.

She had on a snugly tailored gray sharkskin suit over a white blouse and less makeup than she'd worn at the clinic. It made her look tired but younger. Every hair in place, but her coiffure lacked luster.

Her husband had exchanged cowboy duds for a brown-and-tan houndstooth jacket, beige slacks, chocolate suede wingtips, white shirt, and green tie.

She waited until he took her arm. The difference in their heights seemed almost comical but their expressions killed the joke. They walked toward me, matching each other step for step, looking like pallbearers.

"Dr. Delaware," said Leo Gabney. "We've been calling the police department regularly, just received the terrible news from Chief Chickering." His free hand wiped his high brow. "Terrible."

His wife bit her lip. He patted her arm.

"How's Melissa?" she said, very softly.

Surprised by the question, I said, "Sleeping."

"Oh?"

"It seems to be her major defense right now."

"Not uncommon," said Leo. "Protective withdrawal. I'm sure you're aware of how important it is to monitor, because sometimes it's a prelude to prolonged depression."

I said, "I'll be keeping an eye on her."

Ursula said, "Has she been given anything? To make her sleep?"

"Not to my knowledge," I said.

"Good," she said. "It's best that she not be tranquilized. In order to . . ." She bit her lip again. "God, I'm so sorry. I really— This is just . . ."

She shook her head, folded her lips inward, and looked at the sky. "What can you say at a time like this?"

"Horrible," said her husband. "You can say it's damned horrible and feel the pain while resigning yourself to the inadequacy of language."

He patted some more. She gazed past him, at the big house's peach facade. Her eyes seemed unfocused.

He said, "Horrible," again, a professor trying to foment discussion. Then, "Who can account for the way things work out?"

When neither his wife nor I responded, he said, "Chickering suggested suicide—playing amateur psychologist. Pure nonsense, and I told him so. She never displayed an iota of depression, masked or overt. On the contrary, she was a robust woman, considering what she'd been through."

He stopped again, meaningfully. Somewhere, from the trees, a mockingbird imitated a jay. Gabney gave an exasperated look and turned to his wife. She was somewhere else.

I said, "Did she ever mention anything in therapy that would explain why she drove up to that reservoir?"

"Nothing," said Leo. "Not a thing. Driving off by herself in the first place was total improvisation. That's the hell of it—had she adhered to the treatment plan, none of this would have happened. She'd never been anything but compliant before."

Ursula continued to say nothing. She'd loosened her arm from her husband's grip without my noticing.

I said, "Was there any unusual stress she was undergoing—apart from the agoraphobia?"

"No, nothing," said Gabney. "Her stress level was *lower* than ever before. She was progressing beautifully."

I turned to Ursula. She continued looking at the house but shook her head.

"No," she said. "Nothing."

"Why this line of inquiry, Dr. Delaware?" said Gabney. "Surely *you* don't believe it was suicide." Pushing his face closer to mine. One of his eyes was a paler blue than the other. Both were clear and unwavering. Less combative than curious.

"Just trying to make some sense of it."

He placed a hand on my shoulder. "I understand. That's only natural. But I'm afraid the sad *sense* of it boils down to the fact that she overestimated her progress and deviated from the treatment plan. The *sense* of it is that we'll never *make* any sense of it."

He sighed, wiped his brow again, though it was dry. "Who knows better than we therapists that human beings persist in their annoying habit of being unpredictable? Those of us who can't deal with that should study physics, I suppose."

His wife's head made a sharp quarter-turn.

"Not that I'm blaming her, of course," he said. "She was a sweet, well-meaning woman. Suffered more than anyone should. It's just one of those unfortunate . . . things." Shrug. "After enough years in practice, one learns to accommodate to tragedy. One definitely learns."

He reached for Ursula's arm. She allowed him to touch her for a moment, then moved away and walked quickly up the limestone steps. Her high heels clattered and her long legs seemed too decorative for top speed. She looked sexy and awkward at the same time. At the front door she placed her palms flat upon the Chaucer carving and stood there, as if the wood had healing powers.

"She's soft," said Gabney, very quietly. "Too caring."

"Didn't know that was a fault."

He smiled. "Give yourself a few more years." Then: "So, are you taking responsibility for the emotional well-being of this family?"

"Just Melissa."

He nodded. "She's certainly vulnerable. Please don't hesitate to consult with us if there's anything we can do."

"Would it be possible to review Mrs. Ramp's chart?"

"Her chart? I suppose so, but why?"

"Same answer as before, I guess. Trying to make sense out of it."

Professorial smile. "Her chart won't help you with that. There's nothing . . . juicy in it. Which is to say we avoid the typical anecdotal pitfalls—compulsively detailed descriptions of the patient's every twitch and blink, those lovely Oedipal recollections and dream sequences movie writers are so fond of. My research has shown that that kind of thing has little to do with therapeutic outcome. Typically, the doctor scrawls in order to feel he's being useful, never bothers to actually go back and read any of it, and when he does, none of it's useful. So we've developed a method of record-keeping that's highly objective. Behavior-based symptomology. Objectively defined goals."

"What about records of the group sessions?"

"We don't keep those. Because we don't conceptualize the groups as therapy—unstructured group sessions have very little direct treatment value. Two patients presenting identical symptoms may have arrived at their pathology along totally different pathways. Each has developed a unique pattern of faulty learning. Once the patient has changed, it may be appropriate for him to talk to others who've experienced progress. If for no other reason than as a social reinforcer."

"Socializing as a reward for doing well?"

"Exactly. But we keep the discussion on a positive track. Don't take notes or do anything else to make it seem too clinical."

Remembering what Ursula said about Gina's planning to talk about Melissa in group, I said, "Do you discourage their talking about their problems?"

"I'd prefer to see it as reinforcing positivity."

"Guess you'll be facing a challenge now. Helping the others deal with what happened to Gina."

Keeping his eyes on me, he reached into his pocket and brought out a packet of chewing gum. Unwrapping two pieces, he stuck them together and got to work on them.

"If you want to read her chart," he said, "I'd be happy to make you a copy."

"I'd appreciate that."

"Where shall I send it?"

"Your wife has my address."

"Ah." Glancing at Ursula again. She'd moved away from the door, was coming slowly down the steps.

"So," he said, "the daughter's sleeping?"

I nodded.

"How's the husband doing?"

"He hasn't come home yet. Any psychological insights on him?"

He moved his head to one side, shifting into the sunlight, and his white hair became a nimbus. "Seems a pleasant enough fellow. Somewhat on the passive side. They haven't been married long, so he's a Johnny-come-lately, in terms of the pathology."

"Was he involved in the treatment?"

"As involved as he could be. He followed through on the little that was expected of him. Excuse me."

Turning his back on me, he walked briskly toward the steps and took his wife's hand as she descended. Tried to put his arm around her shoulder but was too short to pull it off. Grasping her waist instead, he ushered her toward the Saab. Holding the passenger door open for her, he helped her in. His turn to drive. Then he walked over to me and offered his soft hand.

We shook.

"We came to help," he said, "but it doesn't seem as if there's much for us to do right at this moment. Please let us know if that changes. And good luck to the child. She'll certainly need it."

Madeleine's directions were precise. I found the Tankard without any trouble.

Southwestern stretch of Cathcart Boulevard, just below the San Labrador city limits. Same mix of pricey shops and service establishments, lots of self-conscious mission architecture. The pistachio trees ended at the Pasadena border and were replaced by jacarandas in full bloom. The median was beautifully littered with purple blossoms.

I parked, spotting other non-Labradoran features: a cocktail lounge at the end of the block. Two liquor stores— one billing itself as a wine merchant, the other a PURVEYOR OF FINE SPIRITS. Window banners announcing premium French and California varietals on special.

The Tankard and Blade was a modest-looking establishment. Two stories, maybe a thousand square feet, set on a quarter-acre lot that was mostly parking space. Coarse-troweled white stucco, brown crossbeams, leaded windows, and mock-thatch roofing. A chain blocked the lot. Ramp's Mercedes was on the other side, parked toward the rear, confirming my powers of deduction. (Where the hell was the deerstalker hat and calabash?) A couple of other cars sat farther back: twenty-year-old brown Chevrolet Monte Carlo with a white vinyl top peeling at the seams, and a red Toyota Celica.

The front door was panes of bubbly colored glass set into distressed oak. A hand-printed cardboard sign hanging from the knob said SUNDAY BRUNCH CANCELED. THANK YOU.

I knocked, got no answer. Pretended I had a right to intrude and rapped until my knuckles grew sore.

Finally the door opened and an irritated-looking woman stood there, keys in hand.

Mid-forties, five five, 135. Figure in the hourglass mode, made ostentatious by what she had on: Empire-waisted, bodice-topped, puffed long-sleeve maxi-dress with a square neckline low enough to display a swelling hand's-breadth of freckled cleavage. Above the waist the dress was white cotton; below, wine-and-brown paisley print. Platinum hair drawn back and tied with a wine-colored ribbon. A black velvet choker centered with an imitation coral cameo encircled her neck.

Someone's idea of Ye Olde Serving Wench.

Her features were good: high cheekbones, firm square chin, full crimson-glossed lips, small uptilted nose, wide brown eyes framed by too-dark, too-thick, too-long lashes. Hoops the size of drink coasters hung from her ears.

Protected by barroom light or booze-softened consciousness, she would have been a knockout. Morning assaulted her beauty, pouncing upon overly pancaked skin, worry seams, a loosening around the jowls, pouches of despair tugging her mouth into a frown.

She was regarding me as if I were the taxman.

"I'd like to see Mr. Ramp."

She back-rapped the sign with crimson nails. "Can't you read?" She flinched as if asserting herself hurt.

"I'm Dr. Delaware—Melissa's doctor."

"Oh . . ." The worry lines deepened. "Hold on a second—just wait here."

The door closed and locked. A few minutes later she opened it. "Sorry, it's just . . . You should have . . . I'm Bethel." Shooting her hand forward. Before I could take it, she added, "Noel's mom."

"Good to meet you, Mrs. Drucker."

Her expression said she wasn't used to being called Mrs. She dropped my hand, looked up and down the boulevard. "C'mon in."

Closing the door behind me and locking it with a hard twist.

The restaurant's lights were off. The leaded windows were frosted and thinly spaced and a dishwater-colored haze struggled through them. My pupils labored to adjust. When they stopped aching, I saw a single long room lined with tuft-and-nailhead red-leather booths and floored with honey-brown carpet patterned in mock peg-and-groove. The tables were spread with white linen and set with pewter drink plates, blocky green glass goblets, and stout-looking flat-ware. The walls were vertical pine planks stained the color of roast beef. Bracketed shelves just below the ceiling line housed a collection of mugs and steins—easily a hundred of them, many of them featuring pink-cheeked Anglo-Saxon visages with dead porcelain eyes. Suits of armor that looked like studio props stood in strategic locations around the restaurant. Maces and broadswords hung on the walls, along with still lifes favoring dead birds and rabbits.

An open door at the rear offered a glimpse of stainless-steel kitchen. To its left was a horseshoe-shaped, leather-topped bar backed with a St. Pauli's Girl mirror. A stainless-steel serving cart sat at the epicenter of the *faux*-wood carpet, bare except for a rotisserie spit and a carving set hefty enough to handle bison surgery.

Ramp was at the bar, facing the mirror, brow resting in one hand, one arm dangling. Near his elbow was a glass and a bottle of Wild Turkey.

Clatter came from the kitchen, then silence.

Unhealthy silence. Like most places designed for social intercourse, the restaurant was deathly without it.

I approached the bar. Bethel Drucker stayed with me. When we got there, she said, "Can I get you something, sir?" As if brunch had been restored.

"No, thanks."

She went over to Ramp's right side, leaned low, tried to catch his eye. He didn't budge. The ice in his glass floated in an inch of bourbon. The bar top smelled of soap and booze.

Bethel said, "How 'bout some more water?"

He said, "Okay."

She took the glass, went behind the bar, filled it from a plastic Evian bottle, and put it in front of him.

He said, "Thanks," but didn't touch it.

She looked at him for a moment, then went into the kitchen.

When we were alone, he said, "No problem finding me, huh?" Talking so low I had to move closer. I took the stool next to him. He didn't move.

I said, "When you didn't come home, I wondered. It was an educated guess."

"Got no home. Not anymore."

I said nothing. The St. Pauli girl grinned with Aryan joy.

"I'm a guest now," he said. "Unwanted guest. Welcome mat worn clear the hell through . . . How's Melissa?"

"Sleeping."

"Yeah, she does that a lot. When she's upset. Every time I used to try to talk to her she'd doze off."

No resentment in his voice. Just resignation. "Lots to be upset about. I wouldn't trade what she's been through for twenty billion. She got dealt a lousy hand. . . . If she'd've let me . . ."

He stopped, touched his water glass, made no attempt to lift it.

"Well, she's got one less thing to be upset about," he said.

"What's that?"

"Yours truly. No more evil stepdad. She once rented that from the video store—*The Stepfather.* Watched it over and over. Downstairs in the den. Never watched anything else down there—doesn't even like movies. I sat down to watch it with her. Wanting to relate. Made popcorn for two. She fell asleep."

He heaved his shoulders. "I'm gone, hit the dusty trail."

"From San Labrador or just from the house?"

Shrug.

"When did you decide to leave?" I said.

" 'Bout ten minutes ago. Or maybe it was right from the beginning, I don't know. What the hell's the diff?"

Neither of us talked for a while. The mirror shot back our reflections, sullied by dishwater light. Our faces were barely discernible, distorted by the imperfections in the silvered glass and the painted face of the grinning fräulein. I made out just enough to know that he looked awful. I didn't look much better.

He said, "I just can't see why the hell she'd do it."

"Do what?"

"Drive up there—break her appointment at the clinic. She never broke rules."

"Never?"

He turned and faced me. Unshaven, pouch-eyed. Instant old man; the mirror had been kind. "She once told me that when she was a kid in school, she used to get straight A's. Not because she especially liked to study, but because she was afraid of the teachers getting mad at her. Afraid of *not* doing well. She was straitlaced as they come—even back when we were at the studio and things got pretty loose, she never relaxed her standards."

I wondered how that kind of morality would fare after coming up against Todd Nyquist. I said, "Chickering's pushing a suicide theory."

"Chickering's a goddam ass. The only thing he's got any talent for is keeping things quiet. Which is what they pay him for."

"What kinds of things?"

He closed his eyes, shook his head, faced the mirror again. "What do you think? People making asses of themselves. They come in here and get plastered, want to drive home and get all pissed-off and abusive when I tell Noel not to release their keys. I call Chickering. Even though this is Pasadena, he comes right down and escorts them home—he or one of his troopers, but they do it with their own cars, so no one will see anything out of the ordinary. Nothing gets written up and the ass's car gets delivered to his driveway. If it's somebody local. Same with nice old ladies caught shoplifting, or kids smoking dope."

"What about outsiders?"

"They get put in jail." Grim smile. "We've got great crime statistics." He ran a finger across his lips. "That's why we've got no local paper—thank God for that now. I used to think it was a real pain in the ass from an advertising point of view, but thank God for it now."

He put both hands over his face.

Bethel came out from the kitchen carrying a plate of steak and eggs. She put it down in front of him, then quickly went back in.

After a long time he looked up. "So. How'd you enjoy the beach?"

When I didn't reply, he said, "I told you she wouldn't be out there. Why the hell'd you bother?"

"Detective Sturgis asked me to check."

"Good old Detective Sturgis. *We* sure wasted each other's time, didn't we? You usually do what he asks?"

"He doesn't usually ask."

"Though it wasn't exactly dirty work, right? Drive to the beach, catch some sun, check up on the client."

"It's a beautiful spot," I said. "Get down there much?"

He tensed his jaw. Touched his whiskey glass. Finally said, "Used to. Few times a month. Never could get Gina to go with me." He turned and looked at me again. Stared.

I held his gaze.

"Nothing like the sun at the beach," he said. "Gotta keep the old tan going. Perfect host and all that—got a certain goddam standard to uphold, right?"

He lifted the glass, sipped.

I said, "The last couple of days haven't been a day at the beach for you."

"Yeah." Hollow laugh. "First I thought it was nothing—Gina'd lost her way, would come right back. Then when she didn't show up by Thursday night, I started thinking maybe she *had* taken a drive—wanting to be free, like Sturgis said. Once I put that in my mind, I couldn't get it out. Couldn't stop wondering if it was something *I* did—drove myself *nuts* wondering. So what does it turn out to be? Goddam stupid *accident*, Jesus H . . . I should have known it wasn't us. We were getting along great, even though . . . it was so . . . so . . ."

He made a tortured sound, picked up the glass, and heaved it at the mirror. The fräulein's face cracked; blades of glass tumbled out and shattered on the gooseneck spigot of the bar sink, leaving a trapezoid of white plaster. The rest of the mirror remained bolted to the wall.

No one came out of the kitchen.

He said, "*Skoal. À*-goddam-*santé*. Bottoms goddam up." Turning to me: "What are you here for anyway? See what a secret fag looks like?"

"Touching base. Trying to make some sense of what happened, myself. So I can help Melissa."

"Made any so far? Sense?"

"Not yet."

"You one, too?"

"What?"

"Fag. Gay—whatever they're calling it nowadays. Like him. Sturgis. And me and . . ."

"No."

"Bully for you . . . Good old Melissa. What was she like as a little kid?"

I told him, emphasizing the positive, careful not to break confidentiality.

"Yeah," he said again. "That's what I figured. I would have liked— Ah, to hell with it."

He got up with remarkable speed. Went to the kitchen door and called out, "Noel!"

The Drucker boy came out, wearing his red busboy's jacket over a T-shirt and jeans and holding a dish towel.

"You can go now," said Ramp. "The doctor here says she's sleeping. If you want to wait till she wakes up, that's fine. I've got nothing for you to do here. Just do one thing first: Pack me a suitcase—clothes, stuff, just throw it in. Use the big blue case in my closet. Bring it back here—doesn't matter what time. I'll be here."

"Yes, sir," said Noel, looking uneasy.

"*Sir,*" said Ramp, turning to me. "Hear that? Respectful youth. This boy will go far. Watch out, Harvard."

Noel winced.

Ramp said, "Tell your mom it's safe to come out. I'm not going to eat any of this. Gonna take a nap, myself."

The boy went back into the kitchen.

Ramp watched him. "Everything's going to change," he said. "Everything."

26

Just as I was pulling away from the curb, Noel came out of the restaurant. He spotted me and jogged over to the Seville. He'd removed his red jacket, wore a small backpack over his T-shirt. The shirt said GREENPEACE. He mouthed, "Excuse me."

I opened the passenger window.

He said, "Excuse me," again, and added a "sir."

"What's up, Noel?"

"I was just wondering how Melissa's doing."

"She seems mostly to be sleeping. The full impact may not have hit her yet."

"She's a very . . ." He frowned.

I waited. He said, "It's hard to phrase it."

I shoved the door open. "C'mon in."

He hesitated for a moment, pulled off the backpack, placed it on the floor, and slid in. He lifted the pack and put it on his lap. His face was hungry and hurting.

"Nice car," he said. "Seventy-eight?"

"Nine."

"The new ones aren't nearly as good. Too much plastic."

"I like it."

He played with the straps on the backpack.

I said, "You were saying something about Melissa. Something that was hard to phrase."

He frowned. One fingernail scraped a strap. "All I meant to say was, she's a very special person. Unique. Just from looking at her you'd assume she was something totally different than what she actually is—I mean, I know this sounds sexist, but most of the really good-looking girls tend to be concerned about superficial things—at least that's the way it is out here."

"Out here in San Labrador?"

He nodded. "At least as far as what I've seen. I don't know, maybe it's California in general. Or the whole world. I've never really lived anywhere else since I was a little kid, so I can't really say. That's why I wanted to get out of here—try a different environment. Not all this party-hearty."

"Harvard."

Nod. "I applied to a lot of schools, didn't really expect to get into Harvard. When I did, I decided it was what I wanted, if the financial part could be worked out."

"Was it?"

"Basically. Between what I've saved up, taking a year off to put more away, and some other things, I could have handled it."

"Could have?"

"I don't know." He fidgeted, pulled straps. "I really don't know, now, if going away is the best thing."

I said, "Why's that?"

"I mean, how can I leave when she's going through something like this? She's . . . deep. Feels things more strongly than other people. She's the only girl I've ever met who's really concerned with important things. The first time we ever met, it was unbelievably easy to talk to her."

Pain in his eyes.

"Sorry," he said, reaching for the door handle. "Sorry for bothering you. Actually, I feel kind of dishonest talking to you."

"Why's that?"

He rubbed the back of his neck. "The first time Melissa called you—about wanting to come in and see you? I was there. In the room with her."

I mentally replayed the conversation. Melissa excusing herself a couple of times . . . *Oh, darn, hold on* . . . hand over the phone.

"And?" I said.

"I was against it," he said. "Her seeing you. I told her she didn't need a— She could work things out herself. That we could problem-solve it together. She told me to mind my own business, that you were great. Now here I am, talking to you myself."

"None of that's important, Noel. Let's get back to where we were—Melissa as a unique person. I agree with you on that. What you're saying is you feel a unique rapport with her. And you're worried about abandoning her in her time of need."

He nodded.

"When are you supposed to leave for Boston?"

"Early August. Classes start September. But they want you to get there earlier, for orientation."

"Got a major in mind?"

"Maybe international relations."

"Diplomacy?"

"Probably not. I think I'd prefer something that has to do with actual policy-making. An administrative staff position at the State Department or Defense. Or a congressional aide. If you study the way the government works, it's really the people behind the scenes who get things done. Sometimes professional diplomats do have impact, but often they're just appointed figureheads." Pause. "Also, I think I'd have a better shot at a behind-the-scenes position."

"Why's that?"

"From everything I've read about the foreign service, where you come from—your family, your background, who you know—is more important than what you actually accomplish. Kind of like making the best clubs in high school. I haven't got much of a family. Just Mom and myself."

Saying it matter-of-factly, no self-pity.

He said, "It used to bother me—people put a lot of premium on lineage out here. Meaning money that's two generations old. But now I realize I've actually been pretty lucky. Mom's really supportive and I've always had everything I needed. When you get down to it, a person doesn't need that much, do they? Also, I got to see what happens to lots of the rich kids—the kind of messes they get themselves into. That's why I really respect Melissa. She's probably one of the richest girls in San Lab, but she doesn't act like it. The first time I met her she'd come into the Tankard with some other kids for a French Club dinner and I was busing for my mom. The rest of them acted as if I were invisible. Melissa took the time to say please and thank you, and afterward, when the others went out to the parking lot, she hung back and talked to me, told me she'd seen me at the Pasadena–San Labrador track meet—I used to do gymnastics until it took too much time from my studies. Nothing flirty—she's not like that. We started talking and there was this instant . . . rapport. As if we were old friends. She kept coming in and we got to be really good friends. She helped me with lots of things. All I want is to be able to help her. Is it definite about her mom being . . . ?"

"No," I said. "Not definite. But it doesn't look good."

"That's really . . . terrible." Shaking his head. Scratching the pack. "God, that's terrible. It's going to be so hard for her."

"Did you know Mrs. Ramp well?"

"Not really. I washed her cars every couple of weeks. Once in a while she'd come down and take a look. But to tell the truth, she really didn't care about them. One time I made a comment about how fantastic they were, and she said she guessed so, but to her they were just metal and rubber. Then she apologized right away, said she hadn't meant to demean my work. I thought that was pretty classy. Overall, she seemed pretty classy. Maybe a little . . . distant. I thought the way she lived was . . . Melissa and I used to . . . I guess I should have had more sympathy. If Melissa remembers that, she'll probably hate me."

"Melissa will remember your friendship."

He said nothing for several moments. Then: "Actually, it may have gone beyond friendship . . . at least from my point of view. From hers, I can't really be sure."

Looking at me straight on. Begging for good news.

The most I could offer was a smile.

He picked at a cuticle. Bit it. "Great. Here I am talking about myself when I should be thinking about Melissa. I'd better get over there. Got to pack Mr. Ramp's suitcase. Think he's serious about leaving?"

"You'd probably know that better than I would."

"I don't know a thing," he said quickly.

"He and Melissa don't seem to have the makings of a happy family."

He ignored that, lifted the pack and reached for the door handle. "Well, better get going."

"Need a ride?" I said.

"No, thanks, got my own car—the Celica over there." Opening the door, he put one foot on the curb, stopped, turned to face me again.

"What I meant to ask you in the first place, is there anything I should be doing—to help her?"

"Be there for her when she needs company," I said. "Listen when she talks but don't feel hurt or worried if she doesn't want to talk. Be patient when she gets really upset— don't cut her off or try to tell her everything's all right when it's not. Something bad happened—you can't change that."

He'd kept his eyes on me and nodded as I spoke. Good powers of concentration, almost eerie. I half expected him to whip out paper and pencil and take notes.

"Also," I said, "I wouldn't make any drastic changes in your own plans. Once Melissa gets over the initial shock, she's going to have to pull her life together. Putting your life on hold for her could even make her more upset. Even if you don't intend to, you're obligating her to you. Creating a debt. At this stage in Melissa's life, independence is really crucial. Even *with* what's happened. She doesn't need another burden. May come to resent it."

He said, "I never . . ." He was bouncing the pack. Looking down at it. The canvas was packed tight. It landed on his knee with a dull sound.

I said, "Books?"

"Textbooks. Some of the material I thought I'd be taking this fall. I wanted to get an early start—the freshman competition's really tough. I keep carrying them around, but I haven't read a line yet." Embarrassed smile. "Kind of weenie-ish, I guess."

"Sounds like good planning to me."

"Whatever," he said. "It's just that I feel an obligation to excel—if I go."

"Obligation to whom?"

"My mother. Don—Mr. Ramp. He's putting up any tuition shortfall for the first two years—those are the other funds I mentioned. If I ace freshman and sophomore, I should qualify for some kind of scholarship."

"He obviously thinks a lot of you."

"Well," he said dismissively, "I guess it makes him feel good that we're making progress—Mom and me. He gave her a job when she . . . when things were difficult." Brief flash of pain. Shallow smile to compensate. "Gave us a place to live—the second floor of the Tankard is our home. Not that it was charity—Mom's earned it, best waitress anyone could ever want. When he's not there she basically runs the place, even fills in for the chef. But he's also about the best boss you could have—he bought me the Celica, in addition to my bonus. Got me the job at Melissa's place."

"Melissa doesn't seem to share your feelings about him."

He started to reach for the door, gave a resigned look, and let his arm drop. "She used to like him. When she was just a customer, they'd talk and he'd bring her free Shirley Temples. She's the one who fixed him up with her mom. The trouble started after it got serious. I kept wanting to tell her that he hadn't changed—he was exactly the same person but she was just looking at him differently, but . . ."

Weak smile.

"But what?"

"You just don't tell Melissa things like that. She gets an idea in her head and she just won't shake it—not that it's a terrible fault. Too many kids are wishy-washy, don't care about ideals. She sticks to her principles, doesn't care about conforming or getting into stuff just because everyone else is. Like with drugs—I always knew how bad they were because I . . . because of all I've read. But someone like Melissa, you'd think she might be . . . susceptible. Being popular and good-looking and having plenty of money. But she never did. She stood her ground."

"Popular?" I said. "She's never mentioned any friends other than you. And I haven't seen any come around."

"She's picky. But everyone liked her. She could have been a cheerleader, joined the best service clubs if she'd wanted, but she had other things on her mind."

"Like what?"

"Her studies, mostly."

"What else?"

He hesitated, then said, "Her mom—it was as if being a daughter was her main job in life. She once told me she felt she'd always have to take care of her mom. I tried to convince her that wasn't right but she really got steamed. Told me I didn't know what it was like. I didn't argue with her. All that would've done was get her madder, and I really don't like it when she gets mad."

He walked away before I could respond. I watched him lift the chain to the parking lot, get in the Toyota, and drive off.

Two hands on the wheel.

This boy will go far.

Courteous, reverent, industrious, almost excruciatingly earnest.

In some ways, Melissa's male counterpart—her spiritual sibling. I could understand the rapport.

Did that get in the way of her thinking of him the way he wanted?

A good kid.

Too good to be true?

My talk with him had twanged my therapist's antennae, though I wasn't sure why.

Or maybe I was just filling my head with supposition in order to avoid reality. The topic we'd barely touched upon.

Blue skies, black water.

Something white, floating . . .

I started the Seville, pulled forward, coasted across the San Labrador city line.

Melissa was awake, but not talking. She lay on her back, head propped on three pillows, hair braided atop her head, eyelids swollen. Noel sat by her side, in the rocker Madeleine had filled an hour ago. Holding her hand, looking alternately content and edgy.

Back in her uniform, Madeleine moved through the room like a harbor barge, docking at pieces of furniture, dusting, straightening, opening and closing drawers. On the nightstand was a bowl of oatmeal that had congealed to mortar. The drapes were drawn, warding off the harshness of midday summer light.

I leaned under the canopy and said hello. Melissa acknowledged me with a feeble smile. I squeezed the hand Noel hadn't claimed. Asked her if there was anything I could do for her.

Head shake. She looked nine years old again.

I stuck around anyway. Madeleine swiped a bit more with her dishrag, then said, "I go downstairs, *ma petite choute*? Something to eat?"

Melissa shook her head.

Madeleine picked up the bowl of oatmeal and walked halfway to the door. "Something to eat for you, monsieur doctor?"

The invitation and the "doctor" meant I must have done something right.

I realized I was hungry. But even if I hadn't been, I wouldn't have turned her down.

"Thank you," I said. "Something light would be fine."

"A steak?" she said. "Or some nice lamb chops—I have the double-cuts."

"A small chop would be great."

She nodded, stuffed her dustrag in a pocket, and left.

Alone with Noel and Melissa, I felt like an unwanted chaperon. They seemed so comfortable with each other that three was definitely a crowd.

Soon her eyes had closed again. I stepped out into the hallway, found myself drifting past closed doors. Drifting toward the back of the house—the rear spiral staircase that Gina Ramp had descended that first day, looking for Melissa. Stairs that ascended as well, tunneling upward through the gloom of the hallway.

I began climbing. At the top was a hundred square feet of bare space marked by cedar double doors.

Old-fashioned iron key in the lock. I turned it, stepped into darkness, groped for a light switch, and flicked. Found myself in an enormous, loftlike room. Over a hundred feet long, at least half that amount in width, with dusty pine-plank floors, cedar walls, unfinished beam ceiling, bare bulbs joined to unshielded electrical conduits that ran the length of the beams. Dormer windows on both ends, shaded with oilcloth.

The right portion of the room was filled: furniture, lamps, steamer trunks and leather suitcases that brought to mind the age of rail travel. Groups of objects assembled with loose but noticeable organization: Here a collection of statuary, there a foundry's worth of bronze sculptures. Inkstands, clocks, stuffed birds, ivory carvings, inlaid boxes. A jumble of staghorns, some of them on mounting boards, others bound together with leather thongs. Rolled rugs, animal skins, elephant-foot ashtrays, glass shades that could have been Tiffany. A standing polar bear, glass-eyed, yellowed, snarling, one paw waving, the other clutching a taxidermic salmon.

The left side was nearly empty. Two levels of vertically slotted storage racks ran along the wall. An easel and artist's flat file sat in the center. Canvases and framed pictures filled the slots. A blank canvas was clamped to the easel—not quite blank; I made out faint pencil lines. The wooden frame had warped; the canvas billowed and puckered.

A pine paint box sat atop the flat file. The latch was rusted but I pried it open using my fingernails. Inside were a dozen or so sable brushes, their shanks paint-stained, their bristles stiffened to uselessness, a rusty palette knife, and paint tubes dried solid. Lining the bottom of the case were several pieces of paper. I slid them out. Pages cut out of magazines: *Life, National Geographic, American Heritage.* Dates from the '50s and '60s. Landscapes and seascapes, mostly. Inspirational images, I supposed. A photo between two of the pages. Writing on the back. Black ink, a beautiful, flowing hand:

March 5, 1971
Restoration?

Color photograph—good quality, satin finish.

Two people—a man and a woman—standing in front of paneled doors. The Chaucer doors. Peach-colored stucco around the wood.

The woman was Gina Dickinson's size and shape. Model-slim figure, except for a hard, high swell of belly. She had on a white silk dress and white shoes that stood out nicely against the dark wood. On her head was a wide-brimmed white straw sun hat. Wisps of blond hair fuzzed her slender neck. The face below the hat was encased in a mummy-wrap of bandages, the eyeholes flat and black as raisins in a snowman.

One of her hands clutched a bouquet of white roses. The other rested on the shoulder of the man.

Tiny man. Coming midway to Gina's shoulder, making him four seven or eight, tops. Sixtyish. Frail. Head too big for his body. Arms disproportionately long. Stumpy legs. Goatish features under frizzy gray hair.

A man whose ugliness was so beyond aesthetic repair that it seemed almost noble.

He wore a dark three-piece suit that was probably well cut, but tailoring couldn't compensate for Nature's faulty draftsmanship.

I remembered something Anger, the banker, had said:

Art was his only extravagance. He would have bought his clothes off the rack if he could.

No portraits in the house . . .

The aesthete . . .

He was posed formally, one hand in his waistcoat, the other around his bride. But his eyes had wandered off to one side. Uneasy. Knowing that the camera would be cruel even on special days, but that special days cried out for preservation nonetheless.

He'd kept the picture at the bottom of a box.

Like the magazine photos, inspiration?

I took a closer look at the canvas on the easel. The pencil lines assembled themselves as coherent form: two ovals. Faces. Faces on an equal level. Cheek to cheek. Below, what would have been the sketchy beginnings of torsos. Normal size. The one on the right flat-tummied.

Art as revisionism. Arthur Dickinson's attempt at mastery. March 5, 1971.

Melissa had been born in June of that year. Arthur Dickinson had missed the unveiling of his most prized work by weeks.

Something else about the picture struck me: older, shorter, homely man. Taller, younger, beautiful woman.

The Gabneys. The way Leo had tried, unsuccessfully, to embrace his wife's shoulders.

He was of normal height, the disparity less dramatic, but the parallel remained striking.

Maybe it was because the Gabneys had stood in that same spot this morning.

Maybe I wasn't the only one to have noticed it.

Identification between therapist and patient.

Similar taste in men.

Similar taste in interior decorating.

Who'd influenced whom?

Chicken-egg riddles, which had come to me as I sat in Ursula's office, returned with brain-pecking vengeance.

I went over to the vertical rack. Handwritten labels under each slot listed artist, title, descriptive data, dates of execution and purchase.

Hundreds of partitions, but Arthur Dickinson had been an organized man; the collection was alphabetized.

Cassatt, between Casale and Corot.

Eight slots.

Two of them empty.

I read the labels.

Cassatt, M. Mother's Kiss, c. 1891. Aquatint with drypoint and soft-ground. Catal: Breeskin 149, $13^5/_8 \times 8^{15}/_{16}$ in.

Cassatt, M. Maternal Caress, c. 1891. Aquatint with drypoint and soft-ground. Catal: Breeskin 150, $14^1/_2 \times 10^9/_{16}$ in.

The rest of the six accounted for, framed and glassed. I pulled them out carefully. All black-and-white, no mother and child scenes.

The two best prints gone.

One for the patient's gray room, one for the doctor's. I recalled the way the Gabneys had behaved this morning.

Leo trying to project sympathy. But making sure to tell me that Chickering's suicide theory was nonsense.

Damage control.

Ursula operating on a whole other level.

Touching the Chaucer doors as if they led to a shrine.

Or a treasure trove.

I thought of Gina's unaccounted "petty cash." Two million . . .

Had the gifts gone beyond art?

Therapeutic transference as a pathway to riches?

Dependency and terror could create a cancer of the soul. Those with the cure could name their price.

I thought of gifts I'd been offered. Mostly handmade creations of little children—potholders, popsicle-stick picture frames, drawings, clay sculptures. My office at home was full of them.

In the case of adult offerings, I had a policy of accepting only tokens—flowers, candy. A yellow-wrapped basket of fruit. I turned down anything of significant and lasting value. Doing it graciously was sometimes an ordeal.

No one had ever shoved a piece of rare art in my hands. Still, I liked to think I would have turned that down, too.

Not that accepting gifts was indictable; ethically, it lay somewhere in the fuzzy area between felony and bad judgment. And I was certainly no saint, immune to the pleasures of a bargain.

But I'd gone to school to learn how to do a certain job, and most responsible therapists agreed that any sizable gift, in either direction, reduced the chances of doing the job correctly. Shaking the therapeutic balance by immutably altering the relationship that forms the core of change.

Apparently the Gabneys disagreed.

Perhaps a treatment that involved house calls and open-ended sessions lent itself to a relaxation of the rules; I thought of how much time *I'd* spent in this house.

Foraging in the attic.

But *my* intentions were noble.

As opposed to?

Melissa had reacted to the bond between her mother and Ursula with growing suspicion.

She's cold. I feel she wants to shut me out.

Reactions discounted by everyone, including me, because Melissa was a high-strung kid, dealing with dependency and separation and threatened by anyone who got close to her mother.

Little girl who cried wolf?

Was any of it relevant to Gina's fate?

Another visit to the clinic seemed in order, though I wasn't sure how I'd approach the Gabneys.

Picking up Gina's chart—saving them the price of postage?

In the neighborhood, decided to stop by . . .

And then what?

God only knew.

Today was Sunday. It would have to wait.

Meanwhile, there were lamb chops to deal with. A meal I was willing to bet would be first-rate. Too bad my appetite had waned.

I restored Arthur Dickinson's hideaway to its original condition and went downstairs.

27

I ate by myself in the big dark dining room, feeling more like hired help than lord of the manor. When I left the house at one-fifty, Melissa and Noel were still up in the bedroom, talking in low, earnest tones.

I intended to head for home but found myself driving past the Gabney Clinic. A gunmetal-gray Lincoln and a wood-sided Mercury station wagon were parked in front. Ursula's Saab sat at the mouth of the driveway.

Gina's therapy group, one day early? Emergency session to deal with her death? Or another group led by the dedicated doctor?

Two o'clock. If the one-to-three schedule was adhered to, the session would be over in an hour. I decided to keep an eye on the building, call Milo while I was waiting.

I looked for a phone. Directly across the street were houses. Farther to the south, the neighborhood was completely residential. But cater-cornered a block north stood a row of storefronts: a prewar golden brick building with limestone insets and domed brown awnings over each shop. I cruised past slowly. The first establishment was a restaurant. Then a real estate office, a candy shop, and an antique gallery with hall trees and odd tables out on the sidewalk.

Beyond that, another couple of commercial blocks, then apartments.

The restaurant was my best bet. I turned around, pulled up in front of it.

Cute little bistro affair. LA MYSTIQUE in frosted script on the windows. *Art nouveau* letters surrounded by a garland. Peppermint and white petunias in a box under the window. A banner over the flowers announced *Brunch*.

Inside were eight tables covered with blue-and-white checkered cloths, sprigs of daisies and lavender in blue glass vases, white chairs and walls, European travel posters, an open kitchen behind a low Plexiglas partition in which a Hispanic man wearing a chef's toque labored. Two of the tables were occupied, both by pairs of conservatively dressed middle-aged women. What was on their plates tended toward the green and leafy. They paused to look up as I entered, then resumed playing with their food.

A conspicuously busty, fair-haired woman of around thirty came forward, holding a menu. She had a full, friendly face not quite brightened by a nervous smile. Her hair was tied in a bun and bound with a black ribbon, and she wore a knee-length black knit dress that emphasized her chest but failed, otherwise, to flatter. As she came toward me I could see an undertow of anxiety tugging at the smile.

Brand-new-business anxiety?

Still-in-the-red anxiety?

She said, "Hello. Please sit anywhere you'd like."

I looked around, noticed that the two window tables offered an oblique but clear view of the clinic.

"How about there," I said. "And do you have a pay phone I could use?"

"Right through the back." She pointed to Dutch doors to the left of the kitchen.

The phone was mounted on the wall between the bathrooms. After two rings, Milo's new businesslike message kicked in. I told him I had a few things I wanted to discuss, said I'd probably be back at Melissa's house by four. Then I dialed an art gallery in Beverly Hills that I'd dealt with before and asked for the owner.

"Eugene De Long speaking."

"Eugene, it's Alex Delaware."

"Hello, Alex. Nothing on the Marsh yet. We're still looking for one in acceptable condition."

"Thanks. Actually I'm calling to find out if you can give me an evaluation of a piece—or two pieces really, same artist. Nothing formal, just an approximation."

"Certainly, if it's something I know about."

"Cassatt color print."

Moment of silence. "I didn't know you were in the market for that kind of thing."

"Wish I were. It's for a friend."

"Is your friend buying or selling?"

"Maybe selling."

"I see," he said. "Which particular color prints?"

I told him.

He said, "Just one second," and put me on hold for several minutes. He came back saying, "I've got the most recent auction figures for comparable works right here. As you know, with works on paper, condition is everything, so without inspecting it I can't be sure. However, Cassatt's print runs tended to be low—she was a perfectionist, had no compunctions about burnishing down her initial impressions and reworking the plates—so any decent piece would be interesting. Especially color. If you've indeed got the final states in excellent condition—full margins, no stains—you've got a couple of jewels. I could get a quarter of a million from the right client. Maybe more."

"Both or each?"

"Oh, each. Especially in the current climate. The Japanese are crazy for Impressionism and Cassatt's at the top of their American list. I expect her important paintings to be fetching solid seven figures very shortly. The prints actually reflect a blending of Western and Asian sensibilities—she was highly influenced by Japanese printmaking—that appeals to them. Even three hundred wouldn't be out of the question for a really fine impression."

"Thanks, Eugene."

"My pleasure. Tell your friend he or she's got a blue chip investment, but in all honesty the major appreciation probably hasn't taken place. However, if he or she does want to sell, there's no need to go to New York."

"I'll pass it along."

"*Bonsoir,* Alex."

I closed my eyes and pictured zeros for a while. Then I dialed my service and found out Robin had called.

I called her studio. When she picked up I said, "Hi. It's me."

"Hi. Just wanted to see how you were doing."

"Pretty well. Still out here on a case."

"And *here* is?"

"Pasadena. San Labrador."

"Ah," she said. "Old money, old secrets."

"If you only knew how right you were."

"ESP," she said. "If the world ever stops strumming, I'll get into tea leaves."

"Or stock trading."

"No, not that! Jail isn't my thing."

I laughed.

"Anyway," she said.

"How're you doing?"

"Fine."

"How's Mr. Panic's guitar?"

"Just a scratch, really. It wasn't even close to an emergency. I think he's finally going off the deep end—too much sobriety."

I laughed again. "I'd like to see you again, when things ease up."

"Sure," she said. "When things ease up."

Silence.

"Soon," I said, though I had nothing to back that up.

"That's even better."

I went back into the restaurant. There was a basket of bread and a glass of ice water on the table. Two of the lunching women had left; the other two were settling their check, with a pocket calculator and furrowed brows.

The bread smelled fresh—slices of whole wheat and baguettes tinged with anise—but Madeleine's "light" meal had stuffed me and I pushed it aside. The woman who had seated me noticed and I thought I saw her flinch. I picked up the menu. The two customers left. The woman picked up their credit slip, glanced at it, and shook her head. After wiping the table, she came over to me, pencil at the ready. I ordered the most expensive coffee listed—triple espresso with a dash of Napoleon brandy—and a bowl of jumbo strawberries.

She brought the berries first—truth in advertising, they were as big as peaches—the coffee a few minutes later, still foaming.

I smiled at her. She looked worried.

"Everything okay, sir?"

"Great—terrific berries."

"We get them from Carpenteria. Would you like some fresh cream?"

"No, thanks." I smiled and let my eyes drift across the street. Wondering what was going on behind the Craftsman facade. Calculating the hours of therapy necessary to buy a quarter-of-a-million-dollar piece of paper. Trying to figure out how I'd deal with the Gabneys.

When the proprietress came back a few minutes later, the level of coffee in my cup was one third lower and only two strawberries were gone.

"Something the matter, sir?"

"Not at all—everything's fine." I sipped to prove it,

then speared the most gargantuan of the strawberries on my fork.

"We import all our coffee," she said. "Simpson and Veroni buy from exactly the same source but they charge twice as much."

I had no idea who Simpson and Veroni were, but I smiled and shook my head and said, "Figures." The empathy didn't impress her. If this was her usual interpersonal style, I could see why the public wasn't beating a path to her door.

I took another swallow and began working on the berry.

She lingered for a second, went into the kitchen, and began conferring with the chef.

I resumed looking out the window. Glanced at my watch: 2:35. Less than half an hour till show time. What would I say to Ursula Gabney?

The busty woman came out from the kitchen with the Sunday paper under one arm, sat down at one of the tables, and began reading. As she put aside the front section and picked up the Metro, our eyes met. She pulled away quickly. I gulped down the rest of my coffee.

Without rising, she said, "Anything else?"

"No, thanks."

She brought me the check. I handed her a credit card. She took it, stared at it, returned with a slip, and said, "You're a doctor?"

I realized then how I must have appeared to her: clothes I'd slept in, unshaven.

I said, "I'm a psychologist. There's a clinic across the street. I'm on my way over there to talk to one of the doctors."

"Uh-huh," she said, looking doubtful.

"Don't worry," I said, putting on my best smile. "I'm not one of the patients. Been working a long shift—emergency case."

That seemed to spook her, so I produced my license and med school faculty card. "Scout's honor."

She relaxed a bit, said, "What kind of things do they do over there?"

"Don't really know," I said. "Had any problems because of them?"

"Oh, no. It's just that you don't see too many people going in and out. And there's no sign telling anyone what kind of place it is. I wouldn't have even *known* what it was except one of my customers told me. It just made me wonder what they do in there."

"I don't know much about it myself. My specialty is working with children. One of my patients is the child of a woman who used to be treated there—maybe you noticed her. She used to come in an old Rolls-Royce—black and gray."

She nodded. "I did see a car like that a couple of times, but I never noticed who drove it."

"The woman who owned it disappeared a few days ago. It's been pretty hard on the child. I came over to learn what I could."

"Disappeared? What do you mean?"

"She set out for the clinic, never showed up, and hasn't been seen."

"Oh." A new kind of anxiety, one that had nothing to do with balance sheets.

I looked up at her, fingered the credit slip.

"You know . . ." she said, then shook her head.

"What is it?"

"Nothing . . . It's probably nothing. I shouldn't mix in, in things that don't concern me. . . ."

"If you know anything—"

"No," she said emphatically. "It's not about your patient's mother. Another one—of their patients—the customer I mentioned. The one who told me what kind of place it was. She used to come in here, didn't seem as if there was anything wrong with her. She said she used to be afraid of going places—phobic—that's why she was going for treatment, but she'd gotten a lot better. You would have thought she'd like the place—the clinic—be grateful. But she didn't seem to—not that you should quote me on that. I really don't need any headaches."

She touched the credit slip. "You still need to total and sign."

I did, adding a 25 percent tip.

"Thank you," she said.

"My pleasure. What made you think this woman didn't like the clinic?"

"Just the way she talked—asking lots of questions. About them." Glancing across the street. "Not right away. After she'd been coming for a while."

"What kinds of questions?"

"How long they'd been here. I had no idea, just moved in myself. Did the doctors or any of the other patients ever come in here—that was an easy one. Not even once. Except Kathy—that was her name. She didn't seem afraid of anything. Kind of aggressive, actually. But I liked her—she was friendly, liked my food. And she came in all the time. I really liked the idea of having a regular. Then one day, out of the blue, she just stopped." Snapping her fingers. "Just like that. I thought it was strange. Especially because she hadn't mentioned anything about being finished with her treatment. So when you said this other woman disappeared, it kind of reminded me of that. Though Kathy didn't really *disappear*—she just stopped showing up."

"How long ago was this?"

She thought. "About a month ago. First I thought it was something to do with the food, but she stopped going over there, too. I knew her car. She'd been on a regular schedule: Monday and Thursday afternoon, like clockwork. At three-fifteen she'd be in here for angel hair pasta or scallops, cappuccino royale, and a raisin croissant. I appreciated it because, to tell the truth, business has not been booming yet—we're still establishing our presence. My husband has been I-told-you-soing for three months. I started Sunday brunch last week, but it hasn't exactly raised the dead."

I clucked my tongue in sympathy.

She smiled. "I called this place La Mystique, for mystery. He says the only mystery is when I'm going to fold—so I've got to prove him wrong. That's why I especially appreciated Kathy's patronage. I still wonder what happened to her."

"Do you remember her last name?"

"Why?"

"I'm just trying to contact everyone who knew my patient's mother. You never know what little detail might tell us something."

She hesitated, then: "One sec."

She pocketed the credit slip, went back into the kitchen. As I waited, I looked over at the clinic building. No one entered or exited. Not a hint of life behind the windows.

She returned with a square of yellow message paper.

"This is Kathy's sister's address. She gave her as a reference at the beginning, because she used to pay by check and her own checks were out-of-state. I actually thought of giving a call, but never got around to it. If you speak to her, give her my best—tell her Joyce said hi."

I took the paper and read it. Neatly printed letters in red felt-tip marker:

KATHY MORIARTY
C/O ROBBINS
2012 ASHBOURNE DR.
S. PAS.

A 795 phone number.

I put it in my wallet, got up, and said, "Thanks. Everything was great."

"All you had was berries and coffee. Come back sometime when you're hungry. We're good—we really are."

She walked back to her table and the newspaper.

I got up, looked out the window, saw movement. A stately-looking gray-haired woman getting into the Lincoln. The station wagon already pulling away from the curb.

Time for a chat with Dr. Ursula.

But I was disabused of that notion as I reached the sidewalk. The Saab shot backwards out of the driveway, came to a short stop, and sped northward. So fast, I barely had a glimpse of the driver's tense, beautiful face.

By the time I got behind the wheel of the Seville, she was out of sight.

I sat for a while, wondering what had drawn her away. Opened the glove compartment, took out my Thomas Guide, and looked up Ashbourne Drive.

The house was a generously proportioned used-brick Tudor on a wide, ungated lot shaded by maples and firs. A Plymouth van in the driveway shadowed a scattered collection of toy bikes and wagons. Three brick steps and a porch led to the front entrance. The door featured a tiny brass replica of itself set at eye level.

A bell-ring, the tiny door creaked open, and a pair of dark eyes peered out. A TV cartoon soundtrack blared from within. The eyes narrowed.

"Dr. Delaware to see Mrs. Robbins, please."

"*Wan meen'*."

I waited, straightening my clothes and finger-combing my hair. Hoping my dress shirt and tie would make the stubble look like intentional hip.

West-side hip. Wrong neighborhood.

The little door opened again. Blue eyes. Pupils contracting.

"Yes?" Young voice, slightly nasal.

"Mrs. Robbins?"

"What can I do for you?"

"My name is Dr. Alex Delaware. I'm trying to locate your sister Kathy."

"Are you a friend of Kathy's?"

"No, not actually. But we have a mutual acquaintance."

"What kind of doctor are you?"

"Clinical psychologist. I'm sorry to bust in on you like this, and I'll be happy to show you identification and some professional credentials."

"Yes, why don't you do that."

I pulled the appropriate snips of paper out of my wallet and held them up, one by one.

She said, "Who do you and Kathy both know?"

"It's something I really need to discuss with her personally, Mrs. Robbins. If you're not comfortable giving me her number, I'll give you mine and she can call me."

The blue eyes moved back and forth. The little door slammed shut again and the big one opened. A woman in her late thirties came out onto the front porch. Five six, trim, strawberry-blond hair cut in a bob. The blue eyes deep-set in a long, freckled face. Full lips, pointed chin, slightly protruding ears that the short hair flaunted. She wore a short-sleeved, boatneck top with horizontal red-and-white stripes, white canvas pants, and tennies without socks. Tiny diamonds in her ears. She could have been one of Las Labradoras.

"Jan Robbins," she said, looking me over. Her nails were long but unpolished. "It's best that we talk out here."

"Sure," I said, conscious of every wrinkle in my suit.

She waited until I'd backed away a bit before closing the front door behind her. "So why are you looking for Kathy?"

I considered how much to say. Had Kathy Moriarty's sessions at the clinic been something she'd withheld from her sister? She'd talked openly to Joyce at the restaurant, but strangers were often seen as the safest repositories of confidences.

"It's complicated," I said. "It would really be best if I talked to your sister directly, Mrs. Robbins."

"I'm sure it would, Doctor. I'd like to speak with her directly myself, but I haven't heard from her in over a month."

Before I could reply, she said, "Not that it's the first time, given the way she lives—her career."

"What career is that?"

"Journalism. Writing. She used to work for the *Boston Globe* and the *Manchester Union Leader,* but now she's on her own. Freelancing. Trying to get her own books published— she actually had one out a few years ago. On pesticides—*The Bad Earth?*"

I said nothing.

She smiled—with some satisfaction, I thought. "It wasn't exactly a best-seller."

"Is she from New England originally?"

"No, originally she's from here—California. We both grew up in Fresno. But she went back east after college, said she considered the West Coast a cultural wasteland."

She gave a quick look at the van and the toy bikes and frowned.

"Did she come back out on a writing project?" I said.

"I assume so. She never told me—never talked about her work at all. Confidential sources, of course."

"You don't have any idea what she was doing?"

"No, not in the least. We're not— We're very different. She didn't spend much time here."

She stopped, folded her arms across her chest. "Now that I think about it, how did you find out I was her sister?"

"She used you as a reference in order to cash an out-of-state check at a restaurant. The owner gave me your address."

"Great," she said. "Figures. Thank God the check didn't bounce."

"She have a problem with money?"

"Not with spending it. Look, I've really got to get inside. I'm sorry I can't help you."

She started to turn away.

I said, "So her being gone for a month doesn't concern you?"

She pivoted sharply. "For her pesticide book, she traveled all over the country for more than a year. We never heard from her unless she ran short of cash. Instead of repaying what she'd borrowed, we got a signed copy of the book. My husband's a corporate attorney, handles chemical accounts. You can imagine how much he appreciated that. A few years before that, she went to El Salvador—some sort of investigative thing, very cloak-and-dagger. Six months she was gone, not a call, not even a postcard. My mother was scared out of her mind and we never even saw a story come out of that one. So no, it doesn't concern me. She's out chasing another intrigue."

"What kind of intrigue generally interests her?"

"Anything with a hint of conspiracy—she fancies herself an investigative reporter, still thinks the Kennedy assassination makes for fascinating dinner table conversation."

Pause. Cartoon sounds, from inside the house. She gave a hard swipe at her hair. "This is ridiculous. I don't even know you. I shouldn't be talking to you. . . . In the unlikely event I hear from her soon, I'll tell her you want to talk to her. Where's your office?"

"West side," I said. "Do you have a recent address for her?"

She thought for a moment. "Sure, why not? If she can give out mine, I can give out hers."

I pulled out a pen and, using my knee for a table, wrote on the back of a business card as she reeled off an address on Hilldale Avenue.

"That's West Hollywood," she said. "Closer to your part of town."

Standing there, as if expecting me to answer some challenge.

I said, "Thanks. Sorry to bother you."

"Sure," she said, looking at the van again. "I know I sound hardhearted, but it's just that I've tried for a long time to . . . help her. But she goes her own way no matter who—" She touched her mouth, as if forcefully hushing it. "We're very different, that's all. *Vive la différence*—you psychologists believe in that, right?"

28

I got back to Sussex Knoll by four-fifteen. Noel's Celica was parked in front, along with a brown Mercedes two-seater with a DODGER BLUE sticker on the rear bumper and a cellular antenna on the rear deck.

Madeleine opened the door for me.

"How is she?"

She said, "Upstairs, monsieur doctor. She eats a little soup."

"Has Mr. Sturgis called?"

"*Non.* But others . . ." She cocked her head toward the front room and curled her lips in scorn. A conspiratorial gesture; I was an insider now.

She said, "*They* wait."

"For whom?"

She shrugged.

The two of us crossed the entry. When we got to the room, she veered and kept walking toward the back of the house.

Glenn Anger and a heavyset bald man in his fifties were sitting in the overstuffed chairs, legs crossed, looking clubby. Both wore dark blue sack suits, white shirts and pocket squares, foulard ties. Anger's cravat was a pink mini-print, the other man's yellow.

When I was a few feet away they stood and buttoned their jackets. The bald man was six feet tall, with a power-lifter's build gone slightly to seed. His face was square and beefy above an eighteen-inch neck, his tan every bit as good as Anger's and the one Don Ramp had sported before life had ground him pale. The little hair he had was wispy and colored an insipid brown-gray. Most of it ran around the sides of his head and looked as thin as a greasepaint smear. A tiny, teased puff topped his crown.

"Well," said Anger, "I suppose your work here is at an end." Looking grimly satisfied. To the bald man: "This is one of the detectives hired to search for Gina, Jim."

"Not exactly," I said. "My name is Alex Delaware. I'm Melissa's psychologist."

Anger looked baffled. Then peeved.

I said, "Mr. Sturgis—the detective—is a friend of mine. I referred the family to him. I happened to be with him when we went to your office."

"I see. Well, that's—"

"Sorry for not clarifying, but given the urgency at the time, it didn't seem important."

"Well," said Anger, "I suppose it wasn't."

The bald man cleared his throat.

Anger said, "Doctor—it is *Doctor* Delaware?"

I nodded.

"Doctor, meet Jim Douse, Gina's attorney."

One side of Douse's mouth smiled. He shook my hand, exposing a monogrammed cuff. His hand was big and padded and surprisingly rough—weekends spent away from the desk—and he curled his fingers in a way that prevented much contact between our palms. Reserving judgment on how friendly he wanted to get, or the special care very strong men sometimes exercise so as not to inflict pain.

He said, "Doctor," in a smoker's rasp. The tips of two cigars protruded from behind his pocket square. "Psychologist? I use them from time to time in court."

I nodded, wondering if that was an icebreaker or a threat.

He said, "How's our little girl doing?"

"Last time I saw her she was resting. I'm on my way up there to check."

"Cliff Chickering told me the terrible news," said Anger. "This morning, in church. Jim and I came by to see if there was anything we could do. What a stinking thing—I never actually believed it would come to this."

Douse looked at him as if introspection were a felony, then shook his head in a delayed show of sympathy.

I said, "Has the search been called off?"

Anger nodded. "Cliff said they stopped looking a few hours ago. He's convinced she's at the bottom of that dam."

"He's also convinced she put herself there," I said.

Anger looked uncomfortable.

Douse said, "I've suggested to Mr. Chickering that any further theorizing should be backed up with fact." Lifting his chin, he ran a finger around the interior of his shirt collar.

Anger said, "Damned accident is what it was, that's obvious. She shouldn't have been out there driving in the first place."

I said, "If you'll excuse me, gentlemen, I'm going to see Melissa."

"Give her our condolences, Doctor," said Anger. "If she'd like us to come up, we will. If not, we'll be available whenever she's ready to tackle the transition—just let us know."

"What transition is that?"

"Transfer of status," said Douse. "There's never a good time for it, but it needs to be done as quickly as possible. Routine procedures, paperwork. The government giving itself something to do. Everything's got to be followed to the letter or Uncle Sam gets his dander up."

Anger said, "She's too young to deal with it. The sooner we get everything squared away, the better."

"Too young to deal with paperwork?" I said.

"Too young to deal with the *mechanics*," said Anger. "The burden of management."

"She should be doing other things with her life," said Douse. "Wouldn't you say that—psychologically speaking?"

Feeling as if I'd been beamed down to a Senate subcommittee meeting, I said, "You're saying she shouldn't manage her own money."

Silence dropped like a theater curtain.

"It's complicated," said Douse. "Lots of inane regulations."

"Because of the size of the estate?"

Anger pursed his lips and busied himself with a jumpy-eyed appraisal of the Old Masters on the walls.

Douse said, "Unless it can be shown to me that you'll have an extended role in the matter, I'm not able to go into details with you, Doctor. But speaking generally, let me say this: Without concrete proof of an actual act of decession, it will take substantial time to establish the validity of the heir's tenancy and rights and subsequent transfer of ownership of those rights and the concomitant property."

He stopped and watched me. When I didn't move, he went on: "When I say substantial time, I mean just that. What we're dealing with, here, is multiple jurisdictions. Everything from local up to federal—because of the dynamics of the tax code. And that's just in terms of basic transfer. It doesn't even start to consider the whole issue of guardianship—guarding her rights. There are matters of proxy ownership, various fine points of estate law. And, of course, the IRS always steps in and tries to plunder whatever *it* can, though with the trusts that have been established, we're on solid ground regarding that can of worms."

"Guardianship?" I said. "Melissa's reached her majority—why would she need a guardian?"

Anger looked at Douse. Douse looked back at him.

Ocular tennis match. The ball finally landed in the banker's court.

"Majority," he said, "is one thing. Competence is another."

"You're suggesting Melissa's incompetent to run her own affairs?"

Anger returned his attention to the paintings.

" 'Affairs,' " said Douse, "doesn't even begin to describe it." He swept an arm around the room. "How many eighteen-year-olds would be competent to manage something of this magnitude? I know mine sure wouldn't."

"Mine neither," said Anger. "Add to that the emotional stress. The family history." He turned to me. "You'd have a good handle on that."

It sounded like an invitation. I didn't RSVP.

Douse touched his bald head. "From where I'm sitting," he said, "both as her attorney and as a parent, my educated judgment is that her resources would be put to optimal use just trying to grow up. God knows it's going to be hard enough, considering."

"That's for sure," said Anger. "I've got four at home, Doctor. All teens or tweens—we're going through the wringer. Major-league hormone alert. Give an adolescent lots of money, might as well hand them a loaded gun."

"Do you have kids of your own, Doctor?" said Douse.

"No," I said.

Both of them gave knowing smiles.

"Well," said Douse, playing with a jacket button, "as I said, that's about all I'm free to divulge, barring an extended role for you."

"What kind of role?"

"Should you choose to commit yourself to an extended course of psychological consultation—coordinating the management of Melissa's emotional affairs in sync with Glenn's and my stewardship of the financial aspects of her life, I'd be sure to see that your views were considered at all critical junctures. And well compensated."

"Let me get this straight," I said. "You'd like me to help

you certify Melissa psychologically incapable of handling her own affairs so that a guardian can be appointed to manage her money."

Anger winced.

"Wrong," said Douse. "We don't *want* anything. *Our* welfare isn't what's at stake here—we're only thinking of *hers*. As longtime friends of the family, and as parents and professional managers. And we're in no way attempting to influence your judgment or opinion. This conversation— which I might remind you originated spontaneously— simply reflects a discussion of issues that have acquired a certain sense of urgency due to unforeseen events. Plainly put, Doctor, we need to square things away damned quickly."

"One thing you should be clear on, Doctor," said Anger, "is that the money's not Melissa's yet. Not in a legal sense. She'd have a heck of a time getting hold of it before the process completes itself. And as Jim said, the wheels of bureaucracy grind slowly. The process will take a long time—months. Or even longer. In the meantime, her needs have to be met—the running of this household, salaries, repairs. Not to mention marshaling investments through a web of regulations. Things need to progress smoothly. As far as I can see, a guardian's clearly the best way to go."

"Who'd be the guardian? Don Ramp?"

Douse cleared his throat and shook his head.

"No," he said. "That would contravene the spirit, if not the letter, of Arthur Dickinson's will."

"Who, then?"

More dead air. Footsteps thumped somewhere in the big house. A vacuum whined. The phone rang once.

"My firm," said Douse, "has been of long service to this family. There's a certain logic to seeing that continue."

I said nothing. He unbuttoned his jacket, pulled out a small crocodile case, removed a white business card, and gave it to me gravely, as if it were something of value.

J. Madison Douse, Jr.
ATTORNEY AT LAW

Wresting, Douse, and Cosner
820 S. Flower Street
Los Angeles, CA 90017

Douse said, "The founding partner was Chief Justice Douse."

Leaving out the "my uncle" part. Confusing conspicuous discretion with class.

Anger blew it by saying, "Jim's uncle."

Douse cleared his throat without opening his mouth. The end result was a deep, bullish snort.

Anger hastened to repair: "The Douse and Dickinson families have been bonded by many years of implicit trust and goodwill. Arthur entrusted his affairs to Jim's dad, back in the days when those affairs were even more complex than they are now. It's in your patient's best interests that she be taken care of by the best, Doctor."

"Right now," I said, "it's in my patient's best interests to marshal her emotional defenses in order to deal with losing her mother."

"Exactly," said Anger. "That's exactly the reason Jim and I would like to see everything squared away as soon as possible."

"The problem," said Douse, "is one of procedural transfer—establishing continuity. Every step of the process as it currently operates was contingent upon Mrs. Ramp's approval. Even though she had little to do in terms of a hands-on, day-to-day management role, legally—procedurally—we were required to interface with her. Now that she's . . . no longer available, we're obligated to—"

"Deal with her heir?" I said. "Must be a hell of an inconvenience."

Douse buttoned his jacket and leaned forward. His forehead puckered and wrinkled and he sniffed like a tackle out for a quarterback. "I sense a . . . combativeness here,

Dr. Delaware, that's wholly unwarranted by the facts at hand."

"Maybe," I said. "Or maybe I just don't like the idea of being asked to lie professionally. Even if your intentions *are* good. Melissa's not incompetent—nowhere near it. She hasn't a trace of thought disorder or any other mental disturbance that would impair her judgment. As to whether or not she's mature enough to handle forty million dollars, who knows? Howard Hughes and Leland Belding weren't much older when they took over their parents' estates, and neither of them did too badly. And banks and law firms have been known to screw up handily, haven't they? What're the latest figures on the S-and-L mess?"

"That," said Anger, coloring, "has nothing to do with—"

"Whatever," I said. "The bottom line is, any decision to delegate management of Melissa's money will have to be Melissa's. And it will have to be voluntary."

Douse pressed his fingertips together, withdrew them, repeated the gesture several times. It might have been a parody of applause. His eyes were steady and small.

He said, "Well, there's obviously no need for you to assume the burden of assessment, Doctor. Given your reluctance."

"What does that mean? Bring in the hired-gun expert witnesses?"

His face remained blank as he showed his cuff monogram and consulted a gold-and-rivet Cartier that looked much too small for his wrist.

"Nice meeting you, Doctor." To Anger: "This clearly isn't a good time to be visiting, Glenn. We'll come back when she's feeling more up to it."

Anger nodded but he looked off-balance. None of his trophies had been for Overt Conflict.

Douse touched his elbow, and the two of them walked past me, heading for the entry. And came face-to-face with Melissa, who stepped out from behind a tall bookcase. Her hair was tied in a ponytail. She had on a black blouse over a knee-length khaki skirt, no stockings, black sandals. Something pink was clenched in her right hand—a balled tissue.

"Melissa," said Anger, switching on a loan-denial sadface. "I'm so sorry about your mother, hon. You know Mr. Douse."

Douse held out his hand.

Melissa opened her palm and showed the tissue. Douse dropped his arm.

"Mr. Douse," she said. "I know who you are, but we've never met, have we?"

"Sorry it has to be under these circumstances," said the attorney.

"Yes. How kind of you to come. And on a Sunday."

"Days don't matter when it comes to something like this," said Anger. "We came by to see how you were doing, but Dr. Delaware told us you were resting and we were just on our way out."

"Mr. Douse," she said, ignoring him and stepping closer to the attorney. "Mr. Douse, Mr. Douse. Please *douse* any ideas of ripping me off, okay, Mr. Douse? No, don't even say a *word*—just *leave*. Right *now*—both of you—*out*. My new attorneys and my new bankers will be contacting you shortly."

After they were gone, she cried out in rage and collapsed against me, weeping.

Noel came running down the stairs, looking scared and confused and eager to comfort. He saw her pressed to my chest and stopped midway down the flight.

I motioned him forward with a small backward movement of my head.

He stepped very close to her and said, "Melissa?"

She kept crying, pushed her head into my sternum so hard it hurt. I patted her back. It seemed inadequate.

Finally she pulled away, red-eyed, face blazing.

"Oh!" she said. "Oh, the *bastards*! How *could* they! How could they have the— She's not even . . . oh!"

Choking on her words. She wheeled, ran to a wall, hit it hard with her fists.

Noel looked to me for counsel. I nodded and he went to her. She allowed him to guide her into the front room. The three of us sat down.

Madeleine came in, looking angry but smug, as if her worst assumptions about mankind had been confirmed. Once again. I wondered how much she'd heard.

More footsteps.

The other two maids appeared behind Madeleine. She said something, and they hurried off.

Madeleine walked over and touched Melissa's head. Melissa looked up and pushed a smile through her tears.

Madeleine said, "I bring you to drink?"

Melissa didn't answer.

I said, "Please. Tea, for all of us."

Madeleine lumbered off. Melissa sat hunched under Noel's protective forearm, jaw clenched, tearing the tissue to shreds and letting them fall to the floor.

Madeleine returned with tea, honey, and milk on a silver tray. She served, handing a cup to Noel, who guided it toward Melissa's lips.

Melissa drank, choked, sputtered.

All three of us hurried to attend to her. The resulting flurry of arms was Keystonish; it might have been comical under different circumstances.

When the dust cleared, Noel again held the cup to Melissa's lips. She took a sip, started to gag, put her hand to her chest, and managed to hold it down. When she'd finished a third of the cup, Madeleine nodded in approval and left.

Melissa touched Noel's hand and said, "Enough. Thanks."

He put the cup down.

She said, "The bastards. Unbelievable."

"Who?" said Noel.

"My *banker* and my *lawyer*," she said. "Trying to rip me

off." To me: "Thanks—thanks so much for sticking up for me, Dr. Delaware. I know who my true friends are."

Noel remained confused. I gave him a brief replay of the interchange with Anger and Douse. Each word seemed to inflate his own anger.

"Assholes," he said. "Better get yourself some new ones fast."

"Oh, yeah," she said. "I made it sound as if I already had someone hired—you should have seen the looks on their faces."

Brief smile. Noel remained serious.

Melissa said, "Do you know any good lawyers, Dr. Delaware?"

"Most of the ones I know practice family law. But I should be able to get you a referral for an estate lawyer."

"Please. I'd really appreciate it. And a banker, too."

"The estate lawyer should be able to refer you to a banker."

"Good," she said. "The sooner the better, before those two worms try anything. For all I know they've already been filing some kind of papers against me." Insight widened her eyes. "I'll have *Milo* check them out. He'll be able to find out what they're up to. They've probably ripped me off already, wouldn't you say?"

"Who knows?"

"Well," she said, "they haven't exactly shown themselves to be honorable. For all I know they've been ripping off Mother all these years. . . ." Closing her eyes.

Noel hugged her tighter. She allowed it but didn't relax.

Her eyes opened suddenly. "Maybe *Don* was in it with them—all of them scheming—"

"No," said Noel, "Don wouldn't—"

She cut him off with a slashing diagonal movement of one arm. "You see one side of him, I see another."

Noel was silent.

Melissa's eyes got huge. "Oh, *God!*"

"What is it?" I said.

"Maybe they even had something to do with . . . with
. . . what happened. Maybe they wanted her money and . . ."

She shot to her feet, throwing Noel off balance. Dry-
eyed, hands fisted. One fist rose to eye level and shook.

"I'll *get* them," she said. "The *bastards*. Anyone who *hurt*
her will *pay*!"

Noel stood. She held him at arm's length. "No. It's all
right. I'll be all right. I know where I stand now."

She began walking around the room. Circling, sticking
close to the walls, like a novice skater. Taking wide steps and
speeding her pace till it was nearly a jog. Scowling and
extending her lower jaw and punching her hand with a fist.

Sleeping Beauty roused by the malignant kiss of suspicion.

Anger replacing fear. Incompatible with fear.

I'd treated an entire school that way the previous fall.
Had taught her the same lesson years ago.

This child's anger white-hot. The look on her face almost
savage.

I watched and could think of nothing but a hungry
animal in a cage.

Psychological progress, I guessed.

29

Milo showed up shortly after, wearing a brown suit and carrying a shiny black briefcase. Melissa latched onto him and told him what had happened.

"*Get* them," she said.

"I'll check it out," he said. "But it'll take some time. In the meantime, get yourself a lawyer."

"Whatever it takes. Please. Who knows what they've been up to."

"At least," he said, "they're on notice. If they've been up to something larcenous, they'll probably quit for the moment."

Noel said, "True."

Milo said to Melissa: "How are you doing, otherwise?"

"Better . . . I'm going to get through it. I have to . . . if there's something you need me to do, I can do it."

"What you can do, for the time being, is take care of yourself."

She started to object.

Milo said, "No, I'm not brushing you off. I mean it. Just in case they decide to keep pushing."

"What do you mean?" she said.

"These guys are obviously out to run the show. If they can

convince a judge you're screwed up, they've got a shot at it. I may get dirt on them or I may not. While I'm digging, they'll be stockpiling ammunition. The better you look—physically and psychologically—the less ammunition they're gonna have. So take care of yourself."

He looked over at me. "If you have to scream, scream at *him*—that's his job."

She let Noel take her upstairs. Milo said, "Did it happen the way she said?"

I nodded. "They were a couple of real sweethearts. Came on concerned, then eased into the Grand Plan. Kind of stupid, though, showing their cards like that."

"Not necessarily," he said. "In most cases it would work, because the average eighteen-year-old would be intimidated and agree to let a couple of suits handle everything. And plenty of shrinks would go along with what they offered you. For the right compensation." He scratched his nose. "Be interesting to know what they're really after."

"I'd say filthy lucre's a good guess."

"Question is how *much* lucre. Are they out to totally drain the estate or just maintain managerial control so they can beef up their fees a couple of percent. People who live off the rich get into a rut—start thinking they have a *right* to it."

"Or maybe," I said, "they made some bad investments and want to keep it quiet."

"Wouldn't be the first time," he said. "But the thing we've got to consider is, despite all these maybes, do they still have a valid point—one that would look good to a judge. *Can* she handle that kind of dough, Alex? How's she really doing emotionally?"

"I'm not sure. She's gone from drowsy to enraged awfully quickly. But nothing pathological when you consider what she's been through."

"Say it in court that way, and she's finished."

"Forty million dollars would be tough for anyone, Milo.

If I were King of the World, I wouldn't give any kid that much. But no, there's no psychological justification for declaring her incompetent. I could back her up."

"Anyway," he said, "what's the worst thing that could happen? She pisses it away, has to start from scratch. She's smart enough—could do something useful with her life. Maybe it would be the *best* thing ever happened to her."

"Financial collapse as a therapeutic technique? Good excuse for doctors' raising their fees."

He smiled. "In the meantime, I'll do what I can to check out Anger and the other guy. Though it's gonna be damned hard to pierce that kind of armor quickly. She really needs legal help."

"I thought I'd call someone on that."

"Good." He lifted his briefcase.

"That new?" I said.

"Picked it up today. Got an image to uphold. This private-eye business is heady stuff."

"Did you get the message I left with your machine a couple of hours ago?"

" 'Several things to talk about'? Sure, but I've been a busy little private bee, scooping up honeycombs of information. How about a share-fest?"

I motioned to one of the overstuffed chairs.

"No," he said. "Let's get the hell out of here, breathe some normal air—if it's okay for you to leave."

"Let me check."

I climbed the stairs, went to Melissa's room. The door was partially open. As I raised my hand to knock, I looked through the crack and saw Melissa and Noel, stretched out on the bed, fully clothed, entwined. Her fingers in his hair. His arm around her waist, rubbing the small of her back. Bare feet, toes touching.

Before they noticed me, I tiptoed away.

Milo was in the entry hall, refusing a plate of food from Madeleine.

"Full," he said, patting his belly. "Thanks anyway."

She regarded him as if he were a wayward son.

We smiled and left.

Once outside, he said, "I lied. Actually, I'm hungry as hell and her stuff's probably tastier than anything we're gonna get somewhere else. But the place gets to me—after a while, I OD on being taken *care* of."

"Me, too," I said, getting into the car. "Think how Melissa feels."

"Yeah," he said, starting up the engine. "Well, now she'll be on her own. Any suggestions, cuisine-wise?"

"As a matter of fact, I have just the place."

Start of the dinner hour. La Mystique was empty. As I pulled up in front, Milo said, "Gee. Are we gonna have to wait at the bar?"

I said, "That's the Gabney Clinic," and pointed to the big brown house. The windows were dark and the driveway was empty.

"Ah," said Milo, squinting. "Little spooky." He turned back to the restaurant. "So what's this place, your lookout post?"

"Just a warm, kind resting spot for the weary sojourner."

Joyce was startled to see me again, but she welcomed me as if I were long-lost kin and offered the same front table. Sitting there at this hour would have turned us into a window display, so I asked to be seated at the back.

She took our drink orders and came back with two Grolsches. As she poured, she said, "We've got poached striped bass and veal *vino* for specials," and launched into a detailed speech about the preparation for each.

I said, "I'll have the bass."

Milo scanned the menu. "How's the *entrecôte*?"

"Excellent, sir."

"That's what I'll have. Bloody rare, with double potatoes."

She stepped behind the partition into the kitchen and began cooking.

We touched glasses and drank beer.

I said, "According to Anger, Chickering said the search for Gina is over."

"Not surprised. Last time I checked with the Sheriffs was one-thirty this afternoon. They were pretty much winding down—not a trace of her anywhere in the park."

"Lady in the lake, huh?"

"Looks that way." He ran his hand over his face. "Okay. Time to share. Who first?"

"Go ahead."

"Basically," he said, "it's been hooray for Hollywood. Spent most of my day talking to movie people and ex-movie people and associated hangers-on."

"Crotty?"

"No, Crotty's gone. Died a couple of months ago."

"Oh," I said, thinking of the scrawny old vice cop turned gay activist. "I thought the AZT was working."

"We all did. Unfortunately, he didn't. Sat on the porch of that little farm he had up in the hills and ate a gun."

"Sorry."

"Yeah. In the end, he did it like a cop. . . . Anyway, what I learned in cinemaville: Apparently Gina and Ramp and McCloskey were all pretty chummy back in the good old days. There was this group of contract players at Apex Studios during the mid- to late sixties. McCloskey wasn't exactly part of it, but he hung out with them, started his modeling agency by getting the others photo gigs—pretty faces, both sexes. From everything I hear, they were a wild bunch, lots of boozing and doping and partying, though no one has anything bad to say about Gina specifically. So if she sinned, she did it quietly. Most of them never went anywhere, career-wise. Gina was the most likely to succeed, but the acid thing kiboshed that. The studio knew it was a buyer's market, lots of fresh flesh bused in daily from Iowa.

So it gave these kids shoestring contracts, used them for walk-ons, various ancillary services, then ditched them when the wrinkles started showing."

"Ramp never mentioned knowing McCloskey more than casually."

"He knew him all right, though from what I hear they weren't good buddies."

Milo raised his briefcase to his lap, opened it, searched, and came up with a brown marbled-paper folder. Inside was a black-and-white photograph with the Apex Studios snowy-mountain logo on the lower-right margin. The shot had been taken at some kind of nightclub—or maybe it was just a set. Fluted leather booth, mirrored wall, white-linened table, silver service, crystal ashtrays and cigarette boxes. Half a dozen good-looking people in their early twenties wearing stylish evening clothes. Smiling photogenically and smoking and raising glasses in a toast.

Gina Prince née Paddock sat dead center, blond and beautiful, in an off-the-shoulder gown that photographed gray, and a pearl choker that emphasized the length and smoothness of her neck. The resemblance to Melissa was striking.

Don Ramp next to her, husky and tan and healthy-looking, sans mustache. Joel McCloskey on her other side, slick-haired and handsome—almost pretty. His smile was different from those of the others. Outsider's uncertain grin. A cigarette between his fingers was burned down nearly to the filter.

Two other faces—a man and a woman—that I didn't recognize. And one, at the far end, that I did.

"This," I said, pointing to a sharp-featured brunette in a dangerously low-cut black dress, "is Bethel Drucker. Noel's mother. She's blond now, but this is her—I just met her today. She works for Ramp as a waitress at his restaurant. She and Noel live upstairs."

"My, my," said Milo. "One big happy family." He pulled another piece of paper out of the briefcase. "Let's see, she must be Becky Dupont. *Nom du cinéma.*" Leaning forward, he took hold of a corner of the photo. "Good-looking woman. Voluptuous."

"She still is."

"Good-looking or voluptuous?"

"Both. Though she shows some wear."

He looked toward the kitchen, where Joyce was working next to the chef. "Must be the day for voluptuous. Tell you one thing, old Becky/Bethel liked her dope. Downers and Quaaludes, according to my sources. Not that you need sources—look at those eyes."

I peered closely at the finely wrought face and saw what he meant. Wide, dark eyes half-closed, the lids sagging. The bit of iris visible, dull and dreamy and distant. Unlike McCloskey's, her smile reflected genuine bliss. But the amusement had nothing to do with the party at hand.

"It fits," I said, "with something Noel said to me today. About always knowing drugs were bad. He started to explain, then changed his mind and said he'd read about it. He's a really intense kid, very straitlaced and self-directed— almost too good to be true. If he grew up seeing what wild living did to his mom, that could explain it. *Something* about him got my antennae buzzing—maybe that was it."

I gave him back the photo. Before he put it away, he took another look. "So. Looks like everyone knows everyone knows everyone, and Hollywood has sunk its fangs into San Labrador."

"What about the other two people in the picture?"

"The guy is one of my sources, to remain unnamed. The girl is a would-be starlet named Stacey Brooks. Deceased— car crash, 1971, probable DUI. Like I said, a wild bunch."

"Those *ancillary* services they provided to the studio," I said. "That mean the casting couch?"

"That and related stuff—crowd scenes at various parties, dating potential backers and other pooh-bahs. Basically being available to satisfy a variety of appetites. Ramp was especially versatile—handsome escort for the ladies, sub rosa amusement for the gentlemen. He was a cooperative fellow, did what he was told. The studio rewarded him with a few parts—mostly minor roles in westerns and cop flicks."

"What about McCloskey?"

"My sources remember him as a swaggering tough-guy type. Bargain-basement Brando, toothpick in the mouth, always hinting at pals in New Joisey, but never really fooling anyone. Also, he hated gays, didn't hesitate to say so without being asked. Maybe it was real, maybe he was latent and protesting too much. No one seems to have a clear handle on who he went to bed with other than Gina. What they do remember are his obnoxious personality and his heavy doping—speed, coke, grass, pills. For a while, when his business was failing, he got into dealing. Supplying people at the studio. Then trading modeling services for dope—that finished his agency off. The models wanted to get paid in cash and he didn't have any."

"Did he ever get busted for dealing?"

"No. Why do you ask?"

"I was just wondering if Gina might have had something to do with getting him in trouble with the law. Or if he thought she had. It would have been a reason to have her burned."

"Yeah, it sure would, but no dope record—no previous arrests of any kind before the attack."

Joyce brought bread. When she left, I said, "How about this, then: His homophobia *was* a cover for his being gay. Gina found out and they had some kind of confrontation over it. Maybe she even threatened to blow his tough-guy cover. It set McCloskey off and he hired Findlay to get her. It would explain why he refused to talk about his motives. It would have humiliated him."

"Could be," he said. "But then why wouldn't *she* have let the cat out?"

"Good question."

"Maybe," he said, "it was something a lot more simple: McCloskey and Gina and Ramp got involved in a triangle and McCloskey eventually freaked out. Remember the way they were sitting in the picture? She's the meat in the sandwich. In any event, it's probably ancient history. Probably has nothing to do with her disappearance, other than telling us something about Mr. R."

"Prosperous businessman trying to forget about providing ancillary services."

"Yeah. Even when we were looking for his wife, and McCloskey was a potential suspect, he didn't talk about the bad old days. Even though he was the one pointing a finger at McCloskey. You'd think he'd want to tell us anything that could help find her."

"Unless there was nothing to tell," I said. "If Gina never knew why McCloskey burned her, why would Ramp?"

"Maybe," he said. "What is clear is that Gina had to be aware of Ramp's sexuality when she married him. Bi guys aren't considered prime matrimonial material nowadays— the physical risk on top of the social. But that didn't stop her."

"Separate bedrooms," I said. "No risk."

"Yeah, but what's his allure for her?"

"He's a nice guy. Tolerant of *her* lifestyle, so she puts up with *his*. And he does appear to be a softie—taking in an old friend like Bethel, paying for Noel's college. Maybe after all the brutality Gina experienced, she wanted compassion more than sex."

"Old friend," he said. "Wonder how Bethel feels about hopping tables while her former buddies live in the Peach Palace."

"Noel hinted that he and his mom had been through some really hard times. Hopping tables might very well be a big step up."

"Suppose so," he said, taking a piece of bread.

I said, "You keep coming back to Ramp."

"I went down to the beach today to talk to Nyquist, and the place was cleaned out. Neighbor said Nyquist packed his van last night and headed out for parts unknown. The Brentwood Country Club says he didn't show up for some tennis lessons he was supposed to give today, didn't bother to call in."

"Ramp's folding his tent, too. Asked Noel to pack him a bag. Maybe it's the trauma of losing Gina—he's tired of all the pretense. But it'll be interesting to see if he eventually files a claim against the will or cashes in on some insurance policy no one knew existed. Not to mention the missing two million—who'd be in a better position to siphon that off than the husband?"

"Melissa's suspicions validated," he said.

"Out of the mouths of babes. Ramp's presence is accounted for the day Gina disappeared. But what about Todd? Maybe *he* seduced her to get closer to the two million. In any event, he's someone she would have picked up if his car broke down near the house and she saw him thumbing. And now he and Ramp are both on the move."

"Ramp's still around. I drove by his restaurant before I stopped by the house. His Mercedes was in the lot and I peeked my head in. He was out cold—stinking drunk, Bethel clucking over him like a mama hen. I left and parked across the street, observed the place for a while. No sign of Nyquist."

"One thing, Milo. If Ramp's planning an escape, why would he tell me and telegraph it?"

"No," he said. "That wasn't telegraphing—that was *covering*. Giving himself a plausible motive for leaving: overwhelmed with grief, the poor sucker left with nothing. So no one'll suspect Tahiti with Todd. Not that anyone's likely to suspect him, anyway. Officially, no crime's been committed. And as a one-man shop, I'm spread too thin to check him out while looking for Nyquist and doing the number Melissa wants me to do on Anger and Douse. I can't justify telling her Ramp's a higher priority than Anger and Douse, because I've got nothing to back me up, and those two are *already* moving against her. Also, it would most likely freak her out even further, and I don't see that being constructive right now, do you?"

"No."

He thought for a while. "What I'm gonna do is make a call. Someone I know who happens to have a real private-eye's license but doesn't use it much. Not too brilliant or creative. But patient. He can keep an eye on Big Don while I hit the financial trail."

"What about Nyquist?"

"Nyquist is unlikely to make a move without Ramp."

The food came. Milo cut, chewed, said, "They sure know how to do their tri-G's."

We ate for a few minutes.

"My turn," I said.

"One sec," he said. "Got a couple more tidbits—related to Gina's first husband, Dickinson. Remember Anger's crack about off-the-rack suits? Turns out the reason Dickinson couldn't wear one is he was a dwarf."

"I know. I found a picture of him."

Surprise brightened his eyes. "Where?"

"At the house. Up in the third-floor attic."

"Little freelance archaeology? Good for you," he said. "I couldn't find any pictures of him at all. What'd he look like?"

I described Arthur Dickinson and Gina as a mummy bride.

"Weird," he said. "First hubby an old gnome, second one full-sized but interested in boys. All in all, I'd say the lady wasn't oriented toward the physical."

"Agoraphobia," I said. "The classical Freudian explanation says it's a symptom of sexual repression."

"You buy that?"

"Not in all cases, but maybe this one. It supports my theory of Gina's marrying Ramp because of a need for friendship. The fact that they used to know each other helped their rapport along—once Melissa put them in touch with each other. Old friends reattaching, mutual needs—happens all the time."

"I've got more," he said, "on Arthur. Seems, in addition

to making a fortune with the strut, he also dabbled in the movies. From the financial end. And some of the deals he did were with Apex Studios. So far I haven't been able to connect him to any film Gina or Ramp or any of the other pretty faces worked on, or find proof that he knew them prior to McCloskey's trial. But I'd say it's a decent possibility."

"The old Chief Justice Rag," I said.

"What do you mean?"

"Jim Douse's uncle was Chief Justice Douse."

"Hammerin' Harmon?" said Milo. "Yeah, I remember Anger saying that. So what?"

"Didn't he sit on the court when McCloskey came to trial?"

He thought. "When was that—'69? No, Harmon was gone by then. The soft-hearted guys were already taking over. When Harmon ran things, the apple-green room was real busy."

"Even so," I said, "as chief justice emeritus, he'd have plenty of residual clout. And Arthur Dickinson was a client of his firm. What if Jacob Dutchy's being chosen for the McCloskey jury wasn't coincidence?"

"What if," he said, then repeated it. "You do love your conspiracies, lad."

"Life's robbed me of my innocence."

He smiled and cut more steak. "So what does any of it have to do with our lady in the lake?"

"Maybe nothing. But why don't you ask McCloskey? Given what we know, maybe *you* can open him up. Maybe he *needs* opening up. Despite all our theories about complex financial motives, maybe what happened to Gina just boils down to simple revenge. McCloskey let his anger stew for nineteen years, finally reverted to type and paid someone to get her."

"I don't know," he said. "I do believe the guy's pretty much of a zero, mentally. And from what I've been able to find out, he has no known associates—just hangs out at the mission and plays penitent."

"Suppose the operative word is *plays*. Even bad actors can improve over time."

"True. Okay, yeah, I'll give him another chance at confession. Tonight. Can't do the financial thing anyway till the banks open."

Joyce came over to see how we were doing. Our compliments made her glow. At least someone's day had been made. She brought us coffee and dessert on the house. Milo forked a piece of double chocolate cake and said, "Great. Fabulous. Best I ever had," and she turned incandescent.

When she finally left us, he said, "Okay, your turn."

I told him the value of the Cassatt.

"Two-fifty," he said. "Hell of a transference—that what you guys call it?"

I nodded. "It smells bad. And I'm probably not the only one who suspects the Gabneys of something fishy."

I recounted what I'd learned about Kathy Moriarty.

"A reporter, huh?"

"An investigative reporter. According to her sister, she *really* loved conspiracies, spent her life chasing them down. And she's from New England—worked in Boston, the Gabneys' old stamping grounds. Which leads me to suspect she learned about something they did back there and came to L.A. to check it out. Passed herself off as an agoraphobic and joined the group in order to spy and collect dirt."

"Sounds reasonable," he said, "but they're ultra high-priced. Who paid Moriarty's therapy bills?"

"Her sister said Kathy was always hitting her up for money."

"That kind of money?"

"I don't know. Maybe she had someone behind her, a newspaper or a publisher—she's written a book. Meanwhile, she hasn't been heard from in over a month. That makes two out of four group members gone. Though in Kathy's case, the sister says that's typical. But one thing's for certain—she was no agoraphobic. She had to be spying on the Gabneys."

"What you're setting up," he said, "is financial scam

number two. The Gabneys looting Gina, just like Anger and the lawyer."

"Three, if you include Ramp and Nyquist."

"Step right up," he said. "Jab a needle into the rich lady's vein."

"Forty million dollars," I said, "equals pretty big veins. Even the two million would have been enough to get the gears turning. I especially like the Gabneys, because of the Kathy Moriarty angle. Their move from Boston to L.A. — maybe it was out of necessity, avoiding a scandal."

"*Harvard* avoiding a scandal."

I nodded. "Even more reason to cover it up. But Kathy Moriarty picked up the trail somehow and decided to follow it."

Milo ate some more cake, licked his lips, said, "From what you told me, the Gabneys were pretty well regarded professionally."

"Very well regarded. Leo Gabney would probably be on any psychologist's list of the top ten living behavioral experts. And as a Ph.D.-M.D., Ursula could write her own ticket. But even a successful therapist's earning power is limited. You're selling time, and there are just so many billable hours. Even at what they charge, it would take a hell of a lot of hours to earn a Cassatt. Also, Leo struck me as a bitter man. The first time I met him he spoke of losing his son in a fire. The wound had clearly never healed. He blamed it on the judge giving custody to his wife. On the entire legal system. Maybe he deals with his anger by defying that system."

"Crime as personal vengeance," he said. "The thrill — sure, why not. What about Ursula — she have some axe to grind?"

"Ursula's his protégée — from what I've observed, she does what he tells her. Though Gina's death seems to have really shaken her up, so perhaps she's the weak link. I intended to talk to her today, but she left before I had a chance."

"Protégée, huh? But the print ended up in *her* office."

"Maybe the print was just the tip of the iceberg."

"Art for her, cash for both of them? Course at these prices, a million or two wouldn't buy that much art, would it?"

"We have only Glenn Anger's word on how much Gina received every month. He could have programmed his computer to read any way he wanted."

"Why would Gina give the Gabneys dough?"

"Gratitude, dependency—same reasons cult members give everything to the guru."

"Could have been a loan."

"Could have been, but she's not around to collect, is she?"

He frowned and pushed his cake aside. "Ramp and Nyquist, the button-down boys, now her goddam shrinks. Suspect hit parade. Poor thing was an equal-opportunity victim."

"Like ants crawling over a beetle carcass," I said.

Milo tossed his napkin on the table. "What else do you know about this Moriarty?"

"Just her address. West Hollywood." I pulled out the paper Jan Robbins had given me and handed it to him.

"Hey," he said, "we're neighbors—this is maybe six blocks from my place. Could have stood next to her in line at the supermarket."

"Didn't know you went to the market."

"I was speaking symbolically." He lifted his briefcase to his knee, rummaged, and pulled out his notepad, copied down the address.

"I can stop by," he said, "see if she's still living there. If she isn't, anything further's gonna have to wait, 'cause of all the other stuff I've got to deal with. You want to spend some time pursuing it, that's fine, too."

"Do I get a brand-new private-eye briefcase?"

"Buy your own, ace. We're talking free enterprise."

30

I paid the check and Milo chatted with Joyce, compliment-
ing her further on her food, commiserating on the problems
of running a small business, then somehow easing into the
subject of Kathy Moriarty as if it were the next logical step.
She had no new facts to offer but was able to come up with a
physical description of the reporter: mid- to late thirties,
medium height and build, brown hair cut short, Buster
Brown style, rosy complexion ("like what you'd expect in an
Irish girl"), light eyes—either blue or green. Then, as if
realizing she'd given more than she'd taken, she crossed her
arms over her chest and said, "Why do you want to know all
this?"

Milo crooked his head and led her to the rear of the
restaurant—a needless concealment, since we were the only
customers. He showed her his inactive LAPD badge. She
opened her mouth but said nothing.

He said, "It's important you don't say anything to anybody. Please."

"Sure. Is something—"

"No danger to you or anyone. We're just making a
routine inquiry."

"About that place—the clinic?"

"Does something about the place bother you?"

"Well," she said, "like I was telling this gentleman, it *is* odd so few people come in and out. Makes you wonder what they're really doing in there—this day and age, you've got to wonder."

"Yes, you do."

She shivered and seemed to enjoy the conspiracy. Milo obtained another pledge of silence from her. We left the restaurant and headed back toward Sussex Knoll.

"Think she can keep a secret?" I said.

"Who knows."

"Not that important?"

He shrugged. "What's the worst that can happen? It gets back to the Gabneys that someone's asking questions. If they're not up to anything, it goes nowhere. If they are, maybe they'll get scared and do something rash."

"Such as?"

"Sell the Cassatt, maybe even do some other quick cashing-in that lets us know they've been holding on to some other assets of Gina's."

Gina. He said her name with an easy familiarity, though they'd never met. A homicide cop's intimacy. I thought of all the others he'd never met but knew so well. . . .

". . . so," he was saying, "that okay with you?"

"Is what okay?"

He laughed. "You're making my point for me, champ."

"Which is?"

"Go home and get some sleep."

"I'm fine. What were you saying?"

"That you should catch some Z's and check out Moriarty's place tomorrow morning. If it's an apartment building, talk to the landlord or the manager, if you can find them. Any other tenants, too."

"What's my premise?"

"Your *what?*"

"My reason for asking questions about her—I don't *have* a badge."

"Buy one," he said. "On Hollywood Boulevard, one of the costume shops. Be as legal as the one I'm using."

"Well, aren't we bitter," I said.

He gave an evil grin. "Okay, you want a premise: Say you're an old friend just come out from the East Coast, you're looking her up for old time's sake. Or you're a cousin—the grand Moriarty family reunion's coming around soon and no one can seem to get hold of dear Kathy. Make something up. You met her sister—you should be able to make it sound realistic."

"Nothing like a little deception to spice up the morning, huh."

"Hey," he said, "makes the world go 'round."

As we parked in front of the house, Noel Drucker came out the front door carrying a large blue suitcase with a designer logo.

He said, "She's up in her room. Writing."

"Writing what?"

"Something to do with the bank guy and the lawyer, I think. She's really ticked off, wants to sue them."

Milo pointed at the suitcase. "For the boss?"

Noel nodded.

"Any idea where he's gonna be living?"

"I guess he'll stay with us till he finds a place. With my mom and me. Upstairs at the Tankard. It's his, anyway."

"You rent from him?"

"No, he lets us stay there free."

"Pretty nice of him."

Noel nodded. "He really is a nice guy. I wish . . ." He threw up one hand and said, "Whatever."

"Must be hard for you," I said. "Caught in the middle."

He shrugged. "I figure it's practice."

"For international relations?"

"For the real world."

He got in the red Celica and drove off.

Milo watched his taillights until they disappeared. "Nice kid." As if he'd just tagged an endangered species.

Slapping his briefcase against his leg, he checked his Timex. "Nine-thirty. Gonna make a few calls. Then I'll boogie on down to the mission and try to get a rise out of Mr. Deadbrain."

"If Melissa doesn't need me, I'll go with you."

He frowned. "What about sleep?"

"Too wound up."

He said nothing for a moment, then: "Okay. He's a nutcase—maybe your training will come in handy. But then do me a favor and go home and crash. Don't keep driving on high—the engine burns out."

"Yes, Mom."

Melissa was in the windowless room, sitting at the desk behind a growing pile of papers.

She looked alarmed when we came in, stood suddenly, and knocked some pages to the floor. "Strategy planning," she said. "I'm trying to figure out ways of *getting* the bastards."

Milo picked up the papers, glanced at them, and put them on the desk. Blank. "Come up with anything?"

"Sort of. I think the best way to go is reviewing every single thing they've been doing since . . . since the very beginning. I mean *really* make them open up all their books and go over every line, every number. At the very least it'll freak them out so much they'll forget about ripping me off and I can concentrate on getting *them*."

I said, "Good offense the best defense."

"Exactly." She clapped her hands together. There was color in her cheeks and her eyes glowed, but it wasn't a healthy light. Milo was studying her, but she didn't notice it.

"Did you get a chance to talk to any lawyers, Dr. Delaware?"

"Not yet."

"Okay, but as soon as possible, all right? Please."

"I could try right now."

"That would be great. Thanks." She lifted the phone from the desk and thrust it at me.

Milo said, "I could use something to drink."

She looked at him, then at me. "Sure. Let's go get something from the kitchen."

Alone, I dialed Mal Worthy's home number in Brentwood. A machine with his third wife's voice on it answered. I began leaving a message and he broke in.

"Alex. I was meaning to call you—got a juicy one coming up. Two psychologists splitting up, three *really* screwed-up kids. I've got the wife and it's shaping up as one of the nastiest custody fights you're ever going to see."

"Sounds like fun."

"You bet. How's your calendar, let's say five weeks from now?"

"I don't have it in front of me but that far in advance I don't see a problem."

"Good. You're going to love this—these are two of the craziest people you'll ever meet. The thought of them messing with other people's heads is— What is it with your profession, anyway?"

"Let's talk about your profession," I said. "I need a referral."

"For what?"

"Estate and taxation."

"Word-processing or litigation?"

"Could be both." I gave him a general summary of Melissa's situation, leaving out names, numbers, and identifying marks.

He said, "Suzy LaFamiglia, if your client doesn't mind a woman."

"A woman would be fine."

"Only reason I mention it is, you'd be surprised how many people still come in with rules—no women, no minorities. Their loss, because Suzy's the best. CPA as well as a law degree, worked for one of the big accounting firms and brought in more business than any other associate until they kept passing her up for partnership because she had the wrong genitals. She sued, settled out of court, used the money to go to Boalt—top of the class. She's a real black-hearted litigator. Made her mark working for film people, getting money back from the studios. In situations where the finances are so hairy they go beyond my not inconsiderable skills, she's my main man."

He laughed at his own wit.

I said, "Sounds perfect for my client."

He gave me a number. "Century City East—she's got a whole floor in one of the towers. I'll call you on the other thing. You're going to love it—our little pair of snarling, snapping therapists. I call them the Para*dox. Très à-propos.*" He laughed more heartily.

I hung up without telling him I'd heard the joke before.

Milo came back without Melissa, holding a can of Diet Coke.

"She's in the bathroom," he said. "Throwing up."

"What happened?"

"She just gave out. Started in with more of the tough talk—getting the bastards. I said something to her—then boom, she's crying and gagging."

"I saw you looking at her like a detective. Then you got her out of the room while I called. Why?"

He looked uncomfortable.

I said, "What?"

"Okay," he said, "I have an evil mind. It's what I get paid for." He hesitated. "I didn't want her *out.* I wanted to get her *alone*—get a closer look, without you running interference for her. Because her demeanor, just now, bothered me. It got me thinking—we'd missed one possibility in our little dinner discussion. Very ugly possibility, but sometimes those are the most important ones."

"Melissa?" I said, feeling my gut tighten.

He started to turn away, reversed direction, and faced

me. "She's the sole heir, Alex. Forty million bucks. And she's sure ready to fight for it before the body's even cold."

"There is no body."

"Figure of speech. Don't chew my head off."

"You just come up with this?"

He shook his head. "I guess it's been floating around in the back of my head from the beginning. Because of my training: when there's money involved, look for the person who benefits. But I repressed it, or whatever—maybe I just didn't want to think about it."

"Milo, she's *fighting* because she's channeling her grief into anger. Taking the offensive instead of letting herself be crushed. I trained her to do that in therapy. In my book, it's still good coping."

"Maybe," he said. "All I'm saying is that in a normal situation, I'd have looked at her early on."

"You can't be serious."

"Hey," he said, "I didn't say I thought it was a *probability*. Just something we left out. No, not we—*me*. *I'm* the one trained to think ugly. But I didn't. It wouldn't have happened if I'd been working for the city."

"Well, you're not," I said, raising my voice, "so why not allow yourself a vacation from that kind of thinking?"

"Hey," he said, "don't kill the messenger."

"She had no opportunity," I said. "She was here when her mother disappeared."

"The Drucker kid could have had one—where was he?"

"I don't know."

He nodded, but without satisfaction. "From what I've seen, he digs her enough to eat her fingernail dirt and call it caviar. And he took care of the family's cars. He'd know all about how the Rolls worked. Gina would've picked *him* up, that's for sure. And you yourself said he twanged your antennae."

"I didn't say I sensed anything psychopathic about him."

"Okay."

"Oh, man," I said, feeling a grinding headache coming on. "No way, Milo. No way."

"It's sure not anything *I* want to believe, Alex. I like the kid and I'm still working for her. She was just looking a little too . . . hardbitten, just now. Going on and on about getting the bastards. What I said to her out in the kitchen was 'sounds like you're raring to go.' And she just stopped and fell apart. I felt shitty for making her feel bad, but also better. Because she started looking like a kid again. If I did something untherapeutic, I'm sorry."

"No," I said. "If it was that close to the surface it would have happened sooner or later."

"Yeah," he said.

Neither of us putting into words what we were thinking: if it was real.

Feeling suddenly weary, I sat down in the chair near the phone table. The paper with Suzy LaFamiglia's number was between my fingers. "Just got a lawyer for her. Female, tough, combative—likes to take on the system."

"Sounds good."

"Sounds," I said, "like someone Melissa could grow up to be."

31

Melissa came back to the five-sided room looking a long way from grown up. Her shoulders were stooped, her gait had slowed, and she dabbed at her mouth with a piece of toilet paper. I gave her the lawyer's number and she thanked me in a very soft voice.

"Want me to call for you?"

"No, thanks. I'll do it. Tomorrow."

I sat her down behind the desk. She gazed out blankly in Milo's direction and gave a weak smile.

Milo smiled back and looked at his soda can. I wasn't sure for whom I felt sorrier.

Melissa sighed and put her hand under her jaw.

I said, "How're you doing, hon?"

"I don't know," she said. "This is all so— I feel like I'm just being— Like I've got no . . . I don't know."

I touched her shoulder.

She said, "Who am I fooling—fighting them? I'm a nothing. Who's going to listen to me?"

I said, "It'll be your lawyer's job to fight. Right now you should be concentrating on taking care of yourself."

After a long time she said, "I guess."

Another stretch of silence, then: "I'm really alone."

"Lots of people around here care for you, Melissa."

Milo was looking at the floor.

"I'm really alone," she said again, with an eerie wonderment. As if she'd run a maze in record time, only to find it led to an abyss.

"I'm tired," she said. "I think I'll sleep."

"Would you like me to stay with you?"

"I want to sleep with *someone*. I don't want to be alone."

Milo put the can down on the table and left the room.

I remained with Melissa, saying comforting things that didn't seem to have much of an effect.

Milo returned with Madeleine. The big woman was breathing hard and looked agitated, but by the time she reached Melissa's side, her expression had turned tender. She hovered over Melissa and stroked her hair. Melissa swooned a bit, as if she'd been embraced. Madeleine leaned lower and hugged her to her bosom.

"*I* sleep with you, *chérie*. Come, we go now."

In the car, driving away from the house, Milo said, "Okay, I'm a child-abusing asshole."

"So you don't think her falling apart was an act?"

He braked hard at the foot of the drive and whipped his head toward me. "What the hell was that, Alex? Twisting the goddam knife?"

His teeth were bared. The spotlight above the pine gates yellowed them.

"No," I said, feeling *fear* of him for the first time in all the years I'd known him. Feeling like a suspect. "No, I'm serious. Couldn't she have been faking it?"

"Yeah, right. You're telling me *you* think she's a psychopath?" Shouting now, one big hand pounding the steering wheel.

"I don't know *what* to think!" I said, matching his volume. "You keep throwing theories at me out of left field!"

"Thought that was the *idea*!"

"The idea was to *help*!"

He shoved his face forward, as if it were a weapon. Glared, then sagged against the seat and ran his hands through his hair. "Shit, *this* is a pretty scene."

"Must be sleep deprivation," I said, feeling shaky.

"Must be . . . Change your mind about sacking out?"

"Hell, no."

He laughed. "Me, neither . . . Sorry for getting on you."

"Sorry, too. How about we just forget it."

He put his hands back on the wheel and resumed driving. Slowly, with exquisite caution. Dropping speed at every intersection, even when there was no stop sign. Looking from side to side and in all the mirrors, though the streets were empty.

At Cathcart he said, "Alex, I'm not cut out for this private stuff. Too unstructured—too many blurred boundaries. I've been telling myself that I'm different, but it's bullshit. I'm straight-ahead paramilitary, like everyone else in the department. Need an us-versus-them world."

"Who's *us*?"

"The blue meanies. I *like* being mean."

I thought of the world he'd contended with for so many years. The one he'd be contending with again, in just a few months: being relegated to *them* by other policemen, no matter how many *thems* he put away.

I said, "You didn't do anything out of line. I was reacting from my gut—as her protector. It would have been negligent for you not to consider her as a suspect. It would be negligent not to *continue* considering her if that's where the facts lead."

"The facts," he said. "We don't got us too many of those. . . ."

He seemed about to say more, but the freeway on-ramp appeared and he clamped his mouth shut and gave the Porsche gas. Traffic toward downtown was light, but it created enough of a roar to substitute for conversation.

We reached the Eternal Hope Mission shortly after ten and parked halfway down the block. The air smelled of ripening garbage and sweet wine and fresh asphalt, with a curious overlay of flowers that seemed to travel on a westerly breeze—as if the better parts of town had air-mailed a whiff of better homes and gardens.

The front facade of the mission was swimming in artificial light. That, and the moonglow, turned the aqua plaster icy-white. Five or six shabby men were congregated near the entrance, listening or pretending to listen to two men in business clothes.

As we got closer I saw that the talkers were in their thirties. One was tall and thin and fair with waxy-looking blond hair cut frat-boy short and an oddly dark mustache that hooked down at right angles to his mouth and resembled a fuzzy croquet wicket. He wore silver-rimmed eyeglasses, a gray summer-weight suit, and mocha-colored zip boots. The arms of the suit were a trifle too short. His wrists were huge. A notepad, identical to the ones Milo used, was in one hand, along with a soft-pack of Winstons.

The second man was short, stocky, and dark, clean-shaven and baby-faced. He had a Ritchie Valens pompadour, narrow eyes with lips to match, wore a blue blazer and gray slacks. He was the one doing most of the talking.

The two men stood in profile, neither of them seeing us. Milo walked up to the taller one and said, "Brad."

The man turned and stared. A few of the shabby men followed the stare. The darker man stopped talking, checked out his partner, then Milo. As if unleashed, the homeless men began to drift away. The darker man said, "Hold on, campers," and the men stopped short, some of them muttering. The detective gave his partner an arched eyebrow.

The man Milo had called Brad sucked in his cheeks and nodded.

The other man said, "This way, campers," and corralled the shabby men off to one side.

The taller man watched them until they'd passed out of earshot, then turned back to Milo. "Sturgis. How convenient."

"What is?"

"I hear you've been down here already today. Which makes you someone I want to talk to."

"That so?"

The detective transferred his cigarettes to the other hand. "Two trips in one day—pretty dedicated. Getting paid by the hour?"

Milo said, "What's up?"

"Why all the interest in McCloskey?"

"Just what I told you when I checked in a couple of days ago."

"Run it by me again."

"The lady he burned is still gone. Real gone. Her family would still like to know if there's a connection."

"What do you mean, *real* gone?"

Milo told him about Morris Dam.

The blond man remained impassive, but the hand around the cigarette pack tightened. Realizing it, he frowned and examined the pack, tugging at cellophane, using his fingertips to straighten the corners.

"Too bad," he said. "Family must be shook up."

"They're not throwing any parties."

The blond man gave a curdled smile. "You already rousted him twice. Why again?"

"First couple of times he didn't have much to say."

"And you thought you might convince him."

"Something like that."

"Something like that." The blond man looked over at the dark man, who was still lecturing to the derelicts.

Milo said, "What gives, Brad?"

"What gives," repeated the blond man, touching the rim of his eyeglasses. "What gives is that maybe life just got complicated."

He paused, studying Milo. When Milo didn't say anything, the blond man fished a cigarette out of the pack, put it between his lips, and talked around it. "Looks like we've got business together."

Another pause for reaction.

From half a mile away the freeway rumbled. From half a block away came the sound of shattering glass. Brad's partner kept talking to the derelicts. I couldn't make out his words but his tone was patronizing. The shabby men looked nearly asleep.

The blond detective said, "Seems Mr. McCloskey met with an unfortunate situation." Staring at Milo.

Milo said, "When?"

The detective felt around in his trousers pocket as if the answer were to be found there. He pulled out a disposable lighter, and ignited. The flame cast a two-second hobgoblin glow over his face. His skin was rough-sanded and knobby, with shaving bumps along the jawline. "Couple of hours ago," he said, "give or take." He squinted at me through glass and smoke, as if his releasing the information had made me someone to be reckoned with.

"Friend of the family," said Milo.

The tall man kept scrutinizing me, inhaling and blowing out smoke without removing the cigarette from his mouth. He'd majored in stoicism and graduated with honors.

Milo said, "Dr. Delaware, Detective Bradley Lewis, Central Division Homicide. Detective Lewis, Dr. Alex Delaware."

Lewis blew smoke rings and said, "A doctor, huh."

"*Family* doctor, as a matter of fact."

"Ah."

I tried to look doctoral.

Milo said, "How'd it happen, Brad?"

"What?" said Lewis. "This some kind of a bounty thing? Getting paid for bringing the good news back to the family?"

Milo said, "It won't bring her back, but yeah, I can't imagine they'll mourn." He repeated his question.

Lewis pondered answering it, finally said, "Back alley a few blocks south and east of here—the industrial area between San Pedro and Alameda. Auto versus pedestrian, auto winning with a first round KO."

"If it's hit and run, why are you guys on it?"

"What a sleuth," said Lewis. "Hey—d'you ever do police work?"

Grinning.

Milo didn't talk or move.

Lewis smoked and said, "As it happens, the auto didn't take any chances, according to the techs. Ran over him once, then backed up and did it at least twice more for good luck. We're talking road pizza with all the toppings."

He turned to me, pulled the cigarette out of his mouth, and flashed a sudden, wolfish grin. "Family doctor, huh? You look like a civilized gentleman, but appearances can be deceiving sometimes, right?"

I smiled back. His grin widened, as if we'd just shared a terrific joke.

"Doctor," he said, chain-lighting a second cigarette and grinding out the first on the sidewalk, "you wouldn't by any remote chance have used your Mercedes or BMW or whatever to put poor Mr. McCloskey out of his misery, would you, sir? Quick confession and we can all go home."

I kept smiling and said, "Sorry to disappoint you."

"Darn," said Lewis. "I hate whodunits."

"The car was German?" said Milo.

Lewis kicked the cement with one boot heel and blew smoke through his nose. "What is this, *Meet the Press?*"

"Any reason *not* to tell me, Brad?"

"You're a *civilian,* for one."

Milo said nothing.

Lewis said, "Maybe even a suspect, for two."

"Right," said Milo. "What *is* this, Brad? Fucking *Murder, She Wrote?*"

Turning his stare on Lewis. They were the same height but Milo outweighed Lewis by fifty pounds. Lewis stared back, smoking, stone-faced, and didn't answer.

Milo near-whispered a single word that sounded like "Gonzales."

Lewis's gaze faltered. The cigarette in his mouth dipped, then arced upward as his jaw tightened.

He said, "Look, Sturgis, I can't fuck around with this. At the very least there's a conflict of interest—like if we end up coming out to Pasadena and talking to the *family* about this."

"The *family,* as it stands right now," said Milo, "is an *eighteen*-year-old girl who just found out her mother's dead and doesn't even have a body to bury 'cause it's at the bottom of the goddam dam. Sheriff's just waiting for it to float—"

"All the more reason—"

"That happens, it'll be loads of fun for her, right, Brad? ID-ing a floater? Meanwhile, she's been cooped up in the house for the last few days, tons of eyewitnesses, so *she* sure as hell didn't run the piece-o-shit over, and *she* sure as hell didn't put any contracts out on him. But if you think there's some advantage to coming around and getting her really freaked out, be my guest. Deal with their lawyer—guy's uncle was Hammerin' Harmon Douse. Captain Spain always did appreciate guys taking the initiative."

Lewis puffed and dragged and stared at his cigarette as if it were a thing of wonder. ↘

"If that's where it leads, bet your ass I'll be there," he said, but his voice lacked conviction.

Milo said, "Be my guest, Brad."

The dark detective finished talking to the homeless men and gave a dismissing wave. They dispersed, some of them entering the mission, others drifting up the street. He came over, wiping his palms on his blazer.

"This is the famous Milo Sturgis," said Lewis, between rapid drags on his cigarette.

The shorter man looked perplexed.

Lewis said, "Heavyweight champ from West L.A.—went one round with Frisk?"

Another second of confusion, then insight spread across the shorter man's baby features. Revulsion followed a moment later. A pair of hard brown eyes shifted to me.

"And this," said Lewis, "is the family doctor—family

that's been interested in our d.b. Maybe he can look at that knee of yours, Sandy."

The other detective wasn't amused. He buttoned his jacket and when he turned to Milo, he might have been regarding a floating body.

Milo said, "Esposito, right? You used to be over at Devonshire."

Esposito said, "You came around here earlier and talked to the deceased. What about?"

"Nothing. He wouldn't talk."

"That's *not* what I asked," said Esposito, clipping his words. "Regarding what specifics was your intention to talk with the deceased?"

Milo paused—weighing his words or unraveling the syntax. "His possible involvement in the death of my client's mother."

Esposito didn't appear to have heard. He managed to back his body away from Milo while pushing his head forward. "What do *you* got to tell *us*?"

Milo said, "Ten to one it'll come down to something stupid. Interview the residents of this resort and find out the last person McCloskey short-portioned on the hash line."

"Save your advice," said Esposito, moving back farther. "I'm talking information."

"As in whodunit?"

"As in."

Milo said, "Afraid I can't help you with that."

Lewis said, "The hash-line theory doesn't cut it, Sturgis. The residents of this resort don't tend to have cars."

"They get day jobs once in a while," said Milo. "Driving, delivering. Or maybe McCloskey just met up with someone who didn't like his face. Wasn't much of a face."

Lewis smoked and said nothing.

Esposito said, "Brilliant." To me: "You got something to add?"

I shook my head.

"What can I say?" said Milo. "You bought yourselves a whodunit, for a change."

Lewis smoked.

Esposito said, "And you got nothing that would take the who out of the dunit?"

"Your guess is as good as mine," said Milo. Smiling. "Well, maybe not *that* good, but I'm sure you'll work at improving it."

He began walking past the two of them, heading for the front door of the mission. I tried to follow but Lewis stepped in front of me. "Hold on, Sturgis," he said.

Milo looked back. His forehead was knotted.

Lewis said, "What's your business in there, now?"

"Thought I'd see the priest," said Milo. "Time for confession."

"Right," said Esposito, smirking. "Priest gonna grow a beard, listening."

Lewis laughed, but it sounded obligatory. "Maybe it's not the optimal time," he said to Milo.

"I don't see any yellow tape, Brad."

"Maybe it's still not optimal."

Milo put his hands on his hips. "You're telling me this is a restricted scene because the d.b. once *bunked* here, but it's okay for vagrant scumbags to come in and out? Harmon Junior's gonna love that, Brad. Next time he and the chief meet up on the links they're gonna share a few yucks over that one."

Lewis said, "What is it, three months? And you're already acting like a fucking suit."

Milo said, "Bullshit. *You're* the one with the invisible tape, Brad. *You're* the one all of a sudden turned *careful*."

Esposito said, "We don't have to take this shit," and unbuttoned his coat. Lewis held him back, puffing like a chimney. Then he dropped his cigarette on the sidewalk, watched it smolder, and moved aside.

Esposito said, "Hey."

Lewis said, "Fuck it," with enough savagery to shut Esposito's mouth. To me: "Go ahead. Move it."

I stepped forward and Milo put his hand on the door.

"Don't fuck anything up," said Lewis. "And don't get in our way—I mean it. I don't care how many fucking lawyers you've got behind you, hear me?"

Milo pushed the door open. Before it closed, I heard Esposito's voice mutter, *"Maricon."*

Then laughter, very forced, very angry.

A TV was on in the big aqua room. Some sort of cop show flashed on the screen, and forty or so pairs of drooping eyes followed the crunch-and-rattle fantasy.

"Thorazine city," said Milo, his voice cold as Freon. Anger as therapy . . .

We'd gotten halfway across the room when Father Tim Andrus appeared from around a corner, wheeling a coffee urn on an aluminum cart. Plastic-wrapped stacks of Styrofoam cups filled the cart's bottom shelf. The priest's clerical shirt was olive-drab, worn over faded blue jeans, the knees of the pants scraped white. Same white high-top shoes he'd had on the first time; one of the laces had come loose.

He frowned, stopped, made a sharp turn away from us, and pushed the cart between rows of slumping men. The cart's wheels were loose and kept sticking. Andrus maintained a jerky, weaving progress until he was next to the television. Bending low, he whispered to one of the men—a young, wild-eyed white youth in too-small clothing that gave him the look of an overgrown feral child. Not much older than a child, actually—late teens, maybe twenty, still larded with baby fat and suburban softness under a patchy chin-beard. But any semblance of innocence was destroyed by matted hair and scabbed skin.

The priest talked to him slowly, with exquisite patience. The young man listened, rose slowly, and began unwrapping a cup stack with shaky fingers. Filling a cup from the urn's spigot, he started to raise it to his lips. Andrus touched his wrist and the youth stopped, bewildered.

Andrus smiled, spoke again, guided the youth's wrist so that the cup was held out to one of the seated men. The man took hold of it. The chin-bearded youth stared and released it. Andrus said something and gave him another cup that he began filling. Some of the men had left their seats; a loose queue formed in front of the urn.

Andrus motioned at a scrawny man the color of photo film, slumped in the front row. The man got up and limped over. He and the youth stood side by side, not looking at each other. The priest smiled and instructed, setting up a two-man assembly line. Guiding and praising until a rhythm of filling and distribution had been established and the queue began to shuffle forward. Then he came over to us.

"Please leave," he said. "There's nothing I can do for you."

"Just a few questions, please, Father," said Milo.

"I'm sorry, Mr.— I don't remember what your name is, but there's absolutely nothing I can do for you and I'd really appreciate it if you left."

"The name is Sturgis, Father, and you didn't forget. I never gave it to you."

"No," said the priest, "you didn't. But the police did. Just a while ago. They also informed me you *weren't* the police."

"Never said I was, Father."

Andrus's ears colored. He plucked at his wispy mustache. "No, I suppose you didn't, but you did imply it. I deal with deception all day, Mr. Sturgis—part of the job. But that doesn't mean I like it."

"Sorry," said Milo. "I was—"

"An apology isn't necessary, Mr. Sturgis. You can demonstrate your remorse by leaving and letting me attend to my people."

"Would it have made a difference, Father? If I'd have told you I was a cop on temporary leave?"

Surprise on the priest's lean face.

"What'd they tell you, Father?" said Milo. "That I'd been kicked off the force? That I was some kind of heavy-duty sinner?"

Andrus's pale face took on an angry blush. "I— There's really no sense getting into . . . extraneous things, Mr. Sturgis. The main thing is there's nothing I can do for you. Joel's dead."

"I know that, Father."

"Along with any interest you might therefore have in the mission."

"Any idea who's responsible for his death?"

"Do you care, Mr. Sturgis?"

"Not one bit. But if it helps me understand why Mrs. Ramp died—"

"Why she— Oh . . ." Andrus shut his eyes and opened them rapidly. "Oh, my." Sighing and putting a hand to his forehead. "I didn't know. I'm sorry."

Milo told him about Morris Dam. A longer but softer version than the one he'd given Lewis.

Andrus shook his head and crossed himself.

"Father," said Milo, "when Joel was alive did he say anything to you that would indicate he'd resumed contact with Mrs. Ramp or any member of her family?"

"No, not at all. I'm sorry, I can't take this any further, Mr. Sturgis." The priest looked over at the coffee line. "Anything Joel may have told me was in confidentiality. It's a theological issue—the fact that he's dead doesn't change that."

"Of course not, Father. The only reason I came down here to talk to him again is that Mrs. Ramp's daughter is really struggling to deal with her loss. She's only a kid, Father. A total orphan now. And she's coming to grips with being all alone. Nothing you can say or do will change that, I realize, but any light you might be able to shed on what happened to her mom could be helpful to her in terms of getting her life back together. At least that's what I've been told by her therapist."

"Yes," said Andrus. "That makes sense . . . Poor child."
He thought for a moment. "But no, it can't help her."

"What can't, Father?"

"Anything—nothing I know, Mr. Sturgis. What I mean
is that I know *nothing*—Joel never told me anything that
would ease the poor girl's pain. Though even if he had, I
couldn't tell you, so perhaps it's best that he didn't. I'm
sorry, but that's the way it is."

"Uh-huh," said Milo.

Andrus shook his head and put the knuckles of a fist
against his brow. "That wasn't very clear, was it? It's been a
long day and I lose coherence after long days." Another
glance at the urn. "I could use some of that poison over
there—plenty of chicory in it but we haven't skimped on the
caffeine. It helps the men deal with detox. You're welcome to
some, too."

"No, thanks, Father. Just one more second of your time.
Do you have any idea who might have done it?"

"The police seem to think it was just one of those things
that happens down on Skid Row."

"Do you agree with that?"

"There's no reason not to, I guess. I've seen so many
things that don't make sense. . . ."

"Is there something about McCloskey's death that
doesn't make sense?"

"No, not really." Another look at the urn.

"Was there any reason for McCloskey to be in the area
where he was run down, Father?"

Andrus shook his head. "None that I know of. He wasn't
on an errand for the mission—I told the police that. The men
do take walks—surprisingly long distances for their physical
condition. It's as if staying in motion reminds them they're
still alive. The illusion of purpose, even though they have
nowhere to go."

"The first time we were here, I got the impression that
Joel rarely left the mission."

"That's true."

"So *he* wasn't one of your big walkers."

"No, not really."

"Did he take any other walks you're aware of?"

"No, not really . . ." Andrus paused; his ears were flaming.

"What is it, Father?"

"This will sound very ugly, very judgmental, but my first impression upon hearing what had happened was that someone in the family—Mrs. Ramp's family—decided finally to exact revenge. Lured him away somehow, then ambushed him."

"Why's that, Father?"

"They'd certainly have a reason. And using a car impressed me as a . . . nice middle-class way of doing it. No need to get close. To smell him or touch him."

The priest stared away again. Upward. Toward the crucifix.

"Ugly thoughts, Mr. Sturgis. I'm not proud of them. I was angry—everything I'd put into him and now . . . Then I realized I was being thoughtless and cruel and thinking of myself. Suspecting innocent people who'd had their own share of suffering. I had no right to do that. Now that you tell me about Mrs. Ramp, I feel even more . . ."

Shaking his head.

Milo said, "Did you mention your suspicion to the detectives?"

"It wasn't suspicion, just a momentary . . . thought. An uncharitable thought in the heat of . . . the shock of hearing about it. And no, I didn't. But *they* brought it up—asked me if any member of Mrs. Ramp's family had been by. I said only you had."

"How'd they react when you told them I'd been here?"

"I didn't get the impression they took it seriously—took any of it seriously. They just seemed to be throwing things out—scattershot. My impression was that they're not going to spend a lot of time on this particular case."

"Why's that?"

"Their attitude. I'm used to it. Death is a frequent

visitor around here but he doesn't give too many interviews on the six o'clock news." The priest's face fell. "Here I go again, judging. And there's so much work to be done. You must excuse me, Mr. Sturgis."

"Sure, Father. Thanks for your time. But if you do think of something, anything that would help that little girl, please let me know."

Somehow a business card had made it into Milo's palm. He handed it to the priest. Before Andrus slipped it into a pocket of his jeans, I got a look at it. White vellum. Milo's name, in strong black letters, over the word INVESTIGATIONS. Home number and beeper code in the lower right-hand corner.

Milo thanked Andrus again. Andrus looked pained.

"Please don't count on me, Mr. Sturgis. I've told you all I can."

Walking back to the car, I said, " 'I've told you all I *can*,' not 'all I *know*.' My bet is that McCloskey bared his soul to him—formal confession or some sort of counseling. Either way, you'll never get it out of him."

"Yup," he said. "I used to talk to my priest, too."

We walked to the car in silence.

Driving back to San Labrador, I said, "Who's Gonzales?"

"Huh?"

"What you told Lewis? It seemed to make an impression on him."

"Oh," he said, frowning. "Ancient history. Gonsal*ves*. Lewis used to work at West L.A. when he was still in uniform. College boy, tendency to think he was smarter than the others. Gonsalves is a case he fucked up. Domestic violence that he didn't take seriously enough. Wife wanted the husband locked up, but Lewis thought he could handle it with his B.A.—psych B.A., matter of fact. Did some counseling and left feeling good. Hour later, the husband cut up the wife with a straight razor. Lewis was a lot softer then—no attitude. I could have ruined him, chose to go easy on the paperwork, talk him through it. After that he got harder, got more careful, didn't fuck up again, notably. Made detective a few years later and transferred to Central."

"Doesn't seem too grateful."

"Yeah." He gripped the wheel. "Well, that's the way the Oreo deteriorates."

A mile later: "When I first called him—to scope out McCloskey and the mission—he was frosty but civil. Given the Frisk thing, that's the best I can hope for. Tonight was amateur theater—putting on an act for that little macho asshole he's partnered with."

"Us and them," I said.

He didn't answer. I regretted bringing it up. Trying to lighten things, I said, "Nifty business card. When'd you get it?"

"Couple of days ago—insta-print on La Cienega on the way to the freeway. Got a box of five hundred at bulk rate—talk about your wise investment."

"Let me see."

"What for?"

"Souvenir—it may turn out to be a collector's item."

He grimaced, put his hand in his jacket, and pulled one out.

I took it, snapped the thin, hard paper, and said, "Classy."

"I like vellum," he said. "You can always pick your teeth with it."

"Or use it for a bookmark."

"Got something even more constructive," he said. "Build little houses with them. Then blow them down."

32

Back at Sussex Knoll, he pulled up beside the Seville.

I said, "What's next for you?"

"Sleep, hearty breakfast, then financial scumbags." He put the Porsche in neutral and revved the engine.

"What about McCloskey?" I said.

"Wasn't intending to go to the funeral."

Revving. Drumming the steering wheel.

I said, "Any ideas about who killed him and why?"

"You heard all of 'em back at the mission."

"Okay," I said.

"Okay." He sped away.

My house seemed tiny and friendly. The timer had switched the pond lights off and it was too dark to tell how my fish eggs were doing. I crept upstairs, slept for ten hours, woke up Monday thinking of Gina Ramp and Joel McCloskey— bound together, again, by pain and terror.

Was there a link between Morris Dam and what had happened in the back alley, or had McCloskey been simply another piece of Skid Row garbage?

Murder with a car. I found myself thinking about Noel Drucker. He had access to lots of wheels and plenty of time on his hands during the Tankard's indefinite hiatus. Were his feelings for Melissa strong enough to knock him that far off the straight and narrow? If so, had he been acting on his own, or at Melissa's bidding?

And what of Melissa? It made me sick to think of her as anything other than the defenseless orphan Milo had portrayed to the detectives. But I'd seen her temper in action. Watched her channel her grief into revenge fantasies against Anger and Douse.

I recalled her and Noel, entwined on her bed. Had the plan to get McCloskey been hatched during a similar embrace?

I switched channels:

Ramp. If he was innocent of *causing* Gina's death, perhaps he'd *avenged* it.

He had lots of reasons to hate McCloskey. Had he been at the wheel of the death car, or had he hired someone? The poetic justice would have been appealing.

Todd Nyquist would have been perfect for the job—how would anyone connect a surf-jock from the west side with the downtown death of a brain-damaged bum?

Or maybe Noel was *Ramp*'s automotive hit man, not Melissa's.

Or maybe none of the above.

I sat on the edge of the bed.

An image flashed across my eyes.

The scars on Gina's face.

I thought of the prison McCloskey had sent her to for the rest of her life.

Why waste time worrying about the reason he had died? His life had been a case study in wretchedness. Who'd miss him other than Father Andrus? And the priest's feelings probably had more to do with theological abstraction than human attachment.

Milo had been right to brush it off.

I was playing head-games rather than making myself useful.

I stood, stretched, said, "Good riddance," out loud.

Dressing in khakis, shirt and tie, and a lightweight tweed jacket, I drove to West Hollywood.

The Hilldale address Kathy Moriarty's sister had given me was between Santa Monica Boulevard and Sunset. The house was a graceless box, the color of week-old newspaper, on a thirty-foot lot, shielded nearly to the roof by an unkempt eugenia hedge. The roof line was flat, layered with Spanish tiles painted black. Flat black—it looked like an amateur job, some of the terra cotta showing through in places, the hue that of a poorly dyed brown shoe.

The eugenia hedge ended at a short, collapsing driveway—asphalt struggling with weeds in the couple of feet not taken up by a twenty-year-old, bird-bombed, yellow Oldsmobile. I parked across the street, walked across a dry, clipped lawn packed harder than the asphalt. Four paces took me to a three-step cement porch. Three addresses in black metal letters were nailed to the right of the gray plank door. A piece of adhesive tape, now darkened to the old-paper tint of the house, covered the doorbell ringer. An index card with KNOCK in red ballpoint was wedged between the bell frame and the stucco. I followed instructions and was rewarded, seconds later, with a "Hold on!" in a sleepy-sounding male voice.

Then: "Yeah?" from behind gray wood.

"My name is Alex Delaware and I'm looking for Kathy Moriarty."

"How come?"

I thought of Milo's suggestions of subterfuge, decided I had no stomach for that, and opted for technical truth:

"Her family hasn't seen her in a while."

"Her family?"

"Her sister and brother-in-law. Mr. and Mrs. Robbins, in Pasadena."

The door opened. A young man clutching a handful of paintbrushes in his right hand looked me up and down.

No surprise, no suspicion. Just an artist's eye gauging perspective.

He was in his late twenties, tall and solidly built, with dark hair combed back and tied in a foot's worth of ponytail that dangled over his left collarbone. His face was heavy and soft-featured under a low flat forehead and shelf brows. The gestalt was simian—more gorilla than chimp—helped along by black eyebrows that met in the middle and a wash of black stubble that ran up past his cheekbones, swooped down his neck till it merged with his chest hair. He wore a black polyester tank top emblazoned with the logo of a skateboard company in tomato-red letters; baggy, flowered, orange-and-green knee-length shorts, and rubber beach sandals. His arms were coated with dark, coiling hair just past the elbow. The skin above that was hairless and white and slabbed with the kind of muscle that would pump up easily but looked slack and unused. A dried patch of baby-blue paint stained one bicep.

I said, "Sorry to disturb you."

He glanced at the brushes, then back at me.

I pulled out my wallet, found the business card I'd taken from Milo last night, and handed it to him.

He studied it, smiled, studied me, and gave it back. "I thought you said your name was Del-something."

"Sturgis is in charge. I'm working with him."

"An op," he said, grinning. "You don't look like one—at least not like the ones on TV. Guess that's the point of it, though, isn't it? *Très in*communicado."

I smiled.

He studied me some more. "A lawyer," he finally said. "Defense, not prosecution—or maybe some kind of professor. That's how I'd cast you, Marlowe."

"Do you work in the movies?" I said.

"No." He laughed and touched a paintbrush to his lips. Lowering it, he said, "Though I guess I do. Actually. I'm a writer." More laughter. "Like everyone else in this town, right? But not screenplays—God forbid screenplays."

His laughter rose in pitch and lingered, hovering on the brink of giddy. "You ever write one?"

"Nope."

"Give yourself time. Everyone's got a hot property— 'cept me. What I do for a living is graphic art. Airbrush-photorealism to sell products. What I do for fun is *art*-art— sloppy freedom." Waving the brushes. "And what I do to stay *sane* is writing—short pieces, post-modern essays. Had a couple published in the *Reader* and the *Weekly*. Mood-based urban fiction—how music and money and the whole L.A. experience make people *feel*. The different things L.A. *evokes* in people."

"Interesting," I said, not sounding very convincing.

"Yeah," he said cheerfully, "as if you give a shit. You just want to do your job and go home to your lonely P.I. Murphy bed, right?"

"Boy needs a hobby."

He said, "Oh, yeah," transferred his brushes to his left hand and held out his right and said, "Richard Skidmore."

We shook, he stepped back and said, "C'mon in."

The interior of the small house was prewar budget construction: cramped dark rooms that smelled of instant coffee and takeout food, marijuana, and turpentine. Textured walls, rounded archways, tin wall sconces, all of them bulbless. A brick mantel above a fireplace was piled high with Presto logs still in their wrappers. Thrift shop furniture, including some plastic-and-aluminum-tubing outdoor pieces, was assembled randomly on worn wood floors. Art and its accoutrements—odd-shaped, hand-stretched canvases in various stages of completion, jars and tubes of paint, brushes soaking in pitchers—were everywhere but on the walls. A paint-encrusted easel sat in the center of the living room, amid a mound of crumpled paper, broken pencils, and charcoal stubs. A draftsman's table and adjustable chair were set up in what looked to be the dining area, along with a compressor attached to an airbrush.

The walls were unadorned, but I noticed a single piece of

white construction paper nailed above the mantel. Calli-
graphic lettering at the center read:

> *Day of the Locusts,*
> *Twilight of the Worms,*
> *Night of the Living Dread.*

"My novel," said Skidmore. "Both the title and the opening
line. The rest will happen when the old attention span kicks
in—it's always been a problem for me, but hey, it didn't stop
the last couple of presidents, did it?"

I said, "Did you meet Kathy Moriarty through your
writing?"

"Work, work, work, Marlowe? How much does Boss
Spurgis pay you to get you to be so conscientious?"

"Depends on the case."

"Very good," he said, smiling. *"Evasive.* You know, this
is *really* great, your dropping in like this. It's why I love
waking up in L.A. You can never tell when some SoCal
archetype will come knocking."

Another appraising glance. I started to feel like a still
life.

"Think I'll use you in my next piece," he said, drawing
an imaginary line in the air. "The Private Eye: The Things
He Sees—The Things That See *Him.*"

He lifted several canvases covered with abstract splotches
from a pool chaise and dumped them on the floor unceremoniously. "Sit."

I did and he lowered himself onto a wooden stool directly
in front of me.

"This is great," he said. "Thanks for dropping by."

"Does Kathy Moriarty live here?"

"Her place is in back. Garage unit."

"Who's the landlord?"

"I am," he said with pride. "Inherited it from my grandfather. Gay old blade—ergo the Boys' Town location. Came
out of the closet twenty years after Grandma died, and I was

the only one in the family who didn't cut him off. So when he died, I got all of it—the house, the Bloatmobile, hundred shares of IBM stock. The art of the deal, right?"

"Mrs. Robbins says she hasn't seen Kathy for over a month. When's the last time you saw her?"

"Funny," he said.

"What is?"

"That her sister would hire someone to look for her. They didn't get along—at least from Kathy's POV."

"Why's that?"

"Culture clash, no doubt. Kathy said the sister was Pasadena Whitebread. The kind who'd say uri*nation* and defe*cation*."

"As opposed to Kathy."

"Exactly."

I asked him again when he'd last seen her.

He said, "Same time Whitebread did—about a month."

"When's the last time she paid her rent?"

"The *rent* is a hundred a month, which is stand-up comedy, right? Couldn't get into the whole landlord thing."

"When's the last time Kathy paid the hundred?"

"At the beginning."

"Beginning of what?"

"Our association. She was so happy to get something that cheap—and it includes utilities because everything's metered together and it's too much of a hassle to have it changed—she came up with ten months' worth right at the beginning. So she's paid up through December."

"Ten months. She's been living here since February?"

"Guess so—yeah. It was right after New Year's. I used the garage apartments for a party—artists and writers and terrific fakers. When I was cleaning up I decided to rent one of them and use the other for storage, so I wouldn't be tempted to throw another party next year and hear all that bad dialogue."

"Was Kathy invited to the party?"

"Why would she have been?"

"Being a writer."

"No, I didn't meet her till *after* the party."

"How'd you meet her?"

"Ad in the *Reader*. She was the first to show up and I liked her. Straight on, no bullshit, a real no-nonsense Sapphite."

"Sapphite?"

"As in Lesbos."

"She's gay?"

"Sure." Big smile. "Tsk, tsk—looks like Sister White-bread didn't brief you thoroughly."

"Guess not."

He said, "Like I said, culture clash. Don't be shocked, Marlowe—this is West *Hollywood*. Everyone here is either queer or old or both. Or me. I'm into chastity until something monogamous and heterosexual and meaningful comes along." Tugging the ponytail: "Don't let this fool you—I'm really right-wing. Two years ago I owned twenty-six button-down shirts and four pairs of penny loafers. This"—another tug—"was to make the neighbors more comfortable. I'm already dragging down the property values, not letting them bulldoze and put up another Spa-Jacuzzi-Full-Security."

"Does Kathy have a lover?"

"Not that I saw, and my guess would be no."

"Why's that?"

"Her persona projects as profoundly *un*loved. As if she's just come off something hurtful and isn't ready to juggle with razor blades again. It wasn't anything she said—we don't talk too much, don't run into each other much. I like to sleep as much as I can and she's gone most of the time."

"Gone this long?"

He thought. "This *is* the longest, but she's usually on the road—I mean, it's not weird for her to be away for a week at a time. So you can tell her sister she's probably okay—probably doing something Miss Pasadena doesn't really want to hear about."

"How do you know she's gay?"

"Ah, the *evidence*. Well, for starts, the stuff she reads. Lesbo mags. She buys them regularly—I find them out in the trash. And the mail she gets."

"What kind of mail?"

His smile was a wide, white pin-stripe on wooly stubble. "Not that I go out of my way to read it, Marlowe—that would be illegal, right? But sometimes the mail for the back unit gets put in my box because the carriers don't realize there's a unit back there—or maybe they're just too *lazy* to go back there. A lot of it's from gay groups. How's that for deductive reasoning?"

"After a month you must have quite a bit of it collected," I said.

He stood, went into the kitchen, and returned a moment later carrying a sheaf of envelopes bound with a rubber band. Rolling the band off, he examined each piece of mail, then held on to it for several moments before passing the entire collection to me.

I fanned it and counted. Eleven pieces.

"Not much for a month," I said.

"Like I said, unloved."

I inspected the mail. Eight pieces were computer-addressed postcards and advertisements made out to *Occupant*. The remaining three were envelopes addressed to Kathy Moriarty by name. One appeared to be a solicitation for funds from an AIDS support group. So did another, from a clinic in San Francisco.

The third envelope was white, business-sized, post-marked three weeks previously in Cambridge, Massachu-setts. Typewritten address: **Ms. Kathleen R. Moriarty.** Return address preprinted in the upper left-hand corner: THE GAY AND LESBIAN ALLIANCE AGAINST DISCRIMINATION, MASSA-CHUSETTS AVENUE, CAMBRIDGE.

I pulled out a pen, realized I hadn't brought paper, and copied the information onto the back of a gasoline receipt that I found in my wallet.

Skidmore was studying me, amused.

I turned the envelope over several times, more for his benefit than anything else, finally gave it back to him.

He said, "So what did you learn?"

"Not much. What else can you tell me about her?"

"Brown hair, butch-do. Green eyes, kind of a potato face. Her fashion statement tends to be oriented toward baggy and sensible."

"Does she have a job?"

"Not that I'm aware of, but she could have."

"She never mentioned a job?"

"Uh-uh." He yawned and rubbed one knee, then the other.

"Other than being a writer," I said.

"That's not a *job*, Marlowe. It's a *calling*."

"Have you ever seen anything she wrote?"

"Sure. We didn't talk at all the first couple of months she was here, but once we discovered we had the muse in common, we did do a little show-and-tell."

"What'd she show?"

"Her scrapbook."

"Remember what was in it?"

He crossed his legs and scratched a hairy calf. "What do you call this? Getting a profile on the subject?"

"Exactly," I said. "What kinds of things did she have in her scrapbook?"

"All give, no take, huh?" he said, but without resentment.

"I don't know anything, Richard. That's why I'm talking to you."

"That make me a snitch?"

"A source."

"Aha."

"Her scrapbook?"

"I just skimmed it," he said. Yawning again. "Basically it was articles—stuff she'd written."

"Articles on what?"

Shrug. "I didn't look at it too closely—too fact-bound, no fancy."

"Any chance of my seeing the scrapbook?"

"Like how would that be possible?"

"Like if you have the key to her apartment."

He raised his hand to his mouth, a parody of outrage. "Invasion of privacy, Marlowe?"

"How about you stand right over me while I read it?"

"Doesn't take care of the constitutional issues, Phil."

"Listen," I said, leaning forward and putting major effort into sounding ominous, "this is serious. She could be in danger."

He opened his mouth and I knew he was going to crack wise. I blocked it by holding out a hand and said, "I mean it, Richard."

· His mouth closed and stayed that way for a while. I stared at him hard and he rubbed his elbows and knees and said, "You're serious."

"Very."

"This has nothing to do with collecting?"

"Collecting what?"

"Money. She told me she'd borrowed lots from her sister, hadn't paid any of it back, and her sister's husband was getting pissed—he's some sort of financial type."

"Mr. Robbins is a lawyer," I said, "and he and his wife *are* concerned about Kathy's debt. But that's not the issue anymore. She's been gone too long, Richard."

He rubbed some more and said, "When you told me you were working for the sister, I figured it had something to do with collecting."

"Well, it doesn't, Richard. Her sister—whatever their culture clash—is worried about her and so am I. I can't tell you more than that, but Mr. Sturgis considers this case a priority."

He undid his ponytail and shook his hair loose. It was thick and shiny as a cover girl's, and fanned across his face. I heard his neck crack as he lowered it and continued fanning. When he looked up some of the hair was in his mouth and he chewed it while wearing a thoughtful expression.

"All you want to do is look at it, huh?" he said, pulling strands away from his lips.

"That's it, Richard. You can watch me every second."

"Okay," he said. "Why not? At the worst, she'll find out and get pissed and I'll invite her to find a cheaper place."

He stood and stretched and shook his hair again. When I got up, he said, "Just stay right there, Phil."

Another trip to the kitchen. He came back too soon to have gone very far, carrying a loose-leaf notebook bound in orange cloth.

I said, "She left it with you?"

"Uh-uh. She forgot to take it back after she'd given it to me to look at. When I realized it, she was already gone, so I stuck it somewhere—got so much junk around here—and she never asked about it. We both forgot. Meaning it probably isn't that important to her, right? That's the rationale I'll use if she gets pissed."

He returned to the stool, opened the notebook, and flipped pages. Clinging to his treasure for just a moment before yielding, just as he'd done with the mail.

"Here you go," he said. "We're not talking racy, Phil."

I opened the book. Inside were forty or so double-sided pages—black paper sheathed in transparent plastic. Newspaper clippings bearing Kathleen Moriarty's byline were inserted on each side. There was a flap on the inside front cover. I slid my hand in. Empty.

The articles were arranged chronologically. The first few, dating back fifteen years, were from *The Daily Collegian* at Cal State Fresno. A score or so, spanning a seven-year period, were from the *Fresno Bee*. Next came pieces from the *Manchester Union Leader* and the *Boston Globe*. The dates indicated Kathy Moriarty had stayed at each of the New England papers for only about a year.

I turned back to the beginning and checked out contents. For the most part, general interest stuff, and all local: Town meetings and personality pieces. Holiday features of the clever pet variety. An investigative trend didn't creep in until Moriarty's year at the *Globe:* a series on pollution in Boston Harbor and an exposé of cruelty to animals at a Worcester pharmacologic firm that didn't appear to have gone very far.

The last insert was a review in the *Hartford Courant* of *The Bad Earth,* her book on pesticides. Small press publisher. Good marks for enthusiasm, points off for poor documentation.

I checked the back flap. Slipped out several folded pieces of newsprint. Skidmore was looking at his toes and hadn't noticed. I unfolded and began reading.

Five opinion pieces, dated last year, from a paper called *The GALA Banner* and subtitled "The monthly newsletter of the Gay and Lesbian Alliance Against Discrimination, Cambridge, Mass."

Byline change to *Kate* Moriarty. Title of Contributing Editor.

These essays were filled with rage: male domination, the AIDS plague, the penis as a weapon. A piece on identity and misogyny. Stapled to that one was a scrap of newsprint.

Skidmore yawned. "Almost finished?"

"One sec."

I read the scrap. The *Globe,* again, three years old. No Moriarty byline. No byline at all. Just a news summary— one of those "roundup" items papers run on page 2 of the final edition.

DOCTOR'S DEATH TIED TO OVERDOSE

(CAMBRIDGE) The death of a Harvard Psychiatric Fellow is believed to have resulted from an accidental or self-administered dose of barbiturates. The body of Eileen Wagner, 37, was found this morning in her office at the Beth Israel Hospital Psychiatry Department on Brookline Avenue. Time of death was estimated at some time during the night. Police would not speculate upon what led them to their conclusion, other than to say that Dr. Wagner had been suffering from "personal problems." A graduate of Yale and Yale University Medical School, Dr. Wagner completed pediatric training at Western Pediatric Medical Center in Los Angeles and practiced medicine with the World Health Organization overseas before coming to Harvard last year to study Child and Adolescent Psychiatry.

I looked over at Skidmore. His eyes were closed. I pulled off the article, pocketed it, closed the book, and said, "Thanks, Richard. Now how about giving me a look at her apartment."

His eyes opened.

"Just to make sure," I said.

"Sure of what?"

"That she's not there—hurt or worse."

"No way is she there," he said, with genuine anxiety that was refreshing. "No way, Marlowe."

"How can you be sure?"

"I saw her drive away a month ago. White Datsun—you can get the plates, run some kind of trace, right?"

"What if she came back without the car? You might not have noticed—you yourself said the two of you didn't see each other often."

"No." He shook his head. "Too weird."

"Why don't we just check, Richard? You can stand there and watch—just like with the scrapbook."

He rubbed his eyes. Stared at me. Got up.

I followed him into a tiny, dark kitchen where he picked a ring of keys out of a pile of junk and pushed open a rear door. We walked across a backyard too small for hopscotch to a double garage. The garage doors were the old-fashioned hinge-type. Door-sized inserts were centered in each. Garage apartments. Literally.

Skidmore said, "This one," and led me to the unit on the left. The door-within-a-door was deadbolted.

"Illegal," he said, "converting the garage. You won't tell on me, Marlowe, will you?"

"Cross my heart."

Smiling, he shuffled keys. Then turned serious and stopped.

"What is it, Richard?"

"Wouldn't it smell—if she was . . . you know."

"Depends, Richard. You never can tell."

Another smile. Shaky. He fumbled with the keys.

"One thing I'm curious about," I said. "If you thought I was here to dun Kathy for money, why'd you let me in?"

"Simple," he said. "Material."

Kathy Moriarty's home was a twenty-by-twenty room that still reeked of automobile. The floor was wheat-colored linoleum squares; the walls were white plasterboard. The furniture was a twin-size mattress on the floor, sheet crumpled at the foot, revealing sweat-stained blue ticking. Wooden nightstand, round white Formica table, and three metal chairs padded at seat and back with dollops of yellow Hawaiian-print plastic. One of the far corners contained a hot plate on a metal stand; the other, a Fiberglas water closet no bigger than an airplane latrine. Above the hot plate a single bracket shelf held a few dishes and kitchen utensils. On the opposite wall was a makeshift closet frame of white PVC tubing. A few outfits, mostly jeans and shirts, hung from the horizontal tube.

Kathy Moriarty hadn't spent her sister's money on interior decorating. I had an idea where the funds had gone.

Skidmore said, "Oh, man." The skin beneath his stubble was white and one hand was atop his head, snarled in hair.

"What is it?"

"Either someone's been here or she's packed out on me."

"What makes you say that?"

He waved his hands, suddenly agitated. The kid with the poor attention span, struggling to make himself clear.

"This wasn't the way it looked when she was here. She

had luggage—lots of suitcases, a backpack . . . this big trunk that she used for a coffee table." He looked around and pointed. "Right there. And there was a pile of books right on it—next to the mattress."

"What kinds of books?"

"I don't know—I never checked . . . but one thing I'm sure of: It didn't look this way."

"When's the last time you saw it look any different?"

The hand in his hair clawed and gathered a clump. "Just before I saw her drive away—when would that be? Maybe five weeks. Or six, I don't know. It was at night. I brought her some mail, and she was sitting with her feet up on the chest. So the chest was there—that's for sure. Five or six weeks ago."

"Any idea what was in the chest?"

"No. For all I know it was empty—but why would anyone take an empty trunk, right? So it probably wasn't. And if she packed out, why would she leave her clothes and her dishes and stuff?"

"Good thinking, Richard."

"Very weird."

We entered the room. He stood back and I began circling. Then I saw something on the floor next to the mattress. Fleck of foam. Couple more. Bending down, I ran my hand along the side of the mattress. More foam fell out. My fingers searched and I found the wound: straight as a seam, surgically neat, barely noticeable even from up close.

"What?" said Skidmore.

"It's been slit open."

"Oh, man." He moved his head from side to side, flapping his hair.

He stayed in place while I got down on my knees, spread the lips of the slit, and peered inside. Nothing. I looked around the rest of the room. Nothing.

"What?" said Skidmore.

"Is the mattress yours or hers?"

"Hers. What's going on?"

"Looks like someone's been curious. Or maybe she was hiding something inside. Did she have a TV or stereo?"

"Just a radio. That's gone, too! But this isn't about burglary, is it?"

"Hard to tell."

"But you suspect *nasty,* don't you? That's why you came here in the first place, *isn't* it?"

"I don't know enough to suspect anything, Richard. Is there something you know about her that makes *you* think nasty?"

"No," he said in a loud, tight voice. "She was a lonely dyke who kept to herself—I don't know what else you expect me to tell you!"

"Nothing, Richard," I said. "You've been a big help. I appreciate the time."

"Yeah. Sure. Now can I close up? Gotta go call a locksmith, put on a new bolt."

We left the garage. Once outside, he pointed to the driveway and said, "That'll take you out."

I thanked him again and wished him luck on his private-eye essay.

He said, "Cancel that one," and went inside the house.

33

The first pay phone I found was at a mall on Santa Monica Boulevard. The shopping center was brand-new—empty storefronts, the lot freshly tarred. But the booth had a lived-in smell. Gum clots and cigarette butts littered the floor. The directory had been ripped off its chain.

I called Boston Information and asked for the number of the *GALA Banner.* There was no listing for the paper, but the Gay and Lesbian Alliance had one that I dialed.

A man answered, "GALA." I heard voices in the background.

"I'd like to speak to someone on the *Banner,* please."

"Advertising or editorial?"

"Editorial. Someone who knows Kathy— Kate Moriarty."

"Kate doesn't work here anymore."

"I know that. She's living in L.A., which is where I'm calling from."

Pause. "What's this about?"

"I'm an acquaintance of Kate's and she's been missing for over a month. Her family's concerned, so am I, and I thought someone in Boston might be able to help us out."

"She's not here, if that's what you mean."

"I'd really like to talk to someone on the staff who knows her."

Another pause. "I'd better take your name and number."

I gave him both and said, "That's an answering service. I'm a clinical psychologist—you can check me out in an American Psychological Association directory. You can also call Professor Seth Fiacre over at Boston U.'s psych department. I'd appreciate hearing back as quickly as possible."

"Well," he said, "it may not be that quick. You'll need to talk to the *Banner*'s editor. That's Bridget McWilliams and she's out of the city for the rest of the day."

"Where can she be reached?"

"I'm not at liberty to say."

"Please try to contact her. Tell her Kate's safety may be at stake." When he didn't respond to that, I said, "Mention Eileen Wagner's name, too."

"Wagner," he said, and I heard the sound of scrawling. "As in the composer— No, guess that would be *Vahg*ner."

"Guess so."

I'd forgotten about Seth Fiacre's move to Boston until his name had popped into my head as a reference. The social psychologist had left UCLA for the East last year, when an endowed chair in Group Process had been thrown at him. Seth's specialty was mind control and cults, and the Forbes 400 father of a sixteen-year-old girl rescued from a neo-Hindu apocalyptic sect living in subterranean bunkers in New Mexico had consulted Seth on deprogramming. Shortly after, the money for the chair had come available.

Back to Boston Information. I got the number for B.U.'s psych department and dialed it, was informed by the receptionist that Professor Fiacre's office was at the Applied Social Science Center. A receptionist there took my name and put me on hold. Seth's voice came on a moment later.

"Alex, long time."

"Hi, Seth. How's Boston?"

"Boston is wonderful, a real city. Hadn't been back for any length of time since graduation—kind of a nice homecoming. How about yourself? Do any teaching like you were thinking of?"

"Not yet."

"It's hard to return," he said. "Once you get out in the real world."

"Whatever that means."

He laughed. "I forgot I was speaking to a clinician. What've you been up to?"

"Doing some consulting, trying to put out a monograph."

"Sounds admirably well-rounded. So, what can I do for you? Another bunch of true believers to check out? My pleasure. Last time I gave you data I got two abstracts and a paper in *JPSP* out of it."

"The Touch," I said, remembering.

"They put the touch on lots of suckers. So who're the loony tunes this time?"

"No cults," I said. "What I'm looking for is some information on a colleague. Former faculty at your alma mater."

"The *H* place? Who?"

"Leo Gabney. And wife."

"Dr. Prolific? Yeah, I seem to have heard he was living out there."

"Know anything about him?"

"Not personally. But we're not exactly paddling the backwaters, are we? I remember having to immerse myself in everything he'd written for my Advanced Learning Theory course. The guy was a factory. I used to curse him for turning out so much data, but most of it was pretty solid. He must be—what? Sixty-five, seventy? Little old for mischief. Why're you checking him out?"

"He's a little younger than that—sixty or so. And a long way from the glue factory. He and his wife have a clinic in San

Labrador specializing in phobia therapy. For the rich." I quoted him the Gabneys' fee schedule.

"How depressing," he said. "Here I was, thinking this endowment was serious money, and you've gone and made me feel poor again." He repeated the numbers out loud, then said, "Oh, well . . . What do you want to know about them, and why?"

"They've been treating the mother of one of my patients, and some strange things have come up—nothing I can get into, Seth. Sorry, but you understand."

"Sure. You're interested in his libidinal history, and related matters, when he was back at H."

"That," I said, "and any financial indiscretions."

"Ah . . . *that* can of worms. Now I'm intrigued."

"If you could find out why the two of them left Boston and what kinds of work they were doing during the year or so before they left, I'd really appreciate it."

"Do what I can, though people around here don't like to talk about money—because they lust after it so much. Also, those folks at That Place Uptown don't always condescend to talk to the rest of us."

"Even alumni?"

"Even alumni who stray too far south of Cambridge. But I'll churn the chowder, see what bobs to the surface. What's the wife's name?"

"Ursula Cunningham. She hyphenates it now, with Gabney. She's a Ph.D.-M.D. Gabney was her adviser in grad school and sent her on to med school. Her faculty *appointment* was at the med school, Department of Psychiatry. His may have been, too, as a matter of fact."

"You just raised the hurdle a little higher, Alex. The med school's an entity unto itself. Only one I know there is my kid's pediatrician, and he's only clinical faculty."

"Anything you can learn would be helpful, Seth."

"We're talking ASAP, of course."

"The quicker the better."

"Except in matters of wine, cheese, and carnal pleasure.

Okay, I'll see what I can do. And think about paying a visit some day, Alex. You can take me out to Legal Seafoods for untrammeled lobster gluttony."

My last call was to Milo. I expected a machine but Rick answered with a "Dr. Silverman" that sounded rushed.

"It's Alex again, Rick."

"On my way out, Alex—call from the E.R., bus accident, they're short-staffed. Milo's out in Pasadena. Spent the morning on the phone and left about an hour ago."

"Thanks, Rick. Bye."

"Alex? I just wanted to thank you for getting him the job—he was pretty low. The idleness. I tried to talk him into doing something but I wasn't making much headway until you got him the referral. So thanks."

"It wasn't charity, Rick. He was the best man for the job."

"I know that and you know that. The trick was convincing him."

Afternoon traffic slowed the drive to San Labrador. I spent the time thinking about connections between Massachusetts and California.

The gates at Sussex Knoll were closed. I talked to Madeleine over the talk box and was let in. Neither Milo's Fiat nor Rick's Porsche was in front of the house. A cherry-red Jaguar XJS convertible was.

A woman opened the Chaucer doors before I got to them. Five three, mid-forties, a few extra pounds that rounded her nicely. Her face, in contrast, was lean and triangular under a cap of black curls. Her eyes were the same color, large and round and heavily lashed. She had on a soft pink dress that would have gone well at a Renoir picnic. Bracelets jangled as she extended her arm.

"Dr. Delaware? I'm Susan LaFamiglia."

We shook hands. Hers was small and soft, until she turned on the grip. She wore lots of makeup and had applied it well. Rings graced half of her fingers. A strand of black pearls rested on her bosom. If it was real, it was worth more than the Jag.

"It's good to meet you," she said. "I'd like to talk to you about our mutual client—not right now, because I'm in the middle of talking to her, trying to unravel her finances. How about in a couple of days?"

"Sure. As long as Melissa consents."

"She already has. I've got a release form inside. . . . I'm sorry, did you come to have a session with her?"

"No," I said. "Just to see how she's doing."

"She seems to be doing okay—considering. I was surprised at how knowledgeable she is about money, for someone her age. But obviously I don't know her very well."

"She's a complex young lady," I said. "Has a detective named Sturgis been by?"

"Milo? He was here before, just went over to the stepfather's restaurant. The police came here to question Melissa about this McCloskey character's death. I told them she hadn't been informed of it yet, and that under no circumstances would I allow them to talk to her. Milo suggested they talk to the stepfather—there was a bit of pawing and snorting, but they agreed."

Her smile said success had been no surprise.

The Tankard's lot was so full of cars that it appeared open for business: Ramp's Mercedes, Noel's Toyota, the brown Chevy Monte Carlo, Milo's Fiat, and a dark blue Buick sedan that I'd also seen before.

Milo's hired surveillance was nowhere in sight. Either not on the job or damned good.

As I got out of the Seville, I saw someone exit the rear of the building and run across the lot.

Bethel Drucker in a white blouse and dark shorts and flat sandals. Blond hair loose and flying, chest bouncing. A moment later she was behind the wheel of the brown Chevy, revving noisily, backing out of her space in a squealing fishtail, then speeding down the driveway toward the boulevard. Without stopping, she hooked a sharp right and roared away. I tried to catch a glimpse of her face behind glass but caught only a boomerang flash of hot white sunlight.

Just as the sound of her engine faded, the Tankard's front door opened and Noel stepped out, looking confused and scared.

"Your mom went that way," I said, and he swung his eyes toward me convulsively.

I walked over to him. "What happened?"

"I don't know," he said. "The cops came by to talk to Don. I was in the kitchen, doing some reading. Mom went out and served them coffee, and then when she got back she looked really upset. I asked her what the matter was but she didn't answer and then I saw her leave."

"Any idea what the cops said to Don?"

"No. Like I said, I was in the kitchen. I wanted to ask her what the matter was but she just left without saying anything." He looked down the boulevard. "It's not like her. . . ."

He lowered his head, forlorn. Dark and handsome and forlorn . . . James Deanish. My scalp prickled.

I said, "No idea where she might have gone?"

"It could be anywhere. She likes to drive—being cooped up in here all day. But she usually tells me where she's going and when she's coming back."

"She's probably under stress," I said. "What with the restaurant being closed. The uncertainty."

"She's *scared,*" he said. "The Tankard's been her life. I told her even if worse comes to worse and Don doesn't reopen, she can easily get a job at another place, but she said it would never be the same, because . . ." Shading his eyes with one hand, he scanned the boulevard some more.

"Because what, Noel?"

"Huh?" He gave a startled look.

"Your mom said it would never be the same because . . ."

"Whatever," he said angrily.

"Noel—"

"It's not important. I've gotta go."

Reaching into his jeans, he pulled out a ring of keys, ran to the Celica, and drove off.

I was still preoccupied as I walked up to the Tankard's front door. The NO BRUNCH sign had been replaced with one that said CLOSED UNTIL FURTHER NOTICE.

Inside, the lights had been turned up to cheapening brightness, exposing every raw spot in the wood paneling, every snarl and stain on the carpet.

Milo sat on a stool by the bar, holding a coffee cup. Don Ramp was in one of the booths along the right wall, a bottle of Wild Turkey, a glass, and a cup that matched Milo's within arm's reach. Two other coffees sat near the outer edge of the table. Ramp had on the same white shirt he'd worn at the dam. He looked as if he'd just returned from a guided tour to hell, traveling stand-by.

Chief Chickering and Officer Skopek stood over him. Chickering was smoking a cigar. Skopek looked as if he would have liked one, too.

When the chief saw me, he turned and frowned. Skopek did likewise. Milo sipped coffee. Ramp didn't do anything.

It looked like a chapter meeting of the Big Man's Club gone sour.

I said, "Hi, Chief."

"Doctor." Chickering moved his wrist and a pellet of ash dropped into a tray near Ramp's bottle. The bourbon was two-thirds gone.

I went to the bar and sat down next to Milo. He raised his eyebrows and gave a small smile.

Chickering turned back to Ramp. "Okay, Don, guess that'll do it."

If Ramp responded I didn't see it.

Chickering picked up one of the coffee cups near the edge and took a long swallow. Licking his lips, he came over to the bar. Skopek followed but remained several feet behind.

Chickering said, "Doing some routine questioning for my good friends over in Los Angeles, Doctor. About what happened to the late Mr. McCloskey. Anything you want to add to the current pool of ignorance?"

"Nothing, Chief."

"Okay," he said, then took another swig of coffee. When he finished, the cup was empty. He held it out without looking back, and Skopek took it and placed it on Ramp's table. "Far as I'm concerned, Doctor, it's just deserts. But I'm following up as a courtesy to L.A. So now I've asked you and that's it."

I nodded.

He said, "How's everything else going? With little Melissa?"

"Fine, Chief."

"Good." Pause. Smoke rings. "Any idea who's going to be running the household?"

"I couldn't say, Chief."

"Well," he said, "we were just over there and a lawyer was talking to the girl—lady lawyer. West side firm. Don't know how much experience she's got with this side of town."

I shrugged.

"Glenn Anger's a good man," he said. "Grew up here. Known him for years."

I said nothing.

"Well," he said again. "Got to be going—never a dull moment." To Ramp: "Take care of yourself, Don. Call if you need anything. Lots of people rooting for you—lots of people want to sniff T-bone and New York prime and F.M. on the grill again."

He winked at Ramp. Ramp didn't move.

After Chickering and Skopek had left, I said, "F.M.?"

"Filet mignon," said Milo. "We had a nice little chat about beef just before you got here. The chief's a connoisseur. Buys those packaged steaks from Omaha."

I looked over at Ramp, who still hadn't budged. "He join in the discussion?" I said, very softly.

Milo placed his coffee cup on the bar. The broken St. Pauli Girl mirror had been removed. Bare plaster in its place.

"No," he said. "He hasn't done much of anything except suck bourbon."

"What about Nyquist?"

"Not a word—not that anyone's looking."

"Why'd LAPD send Chickering around?"

"So they can avoid ruffling San Labrador feathers and still say they did the job."

"Chickering have anything new to say about McCloskey?"

He shook his head.

"How did Ramp react to hearing about it?"

"Stared at Chickering, then took a big gulp of Turkey."

"No surprise at McCloskey being dead?"

"Maybe a glimmer—it's hard to tell. He's not registering much of anything. Not exactly your stalwart coper."

"Unless it's an act."

Milo shrugged, picked up the coffee cup, looked at it, put it down. "Don," he called across the room, "anything I can do for you?"

Nothing from the booth, then a long, slow shake of Ramp's head.

"So," said Milo, switching back to a soft tone, "have a chance to go to West Hollywood?"

"Yup—let's talk outside."

The two of us went out to the parking lot.

I said, "Is your surveillance guy anywhere around?"

"Trade secret," he said, smiling. Then: "At this moment, no, but it wouldn't make a difference, believe me."

I told him what I'd learned about Kathy Moriarty and Eileen Wagner.

"Okay," he said, "your Gabney theory's looking better. They probably scammed in Boston, got found out, and came west to scam some more."

"It goes beyond that," I said. "Eileen Wagner was the one who referred me to *Gina*. A few years later, she's dead in Boston, the Gabneys *leave* Boston, and shortly after, *they're* treating Gina."

"Anything in Moriarty's clipping implying Wagner's death wasn't suicide?"

I handed him the scrap.

He read and said, "Doesn't sound as if anyone was going to look into it. And if it developed into something fishy, wouldn't Moriarty have kept *those* clippings in her book?"

"Guess so," I said. "But there's got to be some kind of connection—something Moriarty thought she had. Wagner was studying psych at Harvard when the Gabneys were still there. She probably came into some kind of contact with them. Kathy Moriarty had an interest in all three of them. And all three knew Gina."

"When you met Wagner did anything about her strike you as odd?"

"No," I said. "Not that I analyzed her—it was a ten-minute conversation eleven years ago."

"So you have no reason to question her ethics?"

"None at all. Why?"

"Just wondering," he said. "If she was ethical, she wouldn't have talked to anyone about Gina specifically, would she? Even to another doctor."

"That's true."

"So how could the Gabneys have known about Gina from her?"

"Maybe they didn't. Specifically. But after learning the Gabneys specialized in treating phobics, maybe Wagner talked about Gina's case in general terms. Medical conference—that wouldn't have been unethical."

"*Rich* phobic," said Milo.

"Living like a princess in a castle," I said. "Wagner used those words. She'd been impressed by Gina's wealth. She could have talked about it to one or both of the Gabneys. And when the time came for the Gabneys to seek greener pastures, they remembered what she'd said and headed for San Labrador. And hooked up with Gina because Melissa called."

"Coincidence?"

"It's a real small town, Milo. But I still don't see why

Kathy Moriarty had the clipping of Wagner's suicide in her scrapbook."

"Maybe Wagner was one of Moriarty's sources. About the Gabneys' scam."

"And maybe Wagner died because of that."

"Whoa, that's a big leap," he said. "But tell you what, when I get back, we can pursue it. Get *Suzy* to pursue it— what a gal. If the Gabneys have been bleeding Gina's estate, she'd be the one to find out. The Cassatt could be a good place to start. If it wasn't legally transferred, she'll be on them like a hound on hemoglobin."

"When you get back from where?" I said.

"Sacramento. Suzy's assigned me a trip up there. Seems Attorney Douse has been in some kind of trouble with the Bar recently but they won't talk about it over the phone, and even in person they're demanding proper documentation of need-to-know. I'm booked out of Burbank at six-ten. She's gonna have the papers faxed to me up there tomorrow morning. I'm scheduled to speak to some bankers at one, do my thing at the Bar at three-thirty. After that, she assures me there'll be other items on the agenda."

"Tight schedule."

"The lady doesn't suffer slackers lightly. Anything else?"

"Yes," I said. "Was Bethel listening when Chickering told Ramp about McCloskey?"

"She was in the room, pouring coffee. Why?"

I told him about the waitress's hurried departure. "It's possible it was just sensory overload, Milo. I spoke to Noel a moment later and he said she's been under stress, worried about her job. Maybe hearing about another death was just too much to handle. But I think she was reacting specifically to the fact that it was *McCloskey* who was dead. Because I think McCloskey was Noel's father."

The look of surprise on his face was gratifying. I felt like a kid who'd finally bested Daddy at chess.

"Talk about your leaps," he said. "Where does *that* come from?"

"My quivering antennae. I finally figured it out. It had nothing to do with Noel's behavior—it's the way he *looks*. I saw it just a few minutes ago. He was upset about his mother, lowered his face, and gave this defeated look that was a carbon copy of the expression on McCloskey's face in his arrest photo. The resemblance, once you notice it, is really striking. Noel's short, dark, handsome—almost pretty. Mc-Closkey used to have that same type of good looks."

"Used to," said Milo.

"Exactly. Someone who hadn't known him in the old days would never have spotted it."

"The old days," he said, and walked back inside the restaurant.

"C'mon, Don." Milo propped a finger under Ramp's chin.

Ramp gazed back with cloudy eyes.

"Okay," said Milo, "I've been there, Don. So I know getting the words out is like passing a kidney stone. Don't talk—just blink. Once for yes, twice for no. Is Noel Drucker McCloskey's kid or not?"

Nothing. Then dry lips formed the word *yes,* and a sibilant whisper followed.

"Does Noel know?" I said.

Ramp shook his head and lowered it to the table. Boils had broken out on the back of his neck and he smelled like the bear cage at the zoo.

Milo said, "Noel and Joel. Bethel have a flair for light verse or something?"

Ramp looked up. His facial skin had the texture and color of old custard, and his mustache was clogged with skin flakes.

He said, "Noel because . . . she couldn't." Shaking his head and starting to droop again.

Milo propped him up. "She couldn't what, Don?"

Ramp stared at him, wet-eyed. "She can't . . . She *knew* Joel . . . the way the word . . . looked . . . so Noel . . . three letters the same . . . remember."

He eyed the bourbon bottle, sighed, closed his eyes.

I said, "She couldn't read? She named him Noel because it looked like Joel and she wanted something she could visualize?"

Nod.

"Is she still illiterate?"

Faint nod. "Tried to . . . She couldn't . . ."

"How'd she manage to do her job?" I said. "Taking orders, totaling the check?"

Unintelligible sounds from Ramp.

Milo said, "C'mon, dammit, stop blubbering."

Ramp lifted his head slightly. "Memory. She knew everything . . . the whole menu . . . by heart. When there's . . . a special . . . she . . . we rehearse it."

"And filling out the check?" said Milo.

"I . . ." Look of exhaustion.

"You take care of it," I said. "You take care of *her.* Just like the old days back at the studio. What was she, a country girl, came out west to be a star?"

"Appalachia," he said. "Hill . . . billy."

"Poor girl from the sticks," I said. "You knew she'd never make it in pictures, especially not being able to read lines. Did you help her keep it secret for a while?"

Nod. "Joel . . ."

"Joel blew her cover?"

He nodded. Belched and let his head loll. "Pictures for him."

"He caused her to lose her contract at the studio and then hired her as a model?"

Nod.

Milo said, "How'd she get a driver's license?"

"Written tests . . . memorized all of them."

"Must have taken a long time."

Ramp nodded and wiped his nose with the back of his hand. He lowered his head to the table again. This time Milo let him remain there.

"Have she and McCloskey maintained contact all these years?" I said.

Ramp's head shot up with surprising speed. "No—she hated . . . it . . . not what she wanted."

"What wasn't?"

"The baby. Noel . . ." Wince. "Loved him, but . . ."

"But what, Don?"

Beseeching look.

"What, Don?"

"Rape."

"McCloskey got her pregnant by raping her?"

Nod. "All the time."

"All the time what, Don?" said Milo.

"Rape."

"He raped her all the time?"

Nod.

"Why didn't you protect her from *that?*" said Milo.

Ramp began to sob. The tears landed in his mustache and beaded in the greasy hairs.

He tried to say something, choked.

Milo put his finger under Ramp's chin. Used a napkin to dab the weeping man's face.

"What, Don?" he said gently.

"Everyone," said Ramp, tears flowing.

"Everyone raped her?"

Sob. Gulp. "Had her . . . She's not . . ." Struggling to lift his hand, he tapped his head.

"She's not bright," said Milo. "Everyone took advantage of her."

Nod. Tears.

"Everyone, Don?"

Ramp's head lolled and dipped. His eyes closed. Saliva trickled down one side of his mouth.

Milo said, "Okay, Don," and lowered Ramp's face to the table once more.

I followed Milo back to the bar. The two of us sat and watched Ramp for a while. He began to snore.

"The studio wild bunch," I said. "The dumb, illiterate girl everyone passed around."

"How'd you know?"

"From the way Noel acted just before. We were talking about his mother. He mentioned she said that working anywhere else wouldn't be the same, started to elaborate, and stopped. When I pressed him on it, he got mad and left. That struck me as unusual. He's a kid who controls his emotions—needs to be in control. Typical for someone growing up with a druggie or alkie parent. So I knew whatever it was that made him blow up had to be important. Then when Ramp started talking, it all fit."

"Illiterate," said Milo. "Living that way, all these years, never knowing when someone was going to blow her cover. Ramp taking care of her and the kid out of guilt."

"Or compassion, or both. Guess he is a genuine soft guy."

"Yeah," he said again, glancing over at Ramp and shaking his head.

I said, "It explains Bethel's willingness to wait tables while Ramp and Gina lived like royalty. She was used to being the doormat. Failed at acting and got into heavy dope and God knows what else. Topped it off by getting pregnant by the guy everyone hated. Posed for pictures that probably weren't high fashion. The way she's built isn't exactly suited to *Vogue*. It adds up to *subterranean* self-esteem, Milo. She probably figures what Ramp gave her is more than she deserves. And now she's in danger of losing even that."

He ran his hand over his face.

"What?" I said.

"If McCloskey exposed Bethel, then raped her, why would she freak out when she found out he was dead?"

"Maybe it was still a loss to her. Maybe she harbored some small bit of good feeling toward him. For giving her Noel."

Milo spun on the stool. Ramp snored louder.

"Or," said Milo, "what if it was more than some little *bit* of good feeling? What if she and McCloskey *have* been in contact with each other? Misery loving company. A common enemy."

I said, "Gina?"

"They both could've hated her. McCloskey for whatever reason he had in the first place, Bethel out of jealousy—the haves against the have-nots. What if she wasn't quite so happy playing the underdog? And what if there was another ingredient sweetening the relationship—money? Blackmail."

"Over what?"

"Who knows? But Gina was a member of the wild group."

"You said you didn't uncover any dirt on her."

"So she was better than the others at keeping it quiet—making her secret worth even more. Weren't you the one who told me secrets were coin of the realm out here? So what if McCloskey and Bethel took that literally? If McCloskey had been Bethel's partner in something nasty, it would make *sense* for her to bolt after hearing he was dead."

"Joel and Bethel, Noel and Melissa," I said. "Too goddam ugly. I hope you're wrong."

"I know," he said. "I keep coming up with them. But we didn't write the movie—we're just reviewing it."

He continued to look pained.

I said, "What if Noel ran down McCloskey? He's the first one I thought of when I heard a car had been the weapon. Cars are his thing—he has access to all of Gina's. Think we should open all those garages, see if any of the classics have front-end damage?"

"Waste of time," he said. "He wouldn't have used one of those. Too conspicuous."

"No one in Azusa saw Gina's Rolls drive up to the dam."

"Not true. We don't know that. Sheriff filed it as an accident—no one ever did a door-to-door."

"Okay," I said. "So Noel used some kind of utility vehicle. They used to have one—back when I was treating Melissa. Old Caddy—'62 Fleetwood. She called it a Cadillac Knockabout. They've probably got one like that today—can't use a Duesenberg to pick up the groceries. It's stashed somewhere on those seven acres, or in one of those garages. Or maybe McCloskey was run down with stolen wheels—Noel could know how to hot-wire."

"From too-good-to-be-true to juvenile delinquent?"

"Like you said, things change."

He swung toward the bar.

"Oedipus wrecks," he said. "The all-American kid runs over his old man. How much therapy will it take to patch that one up?"

I didn't answer.

Across the room, Ramp snorted and gasped for air. His head lifted, sank, rolled to the side.

Milo said, "Be a good idea to get him lucid, see what else we can squeeze out of him. Also be a good idea to wait around and see if old Bethel comes back."

He looked at his watch. "Got to be getting over to the airport. You feel like sticking around? I'll check in with you when I'm settled—let's say before nine."

"What about your surveillance guy? Can't he take over here?"

"Nope. He doesn't come out into the open. Part of the deal."

"Antisocial?"

"Something like that."

"All right," I said. "I was planning to play with the phone for a while—check out a few more Boston things. What do I do if Bethel comes back?"

"Keep her here. Try to get whatever you can out of her."

"Using what technique?"

He came around from behind the bar, hitched his trousers, buttoned his jacket, and slapped me on the back.

"Your charm, your Ph.D., bald-faced lies—whichever feels best."

34

Ramp slipped into a deep sleep. I cleared the bottle, glass, and cup from the table, put them in the bar sink, and dimmed the lights until they were no longer cruel. A phone-in to my service yielded no messages from Boston, just a few business calls that I handled for half an hour.

At four-thirty the phone rang: someone wanting to know when the Tankard would be open again. I said as soon as possible and hung up feeling like a bureaucrat. Over the next hour I disappointed lots of people wanting to make dinner reservations.

At five-thirty I felt cold and adjusted the air-conditioning thermostat. Pulling a cloth off one of the other tables, I draped it over Ramp's shoulders. He continued to doze. The great escape. More in common with Melissa than either of them would ever know.

At five-forty, I went into the restaurant's kitchen and fixed myself a roast beef sandwich and cole slaw. The coffee urn was cold, so I settled for a Coke. Bringing all of it back to the bar, I ate and watched Ramp continue to sleep, then phoned the house he'd once called home.

Madeleine answered. I asked if Susan LaFamiglia was still there.

"*Oui*. One momen'."

A second later the attorney came on. "Hello, Dr. Delaware. What's up?"

"How's Melissa?"

"That's what I wanted to talk to you about."

"How's she doing right now?"

"I got her to eat, so I suppose that's a good sign. What can you tell me about her psychological status?"

"In terms of what?"

"Mental stability. These kinds of cases can get nasty. Do you see her as someone who can deal with court without cracking up?"

"It's not a matter of cracking up," I said. "It's the cumulative stress level. Her moods tend to go up and down. She alternates between fatigue and withdrawal, and bursts of anger. She's not stabilized yet. I'd watch her for a while, wouldn't get right into litigation until I was sure she'd settled down."

"Up and down," she said. "Kind of a manic-depressive thing?"

"No, there's nothing psychotic about it. It's actually pretty logical, considering the emotional roller coaster she's been on."

"How long do you think it'll take for her to settle down?"

"It's hard to say. You can work with her on strategy—the intellectual part of it. But avoid anything confrontational for the time being."

"*Confrontational* is mostly what I've seen from her. That surprised me. What with her mother being dead only a few days—I expected more grief."

"That may relate to something she learned in therapy years ago. Channeling anxiety to anger in order to feel more in control."

"I see," she said. "So you're giving her a clean bill of health?"

"As I said, I wouldn't want to see her go through any

major upheaval right now, but in the long run I expect her to do okay. And she's certainly not psychotic."

"Okay. Good. Would you be willing to say that in court? Because the case may end up hinging on mental competence."

"Even if the other side has engaged in illegal activities?"

"If that turns out to be the case, we'll be in luck. And I'm looking into that angle, as I'm sure Milo told you. Jim Douse just went through a very expensive divorce and I know for a fact that he bought too many junk bonds for his personal portfolio. There's talk of some funny business up at the State Bar, but it may turn out to be nothing more than dirt thrown around by his ex-wife's attorneys. So I've got to cover all bases, assume Douse and the banker acted like saints. Even if they didn't, with the way books can be juggled, major skulduggery can be hard to uncover. I deal with movie studios all the time—their accountants specialize in that. *This* case is sure to get nasty, because it's a sizable estate. It could drag on for years. I need to know my client's solid."

"Solid enough," I said. "For someone her age. But that doesn't mean invulnerable."

"Solid's good enough, Doctor. Ah, she's coming back now. Do you want to speak to her?"

"Sure."

A beat, then: "Hi, Dr. Delaware."

"Hi. How're things going?"

"Fine . . . Actually, I thought maybe you and I could talk?"

"Sure. When?"

"Um . . . I'm working with Susan now and I'm getting kind of tired. How about tomorrow?"

"Tomorrow it is. Ten in the morning okay?"

"Sure. Thanks, Dr. Delaware. And I'm sorry if I've been . . . difficult."

"You haven't been, Melissa."

"I'm just— I wasn't thinking about . . . Mother. I guess

I was . . . denying it—I don't know—doing all that sleeping. Now, I *keep* thinking about her. Can't stop. Never seeing her again—her face . . . knowing she never will . . . again."

Tears. Long silence.

"I'm here, Melissa."

"Things will never be the same," she said. Then she hung up.

Six-twenty, still no sign of Bethel or Noel. I phoned my service and was told Professor "Sam Ficker" had called and left a Boston number.

I phoned it and got a young child on the line.

"Hello?"

"Professor Fiacre, please."

"My daddy's not home."

"Do you know where he is?"

An adult female voice broke in: "Fiacre residence. Who's calling?"

"This is Dr. Alex Delaware returning Professor Fiacre's call."

"This is the babysitter, Doctor. Seth said you might be calling. Here's the number where you can reach him."

She read off the number and I copied it down. Thanking her, I gave her the Tankard's number for callback, hung up, and dialed the one she'd given me.

A male voice said, "Legal Seafoods, Kendall Square."

"I'm trying to reach Professor Fiacre. He's having dinner there."

"Spell that, please."

I did.

"Hold on."

A minute passed. Three more. Ramp appeared to be rousing. Sitting up with great effort, he wiped his face with a grimy sleeve, blinked, looked around, and stared at me.

No apparent recognition. Closing his eyes, he drew the tablecloth around his shoulders and settled back down.

Seth came on the phone. "Alex?"

"Hi, Seth. Sorry to bother you at dinner."

"Perfect timing—we're between courses. I couldn't get much on the Gabneys, other than that their leaving wasn't totally voluntary. So they may have been up to something unsavory but I sure couldn't find out what it was."

"Were they asked to leave Harvard?"

"Not officially. Nothing procedural as far as I can tell— the people I spoke to really didn't want to get into details. What I gathered was that it was a mutual thing. They gave up tenure and split, and whoever knew something didn't belabor it. As to what that something is, I don't know."

"Anything on the types of patients they were treating?"

"Phobics. That's about it. Sorry."

"I appreciate your trying."

"I did run a search through Psych Abstracts and Medline to try to find out what kind of work they were doing. As it turns out, not much. She never published anything. Until four years ago, Leo was still cranking the stuff out. Then all of a sudden, it stopped. No more experiments, no clinical studies, just a couple of essays—very soft stuff. The kind of résumé-filler he'd never have gotten published if he wasn't Leo Gabney."

"Essays on what?"

"Philosophical issues—free will, the importance of taking personal responsibility. Spirited attacks on determinism— how any behavior can be changed, given the proper identification of congruent stimuli and reinforcers. Et cetera, et cetera."

"Doesn't sound too controversial."

"No," he said. "Maybe it's old age."

"What is?"

"Getting philosophical and abandoning real science. I've seen other guys go through it when they hit menopause. Gotta tell my students if *I* ever start doing it, take me out and shoot me."

We traded pleasantries for a few more minutes, then said goodbye. When the line was clear, I called the *GALA Banner*. A recording informed me that the paper's office was closed.

No beep for messages. I dialed Boston Information and tried to get a home number for the editor, Bridget McWilliams. A B. L. McWilliams was listed on Cedar in Roxbury, but the voice that answered there was male, sleepy, tinged with a Caribbean accent, and certain he had no relation named Bridget.

By six-forty, I'd been alone in the restaurant for over two hours and had grown to hate the place. I found some writing paper behind the bar, along with a portable radio. KKGO was no longer playing jazz, so I made do with soft rock. I kept thinking about missed connections.

Seven o'clock. Scratch marks on paper. Still no sign of Bethel or Noel. I decided to stick around until Milo reached Sacramento, then call him and beg off the assignment. Go home, attend to my fish eggs, maybe even call Robin . . . I phoned my exchange again, left a message for Milo in case I was out when he called.

The operator recorded it dutifully, then said, "There's one for you, if you want it, Doctor."

"From whom?"

"Someone named Sally Etheridge."

"Did she say what it was about?"

"Just her name and number. It's long distance—another six-one-seven area code. What is that, Boston?"

"Yes," I said. "Give me the number. Please."

"Important, huh?"

"Maybe."

A human being answered, "Uh-huh." Female. Music in the background. I switched off my radio. The music on the other end took shape: rhythm and blues, lots of horns. James Brown, maybe.

"Ms. Etheridge?"

"Speaking."

"Dr. Alex Delaware calling from Los Angeles."

Silence. "I was wondering if you'd call back." Hoarse and husky, Southie accent.

"What can I do for you?"

"I'm not the one asking."

"Did Bridget McWilliams give you my number?"

"Bingo," she said.

"Are you a reporter on the *Banner*?"

"Oh, yeah, right. I interview circuit breakers. I'm an electrician, mister."

"But you do know Kathy—Kate Moriarty?"

"These questions are coming awfully fast," she said. Talking slowly—deliberate slowness. Small laugh at the end of the sentence. I thought I detected an alcohol slur. But maybe being with Ramp all this time had biased my perceptions.

"Kate's been gone for over a month," I said. "Her family—"

"Yeah, yeah, I know that tune. Got it from Bridge. Tell the family not to get bent out of shape. Kate disappears a lot—that's her thing."

"This time it may not be routine."

"Think so?"

"I do."

"Well," she said, "you're entitled."

"If you're not worried, why'd you bother to call?"

Pause. "Good question . . . I don't even know you. So why don't we cut our losses and make bye-bye—"

"Hold on," I said. "Please."

"A polite one, huh?" Laugh. "Okay, you got a minute."

"I'm a psychologist. The message I left for Bridget explained how I could be—"

"Yeah, yeah, I got all that, too. So you're a shrink. So excuse me if that's not real comforting."

"You've had bad experiences with shrinks?"

Silence. "I like myself just fine."

I said, "Eileen Wagner. That's why you called."

Long silence. For a moment I thought she'd left the line. Then: "You knew Eileen?"

"I met her when she was a pediatrician out here. She

referred a patient to me, but when I tried to get in touch with her to talk about it, she never got back to me. Guess she'd left town by then. Went overseas."

"Guess so."

"Were she and Kate friends?"

Laughter. "No."

"But Kate was interested in Eileen's death—I found a clipping she'd put in her scrapbook. *Boston Globe,* no byline. Was Kate free-lancing for the *Globe* at that time?"

"I don't know," she said harshly. "Why the hell should I care what the hell she was doing and who the hell she was working for?"

Definite booze slur.

More silence.

I said, "I'm sorry if this is upsetting you."

"Are you?"

"Yes."

"Why?"

That caught me off guard, and before I found my answer, she said, "You don't know me from Eve—why the hell should you care how I feel?"

"Okay," I said. "It's not compassion for you specifically. It's force of habit. I like making people happy—maybe it's partly an ego trip. I went to school to be a yea-sayer."

"Yea-sayer. Yeah, I like that. Yea, yea, yea—you and the Beatles. John, Paul, Whatsisname, and Ringo. And Shrink. Psyching the crowd . . . I wanna hold your gland."

Brittle laughter. In the background, James Brown was begging for something. Love or mercy.

I said, "Eileen was also a yea-sayer. I'm not surprised she went into psychiatry."

Four more beats of Brown.

"Ms. Etheridge?"

Nothing.

"Sally?"

"Yeah, I'm here. God knows why."

"Tell me about Eileen."

Eight bars. I held my tongue.

Finally she said, "I've got nothing to tell. It was a waste. A fucking waste."

"Why'd she do it, Sally?"

"Why do you think? 'Cause she didn't wanna be what she was . . . after all the . . ."

"All the what?"

"The fucking *time*! The hours and hours of bullshit-trapping. With shrinks, counselors, whatever. I thought we'd put that fucking shit behind us. I fucking thought she was happy. I fucking thought she was fucking convinced she was okay the way God in Her infinite mercy made her. God *damn* her!"

"Maybe someone told her the opposite. Maybe someone tried to change her."

Ten bars of Brown. The song title popped into my head: "Baby, Please Don't Go."

She said, "Maybe. I don't fucking know."

"Kate Moriarty thought so, Sally. She found out something about Eileen's therapists, didn't she? That's what brought her all the way out to California."

"I don't know," she repeated. "I don't know. All *she* ever did was ask questions. She never talked much about what she was doing, thought I was *obligated* to talk to her because she was gay."

"How'd she get in contact with you?"

"GALA. I did all the wiring on their goddam offices. Opened my mouth and told her about . . . Eileen. She lit up like a Christmas tree. All of a sudden we were sisters in arms. But she never talked, only asked. She had all these rules— what she could talk about, what she couldn't . . . I thought we were— But she— Oh, *fuck* this! Fuck this whole *thing*. It's been too fucking long and I'm not putting myself through it again, so fucking for*get* it and fuck *you*!"

Dead air. No music.

I waited a moment, called back. Busy signal. Tried five minutes later, same result.

I sat there putting it together. Seeing things in another light. Another context that caused everything to make sense.

Time to ring another number.

Different area code.

This one was listed. Surname and first initial only. I copied, dialed, waited five rings until someone picked up and said, "Hello."

I hung up without returning the greeting. No air blowing through the vents, but the room felt even colder. After draping a second cloth around Ramp's shoulders, I left.

35

Five minutes of studying the Thomas Guide. A hundred and twenty minutes on Freeway 101 north, following through.

Twilight arrived midway through the drive. By the time I reached Santa Barbara the sky was black. I picked up the 154 near Goleta, found the San Marcos pass with little difficulty, and drove through the mountains all the way to Lake Cachuma.

Locating what I was looking for was more of a challenge. This was ranch country, no street signs or lamps or Chamber of Commerce puffery. I overshot the first time, didn't realize it until I hit the town of Ballard. Reversing direction, I cruised slowly. Despite straining eyes and a heavy foot on the brake, I passed it going the other way, too. But my headlights trapped a wooden sign just long enough for the image to register as I rolled by.

INCENTIVE RANCH
PRIVATE PROPERTY

I cut the lights, backed up, and stuck my head out the car window. Cooler up here. A breeze that smelled of dust and dry grass. The sign was handmade, nailhead letters in pine, swinging gently over a square wooden gate. The gate was low and squat. Horizontal planks in a wooden frame. Maybe five feet high, connected to tongue-and-groove fencing that blocked the entry.

Leaving the engine running, I got out of the Seville and walked to the gate. It yielded a bit when I pushed, but remained shut. After a couple of false starts I found a toe-hold between two of the planks, hoisted myself up, and ran my hand over the inner side of the gate. Metal latch. Big padlock. The view beyond, barely starlit. Below, a narrow dirt road, passing between what looked to be tall trees. Mountains in the background, sharp and black as a witch's cap.

Returning to the car, I edged out and drove a hundred yards or so until I found a spot where the shoulder was shaded by trees. Shrubs, really. Scrawny, wind-whipped things that appeared to grow out of the mountainside and hung suspended over the asphalt. Not concealment but maybe just enough camouflage to shield the car from casual discovery.

I parked, locked, walked back to the gate on foot, recovered my toehold, and was over in a wink.

The road was lumpy and pebble-strewn. I lost my footing several times in the darkness and landed on my palms. As I got closer to the tall trees, I picked up a piny scent. My face began to tingle and itch. Unseen bugs feasting on my flesh.

The trees were packed close together but few in number. Within moments I was in unprotected space. Flat space lit gray by a feeble quarter moon. I stopped, listened. Heard the blood sloshing in my ears. Gradually, details asserted themselves.

A stadium-size plot of dirt, planted, in no discernible pattern, with half a dozen trees. Low-voltage spots at some of the trunk bases.

My nose went to work again. Citrus perfume so strong my mouth tasted summer-vacation lemonade. Unimpressed, the bugs stayed with red meat.

I took a cautious step. Ten more, then twenty. Fuzzy white rectangles appeared through the leaves of one of the trees. I walked around the citrus boughs. The rectangles became windows. I knew there had to be a wall behind them and my mind drew one before my eyes actually saw it.

A house. Modest size. Single story, low-pitched roof. Three windows lit but nothing visible through them. Curtained.

The basic California ranch setup. Silent. Pastoral.

So peaceful it made me doubt my hunch. But too many things fit together. . . .

I searched for more details.

Saw the vehicle I was looking for.

To the left of the house was stake-and-post fencing. A corral.

Behind that, outbuildings. I headed toward them, heard the whinny and snort of horses, filled my nose with the mealy aroma of old hay and manure.

The horse sounds grew louder. I located the origin: stables, directly behind the corral. Behind that—twenty yards back—a tall building that appeared windowless. Feed barn. Farther back, to the right, a smaller structure.

Light there, too. One rectangle. Single window.

I moved forward. The horses pawed and whickered. Got louder. Only a few from the sound of it, but what they lacked in numbers they made up in anxiety. I held my breath, continued. Hooves thudded against soft wood; I thought I felt the earth vibrate, but it might have been my legs shaking.

The horses turned up the volume even further, lathering passionately. I heard a creak and a click from the direction of the smallest building. Pressing myself against the corral, I watched a column of light spread across the dirt as the front door to the building swung open. A screen door whistled and someone stepped out.

The horses kept whinnying. One of them let out a throaty, gaseous rumble.

A deep voice shouted, "Shut up!"

Sudden silence.

The shouter stood there for a moment, then went back inside. The light column thinned to a thread but didn't vanish. I stayed here, listening to the horses panting. Feeling many-legged things tour my hands and face.

Finally the door shut all the way. I slapped at my cheeks, waited several more minutes before moving forward.

Behind the stable walls the horses were whimpering in frustration. I ran past them, kicking up gravel and cursing my leather shoes.

I stopped at the barn door. Sounds—not equine—were coming from the small building. The single window cast a filmy glow on the dust. Sticking close to the barn siding, I inched my way toward the light.

Step by step. The sounds took on tone and form and species.

Human.

A human duet.

One voice talking, another humming. No. Moaning.

I was at the front wall of the small building now, pressing against rough wood but still unable to shape the sounds into words.

Angry tone in the first voice.

Giving orders.

The second voice resisting.

A curious, high-frequency noise, like that of a TV being switched on.

More moans. Louder.

Someone resisting and suffering because of it.

I ran to the window, crouched below the sill until my knees hurt, slowly raised myself and tried to peer through the shades.

Opaque. All I could discern was the barest abstraction of movement—the light-shift of form through space.

The sounds of torment continued from within.

I got to the door, pulled the screen door open, and winced as it creaked.

The sounds continued.

I groped in the darkness for the handle to the inner door.
Rusted knob, loose on its bearings. Metallic jingle. I
quieted it by grasping with both hands. Turned slowly.
Pushed.

An inch of spy-space. I looked through it, heart speeding. What I saw spurred it faster.

My hand pulled the door open . . . in.

The room was long and narrow and paneled with fake worm-
wood the color of cigarette ash. Black linoleum floor. Light
from two cheap-looking swag lamps on opposite ends. Dry,
smoke-flavored heat from a wall unit.

A pair of chipped white barber chairs were bolted to the
center of the floor, set three feet apart, in semirecline.

The first chair was empty. The second contained a woman
wearing a hospital gown, tethered at ankles, wrists, waist,
and chest by broad leather straps. Patches of hair had been
shaved from her head, creating a crude checkerboard. Elec-
trodes were fastened to white scalp-patches and to arms and
inner thighs. Wires running from each site merged to a
central orange cable that snaked across the floor and ended at
a gray metal box, high as a refrigerator, twice as wide. The
box was faced with dials and glassed meters. Some of the
needles on the meters quivered.

The edge of something stuck out from behind the box.
Chrome-shiny, wheeled legs.

A second cable connected the box to a device that sat on a
gray metal table. Paper drum and mechanical arm. The arm
held several mechanical pens. Jagged graph lines peaked and
troughed across the drum, which was rotating slowly. Next
to the machine were several amber pharmaceutical vials and a
white plastic inhalator.

Directly facing the woman was a large-screen television
console. A close-up of a female breast, its nipple apple-sized,
was frozen on the screen. The image shifted: close-up of a
face. A pubic thatch. Back to the nipple.

A man stood next to the set, holding a black remote-control device in one hand, a larger gray one in the other. He was chewing gum. His eyes were hot with triumph that turned to alarm when he saw me.

The woman in the chair was Ursula Cunningham-Gabney. Her eyes were raw and swollen and wide with terror, and her mouth was stuffed with a blue bandana.

The man was sixtyish, with bushy white hair and a small, round face. He wore a black sweatshirt over blue jeans and work boots. His boots were crusted with dried dirt. His eyes widened and blinked.

His wife tried to scream around her gag; what emerged was a thin retch.

He never looked at her.

I moved toward him.

He shook his head and pressed a button on the gray remote. The high-frequency sound I'd heard outside filled the room, shrill as a bird being butchered as the needle on one of the meters jumped. Ursula's body bucked and pitched against her restraints. She kept quaking as her husband's finger remained on the button. He didn't seem to be noticing her at all, was staring at me and inching backward.

The horror made me dizzy. Clearing my head, I took a step.

Gabney's basso voice said: "Stop, damn you," as he pressed another button. The high noise became a shriek and another needle arced to the right. The room smelled of burnt toast. Ursula growled around her gag and shook as if being throttled. Fingers and toes convulsed at the end of pinioned limbs. Her torso rose totally off the seat—only the strap seemed to prevent her from flying away. The veins in her neck swelled, her jaws were forced open, and the gag flew out of her mouth, followed by a soundless scream. Her body was as rigid as cordwood, skin silvery white except for the lips, which looked bluish.

I fought down nausea and panic. Gabney had danced farther away from me, half-concealed behind the big gray box, finger still on the gray remote.

I moved toward the barber chair.

Gabney stopped pushing long enough to say, "Go ahead. Flesh is an excellent conductor. I'll turn up the voltage and cook both of you."

I stood still. Ursula had sunk like a sack of rocks. Wheezing, whistling sounds came from her open mouth. She moved her head from side to side, throwing off sweat-drizzle, chest heaving, panting gutturally through grotesquely swollen lips. Her legs were the last to relax, parting slightly. The electrode between them was attached to some kind of sanitary napkin.

I snapped my head away, looked for Gabney.

From behind the gray box, his voice said, "Sit down—farther back. Even farther—that's good. And keep your hands in full view. Exactly."

He emerged, paler than before, one arm resting on the top corner of the chrome-shiny thing. Took a sidelong glance at the giant breast.

Wondering if he had help, I said, "Quite a setup. A lot for one man to handle."

"Don't patronize me, you insolent shit. Everything's manageable, as long as the proper variables are controlled. No, don't scoot forward or I'll have to deliver more aversives."

"You made your point," I said.

His fingers danced above the buttons on the gray remote but didn't touch them.

"Control," I said. "Is that the primary goal?"

"You call yourself a scientist. Isn't it yours?"

Before I could answer he shook his head in disgust. "Define, predict, and control. Otherwise, why bother?"

"How does that reconcile with your ideas about free will?"

He smiled. "My little disquisitions? How conscientious of you to read them. But if you were half as smart as you think you are, you'd see there's plenty of free will in all of this. This is *about* free will—its restoration." Glancing at the apparatus. "A person shackled by major personality defect can never *be* free."

Ursula groaned.

The sound made his brow crease.

I said, "Where is Gina?"

He ignored me. Said nothing for what seemed like a long time. Looked at the floor.

Pulled on the chrome thing and brought half of it into view.

Bed on wheels. Pull-up caged sides. Adult-sized crib, the kind they use in nursing homes.

Gina Ramp behind the bars. Lying inert. Eyes closed. Sleeping or unconscious or . . . I saw her chest move. Saw her checkerboard scalp . . . cables attached to her, too.

"Listen carefully, idiot," Gabney finally said. "I'm going to go over there and retrieve that bandana. But my hand will remain on the highest-voltage button. If you move, I'll incinerate your precious *Gina*. Fifteen seconds at this level elicits death. Irreversible brain damage requires much less."

Lightly tapping a button, making the prone body twitch.

I said, "I'm not moving."

Keeping his eye on me, he crouched next to his wife's chair, picked up the gag, stood, wadded it, and inserted it in her mouth. She coughed and made choking sounds but didn't resist. The seam of her gown read PROPERTY MASS. GENERAL.

"Relax, darling," he said. Using the black remote, he switched off the TV. Taking a stance in front of the screen, he gave her a look that I couldn't categorize—domination and contempt, lust and just a bit of affection, which sickened me the most. I looked over at Gina, who still hadn't stirred.

"Don't worry about *her*," said Gabney. "She'll be out for a while—chloral hydrate, ye olde Mickey Finn. She responds well to it. Given her history and weak constitution, I've treated her with kid gloves."

"What a guy."

"Don't interrupt me again," he said louder, pressing a button that made the room scream and caused Gina's body to flop like a cloth doll. No conscious perception of pain was evident on her face, but her lips drew back in a toothy rictus that stretched and puckered the skin on her bad side.

When the noise died, Gabney said, "A bit more of that, and all that lovely plastic surgery will have been for naught."

"Stop," I said.

"Quit whining. This is the last time you'll get a warning. Understood?"

I nodded.

The burnt-toast smell filled my head.

Gabney stared at me, contemplative.

"This is a problem," he said, and tapped the gray remote.

"What is?"

"Why the hell did you meddle? How did you find out?"

"One thing kind of led to the other."

" 'Kind of led,' " he said. " 'Kind of led.' Wonderful grammar—who wrote your thesis for you?" Shaking his head. "*Kind* of led—just a loose chain of events, was it? Knocking around aimlessly, damn near random?"

I looked at the machines.

His face darkened. "Don't judge me—don't you damn well dare. This is treatment. You've violated confidentiality."

I said nothing.

"Do you have even the slightest notion of what I'm talking about?"

"Sexual reconditioning," I said. "You're trying to re-channel your wife's sexual orientation."

"Profound," he said. "Just brilliant. You're able to describe what you see. Freshman psych, second part of the first semester."

He stared at me, tapping one boot.

I said, "What am I missing?"

"Missing?" Dry laughter. "Just all of it. The meat, the *raison d'être*, the goddam *clinical* rationale."

"The rationale is that you're helping her become normal."

"And you don't think that's worthwhile?"

Before I could answer he shook his head and cursed, then tightened the arm holding the shock remote. My eyes snapped reflexively to the gray plastic. I realized I'd broken out into a sweat. Waiting for the high-frequency shriek and the pain that was sure to follow.

Gabney lowered his hand, smiling. "Empathetic conditioning. And so rapidly. My, you have a mushy heart—a pity for your patients." The smile dissolved in a pool of contempt. "Well, what you think doesn't matter one goddam iota."

Keeping his eye on me, he inched over toward Ursula. Lifting her gown with the black remote, he exposed her thighs and said, "Flawless."

"Except for the bruises."

"Nothing that won't heal. Sometimes creativity is called for."

"Creativity?" I said. "Interesting way to think of torture."

He stepped directly in front of me, just out of arm's reach. Fingers tapping the buttons lightly. Setting off high-frequency chirps and staccato movements of both women's bodies.

"Are you being intentionally *stupid*?" he said.

I shrugged.

"*Torture* implies intent to cause *harm*. I'm delivering aversive stimuli in order to enhance the rate of learning. Aversives are potent little buggers—only a mushy-hearted moron would question their usefulness. This is no more *torture* than a vaccination is, or emergency surgery."

From around Ursula's gag came the sound a mouse makes when cornered.

I said, "Just speeding up the old learning curve, Prof?"

Gabney studied me, gave the gray remote a couple of quick jabs, and caused both of the women to convulse.

I forced myself to look casual.

He said, "Something amusing?"

"All your talk about treatment, yet you keep using the shocks to vent your anger. Doesn't that break the stimulus-response chain? And why, if you're retraining Ursula, are you shocking Gina? She's just the stimulus, isn't she?"

He said, "Oh, shut up."

"Sexual reconditioning," I said. "It was tried years ago—back in the early seventies—and discredited."

"Primitive crap—methodologically crude. Though it might have developed into something worthwhile if the gay lib agitators hadn't shoved their point of view down everyone's throat—so much for free will."

I shrugged again.

He said, "I don't imagine your mind is capable of opening sufficiently to snare facts, but here are a few, anyway: I love my wife. She *elicits* love from me, and for that I'll always be grateful. She's a remarkable human being—first in her family to finish high school. I recognized how special she was the first time I met her. The flame within—she was damn near *incandescent*. So her . . . problem didn't deter me. On the contrary, it was a challenge. And she agreed with both my assessment and my treatment plan. What we accomplished—together—was totally consensual."

I said, "Fixing her."

"Don't make it sound like something veterinary, you idiot. We worked together to solve her problem. If that's not therapy, I don't know what is. And what emerged from our work together could benefit millions of women. The plan itself was simple—positive reinforcement delivered contingent upon heterosexually induced arousal and punishment administered as a consequence of exposure to homoerotic material. But the application posed a huge challenge—adapting the paradigm to female physiology. With a male subject, measurement of arousal is a snap. Using a penile plesmographic cuff, you record degree of tumescence. Females are structurally more . . . secretive. Our initial idea was to develop a sort of minicuff for the clitoris, but it proved impractical. I won't go into details. It was *she* who came up with the intravaginal moisture probe that she now wears so handsomely. Given proper base-line analyses of secretions, we've been able to correlate bioelectrical changes with perceived sexual arousal. The potential ramifications are fantastic. Compared to what we've done, Masters and Johnson are painting on cave walls."

"Fantastic," I said. "Too bad it didn't work."

"Oh, it *worked* all right. For years."

"Not for Eileen Wagner."

He stroked Ursula again and turned back to me. "Now, that *was* a mistake—my wife's mistake. Poor patient selection. Wagner was pathetic—a cow, a mushy-hearted, bovine do-gooder. Psychology and psychiatry are so full of them."

"If you thought so little of her, why'd you accept her as your fellow at Harvard?"

He shook his head and laughed. "She wasn't my *anything*. I would have sent her to *nursing* school. She rotated for a month on my wife's service. Rounds and didactic sessions and clinical supervision. My wife learned of her sexual pathology and tried to help her. The way *I'd* helped my *wife*. I was against it from the beginning, felt the cow wasn't suitable for our technique—not enough motivation, no willpower. Her obesity alone should have been enough to disqualify her on that account—she was *squalid*. But my wife was too kind. And I gave in."

"Was she your first subject—after Ursula?"

"Our first *patient*. Unfortunately. And, as I'd predicted, she did very poorly. Which says absolutely nothing about the technique."

He gave a sharp look over at his wife. I thought I saw a finger tense.

"I'd call suicide a very poor response," I said.

"Suicide?" His smile was slow, almost lazy. He shook his head. "Bear this in mind: The cow was incapable of doing *anything* for herself."

Strangled sounds from Ursula.

Gabney said, "I'm sorry, dear—I never told you, did I?"

"Harvard believed it was suicide," I said. "Somehow, the med school found out what kind of research you were doing and asked you to leave."

"Somehow," he said, the smile gone. "The cow was a scribbler—tear-stained 'love' notes never sent, stuffed in a desk drawer. Disgusting stuff."

Walking over to his wife again, he stroked her cheek. Kissed a shaved spot on her head. Her eyes were clenched tight; she made no effort to turn away.

"Love notes to you, darling," he said. "Mushy, incoherent, hardly evidence. But I had enemies in the department and they pounced. I could have fought it. But Harvard had nothing more to offer me—it's really not what it's cracked up to be. It was clearly time for a move."

"California," I said. "San Labrador. Your wife's suggestion, wasn't it? Go west for clinical opportunities."

Opportunities arising out of Ursula's supervision of Eileen Wagner. Closed-door sessions that turned into therapy, as supervision often does.

Eileen talking about her past. Her needs. The sexual conflicts that had caused her to switch from pediatrics to psychiatry.

Recounting her experiences, years before, with a beguiling, wealthy agoraphobic. A ravaged princess ensconced in a peach-colored castle, crippled by fear that had eventually spread to her daughter—a little girl so remarkable she'd called for help, herself . . .

An eleven-year-old conversation came back to me.

Eileen in sensible shoes and a mannish blouse, shifting her Gladstone bag from hand to hand.

She's really beautiful. Despite the scars . . . Sweet. In a vulnerable way.

Sounds like you learned a lot from a brief visit.

The color rising in Eileen's cheeks. *One tries.*

Her embarrassment a puzzle. So clear, now.

More than a brief visit had taken place.

A lot more than medical consultation.

Melissa had sensed something out of the ordinary, without fully understanding: *She's my mother's friend. . . . She likes my mother. . . .*

Jacob Dutchy had known, too—made a point of portraying Gina's avoidance of me as a generic fear of doctors.

I'd questioned it: *She met with Dr. Wagner.*

Yes. That was a surprise. She doesn't cope well with surprises.

Are you saying she had some sort of adverse reaction just to meeting with Dr. Wagner?

Let's just say it was difficult for her.

Would it be easier for her to deal with a female therapist?

No! Absolutely not! It's not that at all.

Gina and Eileen . . .

The stirring—the inclinations—that each had fought for so long. Cravings Gina had dealt with by marrying a physically grotesque man who played the role of father. The second time around choosing a bisexual man—an old friend with a secret of his own, whom she could turn to for companionship and mutual tolerance and the outward appearance of married bliss.

Separate bedrooms.

Eileen . . . coping with the self-loathing she'd felt after Sussex Knoll by abandoning her practice, leaving town, and traveling the world as a care-giver, unpressured to defend herself. Devoting herself to saving lives as she waged war with her pain.

Losing too many battles and choosing another strategy—one so many other bright, troubled people have taken: the study of The Mind.

Child psychiatry. Because let's get back to the root of it all.

Harvard. Because let's learn from the best.

Harvard and a blue-collar lover. An electrician with no patience for soul-baring.

Then, rotation on Ursula's service. The mischief gods must have been chortling heartily.

Rap sessions.

Confessions.

Pain and passion and confusion—someone who'd listen to all the things Sally Etheridge never wanted to hear about.

Ursula heard. And was changed herself.

Burying it by playing doctor.

A behavioral nightmare becomes real. The mischief gods beside themselves with glee.

Treatment failure. Of the worst kind.

Bye-bye, Boston.

Time for a move.

California, in search of the princess . . .

In search of the *idea* of the princess. Wealthy phobics Ursula knew she could help.

Playing doctor.

Fee for service. Big fees.

All is well.

Then, the child calls. Again . . .

"Opportunities," Gabney was saying. "Yes, that's basically the way she put it. A business decision. *I* preferred Florida—less expensive; the air's a hell of a lot better. But *she* pushed for California, and not knowing what she was really after, I relented. It's when I relent that things go wrong."

He looked over at Gina, his face befouled with rage—the flailing, mind-searing fury of a man blocked from possessing what he craved.

Because of another woman.

The ultimate insult to the feeble thing known as Maleness.

Suddenly, I was certain Joel McCloskey had been insulted, too.

Thrown over by another woman.

Dirty joke.

Bad joke. Burrowing through *his* dope-softened brain like a spirochete.

Rejection festering. The hatred of homosexuals . . .

Dealing with it by demolishing Gina's beauty—blotting out criminal womanhood.

Too cowardly to do it himself. Cowardly about exposing his motives as well, for fear of what that would say about him.

Had Gina ever understood why she'd suffered?

Gabney emitted a low, angry sound. Staring at Gina. Then at his wife.

"I've never been deceptive with her, but she chose to change the rules—*both* of them did."

"When did you first suspect?"

"Shortly after *that* one's treatment began. It was nothing specific—just nuances. Subtle variations that a man who knew less—or cared less—might never have noticed. Spending more time with her than all the other patients. Extra sessions that weren't necessary from a clinical point of view. Changing the subject and showing odd *resistance* when I challenged her. And abandoning the ranch—she used to come up here regularly. Despite the allergies. Took antihistamines and tolerated the pollens in order to spend peaceful weekends with me. All of that stopped as soon as *she* came into our lives." He smiled. "This is the first time she's been up here since then. All those stupid excuses for staying in the city that she thought I didn't see through . . . I knew damn well what was going on. Wanted hard data to preclude any more lies. So I made a few modifications to our office intercom and began listening in. Heard them"—the round face trembled—"making their plans."

"Plans for what?"

"To leave." He pressed his free hand over his face, as if ironing out grief. "Together."

Giant steps . . .

Melissa, sensing the truth. Feeling edged out by Ursula's possessiveness . . .

Gabney said, "This is how low it sank: My wife accepted a piece of *art* from her—an extremely valuable etching. Now if that's not an inexcusable breach of ethics, I don't know what the hell is. Don't you agree?"

I nodded.

"Money changed hands as well," he said. "To *her*, money means nothing because she's a spoiled bitch, never been deprived of anything. But it was bound to corrupt my wife—she came from a poor family. Despite everything she's accomplished, pretty things still impress her. She's like a child that way. The bitch understood that."

Pointing at Gina: "She gave her money on a regular basis—enormous sums. A secret bank account! They called it their little nest egg. Giggling like stupid schoolgirls. Giggling and plotting to abandon their responsibilities and go gallivanting off to live like whores on some tropical island. On top of the perversity, what a disgusting *waste*! My wife has a brilliant future. The bitch seduced her and attempted to lay everything to waste—I had to intervene. The bitch would have destroyed her."

He pressed a button on the remote. Gina flopped. Ursula watched and made whimpering noises.

Gabney said, "Shut up, darling, or I'll grill her synapses right now, and to hell with the goddam treatment plan."

Tears ran down Ursula's cheeks. She was silent and still.

"If this upsets you, darling, blame yourself."

His finger finally lifted. "If I were a selfish man, I would have simply killed her," he said to me. "But I wanted to give her worthless, spoiled life some meaning. So I decided to . . . apprentice her. As a stimulus, as you've so profoundly pointed out."

"*In vivo* conditioning," I said. "Home movies."

"Science in the real world."

"So you abducted her."

"No, no," he said. "She came willingly."

"Patient to doctor."

"Exactly." He gave a wide, satisfied smile. "I phoned her in the morning, informing her of a scheduling change. Instead of group therapy, she'd be having a one-on-one session with me. Her beloved Dr. Ursula was ill, and I was filling in. I told her we'd make special progress today—surprise her beloved Dr. Ursula with outstanding progress. I instructed her to drive her car out of the gates of her estate and pick me up two blocks away at a precise time. I specified the Rolls-Royce—told her something about consistency of stimuli. Because, of course, it has tinted windows. She arrived right on the dot. I had her slide over to the passenger side, and I got behind the wheel. She asked me where we were going. I didn't answer. That elicited visible symptoms of anxiety—she wasn't even close to being ready for that kind of ambiguity. She repeated her question. Once again, I said nothing and continued to drive. She began to get twitchy and to breathe rapidly—prodromal signs. When I sped onto the freeway she burst into a full-blown anxiety attack. I handed her an inhaler that I'd doctored to contain chloral hydrate and instructed her to take a nice deep breath. She did, and passed out immediately. Which was elegant. I was driving at fifty-five miles per hour, didn't want her thrashing around and creating a hazard. Unconscious, she made a lovely traveling companion. I drove to the dam, where my Land Rover was waiting. Transferred her into the Rover and pushed that ostentatious hunk of junk into the water."

"Pretty strenuous work for one man."

"What you mean to say is strenuous for a man of my age. But I'm in excellent shape. Clean living. Creative fulfillment."

"The car didn't sink," I said. "It caught on a flange."

He said nothing, didn't move.

"Poor planning for someone as precise as you. And with the Land Rover up there, how'd you get back to San Labrador?"

"Ah," he said, "the man is capable of rudimentary reasoning. Yes, you're correct, I did have help. A Mexican fellow, used to work for me up here at the ranch. When we had more horses. When my wife used to ride."

To Ursula: "Remember Cleofais, darling?"

Ursula shut her eyes tight. Water leaked out from under the lids.

Gabney said, "This Cleofais—what a name, eh?—was a big, husky fellow. Not much in the way of brains, no common sense—he was essentially a two-footed beast of burden. I was getting close to firing him—only a few horses left, no sense wasting money—but the transfer of Mrs. Ramp offered him one last chance to be useful. He dropped me off in Pasadena, then took the Rover up to the dam and waited. *He* was the one who pushed the Rolls-Royce in. But he miscalculated, hit that flange or whatever."

"Easy mistake to make."

"Not if he'd been careful."

"Why do I feel," I said, "that he won't be making any more mistakes in the future?"

"Why, indeed." Exaggerated look of innocence.

Ursula moaned.

Gabney said, "Oh, *stop*. Spare me the dramatics. You never liked him—you were always calling him a stupid wetback, always after me to get rid of him. So now you have your way."

Ursula shook her head weakly and sagged in her chair.

I said, "Where'd you take Mrs. Ramp after the Rolls was disposed of?"

"On a scenic drive. Through Angeles Crest Forest along the back roads. The precise route was Highway 39 to Mount Waterman, Highway 2 to Mountain High, 138 to Palmdale, 14 to Saugus, 126 to Santa Paula, then straight down to the 101 and onward to the ranch. Circuitous but pretty."

"Nothing like that in Florida," I said.

"Nothing at all."

"Why the dam?" I said.

"It's a rural spot, comparatively close to the clinic, yet remote—no one goes up there. I know, because I'd been there several times. To sell off horses my wife no longer wanted to ride."

"That's all?"

"What else should there be?"

"Well," I said, "I'd be willing to wager you studied your wife's clinical notes and knew Mrs. Ramp didn't like water."

He smiled.

I said, "I understand about the tinted windows providing cover. But wasn't it risky using a car that conspicuous? Someone might have noticed."

"And if they had, what would they have seen? A car that would have been traced to *her*—just as it was. The assumption would have been made that a mentally ill woman drove up there and either had an accident or committed suicide. Which is exactly what happened."

"True," I said, trying to look thoughtful.

"*Every*thing was considered, Delaware. If Cleofais had reported being spotted, we would have moved on to another spot. I'd earmarked several. Even the unlikely chance of being stopped by a policeman didn't worry me. I would have explained that I was a psychotherapist with a patient who'd had an anxiety attack and passed out, and shown my credentials to back it up. The *facts* would have backed me up. And when she regained consciousness, *she* would have backed me up, because that's all she would have remembered. Isn't that elegant?"

"Yes," I said, causing him to look at me sharply. "Even traveling the back roads, you had plenty of time to set her up here, wait for your wife to call and report she hadn't shown up for group therapy, then fake concern, drive back to Pasadena and make your appearance at the clinic."

"Where," he said, "I had the not altogether salutary experience of meeting you."

"And trying to find out how much I knew about Mrs. Ramp."

"Why else would I bother to talk to you? And for a moment you did have me concerned—something you said, about *her* having plans to make a new life. Then I realized you were just jawing, knew nothing of any importance."

"When did your wife find out what you'd done?"

"When she woke up to find herself in that chair."

Remembering Ursula's hurried exit from the clinic, I said, "What'd you tell her to get her up here?"

"I phoned her, pretending to be ill, and begged her to come up and take care of me. Good wife that she is, she responded promptly."

I said, "How will you explain her absence to her patients?"

"Bad flu. I'll take over their care, don't expect any complaints."

"Two patients gone from the group, now the therapist— given the kind of anxiety you're dealing with, it may not be so simple to reassure them."

"Two? Ah." Knowing smile. "Bonny Miss Kathleen, our intrepid girl reporter? How did you come across that?"

Not knowing if Kathy Moriarty was alive or dead, I said nothing.

"Well," he said, smiling wider, "if you think your evasiveness is going to help her, forget it. Bonny Miss Kathleen won't be reporting anything anymore—nasty little bull-dagger. The arrogance, thinking something as complex as agoraphobia could be faked in my presence. Trying to bluster her way out when I caught her, with threats and accusations. She sat right in that chair." Pointing to Ursula's. "Helped me refine the technique."

"Where is she now?" I asked, knowing the answer.

"In the cold, cold ground, next to Cleofais. Probably the first time she's been that intimate with a man."

I looked over at Ursula. Her eyes were wide and frozen.

"So everything's tied up," I said. "Elegant."

"Don't mock me."

"Mocking you isn't my intention. On the contrary, I had the greatest respect for your work. Read all your publications—shock-avoidance and escape paradigms, controlled frustration, schedules of fear-induced learning. This is just . . ." I shrugged.

He stared at me for a long time.

"You wouldn't," he finally said, "be trying to bull-shit me?"

"No," I said. "But if I am, big deal. What can I do to you?"

"True," he said, flexing his fingers. "Fifteen seconds to deep-fry, you couldn't bear being a party to that. And I've got other toys you haven't even seen yet."

"I'm sure you have. Just as I'm sure you've convinced yourself it's okay to use them. On scientific grounds. Destroy the person to save her."

"No one's being destroyed."

"What about Gina?"

"*She* wasn't much to begin with—look at the way she lived. Insular, selfish, corrupt—of no use to anyone. By using her, I've justified her."

"I didn't know she needed justifying."

"Then *know* it, idiot. Life's transactional, not some fluffy, theological fantasy. The world's getting sucked dry. Re-sources are finite. Only the useful will survive."

"Who determines what's useful?"

"Those who control the stimuli."

"One thing you might consider," I said, "is that despite all this high-minded theorizing, you may not be aware of your true motivations."

The corners of his mouth turned up. "Are you applying to be my analyst?"

I shook my head. "No way. Don't have the stomach for it."

His lips snapped down.

I said, "Women. The way they've let you down. The custody battle with your first wife, the way her drinking caused the fire that killed your son. The first time we met you mentioned a second wife—before Ursula. I didn't get a sense of what she was like, but something tells me she wasn't worthy either."

"A nonentity," he said. "Nothing there."

"Is she still alive?"

He smiled. "Unfortunate accident. She wasn't quite the swimmer she fancied herself to be."

"Water," I said. "You've used it twice. Freudian theory would say it has something to do with the womb."

"Freudian theory is horse shit."

"It could be right on the mark this time, Professor. Maybe this whole thing has nothing to do with science or love or any of that other horse shit *you've* been spreading, and everything to do with the fact that you hate women—really despise them and need to control them. It implies something nasty in your own childhood—neglect or abuse or whatever. I guess what I'm saying is that I'd sure like to know what *your* mother was like."

His mouth opened, and he jammed his hand down on the button.

Machine screams. A higher frequency than before . . .

His voice above the whine—shouting but barely audible: "Fifteen seconds."

I threw myself at him. He backed away, kicking and punching, throwing the black remote at me and hitting me in the nose. Fingers white on the gray module. The stench of burning flesh and hair clogged the room.

I tore at his hands, hit him in the belly, and he gasped and doubled. But his grip was like steel.

I had to break his wrist before he let go.

I put the remote in my pocket, kept my eye on him. He was stretched out on the floor, holding his wrist, crying.

The women didn't stop jerking for a long, long time.

I unplugged the machines, ripped off the electrical cords, and used them to bind his arms and legs. When I was certain he was immobilized, I went to the women.

36

I locked Gabney in the barn, took Gina and Ursula into the house, put blankets over them, got Ursula to drink some apple juice that I found in the refrigerator. Organic. Like everything in the well-stocked fridge. Survival books on a kitchen shelf. Rifle and shotgun in a rack over the table. Swiss Army knife, case full of hypodermic needles and drug spansules. The professor had been preparing for the long haul.

I phoned 911, then put in an emergency call to Susan LaFamiglia. She got over the horror remarkably fast, turned efficient, took down crucial details, and told me she'd handle the rest.

It took half an hour for the paramedics to arrive, accompanied by four cars of Santa Barbara County sheriffs from the Solvang substation. During the wait I found Gabney's records—no great feat of detection. He'd left half a dozen notebooks on the dining room table. A couple of pages were all I could bear to read.

I spent the next couple of hours talking to grim-faced people in uniforms. Susan LaFamiglia arrived with a young man wearing an olive-green Hugo Boss suit and retro tie, had a few words with the cops, and got me out of there.

Mr. Fashion turned out to be one of her associates—I never learned his name. He drove the Seville back to L.A. and Susan took me home in her Jaguar. She didn't ask me any questions and I fell asleep, happy to be a passenger.

I missed my ten o'clock appointment the next morning with Melissa—but not for lack of trying. I was up at six, watching baby koi the size of threadworms wiggle their way around the pond. By nine-thirty I was at Sussex Knoll. The gates were open, but no one answered the door.

I spotted one of the Hernandez sons who was thinning ivy near the outer wall of the estate and asked him where Gina was. Some hospital in Santa Barbara, he said. No, he didn't know which one.

I believed him but tried the door again anyway.

As I drove away he gave me a sad look—or maybe it was pity, for my lack of trust.

I'd just nosed out onto the street when I saw the brown Chevy approaching from the south. Traveling so slowly it seemed to be standing still. I backed up and waited, and when it pulled up in the driveway, I was ready, at the driver's window, greeting a frightened-looking Bethel Drucker.

"Sorry," she said, and put the car into reverse.

"No," I said. "Please. No one's here but I'd like to talk to you."

"Nothing to talk about."

"Then why are you here?"

"Don't know," she said. She had on a plain brown dress, costume jewelry, very little makeup. Her figure refused to be suppressed. I took no pleasure in looking at it. It would be a while before looking would be fun again. "I really don't know," she repeated. Her hand remained on the gearshift lever.

"You came to pay your respects," I said. "That's very kind of you."

She looked at me as if I'd spoken in tongues. I walked around the front of the car and got in beside her.

She started to protest, then, with an ease that bespoke a lifetime of acquiescence, her features assumed a resigned look.

"What?" she said.

"Do you know what happened?"

Nod. "Noel told me."

"Where is Noel?"

"Drove up there this morning. To be with them."

The unspoken words: *as usual.*

I said, "He's a great kid—you've done a wonderful job."

Her face quavered. "He's so damn smart, sometimes I think he's not mine. Lucky for me, I remember the pain—pushing him out. You wouldn't think to look at him but he was a big one. Nine pounds. Twenty-three inches. They told me he was gonna play football. No one knew how smart he was gonna be."

"Is he going to Harvard?"

"He doesn't tell me everything he's gonna do. Now, if you'll 'scuse me, I've got to be going. The place needs cleaning."

"The Tankard?"

"Only place I've got for the time being."

"Is Don planning to open it in the near future?"

Shrug. "He doesn't tell me his plans either. I just wanna clean it. Before the dirt builds up."

"Okay," I said. "Can I just ask you one thing—something personal?"

Her eyes filled.

"Just a question, Bethel."

"Sure—what's the difference, anyway? Talking, dancing, posing for pictures—everyone gets what they want from me."

"Didn't know you were a model," I lied.

"Oh, yeah, sure. Ha! Sure, I was this big famous fashion model. With *these*." Running her hands over her bust and laughing again. "Yeah, I was pretty fancy, just like Gina. We were two of a kind. Only the ones who looked at me weren't ladies buying clothes."

"Did Joel take those pictures?"

Pause. Her hands were small and white around the steering wheel. A cheap cameo ring encircled the ring finger.

"Him. Others. What of it? I was in lots of pictures. I was a picture *star*. Even when I was pregnant and out to here— some people are sick that way, like to see pregnant women."

"Something for everyone," I said.

She turned sharply but her tone was resigned. "You're mocking me."

"No," I said wearily. "No, I'm not."

She studied me, touched her bosom again.

"You saw me," she said. "Driving off yesterday. And now you want to know why."

I began to talk, but she cut me off with a shake of her hand. "Maybe to you it's dumb, getting upset over someone like him—that's the way I felt about it, too. Real dumb. But I'm used to that. Being dumb. So what's the difference, anyway? Maybe to you it was real *real* dumb—retarded— because you think he was pure trash— No, wait a second. Let me finish. He *was* pure shit, no kindness in him. Everything made him mad and crazy—he had to have his way all the time. Some of it was prob'ly the dope. He shot *way* too much speed. But some of it was just the way he was *made*. Mean. So I understand your thinking I'm dumb. But he *gave* me something and no one ever gave me *nothing*—not at that point of my life, anyway. *Since* then, Don came through, and I'd cry for *him* if something happened to him—a hell of a lot more than I cried for . . . the other one. But at that point in my life, the other one was the first one who gave me *anything*. Even if he didn't mean to. Even if he did it because he couldn't have what he really wanted, and he took it out on me. That didn't *matter*—you understand? It turned out good *anyway*—you just said so yourself. Only damn good thing in my life. So yeah, I cried a little for him. Found myself a nice little spot and had a big boohoo. Then I remembered what pure trash he was and I stopped crying. And now you don't see me crying no more. That answer your question?"

I shook my head. "I wasn't judging you, Bethel. I don't think your being upset was wrong."

"Well, aren't you the smart one. So what's your question then?"

"Does Noel know who his father was?"

Long silence.

"If he doesn't, you gonna tell him?" she said.

"No."

"Not even to protect the little missy?"

"From what?"

"Hitching up with a bad seed."

"There's nothing bad about Noel."

She started crying, said, "So much for New Year's resolutions."

I handed her a handkerchief, she blew noisily and said, "Thank you, sir." A moment later: "I wouldn't trade places with that little girl for nothin'. With any of them."

"Neither would I, Bethel. And I'm not asking about Noel in order to protect her."

"What, then?"

"Call it curiosity. Something else I need to figure out."

"You're a real curious fellow, aren't you? Poking around in other people's business."

"Forget it," I said. "Sorry for poking."

"Maybe *he* needs protecting from *her*, huh?"

"Why do you say that?"

"All this." Looking through the windshield at the big peach-colored house. "This kind of thing can eat you up. Noel's head is on real good, but you never kn w. . . . Do you really think the tv of them . . ."

"Who knows?" I said. "They're young, have a lot of changes ahead of them."

"Because I'm really not comfortable with that. You'd think *I'd* be the one who'd want it, but I don't. This isn't real—it isn't the way real people were made to live. He's my baby, I pushed him out with a lot of pain, and I don't want to see him eaten up by all this."

"I know what you mean," I said. "I hope Melissa gets away from it, too.".

"Yeah. I guess it's not been any jar a'honey for her, either."

"No, it hasn't."

"Yeah," she said, starting to touch her bust, but dropping her hand.

I pushed the passenger door open. "Good luck, and thanks for your time."

"No," she said. "He doesn't know. He thinks I don't know, either. I told him it was a one-night stand, no way to ever find out. He truly believes that. I used to . . . do things. I told him a story that didn't make me look real good, because I had to. I had to do what I thought was right."

"Of course you did," I said, and took her hand. "And it *was* right—the proof is in the pudding."

"That's true."

"Bethel, I really meant what I said about Noel. And the credit you get for it."

She squeezed my hand and let go.

"You sound for real. I'll try to believe that."

37

Milo came by my house at four. I was working on my monograph and led him into the study.

"Lots of dirt on Douse," he said, shaking his briefcase and putting it on my desk. "Not that it matters much."

"It might," I said. "In terms of recovering anything he's already looted from the estate."

"Yeah," he said, "let's hear it for private investigation. How you doing?"

"Fine."

"Really?"

"Really. How about yourself?"

"Still on the job—Attorney LaFamiglia likes my style."

"A woman with taste."

"You sure you're okay?"

"I'm fine. There are baby fish down in the pond, they're surviving and growing, and I'm in a great mood."

"Baby fish?"

"Wanna see?"

"Sure."

We went down to the Japanese garden. It took a while for him to see the hatchlings, but finally he did. And smiled. "Yeah. Cute. What do you feed them?"

"Ground-up fish food."

"They don't get eaten?"

"Some do. The fast ones survive."

"Aha."

He sat down on a rock and exposed his face to the sun. "Nyquist showed up late last night at the restaurant. Talked to Don for a few minutes, then split. Looks like farewell. The van was packed up for long-term travel."

"You get that from your guy?"

"Every detail. Along with your departure, down to the second. He's a demon for particulars. If I'd been smart I'd have told him to tail you."

"Would he have been able to help?"

He smiled. "Probably not. We're talking arthritis and emphysema. But he's got damn good handwriting."

He looked at the paper in my typewriter. "What's that?"

"My paper on the Hale School."

"Everything back to normal, huh? When do you see Melissa?"

"As in therapy?"

"As in."

"Soon as possible after she gets back to L.A. I called up there an hour ago. She didn't want to leave her mother's side. The doctor I spoke to said it should be about a week before Gina can be moved. Then there'll be extended care."

"Jesus," he said. "Melissa's sure going to need it— seeing you. Maybe everyone involved in this should go into therapy."

"I did you a real favor, huh?"

"Actually you did. When I write my memoirs this one'll get a chapter of its own. Attorney LaFamiglia said she'd be my agent if I ever do it."

"Attorney LaFamiglia would probably make a good agent."

He smiled. "Balls-in-the-grinder time for Douse and Anger. Almost feel sorry for them. So, you eat recently? If not, I'm up for something solid."

"Had a big breakfast," I said. "But there is something I could go for."

"What's that?"

I told him.

He said, "Christ alive, don't you ever get enough?"

"I need to know. For everyone's sake. If you don't want to pursue it, I'll grope along by myself."

He said, "Jesus," then: "Okay, run everything by me again—the details."

I did.

"That's it? A phone on the floor? That's all you've got?"

"The timing's right."

"Okay," he said, "it should be easy enough to get hold of the records. The question is whether or not it was a toll call."

"San Labrador to Santa Monica is," I said. "I already checked the bill."

"Mr. Detective," he said. "Mr. Private Eye."

The place didn't look like what it was. Victorian house in a working-class section of Santa Monica. Two stories, big front porch with swings and rockers. Yellow clapboard sides with white and baby-blue trim. Lots of cars on the street. Several more in the driveway. Better landscaping and maintenance than the other houses on the block.

"My, my," I said, pointing to a car in the driveway. Black Cadillac Fleetwood, '62.

Milo parked the Porsche.

We got out and inspected the big car's front bumper. Deeply dented and freshly primered.

"Yeah, looks right," said Milo.

We walked up the porch and through the front door. A bell over the lintel tinkled.

The entry hall was filled with houseplants. Sweet-smelling. Too sweet—concealing something.

A dark, pretty woman in her early twenties came out. White blouse, red maxiskirt, Eurasian, clear complexion. "Can I help you?"

Milo told her who we wanted to see.

"Are you family?"

"Acquaintances."

"Old-time acquaintances," I said. "Like Madeleine de Couer."

"Madeleine," she said, with fondness. "She's here every two weeks, so devoted. And such a good cook—we all love her butter cookies. Let's see what time it is—six-ten. He may be sleeping. He sleeps a lot, especially lately."

"Getting worse?" I said.

"Physically or spiritually?"

"Physically, for starters."

"We've seen some deterioration, but it comes and goes. One day he's walking fine; the next, he can't move. It's hard seeing him that way—knowing what's in store. It's such an ugly disease, especially for someone like him, used to being active—though I guess they all are. I'd never even heard of what he's got—it's even rarer than Lou Gehrig's. I had to bone up, and there really isn't much in the medical books."

"How about spiritually?"

She smiled. "You know how he is—but actually he's been real good to have around. He cooks for the others, tells them stories. Prods them when he thinks they're getting lazy. He even orders the staff around, but no one minds—he's such a dear. When he . . . when he can't do those things anymore it's going to be a real loss." Sighing. "Anyway, why don't we see if he's awake?"

We followed her up to the second floor, passing bedrooms, each containing two or three hospital beds. Old men and women occupied the beds, watching television, reading, sleeping, eating orally or intravenously. Young people in street clothes attended to them. The place was very quiet.

The room she stopped at was at the rear. Smaller than the rest. A single bed. *Punch* caricatures on the wall, along with an oil painting of a young, beautiful woman with an unscarred face. A.D. initialed in the lower right corner.

Nothing out of place. Bay rum aroma fighting to assert itself through the sweetness.

A man sat on the edge of the bed, trying to insert a cuff link through French cuffs. Starched white cuffs. Navy tie. Blue serge trousers. All of it much too large; he seemed to be drowning in his clothes. A pair of mirror-black bluchers were lined up at the foot of the bed. Three identical pairs of shoes edged a wood-grain dresser that had been shined far more than its cheap construction merited. Next to the shoes was a four-legged metal walker.

His hair was slicked and right-parted and bone-white. All the plumpness was gone from his face, and his cheeks hung loosely in bulldog jowls. His skin was the color of a plastic skeleton. The cuff links were small squares of onyx.

"People to see you," said the young woman cheerfully.

The man struggled with the cuff link, finally inserted it, then turned and faced us.

A look of surprise passed over his face, then great calm. As if he'd experienced the worst-possible scenario and survived.

He worked hard at producing a smile for the girl, worked harder at getting the words out: "Come in." Voice as fragile as antique crockery.

"Anything I can get you, Mr. D.?" asked the woman.

The man shook his head no. More effort.

She left. Milo and I stepped in. I closed the door.

"Hello, Mr. Dutchy," I said.

Curt nod.

"Do you remember me? Alex Delaware? Nine years ago?"

Eyes fluttering, he struggled to enunciate: "Doc . . . tor."

"This is a friend of mine, Mr. Milo Sturgis. Mr. Sturgis, Mr. Jacob Dutchy. A good friend of Melissa and her mother."

"Sit." Motioning toward a chair. The only other furniture was a walnut drum table of much better vintage than the dresser. Leather top, covered partially by a doily. Tea service atop the doily. Pattern identical to one I'd seen in a small gray sitting room. "Tea?"

"No, thanks."

"You," he said to Milo, taking a long time to get it out. "Look like. A police. Man."

"He is one," I said. "On leave. But he's not here in any official capacity."

"I see." Dutchy folded his hands on his lap and sat there.

Suddenly, I regretted coming and wore it all over my face. Gentleman that he was, he said, "Don't wor. Ree. Talk."

"No need to talk about it," I said. "Consider this a friendly visit."

Half-smile on bloodless, razor-slash lips. "Talk. Any. Thing." Then: "How?"

"Just guesswork," I said. "The evening before McCloskey was run down, Madeleine sat by Melissa's bed and used the phone. I saw it, on the floor. She called you here and told you Gina was dead. Asked you to take care of it. Step into your old role."

"No," he said. "That's. Wrong. Not her . . . nothing."

"I don't think so, sir," said Milo, and pulled a piece of paper out of his pocket. "These are phone records. Made from Melissa's private line that night, itemized down to the minute. Three within a one-hour period to the Pleasant Rest Hospice."

"Circum. Stantial," said Dutchy. "She talks. To me all. The time."

"We saw the car, sir," said Milo. "The Cadillac that's registered to you. Interesting front-end damage. I imagine the police lab would be able to work with that."

Dutchy looked at him, but not with any anxiety—he seemed to be appraising Milo's clothes. Milo had dressed fairly well. For him. Dutchy was reserving judgment.

"Don't worry, Mr. Dutchy," said Milo. "This is off the record. Even if it wasn't, you haven't been notified of your rights, so anything you say can't be used against you."

"Madeleine had. Nothing to. Do. With . . ."

"Even if she did, we don't care, sir. Just trying to tie up loose ends."

"She. Didn't."

"Fine," said Milo. "You thought of it all by yourself. You're a one-man crime wave."

Dutchy's smile was astonishingly quick and full. "Billy. The Kid. What. Else d'you. Want. To know?"

"What'd you use to lure McCloskey out?" said Milo. "His son?"

Dutchy's smile quavered and faded out like a weak radio signal. "Dis. Honest. But. Only way."

"Did Noel or Melissa call him?"

"No." Trembling. "No. No, no. Swear."

"Take it easy. I believe you."

It took a while for Dutchy's face to stop shaking.

"So who called McCloskey?" said Milo. "It sure wasn't you."

"Friends."

"What did the friends tell him?"

"Son. In troub. El. Help." Pause for breath. "Pat. Ernal. Heart. Strings." Dutchy made an excruciatingly slow tugging motion.

"How'd you know he'd fall for that?"

"Never. Know. Po. Ker."

"You flushed him out with the son story. Then your friends ran him down."

"No." Pointing to his starched shirtfront. "Me."

"You can still drive?"

"Some. Times."

"Uh-huh."

"In. Dee. Five. Hundred." Genuine glee on the pasty face.

Milo said, "You and Parnelli."

Reedy laughter.

"I guess it's stupid to ask why."

Ponderous headshake. "No. Not. At all."

Silence.

Dutchy smiled and managed to get a hand on his shirt-front again. "Ask."

Milo rolled his eyes.

I said, "Why'd you do it, Mr. Dutchy?"

He stood, tottered, waved off our aid. It took a full five minutes for him to get into an upright position. I know, because I was staring at the second hand of my watch. Another five to make it to the walker and lean on it, triumphant.

Triumph that went beyond the physical.

"Reason," he said. "My job."

38

"So tiny," she said. "Will they survive?"

"These *are* the survivors," I said. "The key is keeping the grown ones well fed so they won't eat the babies."

"How'd you manage to hatch them?"

"I didn't do anything. It just happened."

"But you must have set it up or something. To make it happen."

"I provided the water."

She smiled.

We were at the edge of the pond. The air was still and the waterfall whispered gently. Her bare legs were tucked under her skirt. Her fingers toyed with the Zen grass. "I like it down here. Could we talk here every time?"

"Sure."

"So peaceful," she said. Her hands left the grass and began kneading one another.

"How's she doing?" I said.

"All right. I guess. I keep waiting for something to . . . I don't know . . . break. For her to start screaming or falling apart. She looks almost too good."

"Does that worry you?"

"In a way. I guess what really worries me is not knowing.

What she knows—what she understands about what happened. I mean, she says she passed out and woke up in the hospital, but . . ."

"But what?"

"Maybe she's just protecting me. Or herself—pushing it out of her memory. Repressing it."

"I believe her," I said. "The whole time I saw her she was unconscious. Totally unaware of her surroundings."

"Yes," she said. "Dr. Levine says the same thing. . . . I like him. Levine. Makes you feel he has plenty of time. That what you have to say is important."

"I'm glad."

"Thank God she got somebody good." Turning to me, eyes wet. "I don't know how to thank you."

"You already have."

"But it's not enough—what you did . . ." Reaching out for my hand, then drawing back.

She looked at the pond. Studied the water.

"I made a decision," she said. "About scheduling. A year here, and then we'll see. Just a semester wouldn't have been enough. So many things to take care of. I called Harvard this morning. From the hospital, before the helicopter arrived. Thanked them for extending the deadline and told them what I'd decided. They said they'll accept me as a transfer if my GPA at UCLA's high enough."

"I'm sure it will be."

"Guess so—if I organize my time properly. Noel left. Came up yesterday to say goodbye."

"How'd that go?"

"He looked a little scared. Which surprised me. I never thought of him as not being in control. It was almost . . . cute. His mother came with him. She looked *really* nervous. She's going to miss him a lot."

"Are you and Noel planning to stay in touch?"

"We agreed to write. But you know how things are—different places, different experiences. He's been a really good friend."

"Yes, he has."

Small, sad smile.

I said, "What is it?"

"I know he wants more than that. It makes me feel . . . I don't know. . . . Maybe he'll meet someone there who will really be right for him."

Leaning closer to the water. "The big ones are coming close. Can I feed them?"

I handed her the feed cup. She tossed in a handful of pellets, far away from the baby koi, and watched the adult fish bob and gobble.

"There you go, guys," she said. "Stay over there. Jeez, what a bunch of gluttons. . . . Do you think she'll really ever be okay? Levine says if we give it enough time, she should be able to function normally, but I don't know."

"What makes you doubt that?"

"Maybe he's just an optimist."

Making that sound like a character flaw.

"From what I've seen of Dr. Levine, he's a realist," I said. Remembering Gina's face framed by hospital linen. Plastic tubing, the far-off clatter of metal and glass. A thin, pale hand squeezing mine. A tranquillity that was unnerving . . .

I said, "Just the fact that she's handling the hospital so well is a good sign, Melissa. Realizing she can be out of the house without falling apart. As bizarre as it seems, the whole thing may end up being therapeutic for her. Which isn't to say there's been no trauma or that it's going to be easy."

"Guess so," she said, barely loud enough to be heard over the waterfall. "There are so many things I still don't understand: *Why* it happened. Where does that kind of evil come from? What did she do to *deserve* that? I mean, I know he's a psycho—the things they say he did. . . ." Shuddering. Kneading. "Susan says he'll be put away forever. Just on the basis of those bodies they found at the ranch. Which is good, I guess. I couldn't stand the idea of a trial—Mother having to face another . . . monster. But it just seems . . . inadequate. There should be more."

"More punishment?"

"Yes. He should suffer." Turning to me again. "You'd have to be there, too, wouldn't you? At a trial."

I nodded.

"So I guess you're glad about there being none."

"It's an experience I could do without."

"Okay. It's for the best. I just don't— What causes someone to—" Shaking her head. Looking up at the sky. Then down again. Kneading. Harder and faster.

I said, "What are you thinking about?"

"*Her*. Ursula. Levine told me she was released from the hospital, went back to Boston—to her family. It's weird, thinking of her as having a family, needing someone. I used to see her as all-powerful—some kind of dragon lady."

Pulling her hands apart. Wiping them on the grass.

"She called Mother last night. Or Mother called her— Mother was on the phone with her just as I arrived. When I heard Mother mention her name I left the room and went down to the cafeteria."

"Does that bother you? Their talking."

"I don't know what she could possibly have to offer Mother, being a victim herself."

"Maybe nothing," I said.

She gave me a sharp look. "What does that mean?"

"Just because they're no longer therapist and patient doesn't mean they have to break all contact."

"What's the point?"

"Friendship."

"Friendship?"

"That bothers you."

"It's not— I don't— Yes, I still *resent* her. And I also *blame* her for what happened. Even though she suffered too. She was Mother's *doctor*. She should have *protected* her—but that's not fair, is it? She's a victim as much as Mother."

"Fair isn't the issue. You have these feelings. They'll need to be dealt with."

"Plenty to be dealt with," she said.

"Plenty of time."

She turned back to the water. "They're so tiny, hard to believe they're able to . . ." Reaching into the bucket, she scooped up more pellets and threw them in, one by one. Staring at the momentary dimple each impact stamped on the water's surface. Flipping her hair. Biting her lip.

"I dropped by the Tankard last night. To bring Don some of his things from the house. There were a lot of people. He was busy with customers—didn't see me, and I didn't wait around, just dropped the stuff off. . . ." Shrug.

"Don't try to do it all at once," I said.

"Yes, that's *exactly* what I'd like to do. Fix everything and go on from there. Fix *him*—the monster. It doesn't seem right that he'll get to live out the rest of his life in some clean, comfortable hospital. That he and Mother are basically in the same situation. I mean, that *is* absurd, isn't it?"

"He'll stay. She'll leave."

"I hope."

"She will."

"It *still* doesn't seem fair. There should be something more . . . finite. Justice—an *end*. Like what happened to McCloskey. May he rot in hell. Did Milo find out anything more about who did it? My offer to pay for the defense still stands."

"The police haven't solved it," I said. "It's not likely they will."

"Good," she said. "Why waste time."

She trickled more food into the pond, rubbed her hands together to get rid of the pellet dust. Began kneading again, her body tense. Rubbing her brow, she let out a long sigh.

I waited.

"I fly up there every day to see her," she said. "And I keep asking myself why is she here, why does she have to go through this? Why should one person who never did anything bad in her life have to go through being victimized by *two* monsters in one lifetime? If there's a God, why would He set things up that way?"

"Good question," I said. "People have been wrestling with various versions of it since the beginning of time."

She smiled. "That's no answer."

"True."

"I thought you had *all* the answers."

"Brace yourself for crushing disillusionment, kid."

Her smile widened and warmed. She leaned forward, holding her hair back with one hand, touching the water with the other.

"You saw things," she said. "Up at that . . . place. Things we haven't talked about."

"There's a lot we haven't talked about. All in—"

"I know, I know, due time. I just wish I knew what *due time* was—could put some kind of number on it."

"That's understandable."

She laughed. "There you go again. Telling me I'm okay."

"That's 'cause you are."

"That so?"

"Very definitely."

"Well," she said, "you're the expert."

Turn the page for an excerpt from
Jonathan Kellerman's
exciting Alex Delaware novel

A COLD HEART

Available wherever books are sold
Published by Ballantine Books

CHAPTER 1

The witness remembers it like this:

Shortly after two A.M., Baby Boy Lee exits The Snake Pit through the rear alley fire door. The light fixture above the door is set up for two bulbs, but one is missing, and the illumination that trickles down onto the garbage-flecked asphalt is feeble and oblique, casting a grimy mustard-colored disc, perhaps three feet in diameter. Whether or not the missing bulb is intentional will remain conjecture.

It is Baby Boy's second and final break of the evening. His contract with the club calls for a pair of one-hour sets. Lee and the band have run over their first set by twenty-two minutes because of Baby Boy's extended guitar and harmonica solos. The audience, a nearly full house of 124, is thrilled. The Pit is a far cry from the venues Baby Boy played in his heyday, but he appears to be happy, too.

It has been a while since Baby Boy has taken the stage anywhere and played coherent blues. Audience members questioned later are unanimous: Never has the big man sounded better.

Baby Boy is said to have finally broken free of a host of addictions, but one habit remains: nicotine. He smokes three packs of Kools a day, taking deep-in-the-lung drags while on stage, and his guitars are notable for the black, lozenge-shaped burn marks that scar their lacquered wood finishes.

Tonight, though, Baby Boy has been uncommonly focused, rarely removing lit cigarettes from where he customarily jams them: just above the nut of his '62 Telecaster, wedged under the three highest strings.

So it is probably a tobacco itch that causes the singer to leap offstage the moment he plays his final note, flinging his bulk out the back door without a word to his band or anyone else. The bolt clicks behind him, but it is doubtful he notices.

The fiftieth Kool of the day is lit before Baby Boy reaches the alley. He is sucking in mentholated smoke as he steps in and out of the disc of dirty light.

The witness, such that he is, is certain that he caught a glimpse of Baby Boy's face in the light and that the big man was sweating. If that's true, perhaps the perspiration had nothing to do with anxiety but resulted from Baby Boy's obesity and the calories expended on his music: For eighty-three minutes he has been jumping and howling and swooning, caressing his guitar, bringing the crowd to a frenzy at set's end with a fiery, throat-ripping rendition of his signature song, a basic blues setup in the key of B-flat that witnesses the progression of Baby Boy's voice from an inaudible mumble to an anguished wail.

> There's women that'll mess you
> There's those that treat you nice
> But I got me a woman with
> A heart as cold as ice.
>
> A cold heart,
> A cold, cold heart
> My baby's hot but she is cold
> A cold heart,
> A cold, cold heart
> My baby's murdering my soul . . .

At this point, the details are unreliable. The witness is a hepatitis-stricken, homeless man by the name of Linus Leopold Brophy, aged thirty-nine but looking sixty, who has no interest in the blues or any other type of music and who happens to be in the alley because he has been drinking Red Phoenix fortified wine all night and the Dumpster five yards east of the Snake Pit's back door provides shelter for him to sleep off his *delerium tremens*. Later, Brophy will consent to a blood alcohol test and will come up .24, three times the legal limit for driving, but according to Brophy "barely buzzed."

Brophy claims to have been drowsy but awake when the sound of the back door opening rouses him, and he sees a big man step out into the light and then fade to darkness. Brophy claims to recall the lit end of the man's cigarette glowing "like Halloween, you know—orange, shiny, real bright, know what I mean?" and admits that he seizes upon the idea of panhandling money from the smoker. ("Because the guy is fat, so I figure he had enough to eat, that's for sure, maybe he'll come across, know what I mean?")

Linus Brophy struggles to his feet and approaches the big man.

Seconds later, someone else approaches the big man, arriving from the opposite direction—the mouth of the alley, at Lodi Place. Linus Brophy stops in his tracks, retreats into darkness, sits down next to the Dumpster.

The new arrival, a man, also good-sized, according to Brophy, though not as tall as Baby Boy Lee and maybe half of Baby Boy's width, walks right up to the singer and says something that sounds "friendly." Questioned about this characterization extensively, Brophy denies hearing any conversation but refuses to budge from his judgement of amiability. ("Like they were friends, you know? Standing there, friendly.")

The orange glow of Baby Boy's cigarette lowers

from mouth to waist level as he listens to the new arrival.

The new arrival says something else to Baby Boy and Baby Boy says something back.

The new arrival moves closer to Baby Boy. Now, the two men appear to be hugging.

The new arrival steps back, looks around, turns heel and leaves the alley the way he came.

Baby Boy Lee stands there alone.

His hand drops. The orange glow of the cigarette hits the ground, setting off sparks.

Baby Boy sways. Falls.

Linus Brophy stares, finally builds up the courage to approach the big man. Kneeling, he says, "Hey, man," receives no answer, reaches out and touches the convexity of Baby Boy's abdomen. He feels moisture on his hand and is repelled.

As a younger man, Brophy had a temper. He has spent half of his life in various county jails and state penitentiaries, saw things, did things. He knows the feel and the smell of fresh blood.

Stumbling to his feet, he lurches to the back door of the Snake Pit and tries to pull it open, but the door is locked. He knocks, no one answers.

The shortest way out of the alley means retracing the steps of the newcomer: walk out to Lodi Place, hook north to Fountain and find someone who'll listen.

Brophy has already wet his pants twice tonight— first while sleeping drunk and now, upon touching Baby Boy Lee's blood. Fear grips him and he heads the other way, tripping through the long block that takes him to the other end of the alley. Finding no one on the street at this hour, he makes his way to an all-night liquor store on the corner of Fountain and El Centro.

Once inside the store, Brophy shouts at the Lebanese clerk who sits reading behind a Plexiglass window, the same man who one hour ago sold him three bottles of Red Phoenix. Brophy waves his arms, tries to get across what he has just seen. The clerk regards Brophy as exactly what he is—a babbling wino—and orders him to leave.

When Brophy begins pounding on the Plexiglass, the clerk considers reaching for the nail-studded baseball bat he keeps beneath the counter. Sleepy and weary of confrontation, he dials 911.

Brophy leaves the liquor store and walks agitatedly up and down Fountain Avenue. When a squad car from Hollywood Division arrives, Officers Keith Montez and Cathy Ruggles assume Brophy is their problem and handcuff him immediately.

Somehow he manages to communicate with the Hollywood Blues and they drive their black and white to the mouth of the alley. High-intensity LAPD-issue flashlights bathe Baby Boy Lee's corpse in a heartless, white glare.

The big man's mouth gapes and his eyes are rolled back. His banana-yellow Stevie Ray Vaughan t-shirt is dyed crimson and a red pool has seeped beneath his corpse. Later, it will be ascertained that the killer gutted the big man with a classic street-fighter's move: long-bladed knife thrust under the sternum followed by a single upward motion that slices through intestine and diaphragm and nicks the right ventricle of Baby Boy's already seriously enlarged heart.

Baby Boy is long past help and the cops don't even attempt it.